CONTROL FREAK

"Laurel," the local air controller said, "you've got traffic coming in."

"The Bat's got the traffic!" he shouted, then fired one round through the control tower's ceiling. Everyone ditched their head sets, scrambling away from the madman.

"Fed Ex 120, proceed to runway six," he said, "then wait for further instructions."

"But you've got Northwest 260 arriving on two-seven!"

Laurel knew that.

He knew 260 would need half its runway to slow and brake.

He knew 120 needed three quarters of its runway to get airborne.

It was simple geometry. Two lines meeting. Closing the gap.

At more than two hundred knots.

And so many unsuspecting lives. . . .

READ ACCOUNTS OF GRUESOME REAL LIFE EVENTS
IN PINNACLE TRUE CRIME

BEYOND ALL REASON   (0-7860-0292-1, $5.99)
My Life with Susan Smith
By David Smith with Carol Calef
On a fall evening in 1994, David Smith began every father's worst night-mare when he learned his two young sons had been kidnapped. Nine days later, his wife, Susan Smith, confessed that the kidnapping had been a hoax, a cruel lie. The truth would be even crueler: 3-year-old Michael and 14-month-old Alex Smith were dead, slain by their mother's own hand.

BLOOD CRIMES   (0-7860-0314-6, $5.99)
The Pennsylvania Skinhead Murders
By Fred Rosen
On February 26, 1995, in a quiet suburb of Allentown, Pennsylvania, 17-year-old Bryan Freeman and his 15-year-old brother David slit their father's throat, stabbed their mother numerous times, and smashed the skull of their 12-year-old brother Erik with a baseball bat. Their hideous mass slaughter led to something even more frightening: the Nazi skinhead movement in America.

LOBSTER BOY   (0-7860-0133-X, $4.99)
The Bizarre Life and Brutal Death of Grady Stiles, Jr.
By Fred Rosen
Descended from a notorious carny family, Grady Stiles, Jr. led an unusual life. With a deformity that gave his hands and feet the appearance of lobster claws, he achieved fame and fortune as "Lobster Boy." But beneath Stiles's grotesque sideshow persona lurked a violent man who secretly abused his family for years. Until his wife and stepson decided to do something about it—by entering a conspiracy to kill.

BORN BAD   (0-7860-0274-3, $5.99)
By Bill G. Cox
On a lonely backroad in Ellis County, TX, the body of 13-year-old Christina Benjamin was discovered. Her head and hands were missing. She had been sexually mutilated and disemboweled. A short distance away was the badly decomposed corpse of 14-year-old James King face down on the creek bank. He had been brutally shot to death. This ghoulish discovery would lead to apprehension of the most appalling torture killer Texas had ever seen. . . .

DARK
RAGE

Lowell Cauffiel

Pinnacle Books
Kensington Publishing Corp.

http://www.pinnaclebooks.com

PINNACLE BOOKS are published by

Kensington Publishing Corp.
850 Third Avenue
New York, NY 10022

First Printing: January 1997

Printed in the United States of America
10 9 8 7 6 5 4 3 2 1

For Lewis, who reinvented himself several times.

The intellect of man is forced to choose
Perfection of the life, or of the work,
And if it take the second must refuse
A heavenly mansion, raging in the dark.

—William Butler Yeats

One

He hated seeing people lined up like that, hunched over those goddamn smorgasbord tables, piling some of everything on their plates, eating until they were sick, only to throw half of it away.

This is what he thought about when she mentioned plans for the holiday.

"Well, maybe we could go up to that place," she'd offered. "Where they have all you can eat."

She read his eyes.

"Forget it, I'll come up with something," she said.

The holiday had no meaning to him. They were childless. He was forty-six; she, two years younger. Her parents had passed, and her sister was in Seattle. Throat cancer took his mother ten years ago. His father was an older story. Maybe they could have the old man over next Thanksgiving, or the following year. It would take that long to find him. If he wasn't dead. He wasn't worth the effort, above or below the ground.

"I'm going to shower," he said.

Afterward, he went out the back door. Left her in the kitchen where she fussed with something. The cool air and Lilac Vegetal tightened his pores. He took five minutes to walk the perimeter of their lot. It was an old habit, inspecting his lot line, eighty by one hundred and twenty feet.

Today, he stopped at the west fence, looking across the other back yards, looking at line after line of chain-link.

Today, he thought about the tin men, the way two of them sold a thousand dollars worth to his mother, even though their bungalow was brick. They'd worked the area real good that summer. They'd sold a couple of truck loads of aluminum awnings, because a lot of houses were like his mother's. He'd taken the damn awnings down when he took title. They served no purpose, really. But everywhere else, most of the tin was still up.

The tin men must have been real good to sell a product so marginal, he thought. They knew their jobs. He had to give them that. In his way of thinking, he'd rather see somebody sell an average product well than do a poor sales job on something of quality. He learned that in the Marines. You did your job, and you did it well, no matter what. He liked that old public service announcement, that TV commercial where a guy signed his name on a line he'd just painted on the street. *"What if you had to sign your name to everything you did? Would you do a better job?"* That's the standard he'd embraced.

At the side of the garage, Laurel Kring slid his key into the dead bolt. He'd removed the big garage door and walled in the front. He'd made the garage his study and workshop, built a fake window with a flower box so his wife could dress it up with flowers. He didn't want some neighborhood punks breaking in, or any niggers. Just last year, two families had moved in up the street. He liked the privacy. He didn't need windows. He liked exploring worlds more vast than all he could gather with a line of sight through glass.

The sound of the cooling fan from the Compaq desktop greeted him. He'd sunk five grand into the PC and its peripherals. He never turned it off. He liked the sound of the running computer when he came through the workshop door.

When he was working, he listened to Coltraine, or Rahsaan Roland Kirk. He had all their works in vinyl. When they were reissued on CD, he'd bought his favorites

and a player for the workshop. He'd been listening since he was a boy, back when WJZZ played beebop and the cool movement, back when he was spending nights alone with the FM in his room. Roland Kirk was a story. A negligent nurse, not doing her job, blinded him when he was two. From this crime and its pain would emerge a prodigious gift. Kirk learned to play forty instruments. He could blow three horns at once. No man could do that. He liked Coltraine's wailing, but he identified with Kirk.

Today, he loaded "A Love Supreme" and sat down at the computer. The sweet dissonance of Coltraine's tenor soon filled the room.

The file was labeled FINAL.LTR. He'd been working on it a little each day, through the first week of his vacation, trying to polish it. The mechanics of writing, conventional sentence structure and organization, had never come easy for him. But he knew his ending. That was good. He was saving it in another file, planning to tack it on the final draft.

Today, he worked again on the part again about his wife. She had been very faithful. He never questioned that. She was there for him when he was discharged in '68. She was the reason he stayed away from the Saigon whores. Because of her, he'd decided not to sign up for a second tour. That's what he remembered most when he thought of the first years of their twenty-five.

As for the long haul, most men would never know such a woman. She didn't run his ass like others he knew, guys who let their wives keep their social calendar, or ran guilt trips when they wanted to do something alone. He never understood that. Women who turned men into little fucking Ken dolls, perfectly good men you could once count on who now had to go to baby showers and birthday parties all the time at their in-laws'. Guys who couldn't go fishing anymore, or whack clay pigeons at the range. Guys crying at work about their wives saying they needed to spend more time together. You're fucking them and sleeping with them seven days a week, he used to tell them. "Doesn't that count as time?" he'd ask. That's how he lost all his friends.

No, his wife *did not* do that shit. And she *did not* deserve to endure any discomfort, as far as he was concerned. When it came to the issues at hand, she was purely innocent. She had stuck by him, regardless.

He wanted to make that clear.

He moved a couple sentences around. Took one or two words out that might be misinterpreted. Then read the entire letter out loud, listening to see if his tongue tripped over any of the words.

When he was done, he removed the North American Arms Mini-Master Black Widow from his desk drawer and inspected it. The .22 revolver had an oversized black rubber grip, but still was easily concealable with its bull cylinder and two-inch barrel. You could easily slip it into a pair of baggy pants, though one had to be careful of its Millett adjustable rear sight. That could hook on clothing if you had to pull it fast.

When he returned to the living room his wife said, "Say hello to Margaret, honey."

"Hello, Margaret."

Margaret half smiled, setting down her coffee. She was sitting on the couch, his wife in an easy chair, folding laundry. Oprah droned at low volume on the TV.

"Would you like something?"

"Yeah, ginseng if we got it." He'd discovered ginseng in the East. It didn't rattle his nerves like coffee.

As the microwave hummed in the kitchen, Margaret, the neighbor, made no conversation. She never said much to him. He'd never heard her say much to his wife, for that matter. Once in a while her mouth would open and produce some mindless statement. Something about sewer work being done up the street or a turn in the weather.

Today, she didn't even seem capable of that.

He stood and watched the people on the talk show, something about mothers who fucked the boyfriends of their daughters. He really didn't care what they were saying. He was wondering why they'd all bothered to dress up, buy new clothes and get new haircuts for that show, only to be presented like circus freaks.

He looked again at Margaret. She had a fat ass, but hardly any upper body. He wondered what his wife got out of visiting with a dumb bitch like that.

When his wife returned with the tea, Margaret said, "I better go."

"I understand," his wife said.

He sat on the couch, but not on the spot where the neighbor had sat.

"Here, take your chair," his wife said.

"No, you've got the laundry."

He liked the way she did the towels. She line dried them right into the final weeks of November. The way he asked.

That was a good woman.

She draped a terry cloth across her lap, taking the corners, folding it neatly. It was very white, he thought, almost glowing. His mouth was dry now, his tongue peppered with ginseng.

"We'll be right back," Oprah said.

He got up now and walked over to her, taking a white hand towel out of the basket, walking behind her. He raised it to his face.

She kept folding.

The towel smelled clean. He felt very clear.

"Smell this."

She held it up to her nose briefly.

"Yeah, so?"

When she turned, he studied her face momentarily. He could see pale skin showing in a crevice untouched by her makeup. He could see a grain of brown in her blue iris, but mostly he saw her smiling. He remembered how she smiled at him like that when he got off the transport from D'Nang. Not all flipped out, just smiling.

"No," he said. "Really smell it. Like this."

He picked up the towel, laying it flat between his hands and his face, inhaling deeply.

She took the towel.

As she breathed in deeply, he slid the Ruger out of his pants, being careful not to hook the Millet sight on the interior of his pocket. He did it in one motion, the tip of the barrel coming to a stop behind her right ear.

"You can smell autumn," he said.

The Black Widow hardly made any noise at all.

A half hour later, he finished the letter, transferring the conclusion from another file, but not letting it stand alone as a separate paragraph. It was from *Profiles in Courage,* by John F. Kennedy. He'd read one part of that book many times: Kennedy's description of the Jap destroyer as it steamed down upon them out of the darkness, cutting the PT 109 in half.

John Kennedy did his job, saved his crew, with hardly anything to work with.

Like the tin men.

Laurel Kring pressed the paste key. The text appeared on the screen.

A man does what he must, in spite of obstacles and dangers and personal consequences—and that is the basis of all human morality.

As he printed out the letter, he could hear Coltraine's notes bouncing off the walls like flies trying to fly through glass.

Two

After the cardiopulmonary technician asked him to open his shirt, she said to Riker, "You're lucky. You don't have a lot of hair on your chest."

"Lucky?" he asked.

She held up one of the sensor pads and peeled off the backing.

"Adhesive," she said.

She slapped seven of them, one by one, on his bare chest. That pattern looked like somebody had sprayed his upper body with a semiautomatic.

"You wouldn't believe some of the hairy guys that come in here. I always offer to shave them, but no, they want to be tough guys."

When she talked he could smell the Juicy Fruit she was chewing.

"There," she said, stepping back to admire her work. "You don't seem like a tough guy. What's your gig?"

"Gig?"

"Yeah, what do you do for a living?"

"Cop."

"Where?"

"At the airport. Metro."

"Well, I guess you *are* a tough guy. But most guys your age, they seem to be trying to prove something."

"My age?" Riker asked, eyeing her.

Riker was forty-six. Give her a bad hangover, deprive her of sleep, she might look twenty-five.

"Maybe," Riker said, "These *tough guys,* as you call them, might just be trying to prove to a young, attractive woman like yourself that they're not about to drop dead from a heart attack. I mean, Christ, they wouldn't be in here, would they, if they were the picture of health."

She held up a handful of wires. "Okay, now we gotta wire you up."

Worker on autopilot, he thought, running her mouth. She just wanted to hear herself talk. He wondered what she'd be like off the job. Put her in jeans and buy her a couple of beers. She had a nice ass. He liked Juicy Fruit.

He looked her in the eyes. She might as well have been looking at the medical certificates on the wall.

"Don't get me wrong," she said. "You're not old or anything. What I was saying was just that some of these guys come in here to get one of these monitors. They don't want to be shaved. But they *do* have to come back in twenty-four hours. You know? What goes on, must come off."

Riker could feel the adhesive on the silver-dollar-size sensors gripping his skin as she snapped the wire harness onto the pads.

"When I take them off, I do it real fast," she continued, mouth running. "It usually doesn't hurt that way. But if you've got a lot of hair, well that's different."

"How different?"

"When you remove about the fifth or sixth one, and you're taking clumps of hair with each one, you get to see somebody's real personality, you know what I'm saying?"

"You're telling me they don't fall on their knees and beg you to stop?"

"Something like that. Most are real jerks."

The technician plugged the wire harness into a data recording device that looked like a cassette recorder.

"Now *this,*" she said, "is your Holter monitor. It's like

a cassette recorder, really. There's a strap so you can carry it like a purse over your shoulder."

He looked at her blankly.

"But most men," she continued, "prefer to wear it on their belts. There's a loop here."

"That's fine."

Riker pulled out his belt a couple loops so he could slip it on.

"Now, on the side there is what we call an 'event' button," she continued. "If you have any symptoms, chest pains, arm pain, light headiness, anything, you press that button and it marks it on the tape that your doctor will analyze later."

"I haven't been having those kind of symptoms," Riker said.

"Well, if you do, that's the button you press."

"I'll be sure to press it before I hit the ground."

She handed him a piece of paper.

"And *this* is your log. On here you note the time from the monitor and what you're doing. See, here's a sample. *Five o'clock: driving. Seven o'clock: watching TV. Seven thirty: jogged.* You get the idea. The more detailed the better."

A log. The goddamn doctor didn't say anything about a log.

"The doc said all I had to do was wear this thing for twenty-four hours," Riker said.

"That's right. But you have to keep a log, too. Otherwise, the cardiologist will not know how to interpret your results."

His heart sometimes felt like it was skipping. That's all he'd told his doctor. Christ, now they were wiring him up like Boris Fucking Karloff.

"I just need you to wear a monitor one work day," the doctor had insisted. "Preferably a stressful one."

Riker picked the day before Thanksgiving. A real ball buster. The busiest day in aviation. The day more shit than ever flowed through what Jack Riker liked to call *the big pipe*.

After the technician taped the wires down, he stood up and buttoned his shirt, moving his torso around to test drive the setup. It was more comfortable than it looked. He hardly felt the sensors anymore on his chest. He reached for his tie. Still wore a clip-on. Been wearing one since he was in uniform. He'd never forgotten what he'd learned at the academy: Real ties looked good, but they gave ass holes something to grab.

The young tech wrote his name and his doctor's at the top of the log sheet, then handed it to him. There were forty-eight lines, designed for "time," "activity," and "symptoms."

She wrote the first entry in for him: *8 A.M. Holter on.*

"Well, I guess I'll see you tomorrow morning," Riker said.

"No you won't. Tomorrow you go to Emergency. They'll remove everything. We've got the holiday off. They'll make sure we get the monitor and the log."

Jack Riker was a little disappointed. He was looking forward to checking out her technique.

As he headed back to Metro on I-94, he wrote *driving* on the log sheet. Jesus Christ, he thought, this was going to be a real pain. He started thinking about what he should write down, what he should leave out. Some things had a tendency to work him up. *Lieutenant had his head up his ass.* Or, *Another bullshit memo from the director of airports.* Better just stick to the routine, or the biological stuff, like, *took a healthy piss.*

He had a 9 A.M. meeting, a favor for the executive lieutenant. The local FAA wanted to talk about a so-called "phantom controller." For the past few weeks, somebody with a radio was butting into tower transmissions with aircraft. Department cruisers had been told to watch out for cars with CB-like antennas, but beyond that, there wasn't much airport police could do. Riker figured it was some introvert who'd spent too much time in a Radio Shack. Don't give him the publicity, he had told the executive lieutenant, and he'd eventually move on to more ambitious pursuits like letter bombs.

Riker liked to leave high-level meetings with high-level officials in other airport agencies to the police brass. He was a detective sergeant, which basically meant he did well ten years ago on a test and got paid better than nonranking detectives. The rank *did not* require him to play politics. He took orders, and gave few, and he liked it that way.

But for the Thanksgiving holiday weekend, the airport brass had gone hunting. The commander, the executive lieutenant and the DB lieutenant had left the night before for the Upper Peninsula. There were only four days left of the Michigan deer season, the commander told anybody who would listen, and goddamnit, they all were going up to his "rustic" cabin and get a goddamn deer.

"How rustic?" Riker asked the lieutenant.

"No telephone," he said. "Thirty miles from the nearest town. But he does have electricity. He said he needed that for the ice maker he put in behind the bar."

The commander extended an invitation to Riker, but he politely declined. Jack Riker hadn't had a drink in five years. And he figured there'd be a lot of that, and not too many deer.

Sometimes people would ask him.

"Oh, I retired champion," he'd say.

He'd quit without some kind of treatment center or AA meetings or some drug that would make him puke if he smelled too much of his Mennen's Skin Bracer. He took care of it the way he took care of most things in his life. He'd done it alone, and took a certain amount of quiet pride in that.

Five minutes from the airport, Riker picked up his cellular phone and dialed the department radio room.

"Leo, this meeting the lieutenant scheduled with the FAA, could you call over there and find out where I'm supposed to meet this guy? His name is Cleage. The lieutenant never passed that along. Is it the new tower, or the old one in the Smith terminal?"

"Do I look like a secretary, Riker?" Leo asked.

Leo was built like an old Packers line backer. He still wore a flat top and bared an uncanny resemblance to the fifties actor, Aldo Ray.

"No, Leo, you don't. But I don't have the number here with me."

"Turn your goddamn radio on."

He hung up before Riker could respond.

Riker didn't use the radio too often, or his handle, which was the number four sixty. He carried a handheld. Too many news organizations monitored the police frequencies. Not that anything he did was all too newsworthy. And other cops listened. He just didn't like his business out on the street.

The county just finished building the new tower for the FAA. The old one sat on top the south terminal, known as L.C. Smith. The new tower was free standing, located in the flat land between runway six, three left, and three center. The old tower looked like an afterthought in faded green aluminum, a relic from the fifties, not four stories higher than the terminal observation deck. The new tower looked like the Seattle Space Needle in cream precast concrete. If the meeting was in the FAA offices under the old tower, Riker knew parking was going to be a pain in the ass.

"Base to four sixty," Riker's radio crackled.

"Yeah," Riker said, ignoring radio protocol, a move he knew would piss Leo off.

"It's in the new tower, four sixty."

Before he could respond, Leo said, "Base clear."

The last time Riker was in any tower was '67, during the Detroit riot. Somebody downtown came up with the idea that a hundred thousand spades were going to drive twenty miles out I-94 and trash Metro. Head right for the tower and cocktail the controllers and their screens. The shift sergeant handed Riker, then a rookie, an M-1 carbine and three fully loaded magazines and stationed him just inside the tower door in the Smith terminal. Riker knew the weapon. He was only a year out of Nam. Two weeks before the riot, Riker had also picked up his first and only sidearm, a .38 Colt bought at a hardware on the east side. He still carried the revolver. But other than the range, he'd never had to fire the gun. The rioters, of course, never came. That the command even thought they would taught Jack Riker early on about the mentality of the brass downtown.

Those controllers were a breed, Riker remembered. Always brought their own food. They had coffee pots and soup cubes and hot plates, browning Smokey Links for breakfast while talking a bunch of inside vector lingo. The controllers didn't give a shit about the riot. They didn't even watch it on their breakroom TV. They never got rattled. Their brains were a bunch of compartments. Those guys might as well have worked on the moon.

In '67, Riker never would have predicted he'd end up back at the airport. He'd worked all the jobs. County road patrol, a one-man car. Solo surveillance. Drug buys. Served on a serial killer hunt, but didn't really like that. He didn't like teamwork. Brass that knew him, knew you got the most of Jack Riker if you turned him lose on his own.

The best assignment was out of the sheriff's department headquarters, in Greektown in downtown Detroit. He worked the organized crime task force, trying to make contraband buys from Sicilians as well as Greeks trying to act like Italians. The command thought with his black hair and black mustache, he could play the part. That was his favorite, back when he still got a good click from Windsor

Canadian on the rocks. He used to drink every night at the Athens Bar in Greektown, putting them down with the guys he was trying to put away.

Riker always was cordial when he made his move. Treat criminals like gentlemen. If he had a philosophy, that was it. You treated your collars with respect. He'd refined this approach in interviews. The other dicks nicknamed it the Spencer Davis routine, the recording artist who did "I'm a Man."

It went something like:

"Look," he'd say, "You're a man, right?"

"Yeah, man."

"And I'm a man, right?"

"Yeah."

"Then, I think we need to deal with this from that perspective. Man to man, why don't you tell me what happened?"

This worked more times than not. Riker believed a good number of people on the low end of the crime chain really wanted to be caught. They didn't want rehabilitation. Rehabilitation required change and hard work. That's why so many ex-cons went back. They wanted a controlled, stable environment with three squares. He'd accumulated enough thank you letters from various Michigan prisons to effectively argue his point.

Rapport. If Riker had a talent, that was it. He had good rapport with criminals. He had good rapport with victims, trying always to send them away from a case with something. He liked being able to meet their needs, whether they knew what they were or not.

As for people untouched by crime, Riker had little patience. Maybe he spent all of his patience on the job. People in general just weren't aware of what was going on around them, he thought, and they created no end of trouble for those who were. When he heard someone say "I like people," he wanted to just slap sense into them. Riker liked

Truman Capote. He read once that the guy kept a book of friends and associates, rating them by importance on three lists. He identified with that. Except if Riker kept a book, he'd have only one inventory, and they'd all be cops.

Perhaps he had everything backward, his ex pointed out more than once. He treated troubled people kindly, but had free-floating disdain for "normal people," as she called them. *Treat a lady like a whore and whore like a lady.* That was the old cop line. Maybe the job had done it to him, or maybe it was some kind of character flaw. He didn't know. Shit, he couldn't remember what he was like before the job.

Riker didn't particularly like the airport because it always had a lot of normal people flowing through it, twenty-two million a year, to be exact, and everybody was short on time. That's why he called it *the big pipe.*

He'd also gotten off to a miserable start. His first day on the job six years ago, an MD-80 went down. Flight 225 to Tucson rose fifty feet off the ground, rolled, clipped the corner of the Hertz building, then dove under an I-94 underpass, killing one hundred fifty six people on board. Riker spent his first six days on the job working with the county medical examiner's body identification team. He still avoided getting off on that freeway ramp.

After the crash, people around him started changing. His wife of seven years started bitching that their two-story in Hamtramck wasn't stylish, the neighborhood too *ethnic.* Riker liked Hamtramck. Pollacks were hardworking and clean, his old man always said. He grew up there. His father moved from Toronto and started a small machine shop that supplied the Hamtramck Chevy plant. Prided himself on getting his American citizenship, prided himself in working for *nobody.* "Son, I don't care what you do with your own life," he always told him. "But unless you work for yourself, somewhere down the line you're going to have to kiss some major ass." That was one good thing about the airport. Mostly he was on his own. The DB didn't have a partner system. And he wasn't spending ten hours a day hunched over a milling machine.

Back then, Riker was a little more sociable. After the crash, he began hanging with a group of Detroit cops who used to meet behind the Conant library every night to have a few pops. A couple of the old dicks from the organized crime outfit, who'd been moved to the Eleventh Precinct, got him going. On hot nights, they drank cheap scotch and bourbon out of plastic cups and told stories. Everyone tossed their empties up on the roof of the library. It was a second-shift custom the Eleventh had observed for years. It came to an abrupt end when a city worker climbed up one day to inspect a librarian's complaints about roof leaks. The city crew took away nearly ten thousand empties, which an engineer determined had begun to jeopardize the structural integrity of the roof. Riker did his drinking at home from then on. His wife started saying things like, "Jack, you're no fun anymore." Started going to Alanon meetings, an outfit one of the guys from the Eleventh called "The Sisterhood of Eternal Vengeance." Almost a year to the date of the two twenty-five crash, she filed.

That's when he quit, but not to get her back. He was trying to protect his livelihood, which perhaps said something about where she ranked. If people wanted to know the details, he wasn't particularly forthcoming. When it came to a man making a fool out of himself, he ascribed to the words of Henry Ford II when he was picked up shit-faced, his mistress in his car. "Don't complain. Don't explain."

That's why he'd retired champion. Like Hank the Deuce, he'd come out of it still on his feet.

There was police work at the airport. In fact, with all the people moving through Metro, it was a wonder there wasn't more. Twenty-two million people came through the big pipe every year. Eleven thousand worked there. There were six square miles of territory and a half of a mile of glass and concrete linking the two domestic terminals, the older L.C. Smith on the south and the modern J.M. Davey on the north. The terminals sprouted six concourses. The International Terminal was a separate building altogether, used for charters as well as overseas flights. There were ninety-four gates, seventeen passenger airlines, and five cargo carriers. There was parking for ten thousand one hundred automobiles in several structures. There were two dozen bars and restaurants, not counting the concourse liquor stands. A bank. A hotel. A duty free shop. A nursery. There even was a Christian Science Reading Room, though the whole time Riker worked at Metro, he'd never seen anyone reading there.

Outside the airport property line, was the city of Romulus, a mix of wood lots and working-class apartments and homesteads. North and east of the airport, Romulus had motels and parking lots and fast food restaurants, but the airport police never did business there. Romulus had its own PD. "The airport police have no jurisdiction here," they often heard when they ventured across the line.

Everything was divided up like that. Romulus PD had its city limits. The airport police had jurisdiction over the roads and physical structures. The DEA had national and international drug trafficking. The state police had the Michigan dope. A private security firm covered the terminal gates and check points. Sometimes investigations suffered. It all stemmed from old territorial disputes, dating back to the days the Wayne County Sheriff's Department policed the airport. Three years ago, Marlon Ladd, the county executive, himself a former county sheriff, took Metro away from the new sheriff and created his own unit called the airport police. The executive offered former sheriff's personnel like Riker full pension and seniority if they jumped. It was an offer no one refused.

The work at the airport didn't change. Riker and four other detectives still served a lot of warrants. They arrested people kiting bad paper and stolen credit cards at airport establishments. They chased down stolen rental cars, investigated petty employee theft and made the terminal pickpockets work for their lifts. A couple times a week a detective and a couple uniformed officers formed what they called a *reception committee,* or just a *committee* for short. This meant waiting at a terminal gate after pilots radioed that they had a passenger who was out of hand.

Their last committee met a professional wrestler. He'd cold cocked a businessman sitting next to him in first class on a Northwestern flight, simply because the suit's evening paper rustled when he turned it. Leo came down from dispatch to get an autograph when he heard the guy was in the building. When Riker talked to him, the wrestler was a perfect gentleman.

"So, man to man, why did you hit him?" Riker asked.

"I don't know. I don't know what came over me."

One of the guys in SWAT theorized steroids. They made people explosive, he said. Riker decided to reintroduce the wrestler to the decked businessman. The wrestler gave him a bunch of tickets to his Cobo Hall event, said his kids could come back to the dressing room. Riker figured he'd saved everyone a lot of time in court.

That's the kind of police work Riker did.

Metro did have a certain quality that could wear at you. At first, Riker thought it was just the ambiance. Up and down the concourses, advertisers went for the people who built and designed cars. Tool companies displayed forgings and assembly machines. A large glass cube in L.C. Smith featured chrome plated die castings. Gears, transmissions, and nuts and bolts filled other showcases.

But lately, Riker decided the place had just become one big goddamn bus terminal, nothing like the way he remembered it as a rookie. Flying no longer had any glamour. Airline labor and management were always chewing at each other's asses. Business travelers were lagged out and pushy.

Bargain fairs brought in a lot of bottom feeders. The flying public streamed through the airport like worried cattle, fed on stories about crashes, lower safety standards, and bad cabin air. The only jet set Riker could identify at Metro hung out in the upscale titty bars in Romulus. They offered free limo service to any out-of-towner who'd pay five dollars for a beer.

Mostly, Riker noticed how the flight attendants had changed. When he was a rookie, he used to sit in Concourse E, watching the gals walk by to their flights. They seemed genuinely excited about what they were doing. Now, when he eavesdropped in the employee cafeteria, he heard a lot of people with attitudes. The young ones bitched about the older ones getting the good trips. The older ones bitched about age discrimination and what the cabin air was doing to their skin.

The freshest material came from the gay attendants, whose numbers had grown in recent years. He'd had a good chat with one the other day while they were both killing time on the bench chairs in Concourse E. The guy had a good take on people who worked at the airport.

"Hey, if I'm going to do shit work like shuttling meals and drinks, at least I can do it on an airplane," the guy told him. "In this business, everybody is always moving. When I work, I feel like I'm going somewhere, too."

Jack Riker didn't think he was going anywhere, for now at least. He wanted to log another two uneventful years, which would give him full pension. He hoped to sneak them in before the big changes hit. Computers in the DB. Evolving rules and regulations. More politically correct crap. A big airport expansion had just started with an eighty million dollar county bond issue. New runways. New access roads. A new terminal.

The new tower was just the first stage.

Two years. Riker's plan was to keep his head down. Then he wanted the hell out.

* * *

He pulled into the access road for the new tower off Eureka Road, on the south end of the airport, stopping to talk to private security in the guard shack. It was already five. Traffic had been bad coming in I-94. The holiday rush was starting its annual build.

"I'm here to see a Dale Cleage with the FAA."

The guard, probably forty-five, eyed a clip board. "Your name?"

"Riker."

"You're with who?"

"Detective Sergeant. Airport police."

"You're not on the list."

Riker showed his badge.

"This is our jurisdiction. I'll just drive in. I can find him when I get there."

The guard didn't raise the gate. "Sorry, can't do that. I'm going to call over."

Riker sighed. Fucking *people.* The guy probably read *Soldier of Fortune.* Boy, that was a nice rent-a-cop patch he had.

"You're here to see who?"

"Cleage. Dale Cleage with the FAA."

The guard repeated the name into the phone.

"You're the lieutenant from the airport police?" the guard asked Riker.

"I'm Detective *Sergeant* Riker. The lieutenant was called away, on business."

The guard said something into the phone, then hung it up. He was writing now, taking his time.

"Well?" Riker finally said.

"Okay, you're all set," the guard said, handing him a laminated parking pass. "Put this on your dashboard. But you're going to need an escort in."

"An escort? What do you mean an escort?"

The guard pointed.

Riker turned around to see an old Toyota Corolla, the same logo on the guard's arm was painted on its door. Inside, Riker could see a guy, maybe thirty. He had a scraggly goatee and long stringy hair.

"Tower," the guard yelled to the car.

The guy didn't hear him. His head was moving up and down to the radio, the car filled with cigarette smoke. Riker assumed it was cigarette smoke.

"Honk your horn, will you," the guard asked.

Riker honked. Where did the security company do it's hiring, he thought, Salvation Army detox? They had one in Romulus.

The guy rolled down the window.

"Tower," the guard said again, lifting the gate now.

He looked at Riker. "Let him escort you there. Follow him. When you're finished just drive out, You won't need an escort coming out."

As Riker waited for the freak in the Toyota, he tried to put the logic together, but for the life of him, could not figure it out. Why he would need an escort going in, and not going out? Did that mean if he was going in there to fuck something up, he could not do it on the way in, but was free to do so on the way out? And what was the neo-hippie going to do if he did?

Shit, Riker thought, I'm the fucking police.

Riker could feel his heart. The arrhythmia felt like a little fish flopping around in his chest.

Before he pulled away, he noted the time on the Holter log.

In the "event" section he wrote:

Late. Held up by some stupid shit.

Three

"Mom," was not an appropriate nickname, Terry Grice protested when she first heard one of the controllers use it.

"Oh, I don't know, I think it fits pretty well," her friend Gerry Russell, head of the Air Traffic Controllers Association local, said when she told him about it over a couple of beers.

"But I don't even have any children."

"What do you call the people who've worn that path in your carpet this year?" Russell said. "Think of it as a tribute. It says basically, we'd be up shit's creek without your motherly care and protection."

Grice still hated it. "Moms don't move a million airplanes a year flying in and out of a major airport."

"You think motherhood is an easy job?" Russell said.

"What do *you* know."

"I know you don't want to be talking that way around my wife."

"That's not what I mean."

"What do you mean?"

"I mean, twenty years in this business. Nobody ever called me anything. And now, all these names going around. And, I get 'Mom.' Why not something with a little more of an edge."

"What do you want? *Bad Ass?* Sorry, it just doesn't fit."

Now, as Terry Grice looked at the clipping from the Detroit *News* on her desk, she was reminded of exactly why the nickname irritated her so much. It was so damned *appropriate*. She had become the resident mother. Now, she was about to assume another motherly role, the one where Mom separates two brawling brothers for the sake of household peace. The trouble with those kinds of fights, is that Mom often got hit with a few stray licks.

The clipping read:

METRO'S RADAR KEEPS GOING OUT

FAA officials scramble to fix the problem in a new system that has failed at least sixty times in first year.

She suspected, no, she *knew*, Gerry Russell had leaked the Monday story. When he hadn't returned her phone call by Wednesday morning, she knew he was distancing himself. Last week the phantom controller, now *this*.

She'd decided to call him again. She had a few minutes before she was due in TRACON, known to earthlings as the radar room, to sub for a supervisor's first shift break.

She was surprised when he answered the phone.

"Gerry, you've got to be the only union official in Detroit who's in his office, diligently working the day before Thanksgiving."

"Well, almost," he said. "I just came down to pick up some things. I've got family coming in for the holiday. My sister and her kids."

"And, you decided you'd also return my phone call, but I beat you to it, right?"

Russell chuckled. "Well, actually, I was going to do that next week."

"I called Monday, and yesterday."

"I figured you'd need a week to cool off."

"You've always been so intuitive."

"Terry," he said disingenuously, "I'm just trying to keep things positive."

She paused. "Is that what you were doing when you leaked this radar story?"

"I didn't leak it. They called me."

She wasn't going to argue that point. "Actually, that's not why I called. It's not just one story, it's the whole thing."

"What *whole thing?*"

She tried her best to sound rational, nonaccusatory. "I'm just trying to look at the bigger picture here, Gerry. I'm just wondering where all this is going to end? Disagreements are one thing, but scaring the crap out of the public isn't going to help your cause one bit."

He sounded somewhat apologetic. "Look, I don't like this kind of thing anymore than you do. But, I thought I was very supportive of the administration in the story."

"What, with this quote?"

She cradled the phone on her shoulder and snapped the clipping between her fingers so he could hear it.

"Said Russell: 'We're not saying it's unsafe to fly out of Metro. The system has a safety margin built into it.' "

"Yes. See what I mean. I thought that was diplomatic."

"What about the next line?"

"Which one?"

She snapped the clipping again.

"Said Russell: 'But these problems are stretching the safety margin to the limit.' "

"I said that?"

"It's got you all over it." She paused. "Look, my point is this. You *know* we solved the problem. We put in a surge suppressor on the ASR-9 two weeks ago. I personally called you to tell you that. The system's working fine now."

"Yes, you did call me, and I appreciate that. But that doesn't negate the fact that for the first six months, my people got the first degree. The Captain was convinced we somehow weren't following specs."

"It could have easily been human error."

"But it *wasn't*. It was the hardware."

"And when we found out, we corrected it. Besides, the new tower has it's own power supply. When we move TRACON over there next week, we won't be seeing these kinds of problems. So why the story? This whole problem is . . . moot."

She wasn't surprised when he failed to answer.

Leaking the story had little to do with the new, eleven million dollar ASR-9 installed two years ago, or the old CENRAP system piped in from Cleveland as a backup during the failures. It had taken them months to find the glitch, a fluctuation of electricity from the airport power plant to the main terminals. It kept knocking out the ASR-9 scopes.

The story was about different stakes. For nearly a year, Gerry Russell, in the name of his membership, had been feuding with the Detroit region's new air traffic control hub director, Dale Cleage. As assistant traffic manager, Terry Grice was trying to be a voice of reason. Sometimes she did feel like a mother, caught between two brawling boys.

Grice knew there were problems. Dale Cleage had been transferred thirteen months ago from Dallas-Fort Worth, where he was assistant director. He'd impressed somebody in Washington with his ability to cut facility overtime and the FAA had given him Metro as a prize. Before Cleage ever set up shop, controllers tapped into the Texas buzz. Cleage had ridden everybody pretty hard at Dallas-Fort Worth, people down there said. He conducted reviews of tower tapes, campaigning to clean up "inappropriate phraseology" between controllers and airplanes. He personally performed over-the-shoulders, the mandatory supervisory review every controller endured every six months. He ordered controllers into retraining seminars, often over minor, harmless mistakes.

"Cleage, isn't that the guy in *The Cain Mutiny?*" a local approach controller said the day the new director toured the Detroit facility.

"No, that's *Queeg,*" somebody else replied.

That day, the nicknames started. For Cleage, "Queeg," and the variations thereof: "Old Man Queeg," "Captain Queeg," or just "The Captain."

Cleage brought a supervisor with him, who controllers nicknamed "Mr. Roberts," though in fact his name was Roberts. Jeremiah Roberts was black, some kind of conservative Texas Baptist, and a humorless technocrat with a fondness for starched white shirts and patternless black ties. "Mr. Roberts" came from the movie of the same name. Same war as *The Cain Mutiny,* different ship, different plot. But once the names started sticking, continuity didn't matter to staff. That was the only bright side of "Mom," Terry Grice decided. It hadn't been lifted from a film script. She considering herself ahead.

Both Terry Grice and Gerry Russell were out of the old school, members of an older fraternity of controllers that predated the 1981 PATCO strike. They'd graduated together from the same academy class twenty years ago in Oklahoma City. Grice was promoted to a first-level supervisor three months before the union walked out. Russell was one of a couple thousand full performance level controllers, or FPLs, who hung onto their jobs. He happened to be on vacation when President Reagan ordered the strikers to return to work. Reagan fired the eleven thousand who didn't. When a new union formed several years later, everyone thought Russell would be a reasonable representative. But, like a lot of controllers, he had a headstrong, independent streak.

Becoming an FPL was a gamut. More than ten thousand people applied to the academy the year they did. After the screening tests and health exams, three thousand candidates were left. Only eighteen hundred made it through the course. Only five hundred got past developmental training. And, despite three years of on-the-job development at a facility, only one third of those five made FPL, meaning they could handle any air traffic control position in the tower or the radar room. Despite the demands of the job, most controllers looked for continuing challenges. Because of the staggered shifts, many had businesses on the side. One controller had an electronics repair shop. Another was a tax accountant. One clearance deliver controller owned a catering service. Another raised goats on his farm, supplying the milk for the feta cheese sold in Greektown.

More than a few controllers were a little eccentric. Harmless horseplay and off-beat terminology kept the stress at bay. Everyone fell into two working groups: TRACON or the tower. The radar operation at the base of the tower was the "Land of the Moles" staffed by the "Traconites." They handled more than two thousand flights a day, or six hundred and fifty thousand flights in a year. The tower, the folks in the sunlight, were "the tower pukes," probably because the job was a little less demanding. They actually *saw* the airplanes and handled less traffic, about four hundred and sixty flights annually, or about fifteen hundred a day. But, if a scope controller wandered up into the tower he might also put up with some good-natured abuse.

"My you're looking pale," a tower puke would say.

"I am?"

"Yeah. I'm surprised your eyes are open, considering all this daylight. You want us to pull the shades?"

Traconites and tower pukes.

"Together we get the job done," everyone said.

For reasons that escaped Grice, Cleage had been chipping away at the esprit de corps. He banned smoking on the L.C. Smith observation deck during breaks. He suggested tower and radar room personnel wear ties, or at least solid color shirts, rather than the plaid flannel shirts long popular with the men. He once issued a memo critical of staff sleep habits. He ordered personal photographs and drawings removed from the break area. He banned the small coffee cup pads some scope operators used to keep their coffee warm during long stretches at the screen. His performance reviews were downright compulsive. On the supervisory level, he changed titles for middle management. Grice was now "Manager for Plans, Procedures & Automation." It hardly fit on her card.

Cleage's style seemed to have infected some of the other supervisors, who were riding the Traconites particularly hard. A month ago, she watched as Roberts pulled a veteran approach controller from the slot, simply because he didn't like the way he'd lined thirty-eight aircraft on his screen during a five o'clock push. Trainees or sick controllers got *pulled*. For a veteran, it was an anomaly.

"Okay, unplug and go," Roberts told the Traconite. "Get me somebody in here who can give me some proper separation."

Everyone heard it, or heard about it.

"This isn't the goddamn post office," Gerry Russell said when he heard about the incident. "People *want* to work here. They *like* air traffic control. They deserve some respect."

The story about the new radar, and more friction between the union and Cleage, couldn't have come at a more stressful time. Terry Grice's priorities needed to be focused on getting the new tower up and running. Devising the transition plan had already caused weeks of debate. There had been two camps among supervisors and controllers: Some argued the radar room and tower cab should become operational at the same time in the new facility. Others argued for phasing them in one at a time.

Mainly, Grice thought, it wasn't prudent to have the two main operations of air traffic control in separate structures, even temporarily. The old TRACON was just a couple stories below the tower cab in the old tower in south terminal. And similarly, the new TRACON would be located on the ground floor of the new tower. The tower pukes used their panoramic view—and tower cab radar if needed—to direct departing and arriving traffic on the ground and within airspace six miles from the airport. The Traconites used scopes to direct traffic between the sixty-mile threshold and the point where aircraft were handed off or received from the regional Air Route Traffic Control centers in Cleveland and Chicago.

The pukes and Traconites handed off the flights back and forth not only by radio communications with flight crews, but something called flight progress slips. The strips, printed out by a computer printer, detailed the flight number, destination, and transponder code. Departure strips arrived in the tower as departing flights fired up their engines. As the flight taxied to the runway, was cleared for take off, and then jetted away, its strip was passed among tower controllers in a plastic baton. Clearance delivery handed the strip to ground control, ground control to local control, then local control sent the strip down to departure control to TRACON, which controlled the flight before handing it off to a regional center.

The old tower employed a pneumatic tube to send the strips to the radar room. They'd put in tubes in the new tower as well. The method was a popular one, though an antique. Efforts to replace the strips over the years had never worked out in facilities that tried to come up with better systems. Controllers saw the strips as a security blanket ever since they were introduced in 1936. Grice remembered how an academy instructor put it: "Considering all the things you have to keep track of mentally, it's just damn nice to have something in your hands."

The word they used a lot was *redundancy*. Everything in the air traffic business was backed up by something else. The ASR-9 radar was backed up by CENRAP, another radar system usually used by the Cleveland center. If CENRAP went belly up, they could always improvise and direct traffic from the tower cab radar scopes. If all the radar failed, there were more contingency plans. Terry Grice once directed traffic from the runway itself when she was stationed in Perioria, Illinois. During a power outage, she sat on her car hood and directed the planes down on a handheld radio. Now, redundancy eliminated power outages. The new Metro tower got its electricity directly from Edison. That was backed up by its own generators, which were fed by a natural gas line. If the gas line ruptured, two large tanks of propane were on standby on the site.

That's what bothered Terry Grice about Dale Cleage's decision to phase in the new tower. There was less *redundancy*. The new cab had been operational all week, but TRACON wasn't scheduled to be moved over to the new tower until next week. This required putting an electronic link in the flight strip chain. Departing flights were coming over from the new tower cab by a data line.

"What if that line goes down?" Grice had argued. "At least with the tubes in the old tower, we could always run the flight strips up and down stairs."

The new tower cab was more than a quarter mile away from the old radar room, across two taxi strips and a major runway.

But Cleage also argued redundancy. "Look, the new tower is largely untested," he said. "If the new tower goes to hell, we can always restaff the old cab and stay in business. But if we move both TRACON *and* visual control over there and there's some kind of hardware failure or big goddamn glitch, then we're pretty much out of it for the duration."

Cleage did have a point. But Grice also wondered whether it was prudent to phase in the new tower at all during the holiday week. Air traffic wasn't particularly higher Wednesday. In fact, it was very low on Thanksgiving day. But the airport itself took on a frantic atmosphere with all the holiday travelers. Sometimes it was contagious. Sometimes even the professionals got a little crazed.

On the phone now, Russell asked her about it. "What do you hear from the new tower?"

"I hear the new tower's fine. It's going better than I thought."

"I hear the old man's been over there himself, supervising."

"That's right. He wanted to get a good look at a push or two."

"Hey, I got an idea," Russell said. "I'll tell you what. I'll make amends."

"How's that?"

"Maybe I could take my niece and nephew up there. I'll get my sister and husband settled, then bring them back and show them the new tower. Even Queeg likes to give the old dollar tour."

"I don't know," Grice said. "He'll be pretty busy."

"Counting strawberries?"

She couldn't help but chuckle. Dale Cleage was the kind of boss who would make everybody's life miserable, but then move on to his next promotion. Gerry Russell would always be a friend.

She couldn't stay mad at him for long.

"How old are the kids?" she asked.

"Ten. Twelve," he said. "Somewhere in there."

Not a bad idea, Terry Grice thought. Put two grown men, who were acting like adolescents, together in the company of much younger children. They'd be forced into mature, civil behavior.

Maybe that would soften them up.

"You know, maybe that *would* be good," Grice said.

"Of course it will be good," Russell said. "Hey Mom, even Adolf Hitler liked kids."

"Gerry," she said. "Please don't call me that."

Thomas Reidy woke up on his back, cold and wondering for a few seconds where the hell he was and what was that

picture of Jimi Hendrix doing hanging on the wall above
his feet.

Reidy sat up, sliding his feet from the overstuffed couch
to the floor. He was in a small apartment with tall ceilings,
one of those old Victorians divided into units. When he
saw the mirror on the coffee table, the long white smudges,
he remembered.

He remembered the way that chick from the blues bar
had licked the mirror with that long tongue of hers, trying
to get the last of the guitar player's blow. He remembered
the way he'd tried to fuck her on the couch, after the guitar
player and the brunette went off to the bedroom. Then he
remembered how his dick wouldn't get hard. He didn't remember her leaving, or passing out on the guy's couch.

Too much coke. Too much scotch. It happens.

Jesus Christ, what time was it?

He looked at his watch, a Rolex.

Shit, he had only an hour to get to the hotel, return the
rental car, then get to the terminal.

Jesus Christ, he had to stop doing this.

Reidy took a very long piss. Started coughing half way
through it, but wouldn't allow himself to hack too much
in fear it would turn into a dry wretch. After he splashed
water on his face, he went back to the living room. Found
his coat. But found only one leather glove in the pocket.
Looked a few seconds for the other one, but never found
it.

Shit, those were good deer skin.

On his way to the door, he knocked gently on the guitar
player's bedroom door, heard a muffled "Come in."

Jimmy. Yeah, that was his name.

The guy named Jimmy turned over in the bed, reaching
for a cigarette on his night stand. He had long blond hair
and fair skin. He smiled through swollen eyes. The chick
from the night before, the brunette from the Ypsilanti blues
bar, was out face down under a blanket.

"Hey," Reidy said. "Gotta go to go to work. Thanks for the blow."

Jimmy was dragging deep on a Kool.

"Hey, dadeo," he said, exhaling. "That other chick still out there?"

"I don't know where she went."

"Well, I'll catch you on the return, maybe."

"Maybe," Reidy said, trying to be polite.

Maybe, but probably not.

Outside, the sky was overcast, but the light hit his eyes like saltwater. On I-94, speeding east, he turned on All News Radio, trying to get a forecast.

". . . today, overcast with a chance of flurries toward evening. No accumulation expected . . ."

That meant probably a fucking blizzard, he decided. They always had it wrong. This early in the year, they seemed to get it all backward. The first sign of a major storm and they went fucking nuts. Warning everyone. Milking the goddamn story for everything it was worth. Those first storms always fizzled. It was the ones they didn't talk about that buried everybody up to their ass.

Snowstorm. Yeah, last night.

He'd met the guy named Jimmy in the bathroom of the blues bar in Ypsilanti's Depot Town. Told the guy he liked the way he played that Strat. Offered him a couple of lines. He'd brought a gram to the bar, playing it safe on a work night. They did it all during the breaks, between the three sets where he must have drank at least a half a fifth of Cutty's. Afterward, when they hooked up with the two chicks, the guy invited everyone back to his place where he said he had a couple grams.

Jesus Christ, he had to stop doing this.

When he got to the hotel, he checked out before he went to his room, leaving the rental car parked right in front of the lobby.

He stopped at the lounge, asked the bartender who was

washing dishes, getting ready for the lunch crowed, to mix him a Bloody Mary.

"How bloody?" he said, after looking him over.

"So you can almost see through it. But put in a big Styrofoam cup with a cap."

He had the next part down to a science. Shower. Shave. Apply two drops of Visine to each one of his eyes. He did it all in fifteen, still finding time to take sips from his drink. He kept his hair short so he didn't have to mess around with it. Could practically comb it with his fingers. Besides, it gave him that clean-cut military look.

At the closet, he hung his Dockers and cotton sweater in the garment bag, then pulled out and put on the white shirt, tie, slacks, and double-breasted coat. He tossed his loafers in the bottom, then balanced on one foot as he put on his dress shoes.

One foot. Not bad. Nothing like hair of the dog to restore some balance.

The car.

The rental lot. He left the empty cup in the car.

The shuttle, straight to J.M. Davey terminal.

Inside, he flagged a Northwest courtesy cart and road to the gate in Concourse E. He sucked on a couple Hall's Mentholyptis. Original flavor. Original flavor, he felt, was the best. He'd even heard it screwed up a breathalyzer, but he hoped he would never have to confirm it. He just knew it made good cover.

At gate E-25, a couple dozen passengers had gathered already. Through the window, he could see the 727 parked at the gate extender. He could see the copilot already in the cockpit, probably getting ready for the preflight.

A boy that he guessed was maybe eight or nine was staring at him as he approached the gate door. Kids always stared. Sometimes adults did, preferably a nice looking skirt with big tits. He'd scored that way before, but not in a while.

Still, the yellow bands on his arms and the hat did have a way of getting attention.

"Hello, Captain," the gate agent said.

He managed a wink to the young boy, then forced his best, sober-looking smile. But the trickle of Halls down his throat now was hitting the vodka and the Mr. Tea's below, the combination producing a sharp stomach cramp as he headed for his airplane.

Jesus Christ, he had to stop doing this.

Four

It took Riker a half hour to reach the top of the new tower from the time he'd pulled into the parking lot. He'd paced in front of the security camera for five minutes, then went out into the frost-covered parking lot and waved his arms to the windows above like a goddamn stranded boater. He walked around to the south side, found another locked door and another security camera, but saw the federal contractor for the new tower had installed the lock in backward. He slipped an ATM card between the latch and the strike plate and walked right in, but found the administrative offices on the ground floor still under construction. He tried the elevator, but it wouldn't respond. So, he'd decided to hike it up the stairwell, counting.

At the top, he wrote in the Holter log: *Walked up 350 steps.*

He found Dale Cleage in the tower cab with a half-dozen controllers, oblivious to everything but the horizon and their equipment. Cleage and a black supervisor were the only two people wearing ties. He was in his mid-fifties, at least six feet two or three, and had Texas in his vowels.

He wanted to make amends. "Sergeant, let me buy you a coffee downstairs. It's the least I can do."

They walked back down to the break room one floor below the cab, at the bottom of a narrow, tight staircase. Cleage offered Riker not only coffee, but breakfast.

"Breakfast?"

"My treat, Sergeant," he said.

Riker saw a microwave. He saw a half-dozen vending machines full of frozen mysteries.

"I'm all set," Riker said politely. "Coffee is fine. Black. No sugar."

Cleage poured coffee from a Bunn, and they sat at a table in front of a large window. To the east, they could see the Renaissance Center and the Detroit skyline twenty-five miles away. To the west, a line of clouds were just starting to show above the horizon.

"Some view," Riker said.

"Our elevation is two hundred and forty-eight feet," Cleage said, as if he were proud of every foot. "Roughly five times as high as the old tower. Some of the controllers who were up here Monday when we had a thirty-knot wind. They swore they could feel it sway."

"The last time I climbed so many steps was the Washington Monument," Riker said. "I was ten."

Cleage apologized again. "You know, I don't know what I was thinking. We have monitors for the two security cameras, but I guess none of us were watching. And from this elevation, you just don't notice the parking lot below. We just had our morning push. I guess it doesn't help to have state-of-the-art security, if we don't use it, does it?"

Speaking of security, Riker told Cleage about the lock.

"I'll have to get someone on that," he said.

Riker took a large swig of the coffee, then said, "So, the lieutenant wanted me just to check base with you on this radio problem. Let me ask you, have you had any of these phony transmissions since the series you reported two weeks ago?"

"No," Cleage said. "And everyone has been looking out for *anything* irregular."

"What do you do, anyway?"

"About what?"

"When this guy with the radio starts talking to airplanes?"

"We have a protocol."

"A protocol? I'm not quite sure I follow."

"Such a situation is specifically addressed in our revised regulations. We broadcast a general alert on all frequencies that phantom controller communications are being received, advising all aircraft to proceed with extreme caution."

Just like that, Riker thought. You have it in the book, therefore *problem solved.*

"But then what?" Riker asked.

Cleage didn't understand.

"Well, you still have two people giving directions to an airplane," Riker explained. "One's an impostor. One's the real thing."

"Well, we hope that the flight crews know the difference."

"Do they? Have they?"

"The transmissions two weeks ago, actually, were pretty authentic sounding. This person obviously had listened quite a bit. Scanners, you know. They're available anywhere."

"But not broadcast equipment, from what I understand."

"No, that's a bit hard to come by. You'd have to build it."

"Well, as you may already know, we're working with the Detroit FCC office on this. They say it would probably be too costly to build something with very much range. They suggested we be on the look out for something portable, operating out of a car. Our cruisers are well aware of the problem, but the lieutenant wanted me to stress to you the importance of calling us the minute you pick up one of these things. Beyond that, I'm not sure there's much more we can do."

"We've put out a letter to airmen."

"What's that?"

"An official administration notice to all commercial air carriers and pilots about the problem. Everybody flying in and out of here will be well aware of the potential."

Riker finished his coffee and stood up. They walked to the elevator, Cleage wondering if they could get a couple of patrol cars when they moved the radar room to the new tower next week.

"Just call the lieutenant," Riker said. "He'll be back by then."

"Where is he, anyway?" Cleage asked.

"Conducting some habitat studies in northern Michigan," Riker said.

Cleage didn't quite know what to say.

Riker was thinking about what Cleage had told him about the phantom transmissions. He remembered the news story about the radar failures.

"Say, you haven't been having any labor problems, have you?"

Cleage activated the elevator with a pass key.

"What do you mean?"

"Disgruntled employees. Pissing match with the controller local. Things like that. I seem to remember your union people squawking in the paper the other day."

Cleage seemed defensive. "I don't understand what you're implying, sergeant."

Riker stepped on the elevator.

"Well, you might want to think about it," Riker said. "Your radar failures. Other problems. Maybe your phantom controller is one of your own."

The Airport Police Department was located in the old county sheriff's road patrol building on Middlebelt, a relic from the 1940s—two stories, red brick, iron windows trimmed in red lead paint, and double front doors with bad hinges that left them perpetually ajar.

When Riker walked into the detective bureau, rookie detective Jimmy Oshefsky was putting something under the DBs Christmas tree. The lieutenant had insisted on pulling the twisted artificial tree out of its box and assembling it a week ago. His premature anticipation of the holidays had so disgusted detectives, they'd decorated it with the worst ornaments they could find, including nearly fifty empty shotgun shells somebody brought over from the gun range.

"Jack," Oshefsky said, when he saw him. "You have . . ."

Riker had his eye on a half a dozen wrapped fifths Oshefsky had placed under the tree.

"What's that?" Riker interrupted, approaching the tree.

"Jack, you ought to know that . . ."

"Oshefsky, just tell me, goddamnit, what the hell are those?"

Oshefsky scratched his bushy cowlick. He was a little stocky, but had the flat belly of a man nearing his thirtieth.

"Okay. They came today. One of the girls from the Landing Strip just brought them over. I guess a couple of the other guys were over there last night and mentioned to the manager we had a tree up."

The Landing Strip was one of the local topless bars. Some of the department cops had made a habit of the place.

"Six bottles, one for everybody," Oshefsky said. "Pretty generous, huh?"

Riker shook his head. "Shit, six bottles wouldn't even last me a week."

"Jack," Oshefsky said.

"What?"

"Mizz Harmon," he said, nodding.

"What about her?" Riker said. "Don't tell me she called again. That woman's becoming a perpetual pain in the ass."

Oshefsky slowly raised his finger, pointing behind Riker. He turned around.

She was sitting at his desk.

Mizz Harmon was Caley Harmon, president of Local 2959 of the International Brotherhood of Teamsters, the union that represented Northwest flight attendants. Everyone in the DB called her *Mizz* Harmon because she'd been hounding the DB on almost a daily basis for the past month, inquiring about their investigation of a missing flight attendant.

"Perpetual, Sergeant?" she said.

He looked back at Oshefsky. Shit, he could have pointed a hell of a lot earlier.

"Jack, I tried to tell you when you came in," he said.

Riker sighed. When he started to walk over, Harmon smiled, picked up his telephone and started dialing.

"I'll be with you in a minute, Sergeant," she said.

Oh, excuse me, he thought. Sorry to interrupt.

Riker walked back over to Oshefsky, who now had sought protection at his desk on the other side of the room.

"Jesus, Jimmy," Riker said quietly. "Why the fuck did you put her there?"

Oshefsky held out his hands. "I told her I didn't know when you'd be back. She took the desk all on her own. She's been using your phone."

"She saw the dancer deliver the booze?"

Oshefsky nodded.

"Great. Where is everybody else?"

"At the terminals. Somebody spotted The Bump."

The Bump was a local pickpocket, known for relieving people of their wallets as he bumped into them in long ticket lines.

Riker sat on Oshefsky's desk and waited, watching her talk.

Caley Harmon was some kind of Teamster. A very attractive woman, everyone agreed. She stood about five feet ten, but came off more statuesque in the pumps and dark suits she liked to wear. While they called her *Mizz* Harmon, Riker had never heard her run the gender angle on anyone.

In its own way, Riker figured, *Mizz* was a title of deference, really. The woman could swear like an iron worker or work you with silence. That was a talent a detective had to respect.

When she sounded like she was going to finish, Riker walked over to his desk to reclaim it. He stood over her now, looking down. He put his hands on his hips, pushing his sport coat back, revealing the butt of his Colt in an unconscious show of authority.

She hung up and pointed.

"What's that on your belt, sergeant?"

She was pointing at the Holter monitor.

"You don't strike me as Walkman type."

When he ignored the question, she stood up and they switched places.

"Thank you," he said.

His chair was warm. She put half of her ass on his desk and hovered over him. Now, he wished he hadn't sat down.

"You know," she said. "I wouldn't have to resort to camping out here and allowing you to embarrass yourself if you returned my damn phone calls."

Riker knew Oshefsky was listening, even though he was looking busy, typing a report.

"Like I told you the last time we spoke, our investigation into the Delesandro matter is continuing. We're doing everything we can to develop and pursue leads, but so far we just don't have anything to report. I told you I'd call you when I did."

"Today is thirty days. She's been missing thirty days."

"Is it? I didn't realize that. Is thirty days supposed to be some kind of magic number? After *thirty days* does that mean we're no longer eligible for the bonus prize?"

She leaned toward him. "Sergeant Riker, tell me. If Nikki Delesandro had a family, would it make any difference?"

"Difference? I don't know what you mean."

"If you had to come in here every day and take phone calls from her mother, or her father, or maybe a husband, which you and I both know she doesn't happen to have back in Minneapolis, would you be handling this case any differently?"

"Yeah. I'd be spending more time on the phone with her family."

"Then, think of me as family."

Riker rubbed his temples. "Look. You know how many people turn up missing in a normal jurisdiction like Detroit?"

"This isn't a normal jurisdiction."

He tried it another way. "This is a Northwest employee from another state. She flies in here for a layover and disappears. The last anyone sees her she's headed out of Concourse E for a shuttle bus to the hotel. She probably passes anywhere from three to five hundred total strangers in the concourse, mostly people who are catching or leaving flights. People who will walk through this airport maybe a couple of times in a year. They're not going to notice her. In uniform, she's just another stewardess."

She interrupted, "They are not stewardesses anymore."

"She's just another *flight attendant*. She doesn't know any of the people who work here. Those she did, the flight crew, tell us nothing that can help us. None of the shuttle bus drivers saw her. No one ever saw her get on the bus. We're *trying.*"

Riker looked up. Caley Harmon said nothing.

Riker continued, "Look, we've got flyers all over the airport. But unless someone calls us, who are we supposed to talk to? Help me here. Hey, I want to find her, too. It's *my* case. You think I want an open file?"

"How about talking to the people who *knew* her," Harmon said. "Mainly, people she flew with. Those are the people who call me."

"We have talked to those people. She did have a lot of . . . relationships."

"What are you saying?"

"I'm not at liberty to discuss her background. That wouldn't be fair to her."

Harmon rapped her nails a couple times on his desk. "So you think she liked to pick up guys. Screw some of the suits she met on trips."

"Well, you said it. I didn't."

"So, is that important?"

"Yeah, it's important. But either myself, or Detective Oshefsky over there, interviewed every passenger she talked to on her last trip. It took us a week to track them all down, check their stories. But so far, that angle has produced nothing."

"No, that's not what you're saying."

"It's not? Tell me *Mizz* Harmon, just what exactly am I saying? I'd love to know."

"No, you're saying that because Nikki Delesandro was a slut, that she isn't a high priority. You know, like some serial killer knocking off prostitutes. Nobody does shit until a half-dozen or so show up dead."

"That definitely is not what I'm saying. I'm saying when you have someone who is indiscreet like that, it just makes the job harder."

Harmon slid off his desk and stood.

She held out her hand, "I'd like to see who you've interviewed."

"What?"

"I'd like to see your investigation. Your file."

Riker shook his head. "I can't do that."

"You could."

"I couldn't, if I wanted to."

"Who can? Who can authorize you to show me the file."

"Well, that would be the commander's call."

"Where's his office?"

"He's not here."

"Where is he?"

"He's killing helpless, defenseless deer. In fact, he's told me this year he was looking for a perfect match for Bambi. He won't be back until next Tuesday."

She reached for her overcoat and started to put it on.

Thank god she's leaving, Riker thought. He got up to show her to the door.

"Mizz Harmon, believe me," he said. "Everyone here in the DB would like to find out what happened to your flight attendant. And hopefully, we will. But it is the day before Thanksgiving. Some people call it the worst day in aviation. You know what that means here at the airport. For us, it's awfully busy around here."

As they walked, she looked over at Oshefsky, who was caught looking, his hands just resting on the typewriter keys. He started typing again.

She stopped at the Christmas tree, looking down at the gift boxes of liquor.

"It doesn't look that busy to me," she said.

"It will be," Riker said.

"Do you realize that is the ugliest Christmas tree I've ever seen in my life?"

Riker smiled. "We went all out."

She shook her head in exasperation.

"Look, I'm really not trying to give you a hard time," he said, softening now. "Come back Tuesday, talk to the commander. If he has no problem with it, I don't. Maybe we can work it out."

She started walking away, but still talking.

"I'm sure we can. But not Tuesday. Today. I'll be back today for the file."

"You will?"

"I'm going to mention it to the director of airports. I'm going to be seeing him later today."

* * *

When Riker went for some coffee, Oshefsky said, "That's turned into a real pain-in-the-ass homicide."

Oshefsky had come over from the county six months ago. He'd scored real high on the county tests, but needed a good three or four years in the job to mature. Riker had been trying to pass some knowledge along where he could. Mainly, he told him he had to get out of the office more, quit relying on his goddamn telephone. "That way you don't have to deal with the lieutenant," he told him. "And you learn the airport. That's how you close cases. You gotta do it face to face."

Riker answered, "It's not a homicide, Jimmy. Not yet, at least."

"Maybe she'll show up as a stinker."

"Maybe, but not 'till spring."

The last homicide Jack Riker worked was a *stinker,* in the parking structure across from J.M. Davey. In fact, every murder case Riker worked at Metro originated in one of the structures, usually on the upper levels where it was more remote.

Leo had come up with the handle *stinker.* He seemed to delight in dispatching one, loved to hear his own voice say it, like a deejay listening to his own voice.

"Riker, we got a stinker. Davey structure, sixth level."

Leo used to work a car, put didn't take the twenty-five and out, opting to stay on in the radio room. Ten years in radio, never seeing anything, only hearing about it. Riker figured that's what happened to you when you hung around past your prime.

"Hey Riker, what's the word on that stinker?"

Riker had to admit, it was damn appropriate. Stinkers showed up in the warm months. Sometimes a car would sit a whole winter, accumulating one hell of a parking bill. Then somebody who parked nearby would mention the odor to the parking cashier, something along the lines of:

"Hey there's something that smells real bad up there where I parked."

The last stinker was named John Wayne Davis, one of the real anuses of the world, everyone agreed. Over the years, the DB had developed three rankings for the human debris they routed out the big pipe. There were anuses, bottom feeders, and mouth breathers.

One morning, sitting around drinking coffee at their desks, they explained the terms to Oshefsky.

"A bottom feeder is just like it sounds," Riker said. "But here's the important distinction. The bottom feeder never sees himself as part of all the scum and muck. A bottom feeder is your basic, marginally intelligent psychopath who gets his sustenance from the bottom. Your basic con man. Somebody who hits dope pads. A blackmailer, or your basic pimp. That kind of thing."

"How does a bottom feeder differ from an anus?" Oshefsky asked.

"Again, Jimmy, listen not only to the sound of the word, but the image it conjures up. Think of the meaning."

Somebody pulled out a *Webster's*. "Here, Oshefsky. It's the excretory opening at the lower end of the alimentary canal."

Riker amended it. "Sorry. Not the meaning. Think of the function. What does an anus do? It produces nothing but shit, and if it is over stressed or on a bad diet, sometimes a little blood."

Batterers. Women beaters. Dope dealers. Muggers. Rapers. Purse snatchers. Pick pockets. Kidnappers. Child molesters. And some disorderly persons. They were anuses, Riker said.

"So, Jimmy," Riker asked him, "Do you think, given some of these explanations, you can guess what a mouth breather is?"

Oshefsky thought about it real hard.

"Man, what the fuck, I don't know," Oshefsky finally said. "You guys are talking over my head."

Riker set down his coffee cup and leaned forward, his elbows on the desk.

"Jimmy, you ever go to K-Mart?"

"Yeah. I mean, I get my fishing gear there."

"Next time, when you're looking at lures, I want you to look around a little, okay?"

"For what?"

"Walk over to the auto parts. The car stereos. They tend to hang out there."

"Who?"

"The mouth breathers. Watch the way some people look at the merchandise. When they read, when they try to *think,* watch the way they breath, the way their jaw hangs open, Jimmy. Mouth breathers are people who are so fucking stupid, they can't think and breath through their nose at the same time."

John Wayne Davis, the last homicide at Metro, was not a mouth breather, but an anus with a little bottom feeder thrown into the genetic mix. They found him in August, the parking ticket in the car indicating the '76 Ford registered to him had been there only a week. Davis was curled up in the trunk, his body blown up from internal decomposition gasses, a Fram oil filter at his feet and an empty Bud can near his head. Somebody had tossed a pair of cheap loafers on top of the body, a fact the medical examiner noted probably meant he was killed somewhere else where he was barefoot. It was hard to put shoes on a dead body, the coroner said. The ankles were the first to swell.

Riker and Oshefsky did a little leg work on John Wayne Davis and found he'd been using the same move for years. He liked to fuck fat chicks, borrow all their money until they were tapped. The last anybody heard, he was running around with some big gal from Brightmore on Detroit's west side. Riker figured he'd finally screwed one who had

some connections. There were a lot of bikers in Brightmore.

They never did find her. Riker didn't complain.

John Wayne Davis was an unusual homicide, as stinkers
went. Most were executed crack dealers who'd been en-
tombed in the trunks of their finest rides.

As for Nikki Delesandro, Jack Riker figured he was doing everything he could to find out what happened to the
woman, considering he also had to handle his regular work
load. The DB didn't have a lot of resources. He figured
she'd probably picked up the wrong guy, probably an anus
or a bottom feeder. Got into some kinky stuff. Got in over
her head.

Riker was getting some heat from the executive lieutenant. That had little to do with Nikki Delesandro and everything to do with the clean image the director of airports
wanted to project. There had been rumors that the county
was considering bringing Indian tribes to run a casino in
the new terminal when it was built. Airport crime could
jeopardize that.

"Won't that be great," Riker said when he heard it. "Dad
can lose his ass on his way home from his business trip."

But directives weren't necessarily accompanied by manpower and equipment at the airport police. Everyone always
cited the cars when such inconsistencies were discussed.
The department had new police cars, but no garage to put
them in. They kept the squad cars parked in a fenced lot
in the back, along with a small assault tank SWAT picked
up surplus. A frigid prevailing wind blew in across runway
three right in the winter. When the snow hit, they assigned
a community service officer to keep everything brushed
off.

"How come we have brand new cars, but no garage?"
the CSO asked.

"Because the director of airports hasn't built us one yet,"

Riker explained. "And the director of airports determines our budget."

"But the entire department just got new uniforms, and we didn't really need those."

"People *see* you in the uniforms. People *see* you in the cars. Once you leave the airport, nobody gives a shit how you look or where you park."

That's the way most business was conducted at Metro, Riker had learned in his five years there. Everything was hooked into the same theme: Look good—inspire confidence in the business of defying gravity. The public saw only meticulously organized news stands, well-lit souvenir shops and overpriced theme bars in the main terminals. The public did not see baggage handlers throwing suitcases at each other or the tired pilots sleeping in the employee cafeterias or the flight attendants bickering over assignments in the airline lounges. Airport designers had concealed the real workplaces in restricted offices below the concourses.

Instead, the public saw a lot of people in uniforms.

"You know why everyone around here wears them?" a ticket agent asked Riker once.

"I always thought it was to identify the company."

"Sure. But that doesn't explain why you'd put wings on an airplane waitress, even give some of them a military rank. It's all part of the show. Nobody really is comfortable flying. Oh, some will tell you they're used to it. But it's always there, in the back of their minds. I see it in their eyes when I sell a ticket: Am I getting on the big one that's going to go down."

The director of airports, James P. Rains, said as much himself in his introductory memorandum to the airport police. Somebody taped it on the bulletin board in the detective bureau. It was full of thumb tack holes from more recent postings, but the words were still legible: "The number one priority of the airport police must be to foster a safe, secure atmosphere that's friendly to the flying public."

James P. Rains was on top of the local chain of command. The commander and the two executive lieutenants kept the paperwork moving and picked up a free luncheon now and then at the local service clubs. But there was no chief, no police board. Only Rains, who had no background in police work and knew practically nothing about law enforcement. Under a federal law giving airports the jurisdiction of a municipality, Rains himself swore in new officers, pinning the badges on their chests himself.

They got badges and a lot of memos from the James P. Rains, a fastidiously dressed man with prematurely gray hair as white as Peter Graves. He took his title, director of airports, from the fact his office also oversaw the operation of Willow Run, a smaller facility twenty miles to the west. The airfield was built for the B-26s Henry Ford rolled off the line in World War II. Now it was largely used for freight transport and specialized corporate flights.

Rains liked to study everything, build coalitions before issuing directives, a style that no doubt worked well with the diverse forces at work in the airport at large, but seemed cumbersome in the quasi-military organization of a police department. When he ordered new uniforms for the airport police, he took bids for designs, then spent another two months securing opinions after one of his female staffers contended that the five-pointed star on their patches conjured up the white male dominance stereotype and was politically offensive.

"Where the hell did she get that idea?" Riker asked the commander when he told him about it after the uniform meeting.

"*High Noon.* You know, with Gary Cooper. She said, and I quote: 'You can't get much more white male dominant than that.' "

"Jesus, Gary Cooper was soft spoken. But it's only a movie. Gary Cooper wasn't a cop. He was a movie star."

People, Riker thought. *People* were so fucked up.

Rains compromised by taking off the rounded ends like the staffer swore she saw in *High Noon.* He detailed the changes in a memo.

"James P. Rains pisses memos," Riker said more than once. "Must have something to do with his name."

When he sat down, there was another Rains memo on his desk:

When on official business only, all nonuniform airport police personnel will use identification signs on the dash of unmarked department vehicles when parking in restricted areas in the airport complex. These signs must display the department star and the name: Wayne County Executive Marlon Ladd. Any vehicles displaying placards of other design and not carrying the county executive's name will be ticketed.

"Why do we need new signs?" Riker asked Oshefsky. "The patrolmen who write the tickets are from our own department. They know who the hell we are."

"I don't know," he said.

"And just where are we supposed to get the goddamn new ones?"

"I don't know. I guess we'll have to get some made up."

Riker pushed the memo aside and made another entry in his Holter log.

"Hey, Riker."

"Yeah."

"Can she do it?"

"Can who do what?"

"*Mizz* Harmon. The file. Does she have that kind of pull with Rains?"

Riker talked as he wrote.

"You remember that stewardess who was murdered about five years back. They found her cut up in her room in the Hilton? It was all over the papers."

"Right. Wasn't that Romulus's case?"

"Yeah, the hotel was in the city limits."

"Okay."

"So, did you ever notice that there's no longer a Hilton here at the airport?"

"You're right."

"Now, it's that low-budget place, across from the freeway." Riker pointed his thumb to the doorway. *"Mizz* Harmon here might have well have changed the signs."

"How do you mean?"

"When they didn't solve the homicide after a couple of weeks, she decided the security at the hotel itself was lacking because the perpetrator had gained entry to the victim's room. Anyway, *Mizz* Harmon decided that the Hilton was no longer going to be on the airline *approved* layover list. No more overnight bookings. You know how much that cost the Hilton?"

"How much?"

"More than one hundred rooms a night, Jimmy. That's *$1.6 million.* They lost $1.6 million that year, just before they went belly up."

"So you think she's got the director's ear, then?"

Riker didn't answer. He figured he already had.

Five

He visited the Landing Strip when somebody papered the parking lot with flyers billing it as the airport's finest topless bar. He went alone. Drove right past the valet stand and parked the car himself.

Somebody chased him, shouting, "Sir, this is valet only."

He parked the car, then rolled down the window. Saw the guy was a nigger.

"I don't need a valet."

"But here you have to valet park," he persisted.

"Well, then, where is the *nonvalet* parking?"

The blue skin laughed.

"There is none, unless you can find some place on the street."

The Landing Strip was on the edge of old Romulus. It was a farm town before the airport. Most buildings didn't exceed two stories. People going about their business at the drugstore and the bank and the barber shop had taken all the street parking. He drove his Wrangler out of their fucking lot, put the Jeep in the lot of a nearby grocery store. He was so angry he didn't see the signs saying "patrons only."

Inside, the club had an aviation motif, most prominently the neon outline of a Boeing 747 flying near the stage where the woman with the big tits that didn't jiggle was dancing. Of course they would pick the largest jet, he thought when he sat down. A big transcontinental special packed with Gooks, winging in over the Pacific, another red eye from Seoul. Get the slant-eyed suits over here for their fucking valets. Separate three bucks from all of them and hustle them inside like water buffalo.

The waitress asked for his order.

"I don't drink," he said.

"You have to drink something. How 'bout a draft."

He asked for a coffee, decaffeinated.

"What kinda business you in, hon?" she asked.

"Aviation," he said.

"You pilots," she said. "You guys have really cleaned up your act."

She didn't know shit. She was looking for a tip.

Aviation.

Laurel Kring liked the word. Some words sounded like what they were. He liked the old meaning, before it degenerated into a cattle call and some tubes of neon on the wall.

Aviation was a quest.

His uncle, his mother's brother, kindled that interest. He spent many Friday and Saturday nights there, at the home of his Uncle Lewis in northwest Detroit. "I need my weekends," his mother said more than once. They built models, and Uncle Lewis told him about being an aeronautical engineer during the war everyone wanted to win. Graduate of Curtis-Wright Technical Institute of Aeronautics in Glendale, California, the school right next to Howard Hughes's hangar. He got seventeen deferments during World War II, so he could work on the planes: The B-19. The Spitfire. The B-36. He hired in as the chief checker at the Detroit Packard plant that built the Rolls for the Spitfire fighter. He designed the B-36's wing assemblies at Consolidated Vultee in Forth Worth, then the world's largest plant. Three hundred drawing boards in one room, he said. He worked with Donald Douglas, Jr., in Santa Monica, building the B-19. "The flying laboratory, the biggest bomber ever

built," he said. They built only one, and on the day they
rolled it out of the hangar, they closed the plant so everyone
could line the runway. It flew off into the cool California
morning and no one ever saw it again. "I think they parked
it in Texas somewhere and it never flew again," Uncle Lewis said.

Detroit Metropolitan Airport bore no resemblance to that
kind of *aviation.*

There were no men like Scott Crossfield, the pilot Uncle
Lewis talked about when the fifties became the sixties.
Crossfield was a test pilot. His aircraft was called the X-15.
They held all the speed and altitude records. Crossfield
flew the X-15 fifty-nine miles above the earth. He poked
the jet's nose through the threshold of space, but faded into
obscurity back on earth. Hysteria over the early astronauts
robbed the man his due.

The X-15 remained Laurel Kring's favorite model. Black
and rapier sleek, its wings were little more than stubs. The
engineers had clipped its wings, but compensated by giving
it sheer engine power. That's how Uncle Lewis explained
it when he gave him the kit on his thirteenth birthday, ten
days before two Detroit niggers killed him for a two-hour
Joy ride in his Buick and a twenty dollar bill.

After the waitress brought the coffee, a go-go whore sat
down across from him.

"Do you want a dance?" she said.

Kring surveyed the club. He could see only a stage, tables and a bar.

"Where's the dance floor?"

She laughed. The second employee to laugh at him, he
thought. Not the way to treat a customer. No way to do
your job.

"No," she said, giggling. "A private dance. You can get
a table dance for five dollars. For ten, I'll do it in your
lap."

"Do what?"

"Dance. It's called a lap dance."

She came around the table.

"Here," she said. "I'll show you."

She straddled his legs and dropped her halter top in one quick motion. Her breasts were smaller than the girl's on the stage. She tweaked her nipples, then put both her hands on his shoulders, leering into his eyes.

Rod Stewart on the sound system, the song *Don't You Think I'm Sexy.*

She began grinding her hips on his penis, never taking her eyes off of him.

She pulled his face into her breasts.

Then back.

Staring at him again.

In his peripheral vision now. The table next to him. Watching. The girl with the tits that didn't move still dancing on the stage.

He could feel the bass lines throbbing in his seat.

"Get off."

"C'mon honey," she said, grinding. "This one's a freebie."

"Get off."

She stopped and pinched his chin. "Honey, you're all tense. You gotta learn to loosen up."

He grabbed her under the arm pits and his forearms extended in one quick motion. When she landed she took the table and his coffee down with him.

The bouncers held him in the back room while they called the Romulus police.

He left that day with two citations. One for disorderly person, the other for illegal parking. Not counting the five dollar cup of coffee, but including all court costs, the visit had cost him two hundred and fifty bucks.

Now, almost one year later, he was about to get it back.

He had a clear view from the window of the small upper flat he'd rented one hundred and fifty yards away. He saw a Lincoln pull up to the valet stand, then watched through his field glasses as men in trench coats got out and headed inside.

When another car pulled up, he lifted his field glasses again. A gray Ford Taurus. That would be better than the Lincoln, he decided. The valets might be more watchful with a Lincoln. A Taurus was just another car.

He watched as the driver stepped out of the Ford. About his height and weight. Dressed casually. He was wearing a tan parka. Kring had a tan parka. He had a dark one, too, if it came to that. He glassed the Ford as the valet parked the car near the back of the lot.

There were two valets working, taking turns. That was good, he thought.

Over the next fifteen minutes, he picked out two more cars with single drivers. A Pontiac LeMans. A Dodge Aires. It was best to have back ups, in case the guy with the Taurus left early. The lot was filling up quickly. This was good. He'd been unsure whether a topless bar would do a big business lunch the day before Thanksgiving.

Now, just wait. Let time work. They were so stupid, he thought. No system. No tags. Just that big wooden box full of keys and their half wits. They didn't even deserve to be car jockeys, those niggers and their precious little fucking lot.

He had this fantasy. Invite them all over to the small flat, one by one, and take them out. Everybody who had wronged him. Cut them up. Hang there body parts around on meat hooks and just let the blood drip on him.

It almost made him hard thinking about it. He could feel his blood flowing.

It was sick. He knew it. That was the thing. He *knew* he was sick now. But he didn't care. He still wanted to kill every last one of the motherfuckers.

He just didn't want to be part of anything anymore.

At the bathroom sink he washed his hands and face. After he dried himself, he pushed the hair back around his right temple, then the left. He lowered his head, looking up at the bald spot on the crown of his head, always checking to see if it had grown.

Back into his own eyes now, then opening his mouth. Studying the scar that ran from the corner of his mouth to his jaw bone. Studying the scar that never changed. It was a clean, straight line, not an eighth of an inch thick. The field surgeon told him that he'd done him a favor.

"After what you've been through, corporal, the least I can do is give you some fine stitching."

The year 1968. Two years after he enlisted to be a pilot. Twenty-two months after he failed to place on the aviator's tests and transferred over to tactics. Liberty Bridge, four miles north of Da Nang. One hundred and twenty-five Marines stormed that night by the NVA. A hundred men were killed in the first fifteen minutes. Most never got to their guns. Another two dozen died in the mess hall. Cornered in that goddamn canteen the final defense. When the shooting stopped, he lay motionless with an empty AR-14 and a .45 caliber Colt semiautomatic. The NVA sent one soldier in to scout the dead. The Gook put the tip of his rifle bayonet in the corner of his mouth and cut him. He lay there, tasting his own blood until the Gook turned his back. When he came up with the Colt, the handgun jammed, so he took him down hand to hand. One of three who survived, he had no use for a semiautomatic since.

It shouldn't have happened. Fucking West Pointers. Fucking ass holes in charge.

He turned off the bathroom light.

In the bedroom, on the mattress with a sheet cover and no blankets, he placed the black leather gym bag he'd brought over from the house. He took out the Mini-Master Black Widow pistol, then arranged three more revolvers in a semicircle, their barrels pointing toward the gym bag, alternating the two blue steel revolvers with the two others in stainless. On the other side of the bag, he placed three Robo alarms which he'd ordered out of the U.S. Calvary catalogue, also laying them out in an arc.

All four revolvers were loaded with half-metal-jacket hollow points he'd poured himself back in his workshop. His experience at Liberty Bridge aside, he did not subscribe to the idea that more was better. A fourteen-round magazine in the hands of a fool was no more effective than a frightened woman with a single-shot Derringer. Most people couldn't hit an elephant at ten feet with a hand-gun. That's why bullshit federal legislation to limit magazine size was such a joke. He pointed this out to his wife during the LA riot, when he saw the footage of that Korean, defending his business with a semiautomatic. The gun looked impressive. Semiautomatics always looked impressive in movies, shells ejecting all over the goddamn place. But he found the sound bite of that Korean funny. Despite all the fireworks, nobody ever reported a body count of dead niggers. "That slant-eyed asshole is just making a lot of noise," he said.

No, all of the weapons on the bed held no more than six rounds, and one of them only five. Next to the Black Widow, was a Smith & Wesson. The Distinguished Combat Magnum Model five eighty-six was a six-shot .357 magnum with a six-inch barrel. Next to it lay a Ruger SP 101, the gun with the five-shot cylinder. The SP 101 was a compact weapon capable of shooting either .38 caliber or .357 magnum. He opted for the larger load. Rounding out the collection was what an ordinary pedestrian might consider his most impressive gun, another Ruger, the Redhawk Double-Action Revolver. Rifled for a .44 magnum, it was the largest handgun made. With a seven-and-a-half-inch barrel, it's total length measured thirteen inches. Its two forty-four grain projectile could knock a two-hundred-pound man off his feet. Anyone standing within fifty feet of the front side of the barrel would be rendered momentarily deaf by the explosion. But the appearance of the weapon was as effective as its firepower. A Redhawk froze most people with its size.

In front of the handguns, he laid out the eight sub-assemblies of his only rifle, a Ruger Mini-14. The two twenty-three was made of heat-treated chrome molybdenum and other alloy steels. Air space separated its hand guard to promote cooling under rapid-fire conditions. With its five-round magazine, the Ruger was not covered under the recent federal ban of assault weapons. But this was not why he preferred it. He liked it because it could be stripped and reassembled in a matter of seconds, and without the use of special tools.

He took the last items out of the gym bag. A photographer's vest from Eddie Bauer. Four boxes of ammunition. A bundle of electrician's wire wraps. He stacked them just behind the pistols. He placed a hip holster on one side. He laid out five additional magazines with the Ruger rifle, then studied the entire arsenal for a moment.

No.

He put the individual boxes of ammo behind each handgun, matching the caliber to the weapon.

This looked much better, he thought.

Before he loaded everything back into the gym bag, he wished he'd brought a camera. The still life looked that good.

Back at the window now, checking his watch, then glassing the Landing Strip, noting that the Ford Taurus was still parked in the lot.

He put on the tan parka, then slid the gym bag under the bed.

Outside, he walked the one hundred and fifty yards to

the topless bar, hesitating just south of the property line until a group of departing customers formed by the valet stand. First one valet ran off to get a customer's car, then the second. Before they returned, he walked quickly into the entrance, but did not venture past the portico inside the door.

There, he waited only a few minutes, listening to the muffled bass from the sound system bleeding from the dancing upstairs. He cracked the door several times, waiting until only one valet was at his station. He wanted the other one. Not the one who'd originally parked the Taurus.

Laurel Kring stepped out and tipped the nigger ten dollars before he said anything. Not that he deserved it. Just a little diversion.

Plus, all us white boys look alike, don't you know?

"The gray Taurus back there, please," he said.

Six

In a day, there are eight pushes—fifteen to thirty-minute periods when commercial aircraft come and go in bunches like flocking birds.

The noon push actually began at 11:30 A.M. and ended just before 12 P.M. As Terry Grice strolled around the darkened TRACON, she didn't need the digital clock on the wall to know the time was nearing the half hour. She knew the push was starting when feeder controller rose three times in five minutes to distribute flight progress strips to four approach and departure controllers working the radar room scopes.

This is what an FAA air traffic control supervisor did. She walked around a lot. She watched and listened. She alone knew the status of all the individual stations: Approach control. Departure control. Feeder control. Final control. Flight data. In a push, each worked at least a dozen birds or more. Terry Grice's charge was the entire flock as it moved through the system. She had to anticipate the bottlenecks and glitches. She had to discern them before they ever had the chance to form.

At eleven thirty-two, she glanced up at the weather monitor. A low-pressure area they'd been expected all day had arrived in the form of a ceiling of stratocumulus clouds at twenty-five hundred feet. Aircraft could safely penetrate the cover with ILS, the FAA's instrument landing system that used beacons and markers to guide pilots in their final run-

way approaches as if they were descending on a set of
electronic rails.

Below the weather monitor, approach controller Jay
Dugan leaned slightly forward at his console, his eyes darting from flight to flight as each sweep of the radar moved
two lines of lights on his scope forward another fraction
of an inch. The lights all had tails, all advancing toward a
large glowing circle in the center. The effect was not unlike
watching orderly columns of fluorescent sperm advancing
toward an egg.

Dugan was lining them up, as the Traconites called it.
He was taking control of flights handed off by Cleveland
Regional Control Center. They were winging in from departures in Boston, New York, and Philadelphia to the east,
and Raleigh, Atlanta, and Memphis to the south. Their
flight paths converged in the dark blue altitudes above Ohio
and Lake Erie. Dugan's job was to fashion these aircraft
into an orderly, three-dimensional lineup, keeping at least
five miles of separation as they glided in for landing on
runway twelve right.

At the scope next to Dugan, another approach controller
was fashioning a second, similar line for arriving westerly
flights on runway twelve left. Both had a dozen or more
flight progress strips that corresponded to the flights showing on their scopes.

Dugan had arranged his strips on the work space just to
the right of his radio transmit switch, inches from his right
hand.

Grice gently laid a hand on his shoulder.

"Looks good, Jay."

Dugan took his eyes off his scope just long enough to
look up and wink.

"Thanks, Ma."

Jay Dugan was good. They all were very good, Terry
Grice thought. If air traffic controllers were the stressed-out
lot portrayed in films and news articles, she'd rarely seen

it manifest on the job. Humor and irreverence dominated most radar rooms and tower operations. Part of the talent of air traffic control was knowing how to stay relaxed.

Grice particularly liked to listen to Dugan when he was working a push. The vectors, the altitudes, and the airspeed rolled off his tongue into his headset with the certainty of a chant. And he was as dependable as the localizer, a transmitter in the ILS that provided horizontal guidance to the foot of the runway.

"N two thirteen, turn right heading two five zero; descend and maintain forty-five thousand. Contact final vector on 118.4"

"Eastern, turn right heading zero one zero; intercept the localizer. Descend and maintain fifteen hundred."

"Northwest, turn right heading three fifty; maintain two thousand."

"U.S. Air, descend to two thousand."

"United, turn left heading three zero zero."

"American, turn left heading three zero zero; reduce to two hundred knots."

"N two thirteen, traffic—an American 727, one o'clock and three miles level at three thousand. N two thirteen, turn right heading two nine zero."

"Northwest, turn right heading zero one zero; intercept the localizer."

"Eastern, cleared ILS twenty-one right approach. Contact Metro tower on 118.4."

After Dugan turned over the Eastern jet to the tower, Grice began to walk toward the bank of phones at the feeder controller's station. She wanted to call the national weather service to find out what they expected for ceilings later in the day. If it fell below two thousand, for safety's sake, they'd have to take landings on one runway instead of two.

"Oh shit."

She turned to look back at Dugan.

His scope was blinking. It blinked two times then disintegrated into bolts of white static, then went completely black.

Voices shouted around the room, all saying variations of the same message.

"Radar out."

"Lost the radar."

"Radar down."

Sixty failures with the ASR-9 in six months. Now they had sixty-one.

Grice shouted, "Stop all departures. Radar's out."

"Again," somebody added.

One of the departure controllers called the tower. Grice walked quickly toward the feeder controller.

"Stop inbounds," she said.

The feeder controller had already snatched up the shout line, a hot phone connection to Cleveland Center. Grice knew the regional control facility would take back a half-dozen planes that were just entering the Metro control space.

She moved back to Jay Dugan.

"You okay?" she asked. "You got 'em?"

He nodded, confirming he'd committed to memory the position of his flights on the scope before it went dark. With the same precision he'd worked the approach, he began contacting his flights, his index finger moving around his flight progress strips as he did.

"American three twenty-one, proceed inbound on the localizer. Hold northeast to the localizer. Right turns. Maintain three thousand."

"N two thirteen, turn right heading zero three zero, holding at three thousand and circle. Visual. We've lost our radar here."

Dugan put six of his planes in circle patterns at even altitudes, still maintaining five miles of separation. The approach controller working the other line of incoming flights fixed his airplanes at odd altitudes.

Two descending flights reported they already had the airport in sight.

"Give them to the tower," Grice said.

"Northwest, maintain VFR and contact the tower."

"Eastern, maintain VFR and contact Metro tower."

The scramble lasted two minutes. Terry Grice knew the same drill was taking place in towers within a hundred miles—at Detroit City Airport, Ann Arbor, Willow Run, and across the river in Windsor, Ontario. All depended on Metro's ASR-9.

When it was over, when every flight was accounted for, they had a dozen flights circling Metro and all outbounds stopped.

Dugan spun in his swivel chair, looking up at Grice.

"I thought we had this goddamn thing fixed," he said.

At twelve thousand feet, flight captain Thomas Reidy banked the 727 to a south by south-east heading per the departure controller's instructions.

"Climb to fifteen thousand, and maintain course. Radar out. We're going to hand you off a little early here to Cleveland Center."

DTW was behind them, thirty miles back below the cloud cover.

"Man, we all just got our ass out of there, didn't we?" the copilot said.

He was about five years older than Reidy, early forties, and a Navy vet. Did his twenty and out on Harriers, then came to the airlines looking for the big buck. Reidy, who'd soloed at sixteen at a little farm airport in his hometown of Temperance, Michigan, was simulator trained. He'd learned to fly the 727s sitting in a box at the Northwest academy, or, as he told the curious, a box decked out inside like a cockpit, one that offered up hundreds of flying scenarios like a virtual reality game. As a result, Thomas Reidy was logging some serious company hours while the guy next to him played fighter jock. Reidy was already pulling nearly eighty K, putting his salary well ahead of the copilot, even if he counted the ten thou that had gone up his nose last year.

"Yeah," Reidy said. "Out by an ass hair."

Secretly he wished they'd been grounded. His stomach felt like shit. Ahead, three landings, four takeoffs: Memphis. Atlanta. Tampa. Miami. The "Vomit Comet," some of the girls in back called it. The prevailing winds sometimes shook the plane like maracas on that Memphis leg. In Miami, they had a four-hour layover. There, he planned to check into some airport dive. Get some rest. Get up, then back to DTW. Back to Detroit after midnight on a special flight.

He no longer wondered how he did it. He just did. He guessed it must have something to do with tolerance, or what he liked to think was his tough constitution. Those blood alcohol levels just didn't apply to him, just like those two pilots the company surprised at the gate at St. Louis with a breathalizer. Or was it Dallas-Fort Worth? One blew a .13, the other a .17. Most mortals passed out when they got into the high ones. Those guys claimed they hadn't touched anything but the beer and Kamikazes they'd been hammering the night before. He believed them. One hundred percent. He'd woken up buzzed many mornings.

Today he didn't have a buzz. He just felt goddamn sick. He had to quit doing this.

At thirteen thousand, the noon sun hit Reidy's eyes like glass darts. He put on his aviator's and turned to the copilot.

"You want to take this?" he said.

"Already?" the copilot said.

"Yeah," Reedy said. "I think I'm coming down with something."

"Really?"

"Or, maybe it was what I ate."

"I'm tellin' ya, you gotta stay away from those greasy eggs."

The thought almost made him wretch.

Three landings. Four takeoffs.

He'd handle them one at a time. He always did.

The copilot took the stick, but looked over again.

"Y'all forgetin' somethin', aren't ya?" he said.

He motioned toward the mike. He hailed from Chicago, but Navy flying had given him one of those authentic Chuck Yeager drawls.

"Don't ya think y'all let 'em know it's okay to stop sayin' their prayers?"

Ready picked up the mike. Hit the goddamn cabin PA switch.

"Ladies and gentleman, good morning. Or, is it the afternoon. I guess it depends on the time zone doesn't it? This is *your* captain Thomas Reidy . . ."

He let up on the key so he could cough, while trying to hold down another wretch.

The copilot looked over again.

". . . *And* I'd like to take this opportunity to welcome you to our flight to Memphis, as well as those of you heading to Atlanta and other points south. We're going to be leveling off soon at an altitude of twenty-eight thousand feet. At that time, I'll probably turn off the seat belt sign, but please pay attention as this leg of the flight has been known to get somewhat bumpy. Real bumpy, in fact . . ."

He decided to throw in something personal.

". . . Myself, I could use a smooth ride today. So let's hope for the best."

The copilot shook his head, half chuckling.

"Hope for the best. Y'all trying to instill some real confidence back there, aren't ya?"

"Fuck 'em," Reidy said.

* * *

Grice shouted to the TRACON coordinator. "Let's get somebody downstairs on this right away. Have them start at the power room. Maybe one of those surge suppressors is bad."

"Already done." The coordinator was holding a phone. "Terry, I have Dale Cleage on the tower line. He wants to know what's going on."

Shit, Grice thought, I don't have time to talk to Dale Cleage right now.

"Tell him I'm jammed," she said. "Tell him what we know. Tell him I'll call him back."

A new drill now. They had to switch over the CENRAP. It wasn't a radar system, but a long-range antenna based twenty miles away in Canton Township. It tracked the flights by beacons and computer-generated targets, feeding them to Cleveland Center. They'd take the CENRAP data from a phone line from Cleveland. Between the CENRAP fixes and the ILS, TRACON could get the traffic moving again until they could get the ASR-9 back up.

The transfer usually took no longer than a couple of minutes. If all went well, they wouldn't have to call the airlines.

Grice picked up the shout phone to Cleveland Center.

"We need a CENRAP feed here."

There was silence.

"Cleveland, I said we need a CENRAP feed."

The voice on the other end of the line said, "Can't do. CENRAP's not available."

"Not available? Why?"

"Well, you did order maintenance on the long-range antenna. CENRAP went off line at ten A.M. That's a four-hour operation. It's not scheduled for completion until this afternoon."

"I didn't order maintenance."

"Somebody there did."

Grice lowered the phone to her chest. "Anybody here know anything about a scheduled maintenance on CEN-RAP?"

She saw only blank faces.

She lifted the phone again. "Look, I don't think we ordered any maintenance here."

"Well, it's getting it, whether you ordered it or not."

"What are they doing?"

"Routine disassembly. Dusting and cleaning."

This makes no sense, she thought. Dusting and cleaning wasn't scheduled until the first of the year.

"Look, I think we'll probably be able to get our ASR-9 back up pretty quick here," she said. "But if we can't, how soon can we get CENRAP back on line?"

"The maintenance is scheduled for completion at fourteen hundred hours. But if you think you're going to be up to your gizzards, I suggest you raise our crew out there at the facility. They have a cellular. I can give you the number, if they've got the phone turned on and you can talk to them, I'll bet they can cut thirty to sixty off that."

She took the number.

"Hold on," she said.

Grice walked the phone number over to the coordinator.

"Get that crew on the line," she said. "If they don't answer, send somebody out there in a car if you have to."

Grice felt like throwing something. She wondered who'd make such a bone head request to move up the maintenance, considering all the problems they'd been having with the new radar system. And why hadn't anyone told her? CENRAP was her bailiwick. Only two other people had the authority to order antenna maintenance. One was an administrator who'd left the day before for a holiday vacation. The other was Dale Cleage.

Grice glanced at the tower phone, but fought the urge

to pick it up. She wanted confirmation before she started throwing stones.

She picked up the phone to Cleveland Center again and asked, "Do you have the maintenance request on that antenna?"

"I've got an internal notice."

"No, I mean the worker order. Our request."

"I'll have to send somebody over to administration. It could take a while."

"Do it," she said. "Then fax it, will you?"

Grice hung up and looked at the feeder controller, who was sitting on a stool next to her in front of the big drawing-board-sized workstation, unwrapping a stick of gum. The printer at his workstation was idle. Normally, it would be churning out two flight progress strips a minute.

The coordinator spoke up. "I reached the antenna crew. They say they can have CENRAP up and running by one fifteen."

Grice looked at the room's digital clock. That was an hour and twenty minutes away. Way too long. They had to get the ASR-9 back up.

Grice walked over to an IBM desktop and began typing in parameters into the FAA's newest piece of equipment, a program they'd put on line only a few months ago. The computer tracked every commercial flight scheduled or underway in the continental United States, reporting them as data or as tiny gray airplanes on detailed regional maps. She zoomed the map of the states to include an area a thousand miles in every direction from Metro, then asked the computer to show all Detroit flights in progress. When the screen refreshed, she could see several hundred aircraft spread across states to the east, west, and south.

Grice typed in a new request: How many inbounds scheduled for arrival in the next ninety minutes?

"Two hundred and sixteen," the computer reported.

She typed again. Departures?

"One hundred and ninety-two."

She took a deep breath and exhaled, trying to let her anger dissipate.

She turned to the feeder controller. "We better start contacting the airlines. Tell them we're looking at a thirty- to sixty-minute hold."

"That ought to make their holiday," he said.

Everyone in the room knew what he meant. The delay would hit the airport like a wave. The backup would start at the gates then spread into the terminal ticket areas. If they didn't get things moving within a half hour, traffic would begin to back up from the freeway, as motorists began circling on the access road, a mile-long loop that connected the terminals.

She reached out her hand.

"Gimme some," she said.

"What?" he said, chewing.

"Your gum. I could use some of that."

After he handed over a stick of Clove, somebody said, "Terry, technicians on line one. He's calling from downstairs. In the power room."

She pushed the gum into her mouth with one hand, taking the phone from the TRACON supervisor in her right.

"Don't tell me one of the surge suppressors failed," she said. "No, on second thought, do tell me that. That's something we can fix."

"Something like that."

She swallowed. The sweetened saliva from the Clove felt good as it coated her dry throat.

"How long?" she asked.

"We're going to have to rewire a harness. We've got an entire AC feed line fried here. I mean, this baby is burned up."

"Weren't the suppressors supposed to cover that?"

"Well, yeah. But I don't think anything could have prevented this. You gotta come down here and see this."

No, she didn't have time to go down there.

"How long?" she asked.

"An hour max, if you hurry."

She stopped chewing.

"Hurry?"

"Yeah, like I said, I think you better hurry down here and take a look at this before I start ripping apart this harness."

"Jesus, guy, I can't come down there now. I've got my own problems."

She had to call the tower, and Cleveland Center again. She had to figure out what to do with a dozen circling airplanes. Then, she had to decide what to do with two hundred more on the ground and another two hundred already headed their way.

The technician was persistent. "No, Terry, I think you have to come down here. And you might want to contact security."

"Security? What the hell are you talking about?"

"I'm talking about vandalism."

"Vandalism?"

"Yeah. Maybe you ought to call the airport cops. I think you'll want to call *somebody,* once you see this mess."

Seven

Gerry Russell knew there were hardware problems when he heard all the laughter as he climbed the last flight of narrow stairs. Only in a control tower could such levity mean that a major piece of equipment was broken.

In the cab, just about everyone was listening to approach controller Michael Garcia, who was gesturing wildly like a stand-up. In just ten years on the job, Garcia had somehow accumulated more aviation stories than most controllers with twice his tenure. In fact, he'd been working the open mike at one of Detroit's comedy clubs recently, and was doing his damnedest to look the part. He had a goatee and a ponytail. Today he was wearing a Red Wings jersey, and a sterling silver peace sign dangled from his pierced ear.

The union rep stopped at the last step, holding his niece and nephew back.

"So, I'm working over at Willow Run, and the call comes in on 118.4: *'Willow Run Tower, Cessna 12345, student pilot. I am out of fuel.'*

"I think, oh man, student pilot. Oh, shit. I better jump on the thing right away, right? You never know how prepared these guys are. I'm thinking this is going to be like *Airport*. I'm gonna have to talk this guy down. Or, if I got time, if he's got the altitude, get somebody in the tower who can.

"I say: *'Roger Cessna 12345, reduce airspeed to best glide! Do you have the airfield in sight?!?'* "

"There's a moment of silence, then the student pilot comes back: *'Uh . . . tower, yeah I have the airfield. I am on the south ramp. I just want to know where the fuel truck is.'* "

Everyone roared.

Russell scanned the cab for Dale Cleage. He was standing near the north window with Roberts, both of them ignoring Garcia's little performance, immersed in their own conversation.

"Garcia, you never worked at Willow Run," a cab staffer said.

"Some say he's never worked, period," Russell chimed in.

Everyone turned.

"Hey, Gerry," Garcia said. "How goes the battle?"

"It goes. You folks look real busy."

"ASR-9 again," somebody else said. "And get this, CENRAP's down as well."

Cleage turned briefly, noticing him now. They made eye contact, but the hub director immediately went back to talking with Roberts.

"Who do we got here?" Garcia asked. "Some new recruits?"

Garcia motioned his niece and nephew forward.

"Shawn and Marie, this is Mr. Garcia. Mike, this is my niece and nephew. They're getting the official tour."

Garcia shook both their hands.

Russell said, "Mr. Garcia talks to the pilots as they approach the airport, giving them directions on how to land. In fact, he probably talked to the pilot of your flight this morning."

"Where did you all fly in from?" Garcia asked.

"We live in Phoenix," the girl said.

Garcia nodded. "Definitely. I handle all the Phoenix flights."

The boy was eyeing the clearance controller's computer screen, but the girl was looking at Garcia with some curiosity. Both kids were mature enough to make a character evaluation, but not sure what to do with it once they had.

"Kids, I want you to notice carefully how Mr. Garcia is dressed today," Russell said. "That's why he's called a tower puke."

"Uncle Gerry," the girl said. "That's not very nice."

The boy giggled.

Garcia had always dressed unconventionally, but since Cleage's dress code memo, he'd responded by pushing the limit every day.

He crouched down, so he could be eye to eye with the kids.

"What you're uncle is trying to say is that this is the type of job where appearances are *irrelevant.*"

He said it loudly. Russell cringed when he realized what he was doing.

"Working on the front lines for the FAA requires mental agility, good judgment, and grace under pressure," he continued, glancing at some of the other controllers now. *"Traditionally,* if you have those abilities, everything else is really secondary."

Garcia stood back up, glancing over at Cleage, making sure he'd heard him. Then he looked at Russell and the rest of the controllers dead pan, before effeminately flicking his earring with an index finger.

"Uncle Gerry, can we look out the windows?" the girl asked, breaking the silence.

"Sure," Russell said. "But I think we better introduce you to the boss first."

Russell hadn't gone into the tower to make trouble. He just wanted give the kids a rather spectacular view.

He guided them over to Cleage and Roberts.

"Hi Dale," he said.

He only nodded to Roberts. In recent months, Gerry Russell had certainly taken issue with Dale Cleage's misdirected priorities, but Roberts was another story. Russell flat out didn't like him. He was half of Cleage's employee relations problem. Roberts seemed to relish being a first-class prick.

Cleage smiled at the kids.

"Well, I see you've brought us some visitors. We might as well open the place up for tours. We're shut down, that's for sure."

The two kids wanted to go to the window.

"Maybe you can sit in those chairs," Russell said. "Just don't touch any of that equipment."

He looked at Cleage. "It's okay, isn't it?"

"I don't think they could hurt anything. You know, that's just how I got into this business. I had an uncle with the administration. I got the same tour when I was a kid."

The kids wandered toward the window. Cleage pointed out to them a new fire house under construction about a hundred yards to the east.

Terry was right, Russell thought. The kids had softened old Captain Queeg right up.

"So, how long you going to be down?" Russell asked.

"I'm not sure. Goddamn ASR-9. I'm still waiting for a report from Terry. We can't go to CENRAP because some idiot in Cleveland ordered a routine maintenance on the long-range antenna. I never received notice. Can you imagine that?"

Russell really didn't want to get into the specifics, but Cleage had brought it up.

"You're thinking it's not the power supply?"

"I don't know. I'm waiting to hear something. Terry's gone to the power room. They assured us the surge suppressors would solve the problem, at least temporarily. But to be quite honest, next week can't get here fast enough.

Once we get TRACON moved over here, get if off that old airport power grid, our tech people say all these problems will disappear."

Laughter erupted on the other side of the cab. Garcia was telling stories again.

Cleage glanced up at the digital clock, then turned to Roberts. "Call over to TRACON again. See if they've heard from Terry Grice yet."

He looked at Russell. "We're going to be in deep voodoo here unless we get something up and running pretty soon."

Russell nodded, then called for his niece and nephew. "Kids, it's time to go."

The girl slid off the swivel chair. "Uncle Gerry, I'm not a kid. I'm an adolescent."

Both Russell and Cleage laughed.

Roberts hung up the phone, saying, "She's still down in the power room. They're all waiting in TRACON. Just like us. You want me to go over there?"

Cleage looked at the clock again. It was 12:32 P.M.

"Maybe you ought to," he said. "I'll handle things over here if we go back up."

Roberts nodded.

"C'mon you adolescents," Russell said, herding them toward the stairway. He slowed to say his goodbyes to Garcia and the rest of the crew. Roberts came up behind him, but then stopped, grabbing Russell firmly by the arm.

"Aren't you in a hurry?" Roberts asked quietly.

Russell pulled his arm away from the supervisors aggressive grip.

"I'd think you'd want to get a phone," Roberts continued.

"Why would I want to do that?"

"Call your reporter friends. This is your chance to make us look like ass holes again."

Before he could tell Roberts where he could put a goddamn telephone, the supervisor slid by him and went hustling down the stairs.

* * *

Riker considered himself very lucky to find a place for his department Dodge on the curb near L.C. Smith. The loop already was thick with cars cruising to meet passengers departing from booked flights and baggage claim. He slid his airport police placard on his dash, then checked his coat, making sure he had a pen. He felt the corner of the Holter monitor log next to his notebook. The thing had been poking him in the armpit all morning. He left it on the car seat.

Inside, Riker took the escalator to the mezzanine level. Terry Grice, the FAA official who'd made the call, was waiting for him just inside the door.

"We need to go downstairs," she said. "The power room is at ground level."

She was in a big hurry.

"I called the FBI," she said on the stairway. "But they said they couldn't get someone here right away."

"Their office is in downtown Detroit," Riker said.

"I know. But they ought to know about this."

"You said vandalism. Actually, we have jurisdiction over the buildings. It's not their case. It's ours."

They turned out of the stairwell and walked to a door with a sign that said DANGER—HIGH VOLTAGE.

Before she opened it, she said, "I don't know if you'd call this vandalism or not."

Inside, an electrician was unscrewing something in a junction box. He was wearing a leather tool belt and was holding a length of new wire in his teeth.

"Just a few more minutes, Terry," he said out of the corner of his mouth. "Then I think we can get your scopes back up."

Grice looked at her watch, then said, "This is detective—"

"Riker."

The technician motioned with his head. "The old harness is over there. On that bench."

Riker looked over. There was a four-feet-long section of cable. It was blackened, obviously fried by a major short. Next to it was a six-feet length of heavy, industrial extension chord, its outer rubber wrap wrinkled from excessive heat.

Riker moved it around with his pen. "What makes you think this was vandalism?"

The electrician motioned with his head again, to an AC outlet near a fuse panel.

"Look over there," he said. "Plugged into that outlet."

Riker walked over. A timer was plugged into the socket, the kind of basic household device people used to turn lights off and on when they were on vacation.

The electrician removed the wire from his mouth and began attaching it to a circuit breaker in the junction box.

"Somebody plugged that utility chord you saw on the bench over there into the timer," he said. "Then spliced it into this ASR-9 feed here. In the box, the circuit breakers were removed and jumped with number eight copper wire. When it clicked on, it added another one hundred and ten volts to the circuit. Major surge. It fried the harness. Blew out the main buss down here as well."

Grice said, "Our entire radar went down."

Riker looked at the timer dial. It was set to click on at 11:45 A.M.

The electrician stepped away from the box.

"Okay," he said. "We're about ready to rock here. But you better get everything off upstairs first before I throw this breaker. You don't want another surge."

Grice said, "Give me five minutes."

She turned to Riker. "C'mon with me Detective."

Riker said he had a few questions first.

"Hey," she said. "I got a couple hundred airplanes waiting on this thing. We'll talk on the way up."

She was nearly running when she hit the stairs. Riker struggled to keep up.

"Who has access to this power room?" he asked.

"You need a DTW ID to get in the lower level."

He knew that. "I mean, the FAA operation here. What kind of security do you have?"

At the top of the stairs at the main terminal level she stopped. "We have a receptionist during business hours out front. There are access doors at the lower level, but they're supposed to be locked."

"I want to get some evidence people over here to take a look at this," he said.

"Fine," she said, walking now again. "Later."

He followed her through the administrative area, then up another flight of stairs. She went through a door marked TRACON.

Inside, it was dark, the only illumination coming from small directional lights at the controller's work stations.

"Okay," Grice announced. "Everybody with a scope. Make sure your power switch is off. We're almost there, folks."

She turned to an FAA staffer in a long-sleeved knit shirt. "Get Cleveland Center on the shout line. Tell them to stand by. We're almost ready here."

Somebody said, "Terry, Cleage and Roberts have been calling every five minutes."

Riker watched her as she walked around the room now, checking every scope.

"Somebody get the tower. Somebody get Cleage for me just as soon as we get some good news."

As she came back in his direction, Riker said he had some more questions.

"In a minute," she said, waving him off.

Riker asked anyway. "Are you having labor problems here?"

She stopped. "Detective Riker, yes we're having some

labor problems. Everybody in this airport has *labor problems*. But right now I've got other priorities. I have several dozen airplanes grounded. Twelve circling. And another two hundred on their way. *If* we can get these scopes back up in the next five minutes, just maybe we won't inconvenience ten or fifteen thousand people in those airplanes, not to mention the grid lock that's building out there with every delayed flight."

She looked at the digital clock. It was 12:38 P.M.

Jesus Christ, Riker thought. Talk about priorities. If she didn't care that somebody just about burned down her goddamn shop, he didn't either.

"Okay," he said. "Let me know when you're ready to talk."

The electrician poked his head in the door. "Terry, you've got your power."

"Okay, everybody," Grice said.

Riker could see the scopes lighting up one by one around the room as staffers pressed the power switches. A small cheer went up. Controllers were putting on their head sets.

A staffer handed Grice a sheet of paper. "Here's that fax from Cleveland Center."

Grice glanced at it. "Shit, Cleage authorized the antenna maintenance." She said to no one in particular.

"Pardon," Riker said.

"Nothing."

She turned to the feeder controller. "Is somebody getting me the tower? Are you getting me Cleage?"

The feeder controller looked at his phone receiver, put to his ear, then rapped it gently on his palm.

"Now what's wrong?" Grice demanded. "Don't tell me the phones are out."

The feeder controller listened again.

"I don't know," he said. "The phone is ringing. But the tower's not picking up."

Eight

Somebody once lit a cherry bomb in the hall of his high school while Mike Garcia was in social studies class.

That is what it sounded like.

A dull explosion. Big at first, as if a large mass of air was being displaced, then instantly absorbed and muffled.

Another.

Then, another. Three in total.

It was exactly 1:15 P.M. Garcia would later remember that, because he'd just happened to look at the tower cab clock, seen the seconds flip over to zeros.

"Was that outside?" somebody said.

Garcia leaned toward the window, looking down at the freshly sealed blacktop. Cars and bright yellow lines pointed at right angles from the tower base. A gray Taurus was parked on the far end, away from the other cars.

He looked south, across runways six and twenty-seven center. Jets were parked at the gates at the south terminal. At the foot of 21 left, a half-dozen jets were lined up, still waiting for the departures to resume.

"There's no crash drill today, is there?" he asked.

Sometimes crash-fire-rescue drilled near the runways. They blew up old fuselages filled with gasoline-soaked mattresses, then put the fire out.

"I don't remember seeing anything," the clearance delivery controller said. She started thumbing through paperwork.

Garcia saw no fire, no fire trucks racing from the Tarmac, their lights flashing. Only runways and pale, dormant grass.

"The new fire house," somebody said. Maybe something exploded on the job site.

He walked over to the east window and looked down at the new building. A welding rig dangled in the air, suspended by a crane. There were no ironworkers on the beams. The pickups parked near the building in the morning were gone.

"I think they knocked off early for the holiday."

"No, people," the traffic manager said. "That sound came from inside."

Dale Cleage was standing up now. "Great. Now we've got stuff breaking up here as well."

"Maybe it was in the powerhouse," Garcia said, heading now to the south window.

Clearance delivery picked up the telephone, saying, "I'll call, but I think the engineer is at lunch."

From the south window, the powerhouse looked just fine.

The traffic manager, a black man of thirty-five named Colin Leaks, was absolutely sure now the explosion was in the ground control radar room, one floor below.

"But there's nothing volatile down there," Cleage said.

"Maybe our furnace isn't worth a damn," Garcia said.

"There's no furnace," Cleage said. "It's electric heat."

"No, man," Leaks said. "That didn't sound mechanical, either."

Garcia knew what he was saying. The intervals had certainty. Like a statement,

Mechanical malfunctions didn't make statements.

"I'm going downstairs to check it out," Leaks said.

He hustled down the narrow tower stairs, running his hands along the railing, pounding his feet like an athlete on the down leg of a stairway work out. At the bottom he pushed open the door into the hallway. The break room was on his left, the entrance to the ground radar equipment on the opposite end of the hall, past the elevator.

Leaks turned right. On his second step, he noticed the light reflecting off the stainless edge of the elevator door jam.

The door was open.

Five feet later, Leaks saw blotches of red across the carpeted floor in front of the elevator. Smeared blotches and a pool, standing tall on the new carpet's stain-guarded nap.

Colin Leaks thought of a V-8. Somebody had bought a can of V-8 in the break room and spilled it all over the floor.

Four feet from the elevator, this notion left as quickly as it came. The sole of a wing tip lay across the elevator threshold. It was moving in a slow rhythm, pushed by the elevator door bumper as it rammed the shoe at the ankle.

Over and over again, in one-second interludes.

Now, something told him to run. Run hard for the stairs. But his body took one more step. Roberts was face down, his body caved in on itself, as if he'd been hurled into the elevator with such force that his forward inertia left him in the beginning of a somersault.

Leaks heard the rustle of clothes. Behind him.

From the break room.

He saw the handgun when he turned.

Everything was very slow now. He found himself evaluating the weapon, not caring about the face of the man who held it. The barrel was very black, its tip very flat and shiny. Freshly oiled, Leaks thought. That gun is freshly oiled. He could see the rifling grooves.

"What are you doing?" Leaks asked.

He didn't mean to shout. It just came out that way. Now he wanted to explain this, but everything was moving so very slowly.

"I'm looking for bosses."

"You're looking for bosses?"

Colin Leaks raised his hand, half pointing to the elevator.

"Why?"

His own eyes were pleading, but he saw only dead calm.

"And, I'm looking for niggers, too."

Riker and Terry Grice stood just behind departure controller Jay Dugan as he kept repeating various versions of the same request on 118.4 megahertz, the primary tower frequency.

"Metro tower this is Detroit departure control, do you read me?"

"Metro tower this is departure control. We have a land line problem here, please copy by radio."

"Metro tower . . ."

Riker looked around the dark room. A half dozen controllers were waiting, watching Dugan, watching Terry Grice.

"Terry, Cleveland Center says they're ready when you are," the feeder controller said. "They say they're stacked up pretty good."

She touched Dugan on the shoulder.

"Try 118.9," she said.

He punched in the new frequency and began again.

"Metro tower this is Detroit departure control. Do you read me?"

Thirty seconds later she said, "Where the hell did they all go up there? They picked a hell of a time for a break."

"Another equipment problem?" Riker asked.

"I don't know," Grice said.

Riker followed her over to the TRACON coordinator's station.

"I'm going upstairs for a minute," she told him.

She looked at Riker. "You can come if you want."

Outside TRACON, she darted into a small supply room, then emerged with a pair of field glasses. He followed her up two flights of stairs, then to a circular stairway leading to the old tower cab.

Jack Riker was starting to feel like a goddamn dog.

At the top, he squinted as the light poured in from all directions. Terry Grice walked to the north window, picking up the binoculars.

She looked, nodded, then handed them to Riker.

"Tell me, are those people I'm seeing out there or what."

Riker lifted the field glasses. He could see shapes behind the glass of the new tower. Two standing at the north window, another moving around deeper in the cab.

Before he could answer, Grice headed back down the stairs.

Back in TRACON, she said to the coordinator, "They're up there, all right. Who do we have that we can send over to the tower? Find out what the hell is going on."

Riker knew little about terminal radar or phone lines or the radio frequencies of the Federal Aviation Administration. But he did know a deteriorating situation when he saw one.

He motioned for the phone. "Let me."

When he reached Leo, he asked him to send a patrol car to the new tower to investigate. "Have the officer locate tower personnel, then call me on my radio."

Riker reached down and turned up the volume on his hand held. He'd brought it in on his belt, next to the Holter monitor.

The monitor, he thought. He'd been up and down a couple of flights of stairs. When he got out of there, he'd have to write that down.

He turned to Grice, "Now, you're saying you don't think *this* is an equipment problem?"

"Well, both the land line *and* the radio. That's unusual."

"Maybe the tower's lost power."

"The telephone is a phone company feed."

She looked at him blankly for a few seconds, then started walking rapidly in the direction of the coordinator. "Let's get the tech from downstairs and get him over to the new tower."

Riker had enough. He wasn't going to chase her anymore.

"Let's just all hold on for a minute here," he said, saying it loud enough so the coordinator heard him.

He walked over to Grice, saying "I need to talk to you outside."

In the hall, he said, "Now, you called the airport police. Said you had a problem over here. And you do. Somebody, someone with access to that power room down there, blew out your radar. I don't know why. And neither do you. But now you can't talk with your own tower. Call it a wild guess, but maybe this *is* related. And we ought to get a handle on it before you plunge any deeper into trouble here."

"Just what are you saying?" She was still brainstorming, and impatient.

"I'm saying you all need to slow down here for a second."

She came right back. "I have nearly four hundred aircraft scheduled to land or take off at this facility in the next hour. I'm already two hundred flights behind. In total, we have nearly three thousand flights scheduled over the next twenty-four hours. Now, I'd love to stop everything, sit down with you, and probe the subtleties of some of our management-labor problems. But there just isn't *time* for that. And, we *are* working under an unusual arrangement here with the new tower. We expected some problems. I just don't know what they are yet."

"Okay. Three quick questions."

She looked at the TRACON door and took a deep breath. "Okay, but quickly."

"Have you had problems? Disgruntled staff. That kind of thing."

She nodded. "Yeah, it's been a little tense."

"Have you ever been sabotaged before?"

"Not since the PATCO strike. And then, it was just punctured tires. That kind of thing. I don't think any controller would ever endanger flight crews or the public."

"Okay. You say you have to be FAA to gain entrance to this facility."

"Right."

"The new tower. I was up there this morning. You have a key code lock there. Who has the code?"

"We have the code."

"We, *who?* Exactly who?"

"Well, the entire air traffic control staff. We distributed the combination to everyone this month, both tower personnel and TRACON people, in anticipation of moving the radar room over there next week."

A staffer came out the door.

"Terry, it's the director. It's Rains."

"Somebody talk to him," she said.

"He says he wants to talk to you."

"Okay, hang on."

She turned to Riker, her hand holding the TRACON door half open. "Is that it?"

"Look, I'm going to go over there myself. I've got a cellular in the car and I'll call you just as soon as our people make contact over there. It shouldn't be more than ten or fifteen minutes. In the meantime, I do not want you sending your technical people, okay? Send them to the gate, if you want. But just let us do our job first."

"Ten minutes," she said.

"Or fifteen," Riker said, as she disappeared into the dark.

Outside L.C. Smith, a TV cameraman was panning a patrolman moving traffic and the long lines of cars snaking toward the terminal from the north. Near the door, under the overhead heater for Sky Caps, a reporter was looking over notes for her stand up. Every year, TV crews came out to do the annual holiday crush story. Riker pushed through a small crowd watching the crew and headed straight for his car.

He used his horn to squeeze through two lanes of traffic. Only when he got moving in the outside lane did he notice the parking ticket flapping under the right wiper.

"Fucking Rains," he mumbled.

He road the bumper of the car in front of him, his right hand searching for his Holter monitor log somewhere on the front seat. It must have slipped into the cushion.

Screw it, he thought. He'd find it later.

Controllers, Riker thought. The situation in the tower reminded him of a story an airport EMT told him a couple years back, about the time a controller hit the carpet with a heart attack during a morning push. When the emergency crew arrived at the radar room they turned on the lights, so they could see to intubate the poor son of a bitch. Everyone raised so much hell about the glare on the radar screens, they lost five minutes arguing and dragging him out. "The guy didn't make it," the EMT said. "But they sure got those planes landed in time."

At the traffic light near the International Terminal, Riker turned right, leaving the congested access loop. He sped past the Delta Hangar and the car rental companies on Lucas Drive, headed for the airport's eastern border at Middlebelt Road.

He cued his car radio. "Leo, has the car reported from the new tower?"

"Negative."

"Who did you send."

"Four thirty-one."

Riker raised the squad car. "I'm near Lucas and Middlebelt, heading to the tower. You're location?"

"We're jammed up here just north of the Davey Terminal," a patrolman came back. "We've got a real mess out here."

Riker could see the traffic on the freeway when he reached Middlebelt. The delayed flights were now backing up cars a mile onto I-94. He knew the patrol car was in the middle of the traffic jam.

"You running code?" Riker asked.

"Negative."

"You might want to do that."

He also knew lights and sirens would be of little help on a grid-locked access road. Riker knew he'd get there first.

He called dispatch again.

"Leo, where is Stupek?"

Vince Stupek was the department's special operations director, another former county cop who'd made the jump to the airport police.

"He's at the pit."

Or the Uzi Pit, as they called it. A year ago, Stupek and SWAT framed up a small building in the southeast corner of airport property, lined it with old tires and used it for weapons training. When SWAT wasn't at the pit, they were drilling at training seminars in crisis resolution. Riker had attended a dozen himself over the years. But there'd never been a crisis to resolve at Metro. No barricaded gunmen. No hostage situations. Not even a run-of-the-mill psycho wandering down a runway, trying to kill himself with a 747.

As he sped toward the check point for the new tower, Riker didn't think they were about to break new ground. He suspected more sabotage, another power failure. Probably the work of some pissed-off, passive-aggressive controller breaking things in lieu of a Christmas bonus. Saboteurs, by nature, worked from the shadows. Riker had never known one to confront anybody eye to eye.

Still, Riker thought, it couldn't hurt to notify Stupek and his crew.

He keyed the radio again. "Leo, see if you can get Lieutenant Stupek on his pager. When you get him, call me on my cellular."

"What do you want me to tell him?"

"Just tell him to stand by."

Three minutes later, Riker turned into the access road off of Eureka Road. When he saw the guard shack, he started thinking about what he was going to say to the guard, how this was a police emergency, and what he and that fucking hippie escort could do with themselves while he made this particular police run.

At the check point, there was no guard, only the top of his stool poking above the solid partition on the guard shack. Ahead, the Toyota idled, blue smoke puffing from its tail pipe.

Riker got out and walked to the compact. He could hear a Bad Company guitar riff booming from the speakers inside. The hippie's head was tilted back on his head rest, the way he'd been earlier in the day.

When he reached the car, he banged on the window. Twice.

Riker opened the door to wake the ass hole.

The hippie fell out with the third chord change to "I Can't Get Enough of Your Love."

When he hit the pavement, Jack Riker saw the small red hole behind his ear.

Nine

Lt. Vince Stupek arrived at the Nomads hangar just ahead of the SWAT van loaded with banquet tables, telephones, and several thousand feet of phone wire.

Inside, he grabbed a Styrofoam cup off the receptionist's desk, poured out the cold coffee into a nearby waste basket, then turned it into a portable spittoon for the Copenhagen packed under his lower lip. He was a tall man with a handlebar mustache and a hairline that started just in front of his ear.

"Where's the switch to that garage door on the street side of the building?" he asked the receptionist.

She pointed. "Right inside that door there."

She was the only staffer in the building. "Is there anything I can do?" she asked.

"You can take the rest of the day off."

He was already somewhat familiar with the building. The Nomads, a travel club with its own Boeing 727, had cooperated in emergencies before. Located right next to the department, the building housed the club's business offices and a hangar that opened to the taxiway to twelve center. Outside was a sprawling fenced parking lot.

Stupek would have preferred to be closer. A mile of open airport separated the hangar from the new tower. The new fire house would have been ideal, but it was inaccessible under the circumstances and still under construction. Simply, the Nomads was the closest available building. With the club's jet gone on a holiday excursion to New England, the building had plenty of room. That's what Stupek needed *right now.* In less than an hour he would turn the Nomads into an emergency operations center. Or, in the acronym-filled field that was his expertise, he would turn the hangar into his fully operational EOC.

The garage door opened and the van sped inside. Stupek put a six-member SWAT team and a dozen other cops to work. He wanted SWAT to set up in the hangar. He wanted the TOC, or tactical operations command, to set up in the club's business offices up front. Folding tables and chairs were set up in both locations. In the offices, cops taped poster boards to the building's white cinder block walls.

Stupek pointed to a large office with an interior window. It belonged to the travel club director, who was gone for the holiday.

"I'll take that one."

Somebody pasted a sheet of paper on the glass, writing "OSC" on it—on scene commander.

When he walked into the hangar, Reed Johnson, the SWAT field commander, was unrolling phone line. He was a tall, thin black man, in his late thirties. He was wearing fatigues and a brown baseball cap that read APD-SWAT.

"Where do you want these CNT lines, Lieutenant?"

The crisis negotiation team had to be in a separate room, away from the noise and activity of SWAT and the TOC.

Stupek pointed to a door on the other side of the hangar. "What's in there? That room with all the windows."

"Some kind of lounge. Looks like one of the waiting areas you'd see over at the terminal, except its got its own bar."

"How about quiet?"

"It's all carpeted."

"Put it in there."

A fifty-two-year-old former Detroit cop named Tommy

Monsorta waddled through the open garage door in the front of the hangar, shaking off the outside chill.

"Somebody close that goddamn door," Stupek shouted.

He motioned to Monsorta. "Tommy, I'm putting you in that lounge over there. Phone company is patching us a line."

Monsorta was a rotund man who moved slowly, more a function of his disposition than his size. Stupek considered him a real find. The department had hired him as a part-time civilian in the radio room. It was a sweet deal, considering he'd retired with full pension after twenty-five with Detroit PD. Monsorta had spent fifteen with Detroit's hostage negotiation unit, dealing with an average of five barricaded gunmen situations a month. Stupek had convinced the airport command that one day they just might need a guy like Monsorta coming off the bench. Now that day had come.

They all had showed up from other jobs. The DB. Evidence. Dispatch. Patrolmen. Dispatch was trying to reach others off duty. The department had rehearsed the drill many times. The drill was designed to respond to any hostage taker, or HT. The drill did not vary, whether the crisis situation was in an aircraft or a building, whether there was one HT, or three or four. Staffing was highly specialized. The CNT in the lounge would have a commander, a primary negotiator, a secondary negotiator, and a police psychologist. The TOC would have a commander, investigators, and information handlers. Their mission was to receive and record data, evaluate its validity, interpret its significance and predictability, then disseminate it to SWAT and the CNT. All the commanders reported to Stupek.

He'd spent no less time and energy preparing. Some said he'd spent an entire career. He spent ten years crashing through doors on the narcotics squad back with the county, before he became interested in special tactics and weapons. While most narcs hit an Irish bar on Southfield Road after a night of ramming dope pads, Stupek went home and pumped iron in his basement. "That's just the way Vince winds down," everybody used to say.

Stupek had made this his personal challenge, his path to professional and personal growth. He'd learned to reign in his primal urge to attack, and attack hard. This quest led him to the prevailing philosophies of crisis situation management. West Coast and East Coast, tactics experts called them. West Coast was military oriented, an ironic tendency considering its laid-back California home. West Coast saw hostage negotiation as nothing more than a tool to aid the tactical team. The West Coast negotiator's sole purpose was to position the hostage taker for termination by sniper fire or full assault. The East Coast philosophy was the more ponderous. Contain and negotiate, East Coast said. Negotiate a solution and use SWAT as a last resort, as long as nobody gets hurt.

Stupek had found the middle ground in the philosophy of the Michigan state police. Once a siege was on, state police crisis experts believed the bad guy was no longer motivated by his cause or his emotions, but by the subconscious realization that if he made the wrong move he was a dead man at the hands of an attacking SWAT team. The role of the negotiator was to become a partner with the bad guy. Together they fashioned a leash to control the growling killer called SWAT. One inappropriate move and the killer could break loose. This nudged the HT to negotiate a peaceful solution, as long as the leash was kept very taut.

Stupek believed in the state police model. He'd convinced the department commander and the director of airports that the program at the Michigan State Police Academy was the only way to go when he asked them for the training funds. "Give me a year and I'll have a fully capable stand-by crisis team using existing department personnel," he told them.

Now, Vince Stupek was going to get his chance to make it work.

The walls of the Nomad's lounge were papered with murals, blown up travel shots of Bahamian white sands and a cityscape of London and Big Ben. In one corner, there was a display case with souvenir cups and glasses. Near it, a couple racks of T-shirts. In the middle of the room, rows of orange seats on blue carpet.

"Christ, they got everything you need in here," Monsorta said to no one in particular when he returned to the CNT.

He was standing in front of a stairway that led to a small connecting ramp for the club jet, small version of what everyone used at the main airport gates.

"The wife and I checked into the Nomads once," a SWAT officer said.

He'd just walked in with what looked like a large aluminum briefcase.

"They got something like eleven thousand members. They fly everywhere. All year long. Three hundred bucks to join. Ninety a year. Not a bad deal, if you like to travel."

Monsorta walked to the lounge bar. Slightly struggling with his weight, he mounted one of the plushly padded stools at the rail. He was looking at a bar clock, a lit bottle with the words MILLER TIME underneath.

"Where do you want this?" asked the SWAT officer, holding up the briefcase.

"I don't like airplanes," he said. "But I like this. Put that thing up here."

"You sure?"

"Yeah, I'm sure. That way, when this is over, I won't even have to move."

The SWAT cop didn't laugh. He thought guys like Tommy Monsorta were police relics. Considering the way he looked, it was a miracle the guy was still alive.

He placed the aluminum briefcase on the bar and opened it. Inside, was a control panel and a telephone handset. Across the top was HOSTAGEPHONE, and just below it, the AT&T telephone logo. There were four jacks: "hot line," "intercom," "outside," and "administrative phone." There was a red light, which would blink when the hot line rang.

"You know," Monsorta said, "I always wondered what it would be like to be the guy who builds these things for AT&T."

"What do you mean?"

"I mean, you're at a party and somebody asks you, 'Hey, so what do you do for a living?' And you say, 'I build hostage phones for AT&T.' And the guy says, 'Hostage phones. Whataya mean by that?' And you say, 'You know, the phones they use to talk to people holding women and children hostage. Psychos that cops gotta talk down before the goddamn shooting begins.' Now, can you imagine saying that at a party?"

Monsorta laughed deeply.

The SWAT officer was plugging in the phone wires into the "hot line" and "outside" jacks.

He stopped to answer. "I guess I don't get it."

Monsorta pulled out a pack of Chesterfield kings, tapping the entire pack against the bar rail to tighten up the tobacco.

After he lit one, he said, "Hey, I'm not trying to old soldier you or nothin.' But you're gonna have to lighten up a little. Especially when that phone is not blinking."

"Lighten up? Why?"

"You're gonna be in pretty bad shape by the end of the day if you don't."

In the radar room, the Traconites had both CENRAP and the ASR-9 up and running, but now they had no tower.

Per the request of local authorities, Terry Grice did not tell the airlines this. She cited "continuing radar failure" when she extended the hold on all local traffic until 2:30 P.M. Cleveland Center diverted nearly fifty inbound flights from Metro, sending them to O'Hare, Kalamazoo, and Toledo Express.

Then, she called the FAA in Washington. She decided national ought to know that Dale Cleage was in that tower. She thought they ought to know that by default, she was left in charge.

"All the airport police have told me is we have an apparent hostage situation up there," she said in a conference call with the regional director and three other Washington people. "We've been asked by local authorities not to respond to the tower lines, or attempt to make any contact. We've also been asked to release no information to airlines or other third parties."

"Do they know who's responsible?" one of the Washington officials asked.

"I don't think so."

"Who do they suspect?"

"I don't know."

"What about you, Ms. Grice? What do you suspect? Or, should I say who? Do you suspect one of your people?"

She couldn't ignore the sabotaged radar.

"We've had some adjustment problems with the new hub director," she said. "But I never thought it was anything that was out of control. I can't, offhand, think of any one individual who displayed that kind of potential. And I think, of all people, I would have heard something."

Hell, she thought, they all called her their mom.

There were several seconds of silence.

"Well, on this end we will be informing the FBI," one official said. "We're going to have to figure out where federal jurisdiction begins and local jurisdiction ends."

"What about local traffic?" somebody asked.

Well, she explained, Dale Cleage had left a contingency plan because of the tower move. She could call in personnel on overtime. She could staff the old tower cab with minimal equipment, as long as visibility held up. They might be able to be operational by the time they were scheduled to lift the hold.

The regional director was noncommittal. "You work with local authorities," he said. "You assess the situation. As for the local traffic, for now that will be your call."

After the conference call, Grice and a half dozen staffers scrambled to put the equipment together, pulling most of it out of the storage room where it had been placed only a few days earlier. At 1:45 P.M., they climbed the old tower's circular stairs. She carried a box of vacuum tube containers in her arms. A pair of field glasses dangled from her neck. Others carried the old tower's radio transmitter, others head sets, an IBM, and a printer.

At the top, she set down the box and took a moment to collect her thoughts. There would be no time to contemplate much of anything in the next few hours if everything went as she expected.

The tower was cold, like a big old empty house in winter. As staffers headed back down the circular staircase for more hardware and materials, she reminded someone to turn on the heat. Alone now, she thought the old tower looked worse than she'd ever remembered it. They'd painted the old acoustic wall and ceiling tile flat black years ago to reduce the glare. Only now, with it empty, did she realize how badly chipped it was, how the years had made so many scars in white.

Outside, to the west just below her, Grice could see the long traffic jam in front of the terminal. Those who'd finally made it to the departure drop-off point were unloading baggage. She watched a man lug two large suitcases from the trunk of a Ford, while a woman from the car escorted a silver-haired senior with a walker. She could

hear car horns, muted, but audible nonetheless. Here and
there, she heard a shout or a voice from the crowd below,
carried up like spirits in the wind racing by the tower glass.

At first, the notion of looking south frightened her, but
she forced herself. She raised her binoculars and aimed the
lenses toward runways six and twenty-seven center. They
were already in focus. She could make out unidentified
shapes in the new tower cab, but unlike the last time she
glassed it, they were moving. A lot of movement. Not the
way controllers usually moved.

Somebody in a dark shirt, near the northeast window.
His arm raised. Somebody in a light shirt. Running quickly.

Then disappearing.

Her body shuddered.

She began questioning the wisdom of opening up the
old tower. She remembered what the detective had said.

"You need to slow down for a second."

Those were her people out there.

She should have shut it *all* down. When she saw that
power room. That sabotaged wire harness.

"Are you Terry Grice?"

The voice came from behind her.

She set the binoculars on the desktop and turned to see
a young man standing at the top of the circular staircase.

"I'm Terry Grice."

"Detective Oshefsky."

He pulled one of his hands out of his jacket pocket and
shook hers quickly.

"I've been sent over here to take you to our EOC."

The dispatcher Leo ran over the dub from the crash-fire-
rescue line. Now he was looking for a place to plug in the
cassette player near the OSC's desk.

Lefty Thompson, the TOC leader, slid his chair over, exposing an outlet. Lefty was short for Leftover, a name he'd

earned as the night-side lieutenant, always showing up with curious looking leftovers his wife had packed in Tupperware.

"You ready?" Leo asked, plugging the chord into the socket.

"Where's Tuck?" Stupek said.

Tuck Conrad, the radio room supervisor, was assigned to lead the CNT.

"He's caught in that freeway jam up," Leo said.

Stupek walked to his door and yelled to no one in particular. "Get Monsorta in here."

Thirty seconds later the negotiator arrived, taking a chair close to the cassette deck.

"Okay," Stupek said. "Let's go with it now."

Leo had taken the call himself from the red phone devoted exclusively to air emergencies at his console.

"I logged this in at thirteen twenty-one," Leo said.

He pressed the play button. The quality was a little muddy from the slow recording speed on the original, but the words were audible.

"Crash-Fire-Rescue."

"Tell that goddamn police car and the Dodge to turn around. Now! Or, everybody up here is fucking dead!"

The caller was raving, his volume distorting the recording.

Stupek didn't like the way he said *everybody.* He said it as if some already were.

"Who is this?" Leo's voice asked.

"This is the tower. Who the fuck do you think it is?"

There was five seconds of silence.

"Is this some kind of joke, tower?" Leo finally said.

There were three very loud explosions. Then, some background voices.

First, a woman's voice: *"No, please."*

Then, a male voice, pleading, *"Listen to him, please."*

Then, some crying.

"Does that sound like some kind of fucking gag, crash-fire-rescue?"

"No, it does not."

"Then turn back the cars. I don't want nothing moving around this tower, you fucking hear me? I can see everything you motherfuckers do from up here."

The tape was silent for several seconds.

Leo hit the pause button and explained, "At this point, I knew Detective Riker and the squad car had reported a double homicide at the gate. They had already requested back up and informed me they were headed to the tower to investigate. I radioed Riker and car four thirty. Told them to get the hell out of there."

"Good," Stupek said.

Leo rolled more of the tape.

More background noise. They could hear more whimpering.

"Very good, CFR," the caller said. *"Now you're getting with the fucking program."*

"Who is this?"

"This is the tower, CFR. Who the fuck do you think it is?"

"Okay."

"So nothin' moves around here. You got that?"

"I've got it."

"Anything moves out here and you're gonna have a lot of people dead."

Then the line clicked.

The dispatcher hit stop and said, "After that, four thirty and Riker confirmed they'd left the area. You know the rest."

Riker had called in the rest to Stupek. All he'd managed to get was the tag number off of a gray Taurus in the tower parking lot. The car didn't have a DTW parking tag, he said.

Stupek asked, "You're sure none of this, or any of the

communications with Riker or the patrol cars went out on the air?"

Leo shook his head. "CFR is a land line. And Riker called us on the phone from the security shack when he found the guard laying there on the floor. Everything else was code, including the back up cars before they were re-called."

Stupek knew local news media sometimes monitored police frequencies. Already, he'd ordered no lights and sirens at the Eureka Road entrance to the tower. He didn't want to draw attention to the guard shack were the two security people were killed.

Stupek pointed to the deck. "I want to hear that one part again. The part with the gunshots."

He tucked some more Copenhagen into his mouth as the dispatcher rewound.

"Is this some kind of joke, tower?"

The gunshots.

The shouting in the background.

Then the crying. On the first playing, Stupek had thought it was the voice of a whimpering woman.

"Again," Stupek said.

Leo hit review, the sounds screaming at a high pitch as the tape raced across the play head.

"Is this some kind of joke, tower?"

Stupek stopped it himself after hearing the crying part. He looked at the dispatcher.

"What does that sound like to you?" he asked.

Leo shook his head. "Well, it doesn't make sense to me, considering who works up there. But it goddamn sounded to me like a crying kid. A little girl, maybe."

Monsorta had been silent, just listening.

"Tommy?" Stupek asked.

"Definitely. Definitely a kid."

Stupek spit. "Yeah," he said. "That's what it sounded like to me, too."

Ten

"Where the hell is Riker?" Stupek asked. "I want him in on this."

In Stupek's plan, Riker was the TOC's lead investigator.

"I talked to Riker down at the guard shack," Oshefsky offered. He'd just delivered Terry Grice. "He said when he got done with the scene, he was going over to the old terminal."

Lefty Thompson said, "Doesn't Riker know the drill? Everyone meets here first."

Oshefsky covered. "He said he wanted to talk to some people over there. I think he had something going."

Stupek's office was crowded and tense. Thompson's frustration extended beyond the missing Riker. He was having trouble finding personnel because of the holiday. Tuck Conrad, the negotiation team leader, had fought his way through traffic in his family car. No one could vent their frustrations in a tirade of profanity. That was not necessarily because of Terry Grice, who took one of a half dozen folding chairs along the wall.

"I presume everyone else here is familiar with our director of airports," Stupek said, motioning to the man in the seat next to her.

James P. Rains nodded his head, smiling like he was getting a banquet introduction.

Oshefsky started to leave.

Stupek stopped him. "Oshefsky, you're working with Riker in intelligence, right?"

He nodded.

Stupek tossed him a yellow legal pad. "Then sit here and take notes. Brief Riker when he shows up. You're going to need to hear this to get started."

"By the way," Thompson said. "We already got a make on that Taurus. Something just came over from Romulus PD. The guy who owns it reported it stolen from one of the topless joints. Not even an hour ago."

"Okay," Stupek said. "You might want to work that later. There may be something there."

"Right."

Stupek addressed the entire room. "Now, I don't want to spend a lot of time on this, because we're still getting set up here. But this is probably going to be the only chance we're going to have to get on the same page while we try to find out what's going on up in that tower. And, each time that phone rings in that lounge back there, everything can change real quick."

"There's been contact?" Rains asked.

"Not yet," Conrad said.

Stupek looked at Rains. "And there's no need to push it. Not yet, at least."

Rains said, "You should know I've spoken with the county executive. He's up on Mackinaw Island with his family. Obviously, that's several hours away, but should we need him here—"

"That's not necessary," Stupek interjected.

"But I do plan to keep him informed. He wanted me to pass along that he has full confidence in the department's ability to handle the situation."

Stupek let a moment of silence pass, then said, trying his best not to be sarcastic, "Well, Director, that's real good to know."

"Now," Stupek continued, looking at Grice, "Can you

tell me exactly how many people you had assigned to that tower at the time we heard from the HT?"

"The what?"

"The hostage taker."

Grice sighed, placing her hands palms down in her lap. "Well, as far as working staff goes, there would be six. Two on local control. Two on ground control. One on clearance delivery. One traffic manager. But today, he had two more people, which would have included Dale Cleage and another supervisor. They were there because of our phase in—"

"I don't need to know what they do," Stupek interrupted. "Right now, I need to know how many."

"Eight people."

"Men or women?"

She thought for a second. "One woman. The clearance delivery controller is a woman."

"Okay, good. Later we're going to ask you to provide Detective Oshefsky here with names and detailed descriptions of these people. We're also going to send somebody over to get everything you've got on that new tower. Security plans. Blue prints. Construction specs."

"I've got all that back in my office."

Stupek held up his hands. "Fine. But before we go down that road, let me just ask you one question: Is there any reason, can you think of any reason, that a child would be in that tower, especially on a busy day like this?"

She was speechless.

"Ms. Grice?" Stupek asked again.

Grice looked around the table, then answered. "The local controller's association rep, Gerry Russell, told me earlier in the day he wanted to take his niece and nephew up to the new tower and show them around. Why?"

"Two children?"

"Yes. Why?"

Stupek motioned to Tuck Conrad, who was sitting by the tape player. "Punch that up, will you."

They all listened to the tape.

When it was over, Stupek said, "Actually, this may not be as bad as it sounds. Those kids could help us later on."

"Help you?" Grice asked.

Conrad answered. "Kids make good bargaining chips."

Grice look horrified.

Stupek didn't want to get bogged down in explanations. He wanted to get what he needed from these people, then get them the hell out of the EOC.

"Ms. Grice, you don't recognize that voice?" he asked. In his lap, he opened his can of Copenhagen.

She had her face in her palms. She was looking down at the floor. "I can't say I do."

"How familiar are you with your staff?" He was holding the dip in his fingers, waiting for an opportunity to discreetly slide it into his lip.

She looked up. "Reasonably familiar. But screaming like that, I don't think I could recognize my own voice."

"I understand," Stupek said.

"Lieutenant, is it?" she asked.

"Yeah. Vince. Whatever."

"Lieutenant, why would somebody want to take hostages in our new tower? It has no real value. I mean, it's not like you can fly it to another country and ask for sanctuary."

He responded coldly, "We haven't had a terrorist-hostage situation connected with aviation in the United States in years."

"So?"

"That's why I'm trying to quickly determine here whether it's one of your people. Some things point to that, and I was hoping you could have confirmed it for us."

"What makes you say that?"

"Well, until we establish communication, we may not know. Though, if it is a single individual and not any organized group, it's to our advantage to have him identified before we do."

"No, I mean what makes you think it's someone with air traffic control."

"Our dispatcher reported that you told Detective Riker you had labor problems. Plus, you heard the tape. Listen to the terms. *CFR*. The way he uses the word *tower*. That caller is real comfortable with that language. He may not be one of your people, but the man on that tape certainly works in aviation or one of the various support operations."

"I understand."

"On the other hand, there is the matter of your radar outage. Those kinds of things typically aren't associated with workplace violence. Workplace situations aren't usually that covert."

Stupek slid the Copenhagen in.

Rains spoke up. "What about the airport?"

"What about it?" Stupek said out of the corner of his mouth.

"Well, I did discuss that with the executive, and we felt that, if at all possible, we should try to keep the airport functioning. We *have* managed to keep the lid on this."

Stupek's face showed nothing. "The fact we've been lucky to maintain a blackout on news coverage has nothing to do with our operation here wanting to keep the airport running. Once you get the cameras involved, it gives the HT another string to pull. In fact, there may be a request for news coverage from that tower before this is over."

Stupek turned to Grice. "Tell me there isn't a TV up there."

"There's six," she said. "Five are security monitors. Plus the union thought it would be a good idea to put a Sony in the break room."

Stupek looked at Rains. "You see what I mean?"

Rains asked Grice, "Terry, can that new tower pose any threat to aircraft, to the flying public?"

"Well, not when it's not controlling the traffic."

"Then," Rains continued, looking at his watch, "Then there's no reason why we can't lift the hold at two thirty and start moving people. We've got a real mess out there."

Stupek blinked a couple of times. "You've got an armed perpetrator out there. Maybe more than one."

Rains was undeterred. "But the tower itself is hundreds of yards from our main runways. It's nearly a quarter of a mile from the nearest terminal. There's not an exterior access on the tower cab is there, Terry?"

"Not unless somebody goes through the trap door on the roof," she said.

"If there's that kind of movement, wouldn't you have plenty of prior notice?" Rains continued. "Wouldn't you be able to take precautions?"

"That's not the point," Stupek said.

Rains continued, "Lieutenant Stupek, I'm not going to sit here with lives of more than a half dozen airport employees at stake and plead financial considerations, even though they would be considerable if we put a stop to the nearly two thousand arrivals and departures expected here, before this day is done. But I have to think of the flying public, the people who use this airport. The taxpayers who have funded our expansion. These people are holiday travelers. Think of the families. Put yourself at the table of all those holiday dinners."

Stupek snapped, "This isn't a goddamn Norman Rockwell painting we're dealing with here. In fact, we don't even know what we're dealing with."

"Why don't we?" Rains said.

Stupek took a deep breath. He didn't want to start a battle. He'd called the meeting to avoid misunderstandings, not create them.

"There is a protocol we follow here. A model. People spend a lot of time and effort figuring out various proven strategies for these types of situations. You personally approved the budget for the training, if you'll recall. But no matter how much training you buy, there's no crisis team anywhere in this country that can be set up and at full steam in less than an hour. We have a lot of people in the department on holiday leave. And SWAT hasn't even found a suitable base close to the tower to launch an all out rescue assault."

Rains nodded. "I wasn't implying negligence."

"I'm not implying you did. And believe me, if it were up to my basic instincts, I'd personally like to go up there and break down that goddamn tower door myself. But one of the things we've learned is that the key to minimizing the loss of life, in the early stages at least, is not necessarily how fast we can work, but how much time we can buy. We buy time with intelligence, but acquiring knowledge also takes time and manpower. Do you follow what I'm saying?"

Rains listened carefully, then asked. "Why can't you initiate contact with the tower? That lunatic on the tape could have killed everyone by now."

"Yes he could have, but storming the tower forty-five minutes ago would only have guaranteed that he did. And initiating contact before we're ready only increases the same risk."

"Ready for what?"

"We're still waiting for a psychologist for our negotiations unit, among other things. Plus, there's something else to consider." Stupek looked Rains dead in the eyes. "With all due respect, sir, I think you're heading down a road here that can create real problems for us."

"What do you mean by that?"

"Well, in my experience with high-profile negotiations back when I was with the county, as well as everything I've learned about this in recent years, the problems we run into in a crisis situation like this never really come from the incident itself, they tend to come from the out-side."

"I'm not following you," Rains said.

Stupek continued as diplomatically as he could. "Well, a hostage crisis is really a rather simple situation. As I was saying earlier, we have proven methods to resolve the situation, to save lives and end it, but the team members have to be allowed to do their jobs. When these operations fail, it's the peripherals that always foul things up. Pressure from outside the operation. Media reports. Administrators. Even pressure from the hostages' families. Those *outside* pressures can erode the patience and disciplined decision making that is absolutely required here. And when that happens, that's when people get hurt."

Rains didn't seem to get the message. He wanted to know more about publicity. "You said coverage can be a problem?"

"It can be, in the early stages. Until you get it under control."

"Well, my office is already getting inquiries. And if we face a major delay here, I'm going to have to announce something. It is the day before Thanksgiving, our biggest travel day of the year. Just what do you propose we use as an excuse?"

Stupek looked at Grice. "Your radar is screwed up, right?"

She said nothing. The eyes of the other cops in the room glanced back and forth between Rains and Stupek. No one was taking notes any more.

"What happens if we do that, Terry?"

"For how long?" she asked.

"Lieutenant Stupek, how much time do you need?" Rains asked.

"I'd like at least two hours. Time for intelligence. Time to make contact. Time for my primary negotiator to establish some rapport."

Grice made a few mental calculations. "Two hours would put us well into the late afternoon push. Total, I'd say about thirty to forty percent of today's flights would have to be rerouted, counting what we already have in the air."

"And if we lift the hold at two thirty?"

"Ten percent," she said.

Rains looked at the clock. It was almost two fifteen.

Rains sighed. "Well, that just strikes me as unacceptable. I'm going to have to confer with the county executive directly on this."

"Do you need a telephone?" Stupek asked.

Rains nodded.

"You can use one of the other offices here."

Stupek spit into his cup as Rains started to get up.

"Is there anything you want me to tell him?" the director asked.

"Who, the county executive?"

Rains nodded.

"Yeah, you might also tell him we don't have a tower. You need a tower to fly airplanes in and out of here."

Rains turned to Terry Grice. "What about the old facility, Terry?"

She wished he hadn't asked.

Jack Riker had his reasons for avoiding the Nomad's hangar, but he also felt he had a lot of unfinished business back at the FAA facility in L.C. Smith. After he got the two bodies at the check point squared away with the van from the medical examiner, he headed back to the terminal. He wanted to talk to Terry Grice again before he reported into the EOC.

Riker skirted the airport traffic, using the east service drive, then driving through the fuel truck gate. He walked into L.C. Smith through one of the baggage docks, showing his badge to a guy with ear protectors who tried to stop him. The idling jets outside rang for a while in his ears.

Inside the door marked TRACON, Riker found more controllers than his first visit. When his eyes adjusted to the low light, he could see a couple with their feet up, telling stories, doing what people do when work stops and everyone waits for word as to what was going to happen next.

He didn't see Terry Grice.

"When is she coming back?" he asked.

A bearded guy in a blue flannel shirt shrugged. "We thought she was with you, or your people. We were hoping you could tell us something."

"At this point, I don't know much more than you," Riker said.

"No," somebody else said. "Some guy, Olzewski or somebody, came for her. She said she'd be calling in."

Oshefsky, Riker thought. Shit, maybe he should have gone directly to the Nomads.

Jay Dugan, the local controller Riker remembered seeing on his first visit, slid his chair closer on its casters.

"Somebody is going to have one hell of a mess on their hands with these airplanes," he said. "It would be nice to know if it's going to be us or Cleveland Center."

Blue flannel looked at Riker and said, "Hey, you're a detective, right?"

Riker nodded.

"Maybe you can settle a little debate we've been having here. We were all wonderin' here what you guys are going to do with The Bat when you get him down from that tower."

"The who?"

"Kring, one of our controllers. We call him The Bat. We always figured he'd be the one to go."

Dugan chimed in. "Hey. He can't answer that. That depends if he's killed anybody. We don't know that yet."

Jesus, Riker thought, they must have made the ID on

the perpetrator. No wonder they sent Oshefsky over. They probably needed Grice for quick background so they could start to work the guy on the hostage phone.

Riker didn't want to look out of the loop.

"Well, it's hard to say," he told blue flannel. "Depends on his background."

Dugan suddenly dropped his chin to his chest, letting his eyes roll up slightly under their lids. He put his thumb and index at a point just behind his right ear, then started turning his hand, like he was driving a screw into the back of his head.

Several controllers chuckled.

"An in-house joke," blue flannel said.

Riker's eyes told them he didn't get it.

Blue flannel explained, "Okay, Kring works in the training unit now. But he used to be one hell of an FPL. That's how he got the name The Bat. Everyone figured he had his own radar, though he always was a surly bastard."

"What do you mean, FPL?" Riker asked.

"Full performance level controller. Guy who can do anything. Local. Departure. Ground. Any job in here. Anyway, like I said, we have figured in here if somebody went, Kring would be the one who would go."

"Go where?"

"You know, go postal. I mean, you just never knew where The Bat was coming from half the time."

Riker pointed to his own head. "What's this thing he was doing?"

"You tell him," blue flannel said to Dugan. "You came up with it."

"Well," Dugan said. "Like he said, it's kind of an in-shop joke. Some of the people here said that Kring was so intense, that the shrinks probably had to hard wire the guy to keep him in check. I came up with the thing that they put a rheostat behind his ear."

Dugan put his hand up again and turned the imaginary

rheostat. "When The Bat came to work," he said. "He had to dial himself down to get through an entire shift."

"Just a joke," blue flannel said.

Riker looked around. A half dozen controllers were standing around him in the darkness, waiting for his response.

"Okay," Riker said, half chuckling.

Controllers, he thought. They all were around the bend.

"So, when did my department contact you about this? Who told you it was Kring?"

"Oh, nobody," blue flannel said, matter of factly.

"Nobody? Then how do you know?"

"We don't," blue flannel said.

"It's pure speculation on our part," Dugan added. "As far as we know, he's home on holiday leave."

Eleven

In a negotiator's ideal world, the hostage taker called. A call meant he wanted something. If he wanted something, that put the negotiator in a better position to deal.

Tommy Monsorta liked making deals. If he hadn't been a police negotiator, he'd probably done well on a car lot, or one of those big appliance stores, though he really wasn't sure he could jump on people the way some did, the minute they came in the door. He'd prefer to wait, to lay back. Let the customer admiringly run his hand across a stove or refrigerator, set his own hook, before he'd introduce himself and reel him in.

Stupek said they couldn't wait.

"Tommy, these people want to try to open the airport."

He could tell by the look on Stupek's face that he had put up a battle trying to dissuade whoever wanted to do this.

"How bad do they want to open it?"

"The county executive."

"The county executive is a former sheriff. Doesn't he know we're dancing in the dark here?"

They didn't even know if they had one hostage taker or a half dozen terrorists packed into that Ford Taurus.

Stupek set his portable spittoon on the bar.

"If you knew the man," Stupek said, "You wouldn't even ask."

Monsorta was glad that he wasn't paid to make those

decisions. He was glad that he wasn't paid to fight them, either.

"How soon?"

"They're ready to go any time after two thirty."

He spun around in his bar stool. "Christ, that's ten minutes. We're still waiting for a shrinker."

Stupek looked like he might spontaneously combust if he stuffed any more anger. Monsorta backed off.

"But what the hell," he added. "I worked without a shrinker for years."

"Obviously, we're not doing anything until we make contact," Stupek said. "I need you to feel the situation out."

Stupek explained the FAA's plan to use the old tower.

"What do you think?" he asked.

"Depends what whoever's taken the tower cares about. We don't know if that's the building, or what it does. One thing about these people, they're are always trying to make some kind of statement. Sometimes they just go for the biggest thing they can find."

"Once we get into it, if it looks doable, we can start with one airplane, move a commercial carrier from the gate area. Or, we can start with a bunch."

Stupek handed a slip of paper to Tuck Conrad. "Here's the phone number to the L.C. Smith tower. If it looks good, they'll roll the planes on our signal. You can call from my office."

"One aircraft?" Monsorta asked.

"What do you think?"

"You might as well send everything. It makes it easier for me if the decision looks bigger than all of us. I can work with that."

Stupek nodded. "That would be my call as well."

Monsorta stuck a Chesterfield in the corner of his mouth.

"Ten minutes," he said. "That doesn't give us much time for an assessment. Where is the shrinker, anyway?"

Conrad answered. "TOC is working on it. Goddamn holiday. Nobody is where they're supposed to be."

Monsorta reached for a match.

"If it's one guy," Stupek continued, "and he's real shaky, play it out. Then I'll make the call."

"Sometimes a disturbed individual may seem perfectly fine," Monsorta said. "Sometimes it's only when you try something you find out how mental they are."

Monsorta lit the smoke.

"I understand," Stupek said.

"What about after the traffic rolls? What are we looking at if he flips out?"

"At that point, we're pretty committed. They tell me it will take at least five minutes to pull the planes back. Like I said, if it's not right, we won't send the plane."

Lt. Vince Stupek also knew if he didn't try to send the planes, and could not demonstrate a good reason, the county executive would make him pay for it somewhere down the line.

"Right," Monsorta said, exhaling. "Assuming . . ."

"Assuming what?"

Monsorta pointed at the AT&T hostage phone. "Assuming that when I make the call somebody picks up the god-damn phone."

When everyone was ready, Conrad, Stupek, and a dispatcher from the radio room, who was the secondary negotiator, took places near a monitor speaker at the far end of the bar. They had a couple of legal pads and two telephones with two lines, one to crash-fire-rescue, the other an outside exchange. The local phone company had patched the hostage phone directly into one of the tower lines.

Tommy Monsorta opened up a thick loose-leaf binder, its pages dog eared, some of them stained with various drinks and fast-food condiments. He turned pages until he reached a section titled: *Profiles.* Each page was headlined by categories:

Terrorist Hostage Taker.

Criminal Hostage Taker.

Psychologically/Emotionally Disturbed Hostage Taker.

Under the last, there were four subcategories: *Inadequate Personality. Psychotic. Severely Depressed. Hostile Depressed.*

Each page had a check list of behaviors. Each page had a list of strategies. Monsorta had internalized the book, but felt no need to demonstrate that to anyone. It had been two years since his last negotiation, an auto worker who boarded himself up in a west side bungalow and began shooting up the neighborhood with a small arsenal after losing a Friend of the Court hearing. It took him an hour to talk the guy down. It took another four to convince him his kids could exercise his visitation rights in jail. Not that Monsorta worried he was rusty. He just liked to have the written word to fall back on, like a salesman working from a price list when a customer started to get the edge.

On a hunch, Monsorta left the binder open at *Hostile Depressed.* Then he swiveled toward the two other men at the other end of the bar and pointed to the mural behind them.

"You know they say it's pretty goddamn cold over there," he said.

They stared back, not understanding.

Monsorta punched the record button on a tape deck tapped into the hostage phone, then dialed a secured line to the tower.

"Yeah, I hear it's not the temperature, but the humidity."

The phone rang once.

"Tommy, what the fuck are you talking about?" Conrad asked.

The phone rang again.

"London," Monsorta said, pointing. "On the wall."

The two men turned around, looking at the mural.

"You know, there ain't nothin' worse than a damp cold. You can put on ten pairs of pants, but you still can't get fuckin' warm."

During the third ring, the line picked up and there was silence.

"Hello," Monsorta said.

More silence.

"Hello, my name is Tommy Monsorta. I'm with the airport police. Who am I speaking with, please?"

More silence.

"All right, you don't want to talk. Fine."

"I told you *I'd* be in *fucking* touch."

The voice was quiet and controlled, unlike the dispatcher's tape. He might have thought it belonged to a different man if he hadn't heard hatred spilling out of the words.

He eyed the telephone, as he would someone's face.

"Yes, you did. And I did get that message. But I thought making some kind of contact would probably be in all our best interests."

"What the *fuck* do you know about *my* interests?"

He seemed to relish calmly saying profanities.

"Well, specifically, I guess I don't know very much. But, as I'm sure you know, when people don't talk, that's how misunderstandings start. And when you got misunderstandings, sometimes things get out of hand."

"You want *out of hand.* You send anybody up here and you'll see what *out of hand* is." Louder, more excited now.

Monsorta paused. Act, don't react.

"Well, that won't happen as long as I have a say here. But that also depends on you. Like I said, most problems can be nipped at the bud. But we have to be talking to do that."

"That's real *fucking* big of you."

"As I was saying, my name's Tommy. What shall I call you?"

"You'll know my name. *Everybody* will, soon enough."

"A first name would be good for now. That's all."

"Are you an officer?"

"A what?"

"You know, a sergeant? Maybe a *major.* I'll bet they gave you a good rank." He sounded almost jealous.

Monsorta fell back on the Mark Twain principal: *When in doubt, tell the truth. It will confound your enemies and astound your friends.* Negotiators embraced it, when dictated by the situation.

"As a matter of fact, they never got around to giving me one of them things here. I checked into this outfit as a civilian."

"But I bet they pay *you* good."

"It's a living."

"Well, I think *you* deserve a rank, considering what you do."

"You might have a point there. Now, how about a name?"

Silence.

"You can give me a name, or I can give you one. But, hey, I don't want you getting angry now if it's something you don't like. It's your choice."

There was a moment of silence, then, "You can call me Bat."

"Okay. That's short for Matthew, I guess, huh?"

"*Bat* is not short for anything."

"Oh, *Bat.* Like Bat Masterson. Yeah, I used to watch that show."

"Never saw it."

Monsorta pushed on with the small talk. "Yeah, who was that? Gene Barry. Played some kind of gambler or something. I think they're doing reruns on cable or something. I watch a lot of cable."

"Those shows are a waste of time."

He was trying to get a fix on the guy's age. "I'm just saying there was a bunch of good shows back then. You remember? 'Maverick.' 'Rifleman.' What was that one with Steve McQueen?"

"Like I said, I never saw those shows."

"Yeah, and I could probably find some better pursuits myself."

"Are you in a position of *authority?*" He seemed to relish using the word.

"Not really. But I can get in touch with those kinds of people."

"Well you can tell *those* people all this didn't have to happen. You can tell *those* people they've brought all this upon themselves."

"Brought what, Bat?"

"This."

"Well, we can talk more about that. And I will pass that along."

"You know there's a *fucking* price to pay. There's always a *fucking* price. People are going to know that."

"I'm not following you, Bat. But considering what you've done here, I think they already do."

"You do your job, Major Tom. You just do your job."

"Okay."

"We can talk more about that." The voice on the line was snotty now, as if he was mimicking.

Monsorta was intrigued by his curious demeanor, his sarcasm. Usually, HT's had a lot of adrenaline flowing. Usually, they shouted and carried on a lot, just to prolong the high.

Monsorta continued, "Well Bat, I'll tell you one thing, I *am* going to do my job. And the first thing I need to know is, what do you want?"

"What do I want?"

"Yeah. You've got the tower. You apparently went up those stairs and took it. Or did you take the elevator?"

"I walked."

"The point is, it's all your's. So what do you want? What do you expect to do with it?"

There was silence, then he responded slowly, calmly. "I want to be left alone. That's all I ever asked."

"So we're talking about some problems at work, or what?"

"The work's not a problem. Not for me, at least."

"So you work up there in the tower, then?"

"I didn't say that."

"Okay, then the radar room, I guess. I hear that's pretty rough."

"I wouldn't know."

"So you work at the airport, I'm guessing."

"You could say that."

"Well, what kind of work are we talking about then?"

"What, you think I'm *fucking* stupid. You think I'm just going to sit here and give you some big goddamn *biography* so you can start pushing buttons, Major Tom? I know your game. Fuck you! And fuck your people too!"

Monsorta looked down at Stupek and Conrad. The guy was a mental. He was all over the place. Give him enough slack, and he'll take himself out before sunset. He wondered if there was anyone else in that tower left alive.

Monsorta waited until he stopped yelling. He waited till his breathing normalized.

"All I was saying was I don't know anything about you," Monsorta continued. "I just was wondering why you would want to take that control tower. You'd be curious too, if you were in my shoes."

"Maybe I don't like it."

"Why?"

"Maybe I don't like *gambling*. Maybe I don't like all the big *fucking* plans your *people* have for this place.

"Hey, I don't like the gambling thing, either. A lot of us don't."

"Like I said, I just want to be left alone."

Monsorta thought, religious zealot? Terminal paper pusher? He felt like the guy was playing "What's My Line?" Monsorta wanted to play, but he also knew he had other limits to test.

"Work with me here, Bat," he said. "And you will be left alone."

"Work with you?"

Empower him, he thought. That's what these guys wanted. Give him all the power, then gently show him how to use it.

"Yeah, you're the man with the tower. You're the man in charge. And hey, anytime you want, you can walk right out of there. It's your decision. And no harm will come to you. *That* I can arrange."

"It's too late for that now."

"It's never too late. We can do it right now, if you want."

"I'm not going anywhere. And neither are you."

"Well, we can talk about that."

"Maybe. Maybe not."

"Right now, let's stick to basics. Like, are you all okay up there?"

"Anybody who is living and breathing is doing just *fucking* fine."

"Do you need any medical attention? I can get that for you if you need it. No strings attached."

"Hey, *Major Tom,* all things considered, I said I'm just fucking fine."

"And everybody else?"

"Nobody needs any medical attention. Do you think I would let you send somebody if they did?"

Suddenly, he began shouting, at somebody in the tower. "Hey. I told you to ditch that *fucking* peace sign, didn't I?"

The monitor speaker crackled.

Monsorta heard two voices in the background, but couldn't make out the words.

"Hey, Bat, what's with all the yelling?"

A second or two of silence.

"Bat?"

Silence, then, "What?" Very calmly.

Peace sign? Jesus, Monsorta wondered what the hell that was all about, but he couldn't think of a graceful way into it. Plus, there was no time to get sidetracked.

"Bat, look, if you want to yell, that's fine. But if you're going to yell, yell at me. I can handle it. People give me shit all the time."

He barked at somebody in the tower again. "Put it in the goddamn garbage. *Fucking asshole."*

A sigh. An aggressive sigh.

Monsorta looked at the other end of the bar. Everybody was thinking the same thing. There were at least two other people in the tower alive.

"Bat, are you with me?"

"What?"

Just breathing now. Through his nostrils.

"What I'm trying to say here is, as far as I'm concerned, what has happened up there has happened. Nothing you and I do right now is going to change that. But there's no need to make it worse."

"Worse?"

"Yeah, my concern right now is you. I don't want to see you dig yourself into a hole you can't get out of. You see, you and me. We're in the same boat here. In the same situation, so to speak."

"You're saying you're *my* equal?"

"No, I'm saying that if you and I do this right, nobody is going to get hurt. But to be perfectly frank, you're the one in control here. You know that. I know that. I'm just here to help."

"You can't help me. Not now."

"Well, I think I can. For one, I can keep this situation from getting out of hand on this end. But you've got to keep it from getting out of hand on your end. I think that's a fair deal for now, don't you?"

"And just how am I supposed to do that?"

Good, Monsorta thought. He asked a goddamn question he could work with.

"Well, we'll have to put our heads together. I'm just guessing at this point, but I think you really want to work this out."

"I just want to be left alone."

"And you will be."

Monsorta glanced down at his binder. He hadn't moved from the page headlined *Hostile Depressed*. He'd been checking some of the points on the page: *Social withdrawal. Irritability. Less talkative than usual. Pessimistic attitude. Whining.* There had been no *Crying,* but he guessed that was just a matter of time. But it bothered him that the HT had given up so little information. Only time would tell him if that was by design or pathology. He wished they had shrinker on the team.

He looked down the bar at Stupek. He was pointing to his watch. Then his pager went off.

"Fuck," Stupek mouthed, reaching down and turning it off, ignoring it.

Okay, Monsorta thought. Try going straight at him.

"You know, Bat, I'm not going to bullshit you, okay? That's not my style."

Silence.

"You know even though we hardly know each other yet, you strike me as a guy who doesn't go for a lot of nonsense. That's good, because I want to be straight with you. That way, if we keep the lines of communication open, when things happen, you won't think anybody here is trying to pull a fast one."

"You pull a *fast one,* Major Tom, I'm going to finish this thing. *Right here. Right now."*

Monsorta paused again. It was time to let out a little leash.

"What you need to understand, Bat, is there's some people down here who have their own ideas about what a *finish* is. And it's not a very pleasant scenario."

"That's a given."

"So now that we understand each other completely, I'm going to share something with you, just so there are no misunderstandings. Can you see the terminals from where you are?"

"This is the tower, isn't it?"

"Okay, if you can see the terminals you can also see the runways."

"I can see a lot more than you think."

Monsorta glanced down at Conrad and Stupek. Everyone wondered what *that* meant.

"Well, then, in a couple of minutes, you're going to see some activity out there at the terminals."

"I don't understand what you're talking about."

"In a few minutes you're going to see activity. I'm not talking people. I'm not talking police. Nothing like that. Just aircraft pulling away from the gates, heading toward the runways."

"Why?"

"Well, that's what I mean. This is my way of showing you I got nothin' to hide here. They tell me they had a radar problem over at the FAA, but now they got it fixed. So, they're just about ready to open this airport back up. And I wanted you to know about it."

Silence.

Monsorta glanced at Stupek again. He was standing with his arms folded, holding his foam cup.

"So, you're going to see jets taxi out there. And take

off. And pretty soon, I'm told, they're going to start landing aircraft here as well."

"How you going to run an airport without a control tower?"

"These people say they can. And that's the main reason I didn't wait for your call. I didn't want any surprises for you. I didn't want any trouble over surprises."

"There's no trouble. Not now."

The voice on the line sounded as if it were deflating, like the reality of what he'd done was hitting him.

"That's good. Because we don't need any misunderstandings over what's really just the normal course of business here."

"You want to open the airport, that's *your* decision. Not mine, Major Tom."

"Well, it's not my decision. It's the decision of people who get paid a lot more than I do."

There was a moment of silence.

"Do what you want," he said, sounding more depressed now. "I need some time to think."

When Monsorta looked down the bar, Conrad was already headed for the lounge door, the number for the FAA in his hand.

Twelve

For three years, Marlon Ladd had sat in his office in the City County Building, watching cars stream into the tunnel to Canada, wondering which ones were headed to the Windsor casino with money to be gambled and taxed. So, he commissioned a study and announced the results at the Detroit Economic Club luncheon.

"Most certainly, gambling is evil," he said in response to a question from the audience. "But it might as well be ours."

The Sault tribe of Ottawas and Chippewas didn't think gambling was evil. At least that's not how they'd described it to the county executive this morning when he met with tribe leaders in a Grand Hotel conference room. Ten years ago, the tribe had started with bingo games in Sault Ste Marie and a savvy treaty attorney who argued Indian sovereignty superseded state gambling laws. Now the Sault tribe was running two large casinos in the Upper Peninsula. They had two thousand slots and most Vegas games of chance. They also wanted to expand.

"After all," one tribe leader said, "our people ranged the entire state looking for shelter and food at one time."

The beauty of the plan, in the opinion of county legal counsel, was the marriage that could be made in the twilight zone of federal laws. Federal law had empowered Marlon Ladd to put Detroit Metropolitan Airport directly under his control. He'd wrestled public safety away from the county sheriff, as well as grab a half dozen other fief-doms controlled by the county's various factions. Now the same statutes could bring tribe gaming to the new South Terminal Complex. But he had to go slowly, and carefully. He needed the governor's approval.

"But for Chrissakes, Marlon," his wife said. "Even the governor isn't stupid enough to come up here this time of year."

She wasn't talking about gambling. She was talking about Mackinac Island in the off season. She'd found all the shops closed, the streets deserted. Now she was sitting against a stack of pillows on the bed of their Grand Hotel suite.

"You know what I've been doing all morning?" she asked.

"What, dear?"

He was sitting at a French provincial parlor table, work-ing on figures the Sault tribe had given him, waiting for Jim Rains to call back about the airport situation.

"On an island known for its 'nineteenth-century charm and horsedrawn carriages,' I've been fucking channel surf-ing," she said, tossing the remote at her feet. "And this cable station isn't worth a goddamn."

"But you insisted on coming," he reminded her.

She was his second wife, twenty years younger. Her trade-in moved back to New York when their children left for college. He was a tall, lanky man, as slim as his ten years as sheriff. Today, he had dressed in charcoal slacks and a black V neck. He rather liked being away from the City County Building. He enjoyed not having to wear a suit.

"I just wanted to be with you," she said.

"And you're with me, all right?"

He had a hint of the Caribbean in his speech. He was raised in New York, but his mother was from St. Martins. Every election his handlers hauled out the tale: He'd come up from nothing, son of a Harlem dry cleaner. Full merit scholarship to the University of Michigan, then its law school. Recruited by Hoover himself. Detroit FBI bureau chief. Wayne County sheriff for ten years. Now executive of a county government larger than twenty states. "Very goal oriented," the profiles went.

That certainly was the case with Metro. Just another airport, until the big bond issue. Earlier planners drew up new buildings and runways, calculating their relationship to lower ticket prices, more airlines, and increased numbers of flights. Ladd thought of twenty-two million people moving annually through the county's biggest economic entity. The new South Terminal Complex, he decided, would not only be a place to board airplanes, but a way to separate and tax dollars from travelers. *Serious* dollars. He didn't want junk shops and news stands. He wanted national stores found in most shopping malls. He wanted good chain restaurants and a cinemaplex. The expansion was going to pump another billion into the county economy, he promised voters. He planned to surf the gambling proposal through the governor's office on a wave of positive airport news.

Ladd slid the papers aside and turned to his wife.

"Why don't you go for a carriage ride?" he said.

"It's twenty degrees out there, Marlon."

She picked up the remote and walked over, resting her chin on his shoulder from behind.

"Why don't you come with me. We'll get under one of those wool blankets. That's why I came. I figured I might be able to see you more than a couple of hours up here."

He pulled the paperwork in front of him again. "I'm going to have to go back downstairs after Jim calls. Maybe later."

She threw the remote to the bed, then followed it there. He kept his nose in the figures. Under normal circumstances, if her harping continued, he would have sent her back to the ferry and St. Ignace Airport. Let the taxpayers fly her home so she could spend the evening with her friends.

Normal circumstances depended on the phone call from the director of airports.

He looked up at her. She was pouting at the bed.

"Why don't you just be patient," he said. "There is a chance we might have to leave early."

She sat up in the bed, her spirits brightening.

"Really?"

"Really," he said, smiling.

He was thinking about her leisure time. He was thinking about the airport and his meeting downstairs, his version of Thanksgiving with the Indians.

A lot more was at stake than squash and corn.

Riker headed for the small door. He walked to the small door that lead directly into the hangar because that was the one he always used, though he hadn't stepped foot inside the Nomads in six years.

Inside, the SWAT team was sitting in a circle, cross-legged on the smooth concrete, the field commander briefing them like a coach talking to his team in the middle of a gym floor.

Riker took a couple steps forward, but stopped, looking up at the lights, the mercury vapor lamps buzzing. He remembered how they buzzed those six days in August like a swarm of hungry flies.

That's why he didn't go there. He didn't like to remember.

During two twenty-five, they just called it *the hangar*.

"I'm heading over to the hangar," they'd say, or, "Take it to the hangar."

Everyone who worked the crash knew what was being done there. The county commandeered the Nomad's hangar because that week the club's 727 was gone for an excursion

to Europe. Outside the large door that opened on the runway side, the medical examiner parked five refrigerated
trucks the county rented from two Eastern Market meat
companies. They parked them on the runway side so the
families couldn't see the vehicles when they passed or entered on the Middlebelt Road side.

Inside, where Riker stood now, a county task force accumulated, tagged and attempted to identify one hundred
and fifty-six bodies. Inside, there was no refrigeration. Inside, there was little they could do about the smell.

The numbers were hard wired into Jack Riker's head. The
oldest, nearly eighty. The youngest, four months. Thirteen
couples. Four families of three. Three families of four. A
family of six. A family of seven, ages four months to thirty-
two. Back then, they worked up other numbers: Seventy-nine
adult males. Forty-five adult females. There were twenty-one
children, ages two to sixteen. There were four children
younger than two.

The task force had seventy-five people. They worked
eighteen hours a day for six days. Pathologists. Doctors.
Dentists. Detectives. Morgue investigators. FBI fingerprint
specialists. Off-duty EMS personnel. Even the two sons of
the chief medical examiner showed up as volunteers. There
was a lot of lifting to do. In the beginning, everyone did
a lot of lifting.

As Riker remembered it, that's why they started the assembly lines. The August air was hot and thick. It became
clear to everyone they would all be there for weeks just
trying to move the bags around. The pathologists made the
decision to use small, stainless steel circular saws. They
cut the jaws out in big frozen wedges, tagged them, and
kept the line moving to a half dozen dentists as the charts
came in from all over the country by Fed Ex. When the
FBI print people saw this, they started asking for hands.
They hacked off the hands with stainless cleavers, then did
the printing.

But for some, even this wasn't fast enough.

Families mostly. Jack Riker was working with the families. They wanted the remains of their loved ones. Riker took calls from mothers and daughters and sons and fathers. He took calls from sisters and uncles and relatives who were in law enforcement, who thought by being in the field they could speed the process along. By mid-week, the politicians were calling. First the Michigan legislators, then the calls from Washington.

"You have the remains of one my constituents," a senator would say.

Riker turned the Washington calls over to the chief medical examiner, an astute pathologist with a thick German accent. He always sent them on their way with the same line: "Which part shall I release, Senator? I have a jaw. What happens when I find the leg?"

The crash left less than a dozen bodies intact.

Everyone took some damage with them. Some talked about it.

Some, like Riker, did not.

For Riker, the last day was worst. Nearly two dozen names on the passenger manifest remained unmatched with remains. So they set up banquet tables and covered them with paper tablecloths. On these, they spread out watches and rings and earrings and money clips and necklaces and smoke stained contents from purses and wallets. They spread out all the personnel items found on parts or in the charred earth and pavement of the crash grid. They needed more than a dozen eight-feet banquet tables for this.

Jack Riker brought them in, one family at a time. The loved ones of the people who remained unidentified. The loved ones who all week had been pleading with him on the phone.

"Look among these items. If there's anything you recognize, I need you to point it out and tell me."

This was how they confirmed the last names.

"When can we have the body?" every one of them asked.

"I'm sorry, there's nothing to release," Riker said.

They all wanted to leave with a watch or a necklace or a half burnt Lion's Club card.

"I'm sorry, we can't release anything yet."

Couldn't do anything for anybody. When the day was over, he felt like he'd previewed a flea market for the dead. That's what got to him.

That's why he didn't like to remember.

Reed Johnson walked over and said, "Jack, you need to go up front. TOC is up there in the business office."

"What?"

"C'mon, I'm heading that way."

Johnson was in SWAT clothing, his jaw moving mechanically on a thick wad of bubble gum.

"You smell anything funny?" Riker asked.

He shook his head.

"You sure?"

He stopped chewing momentarily. "No, can't say I do."

Riker could swear he did.

In the TOC, Johnson picked up blueprints of the new tower from a patrolman who brought them over from the FAA, and jogged back into the hangar. Riker had seen the drill many times. SWAT would chalk out the floor plan of the tower on the hangar floor, then begin rehearsing an assault.

A few minutes later, Riker was trying to explain to Lefty Thompson what the controllers in TRACON had told him, when Vince Stupek came walking out of the CNT in the lounge. He stopped momentarily, as the distant wine of a Boeing 737 heading for runway three center bled through the hangar's south wall.

"Okay, folks," he said. "As you can hear the airport is resuming operations. This does not mean we are any closer to resolution. It just means the CNT is making some headway. Go forth and do likewise."

A telephone on the receptionist desk was ringing, but everyone was ignoring it. The TOC had wired in its own lines, but no one was on the phone. Investigators were hurriedly working with a shift sheet also sent over by the FAA. They were writing the names of hostages on the poster boards on the wall. Below the names, they left space for photographs and clothing descriptions.

Another poster board, labeled "HT," remained blank.

Spaced down the wall were more boards with other key categories in Magic Marker, all waiting for details:

Location/Target.
Weapons.
Explosives.
Demands.
Deadlines.
Medical Problems.
Witnesses.
Vehicles.
Target Photos.
Light/Weather Data.
Time/Event.

Conrad was trying to direct all this, which is why Riker probably wasn't getting through to him.

Stupek walked over when he saw Riker.

"Where the hell have you been?"

Riker ignored the question and said, "You know I was up in that tower this morning for the executive lieutenant. You could see this coming. They've got big problems over there in the FAA."

Stupek was thinking tactics. "We're gonna want to get you with SWAT then, so we can confirm those building prints. Anything you can tell them will help."

"Right, that's not going to be a good situation over there for them."

"I figured."

Everyone could hear the 737 rolling now, getting louder. Runway three center began forty-eight hundred feet directly southwest of the Nomad's hangar, ending not six hundred feet from the hangar door.

Stupek was looking at the posterboards now.

Riker tried to push the sound of the approaching jet from his mind, get Stupek's attention again.

"Vince, listen to what I'm saying."

"I'm listening," he said, but he was reading the posters.

"You remember when that letter carrier lost it and killed those three supervisors at the Royal Oak Post Office lost it a couple of years ago?"

"Yeah. What about it?"

"Remember the first news reports? The way management said they had no indication the guy was a time bomb? But as it turned out, every mail carrier in the goddamn peace knew he was ready to blow any day."

"Isn't that the case where a cheer went up at the union hall when the TV started naming the victims."

"Right. But if you'll remember, people were telling cameras outside the building the carrier's name before they even had an ID."

Riker couldn't shake the sound of the jet. And now he felt his heart skipping. A small, dying fish was flapping around inside his chest. He reached for the Holter monitor, as if touching it would somehow make it stop.

Stupek turned. "Jack, what are you saying?"

The jet hurtled by the hangar, going airborne.

Riker looked away from Stupek. His eyes focused on the banquet tables, where the other investigators were working.

They were using the same goddamn tables. The fucking smell. It was up here, too.

He forced himself to look back at Stupek. Saw him smashing his Copenhagen real hard with his lower lip.

"What's wrong, Jack?"

"The air in here."

"I know."

Stupek had worked in the hangar, too.

He pulled out his can of dip. "Here, this helps."

Riker shook his head.

"Jack, it was the only goddamn place available."

Anxiety attack, Riker told himself. Breathe slow. Real slow. Look normal. Not like some goddamn fruitcake.

"Royal Oak, Jack. Talk to me."

Fuck it, Riker told himself. He was going to go belly up, so be it. He reached inside his sport coat and pushed the event button on the monitor. At least he'd have it marked on their goddamn tape.

He began again, wanting to get it right. "I talked to a bunch of guys over there at the FAA."

"That's what they told me."

"Vince, they sounded like those mail carriers. In Royal Oak. They say the guy's name is Kring. Laurel Kring. He's had a lot of problems. They all think it's Kring in the goddamn tower."

"A controller?" Stupek asked.

"Yeah. A real good one. But they busted him down to a shit office job earlier this year. They even had a name for the guy. They call him The Bat."

Stupek almost yelled, "Why the fuck didn't you call that in?"

"I had Leo page you on my way over. Nobody answered the Nomad's phone."

Stupek spit into his cup. "Shit. I told those assholes this was a goddamn employee."

Riker was already walking to the door. He needed some clean air.

Before he got there, the Nomad's travel lounge flew open. Tuck Conrad poked out his head.

He shouted. "We've got a problem in the tower!"

Stupek walked toward him. "Which tower?"

"Both. I've got the FAA on the line in here. They're telling me somebody lifted the hold."

"You told them to lift it."

"No," Conrad said. "They say the *new* tower lifted it. They're picking up radio transmissions. They're moving goddamn traffic up there."

Thirteen

The ASDE monitor glowed in shades of green, the predominant hue the color of a U.S. Army field jacket. Terminals and hangars and service buildings showed up as lime lines—rectangles, squares, and trapezoids. Runways and taxiway, which were flat and sent back no echo, were electronically superimposed on the screen.

He was not watching the runways. He was studying the small green dots that moved deliberately on the periphery. They were trucks and cars and mostly, but they moved on the screen like hungry mosquitos in the swamps at twilight. The ASDE prevented ground collisions in low visibility. It detailed the movement of everything above surface grade within three miles of the tower. The antenna was one floor below, its electronic eyes peering out in all directions behind the black glass that encircled the tower cab.

The ASDE was very good at ground surveillance when the airport was socked in with fog. He had been very good at ground control. His favorite was when the tower was above the thermal line, the cab bathed in the morning sun, the runways below covered by a dense cloud. It felt like sorcery, the way you could move arrivals and departures in and out of that soup.

This had always been his talent. Laurel Kring understood spacial relationships. He understood time and distance and speed. He saw the give and take. He saw unlimited possibilities and combinations. He saw order in what most others would interpret as chaos.

Chaos came to him in patterns.

"The way your mother and father are always beating on each other, I'm surprised you're so quiet."

His Uncle Lewis said it.

In silence, he discerned patterns.

Mother always took off her blouse about half way through her gin. Did the last of her drinking in her bra. Those points soaked in puked Seagram's when he used to find her in front of the snowy TV. When he led her to her own bed.

A child should not have to learn this kind of predictability. He blamed *them* for that. He blamed them for the apologies that *always* came before dinner. When truces were declared.

"I'm sorry, honey, I cut you."

"Shit, hon, we can always get a new hi fi."

Before dinner, he learned to invite friends over, the one or two he had in a block of boomers. Before dinner, the house was very quiet. They were always good for a couple of hours.

After the evening news, the music started. Some bad Steve and Edie, usually. Their favorite. Celebrating over making up. Starting a new cycle.

Patterns.

It wasn't the liquor that drove his father away. Or the chunk she took out of the old man's scalp, the glass she broke a half inch into his belly.

It was the other men.

Patterns.

His greatest memory bore more chaos.

"I'm going to get a pack of smokes."

They were the last words he heard his father say. In retrospect, he wondered how it ever lasted as long as it did.

Early on, he learned that it was only a reorganization. A metamorphism. Into more chaotic predictability. Just him and her. More intense now. But discernible. Requiring more thought.

Different men, but the same music. Sometimes, two or three a week.

"You're so quiet."

The patterns were not linear. Not geometric.

He discerned in quantums. Coltraine came at you in quantums, pulsating with discordant triads and augmented fifths.

So did Rosan Rollin Kirk. He saw the saxophonist when he was stationed in Germany. One of those basement joints. A giant black man in black sunglasses. Kazoos and cow bells and noisemakers of all kinds pinned to his dashiki. On that smoke choked stage in Berlin. From his baritone he heard his patterns. He couldn't imagine one of those stupid fucking niggers in the barracks carrying genes from that man. And the white trash. He laughed when he thought of the white trash. Imagined what they'd do if they woke up one night in the darkened barracks. Saw Rosin Rollin Kirk, in that dashiki and shades, blowin' chaos at the foot of their fucking beds.

"Kring Ding, how can you listen to that fucking noise?"

Noise was Conway Twitty and Sam and Dave and Jefferson Airplane. Minds numbed with weed and China white needed shit like that.

Kirk and Coltraine were two Fourteens on a napalm run. Red smoke and black smoke. The balls ballet as the Hueys came in. Fucking lead spitting out of open windows. The Gook bastards laying in their own dead pants full of shit.

Hide in the trees. Turn the sonovabitches into worm food.

"We leave no one. We always pick up our own."

Or, in the simplicity of darkness.

Like TRACON.

Or the tower cab at night, when in his mind's eye he

could see the big transcontinentals winging their way in, their 747 bellies lit by the gray moon reflecting off of the great lakes.

Aptitude.

Aptitude made the tower cab now an effortless improvisation.

He'd set a large work table at the south side. Took the traffic manager's high back swivel chair and placed it behind the table. Facing north. On top, six security monitors. Bring the Sony up from the break room, too. The telephone on his left. The Ruger Redhawk on the right. Make sure the big barrel is clearly visible to everyone.

The ASDE was in the center. If they came, they would come from the south. From the access road and the Eureka check point. This was at his back now. Behind the black swivel chair. But he had confidence in the ASDE, or any piece of well-maintained equipment. Twenty-four years with scopes of all kinds. Radar expanded him. Beyond the conventional senses. A predictable world. No surprises. No ignorant fucking bureaucrats and their mindless regs. No trips to the store for smokes.

He was the goddamn best. They all knew it. Before the changes. When a controller could do anything he deemed necessary in his own space.

He knew that's why they called him The Bat.

He had not expected the children, nor the rep. They had created a cursory challenge.

He'd ordered the children into the break room, hanging one of the Robo alarms from U.S. Cavalry on the outer door knob. The rep begged to remain with the children. No wonder the rep couldn't do shit with the administration. People don't do shit for you if you beg like that. He put him in the room as well. Explained the Robo, how it would produce a loud piercing sound if the door was opened. Or, if anyone moved outside the door within a range of fifty feet.

The girl asked a question. Her mouth was dry. She wanted change for the vending machines.

The rep told her to be quiet.

"Uncle fucking Rep," he told him. "All you have to do is ask."

All the other pukes emptied their pockets. The girl went to every one of them, her hands cupped in front of her. She must have scored ten bucks in silver.

The boy was different. Saw him looking at the Robo alarm, studying it. Genuine curiosity. He reminded Laurel Kring of himself at that age.

In retrospect, putting all three of them in the break room was a good idea, he decided. The extra Robo was good. Keep the children out of harm's way. And with the rep there, he wouldn't have to listen to a bunch of union shit.

As for the primary Robo, he'd hung it on the knob of the door to the tower stairs. Facing inside. Move the door an inch and it goes off. Nobody comes through that door without him knowing. Should they find a way through the ASDE, past the security cameras. Facing it toward the stairwell was useless. He wouldn't hear it, and they might find a way to disarm it. This way he had the element of surprise.

Garcia had moved the bodies. He'd specifically picked Garcia. Put the rest of the pukes at the other end of the hall and made them watch. Held the Ruger Redhawk over the sniffling spic while he dragged the dandy ass supervisor into the ground radar room. Then made him go back for Roberts.

"We got a real affirmative action detail here," he said, waving the Ruger. "We got a spic dragging a nigger, soon to be joined by his asshole boss."

He'd never liked the way Garcia looked. And he had his eye on him now. He'd taken the woman named Sanders out of flight data and assigned Garcia to that slot. A good job for him, shuttling strips and flight info. He'd be real busy, but in no position to fuck things up. If anybody was going to go stupid, he figured it would be the spic.

The woman Sanders was going to be a good FPL. He remembered when she was in tower training, how she'd shown a genuine interest when he explained how Uncle Lewis taught him to forecast the weather by studying the horizon.

"Red sky at night, sailor's delight. Red sky in the morn, sailors take warn."

"Sounds like he was an important person in your life," she said.

He respected some thoughtful insight, but appreciated more that she hadn't pushed. People should be allowed their space. He hated people who were always looking for a handle. Looking to fucking use it against you behind your back.

He put the woman Sanders in clearance delivery where she would take requests from pilots on the routes they wished to fly. And the rest of the crew was perfectly capable.

In their positions now.

Four local controllers to work local and ground control in the push. During the slow periods, he'd cut the local control staff to two. Give the others their allocated breaks, just like normal.

As for traffic coordinator, the position he had vacated with the .357 Smith, he had his candidate. Someone he'd been considering for some time. The traffic coordinator had to discern potential conflicts among traffic being worked by the others. Several years ago, a 727 was shooting the gap when it almost sheared the top off of a Casa on three center. Coordinator had failed to discern that one of the ground controllers was sending the Casa across the runway, while local was landing the 727 between departing flights.

Dale Cleage, traffic coordinator. A natural marriage. Feel

the pressure Captain Queeg. Maybe before the day was over, he'd even over-the-shoulder his ass.

He could see the patterns now. The separate activities he'd set into motion in the tower. Clearance delivery contact Cleveland Center and central flow in Washington. Lift the hold ten minutes early. Tell the waiting flights to go ahead and file their plans. Into the system now. Clearances being received from the ARTCC. Clearance delivery and local control make radio contact with the planes running their engines at the gates.

"Northwest two forty-two proceed to runway three center and hold," the ground controller said.

Then, "Delta five thirty-four proceed to runway three center and hold."

He motioned Cleage into position with the barrel of the Redhawk. Cleage was like a fucking West Pointer. One of the guys who hit the deck. Came apart when things got hot. A man, who in his guts, needed to be led.

"Stand by to coordinate with expected arrivals."

He knew that in a matter of seconds TRACON would be inundated with requests for landing coordinates by pilots being handed off by Cleveland Center.

Cleage protested. "Laurel, the last time I've done anything like this was PATCO. I've been supervising for years."

He waved the Redhawk.

"You think you pass a goddamn test, and that qualifies you to be a leader of men?"

"That's not what I meant."

He pointed the Redhawk.

"You're looking at the supervisor."

He leaned back in the black leather swivel chair, his eyes darting back and forth between the controllers. He committed the ASDE and security cameras to peripheral vision, but he could sense them.

Becoming The Bat now.

"Northwest two forty-two cleared for takeoff," said local control.

A pause.

"Northwest two forty-two, cleared for takeoff, do you copy?"

He listened not only to the content, but the tone of the transmissions. The musical rhythm. Only the discordant notes required attention.

One of the local controllers spun around. Looking at him, holding his headset with his right finger.

Kring said, "Request Northwest flight switch from 118.6 to frequency 135.00."

"Northwest two forty-two switch to 135.00 and stand by."

He nodded his approval.

"Northwest two forty-two, cleared for takeoff."

Then, seconds later. "Northwest two forty-two contact departure control."

When he heard the transmission he knew. He didn't have to look out the window. Northwest two forty-two had released its brakes. The aircraft was either airborne or well into its takeoff roll.

"Delta five thirty-four proceed to the foot of three center and hold."

He spread his arms, then reached down and picked up the ringing tower phone.

Fourteen

People were passing notes down the bar in the Nomad's lounge faster than drinks on payday. Tommy Monsorta arranged the slips of paper in front of him as he cradled the AT&T hostage phone under his ear.

"You've got to help me here," he said. "I've got people all over my ass."

"Help you?"

"Yeah, help me."

"I *am* helping you. You said you wanted to open the airport. I have *opened* the airport."

The man who called himself Bat didn't sound depressed anymore.

The old L.C. Smith tower was only monitoring traffic, the notes said. It would not attempt, in the next few minutes at least, to wrestle flight control from the besieged tower staff. That would only unleash confusion among two dozen aircraft that had left their gates already. The more urgent problem was the flock of descending flights released from Cleveland Center and headed into the Metro airspace.

One slip of paper read: "Likely ID on HT: Laurel Kring. Controller."

Monsorta said, "Bat, what I told you was that people here wanted to open the airport. You said you didn't work in the tower. You said you didn't work in radar."

"I don't."

Another note came down: "Transferred six months ago."

"If we're going to play these kind of games, Bat," Monsorta said, "there's not a whole lot I can guarantee."

"You're doing your job, Major Tom. That's good. But I gotta say, your people are a little slow."

"Slow about what?"

He didn't answer.

Monsorta felt himself struggling.

"Well we've got a real mess now, don't we?" he said.

"These people here don't do messy work, if you leave them alone."

Another jet rumbled by outside. Flights were leaving every two minutes.

"They're telling me there's a problem in the radar room. Over at the other terminal. You apparently called someone and started these inbounds. Over at the radar room, they weren't prepared for that."

"Let them do their jobs. They can handle it."

"Well, I'm sure they can. But they're telling me they can't deal with the inbound traffic. They say they really have no coordination here."

"Let the system work. The system has plenty of coordination."

Stupek was at the bar rail now, conferring with the rest of the CNT. Another note came down the bar.

"Bat, it's my understanding here that the inbounds have been canceled. In fact, they're telling me we're going to have to shut the airport back down."

He started yelling. "Shut it down and you're going to need *fucking* janitors!"

"Janitors?"

"Yeah, *Major Tom,* to clean up the *fucking* mess I'm going to make up here."

"Now that's not going to help your situation, is it?"

"This isn't my *situation,*" he said, mockingly. "This is your *situation.* The choice is yours. Not mine."

"What do you mean, *choice?*"

"It's your *choice* what happens to everyone up here. Including the kids, Major Tom. Can *your people* sleep at night with that? I'll tell you, I can. I *fucking* can."

Monsorta remained calm. He sounded calm, at least.

"No one here wants that. I don't think you do, either. I'm talking about preventing confusion. We have to make things safe out there for those planes."

"I can end the confusion. Real quick, if I don't see those inbounds. *Now!*"

Monsorta looked down the bar at Stupek. He had a note pad and pen in his hand, but had run out of things to write. Monsorta didn't need a note to discern what he was thinking. They needed time. Time to develop an assault plan. Time to profile the hostage taker. Time to test his limits on minor issues where the stakes weren't so high. If shooting started in the tower, SWAT was in no position to move, to cut the losses. Monsorta could see only impasse if he kept pushing. You avoided an impasse at all costs. The decision was the OSC's alone now. Stupek didn't need a conference with the director of airports or the FAA or Marlon Ladd himself. When they opened the airport, they had put Metro on the bargaining table. No meeting could take it off. Only a slaughter in that tower, or time and negotiation, could get it back.

Stupek motioned with his hands. *Back off.*

"Well, maybe I can talk to some people here, Bat." Monsorta said. "Maybe I can get them to reconsider."

"I think you ought to do that. Quickly, *Major Tom.*"

"But you've got to give me something to work with."

"Give you something?"

"Yeah, these people on my ass here, I got to have something to convince them. You can understand that, can't you?"

"How about I shoot a fucking spic. Is that convincing enough?"

Everyone heard a click. It sounded like a revolver's hammer.

Monsorta ignored the threat.

"No, I mean convince them everything is safe."

"Safe? Safety is our business."

"Well, I'd like to send—"

"You're not *sending* anyone up here. I already told you that."

"You've got to let me finish, Bat. I was saying I'd like to send someone, just to make sure everyone was okay up there, but I already figured you wouldn't go for that. But there are other ways to do it. I could talk to someone. That might be a good start."

"Talk? Talk to who?"

"Talk to somebody. On the phone."

"About what?"

"To somebody who can assure these people things are okay up there."

"That has nothing to do with the airport."

"Oh, I think it does."

Monsorta paused.

"What I'm saying, is that it would go a long way with these people here if I could give them, let's call it, a second opinion."

"I don't think you need that."

"No, I think *you* do, Bat. I'm going to be perfectly honest with you here. These people I have to deal with have a lot of questions. As far as they know, you may not have all the people you say you do up there. Put yourself in their shoes. Would you put innocent people in those airplanes at risk if you didn't know the situation in that tower?"

"Innocence never stopped them before."

What did *that* mean, Monsorta thought.

"And Bat, you brought up the kids. As far as they know, those kids are *not* okay. And, to be frank, I don't have any confirmation of that as well. So it makes it hard. No, it makes it impossible for me to sell anything to these people without some confirmations. You can understand that, can't you?"

Everyone at the other end of the bar was looking at the monitor speaker. Ten seconds passed.

Finally, he responded, "Who do you want to talk to?"

"Well, how about someone in authority?"

Monsorta immediately wanted that word back.

"I'm the fucking *authority* up here!"

Monsorta backpedalled. "Bat, I'm talking about someone these people might call an authority. You've got to try and put yourself in their shoes. You know what these people are like."

"They ought to change their thinking," he responded, quietly now again.

"I understand. They're not like us working stiffs. They understand only titles."

Somebody handed Monsorta a list of possible hostages from the intelligence unit in the TOC.

"Alright, Bat. I got a list here. How about if we go through it. You and me. How about if I talk to a man named Roberts?"

"He's . . . unavailable."

Monsorta drew a line through his name.

"How about Colin Leaks?"

"He's taking a break. A long break."

Another line.

"Okay, it's my understanding you have a man named Cleage up there."

"Yeah, he's here. He's pretty busy. He's being a good little goddamn worker, in fact."

"Well, Mr. Cleage would be good."

"But you haven't told me what I get."

"What do you mean?"

"I let you talk to Captain Queeg here, I want some guarantees."

"What kind of guarantees?"

"I want these people up here to be allowed to do the jobs they were trained for. That means departures *and* arrivals. Don't you know it's the holiday, Major Tom. You're keeping people from their fucking turkey dinners with all your bullshit."

"We might be able to work something out. I'll have to talk to—"

He interrupted. He sounded real tired of all the talk. "Oh, that's just a lot of bullshit. I want both arrivals and departures within the next five minutes. I want this tower fully operational, as long as *I* say so. You sell that deal to your *people.*"

"I don't know if I can."

"Then you pay the consequences. Everyone pays."

Monsorta kept dealing as he acquiesced. "Well, maybe I can sell them on the idea if we do this an hour at a time. Let's say your people can do their jobs for the next hour. Get all this congestion taken care of. Then, we'll evaluate. I mean, Bat, my guess is that you may want a break at that point anyway."

"What makes you think I'll need a break?"

"Well, I mean, that is a high-pressure job up there."

"That's a lot of old PATCO shit."

"I'm just saying let me see if I can get them to try this for one hour, but first you're gonna have to put Mr. Cleage on the phone."

"*No* trial period. *No* Captain Queeg. *No* talking to your people. Either I start seeing those goddamn arrivals or you get the janitors ready."

Tommy Monsorta had one more move. "Okay, Bat. Okay. Listen, I tell you what I'm going to do. I'm going to make you a deal. *I'm* going to try and get you not one hour, but two hours with these people."

Monsorta looked down at Stupek. He was nodding his approval. The TOC and SWAT could get a lot done in two hours. In two hours, they'd have some options.

Stupek held up three fingers.

"Who knows, Bat," Monsorta continued. "Maybe I can get you three. But, as I was saying, I'm going to have to go in there myself and make your case. Now, I can't do that, I can't make my case, if something screws up. I'm going to be in no position to argue for you if we start having problems. Do you understand what I'm saying?"

"We don't have any problems up here. As long as we're left alone."

"Okay, good. Then we got a deal. You put Cleage on the phone and you've got my word. I think you'd agree that's extremely fair."

More silence, then, "It's fair enough."

"After I talk to Cleage, we'll talk again. Touch base along the way."

"I wouldn't make it too long."

"Well, it won't be three hours. We'll probably be talking before that. And if there are problems, I want you to call me right away. Somebody is always at this phone."

"That's not what I meant. I meant don't be too long with Captain Queeg."

"Why's that, Bat?"

"The Captain here has got a lot of work to do."

Within thirty seconds, Tommy Monsorta introduced himself to a new voice on the line.

"And, I'm talking to Dale Cleage?" Monsorta asked. "Please answer just yes or no."

"Yes. This is Dale Cleage."

"Can I speak with you and Bat on the same line if need be. Right now?"

"No."

He hoped Cleage was bright enough to understand that meant: Is Bat listening?

"Are you okay?"

"Yes."

"Is everyone okay up there?"

"No. Everyone here in the tower cab is okay."

"Does anyone need medical attention?"

"No."

"It's our information that the man calling himself Bat is Laurel Kring. Correct?"

"Yes."

"Alright, do you have homicides?"

"Yes."

"Say anything you want when I reach the number. One . . . Two . . ."

"We could do that. I'm sure we could. It's a matter of TRACON and the tower working together."

"Does he have a lot of weapons?"

"Yes."

"Does he have handguns and spare ammunition?"

"Yes."

"Rifles?"

"Yes. I think I better go now."

"Explosives."

"I don't know. Do you have any more questions?"

Tommy Monsorta had dozens. What was he wearing? Did he have early warning devices? Where was he located in the tower. How was he guarding people? But there was a limit to the yes and no questions and he already was pushing it.

"Okay, let's talk about staff. Elaborate if you will. Are you in a position to run that tower?"

"We have a full staff up here. I don't see a problem. Everyone up here is fully trained."

"Is he in any position to cause harm to the aircraft?"

"No. All of us are dealing with the aircraft. He's observing, more or less. The traffic should be fine."

"Are you sure?"

"I'm absolutely sure. And we all would appreciate it up here if you goddamn do what he says. We'll hold up our end."

Another jet was roared toward the Nomads hangar as Tommy Monsorta heard the hostage taker snatch away the phone.

Fifteen

Riker was sitting in the DB's supply room, filling out the Holter monitor log, guessing at the exact times for the events of the past two hours. He was waiting for a signed search warrant from a local district judge to roll off the fax machine.

Time: *1 P.M.* Event?

Run out of parking lot by barricaded gunman, Riker wrote.

No, he thought, the guy didn't have a gun on *him.* Radio told him to get the hell out.

Screw it. Let the cardiologist figure it out.

Time: *1:30 P.M.* Event?

Went to FAA. Learned possible identity of gunman.

Time: *2:30.* He put a question mark next to it. Jesus, he was missing a lot now. Event?

Pressed event button. In hangar. Palpitations.

Christ, he thought. How do you explain it? *Flipped the fuck out. Had flashback.* No way. He didn't know who was going to see this log. Nobody in the department was going to write him up as a psycho, not officially at least.

Riker began unbuttoning his shirt. It was coming off. The Tape. The wires. The sensors. What little hair he had and all.

Half way down the buttons, he heard voices. He heard the unmistakable sound of a woman's heels.

Jimmy Oshefsky said, "He's right in here. But I'm telling you, he's pretty busy right now."

Caley Harmon stopped at the supply room doorway, holding her briefcase to her breasts. She looked him over head to toe.

She laughed.

He started buttoning his shirt.

"You should have told me earlier you were wired," she said.

"It's just some kind of test."

"Oh, I know. I wasn't laughing at you, really. You just looked kind of funny there in the corner with your nose in your navel. I've seen them on pilots for their flight physicals. They're more common than you might think."

"They're a pain in the ass," he said flatly.

Buttoned now.

She smiled. "I just thought I'd drop by for the Delesandro file. The director said he had no problems with you releasing it to me."

Riker stood.

"I'm afraid I don't have time for that now."

Please, he thought. Just go away.

"Look, I know you're busy. But I've got a couple of days off here, and I'd like to read it over the weekend. I promise, once I get the file, I'll leave you alone until next week."

"To next week? How about until next month? How about until I call you?"

Riker heard the fax machine go on behind him. He turned and glanced. The seal of the district judge was feeding out on the top of the cover page.

"We're in the middle of some serious business here."

"Nikki Delesandro is serious."

"That's not what I meant."

"Anything I could help you with?"

"I'm afraid not. You see, as soon as this search warrant

comes off the machine, that young detective you were speaking to out there and I have to serve it. It would take me at least a half hour to pull that file together and make copies. And right now, *Mizz* Harmon, I just don't have that kind of time."

"Why do you call me that?"

"Call you what?"

"Mizz Harmon. I'd prefer Caley."

"Okay, *Caley.*" He had the warrant now.

He walked right at her, headed out the supply room, making her step aside. She followed him over to the county map on the DB wall.

He placed the street finder on the map, lining up the numbers and letters specified for street named on the search warrant. His eyes focused on the border between the cities of Wyandotte and Trenton. He was doing his best to ignore her, really heaping on the ice. But he could feel her looking over his shoulder. Smelled her perfume. Not flowery. Something earthy, filled with spice.

"What are you looking for?"

"A street."

"You sure I can't help."

"That's why the county executive bought us a map."

He found Kraus Street. Laurel Kring's house was no more than fifteen minutes away.

"Don't you have clerical staff?"

"This is the police department. I don't need a secretary to look at a goddamn map."

"No, clerical staff who can copy it? The file. I'd be able to stop by later. Pick it up."

He turned around. She wasn't more than two feet away. He could see light brown freckles on her nose, under her makeup. But there was also something just a little unwholesome about her. She had a few miles on her, and not all of them were frequent flyer. He liked that. The medical tech back at the cardiologist's office was a girl. Caley Harmon was a *woman*. Maybe under different circumstances . . . but right now, he wanted her off his goddamn back.

He pointed with the faxed warrant, which now had curled half way around his hand.

"You see all that stuff over here?"

He was looking at four or five dozen legal file satchels. They were stacked in rows along the wall. They looked like something somebody had tossed in a badly organized basement.

"Well, *that* is our file system. Your friend, the director of airports, has yet to release funding for file cabinets. Last year, we got cellular phones. This year we were hoping for file cabinets for Christmas. We're supposed to get computers, too."

"Maybe you need a union."

"We got one. It's not worth a shit."

"The file is in there?"

"No, that's not what I'm saying. What I'm saying is look at the place. I ask you, does this look like the kind of operation that has a clerical staff?"

"I'll copy it."

"What?"

She put her hand out.

"Give it to me, and I'll copy it. Where's your Xerox? You have one of those don't you, or are you going to tell me now that you're still using carbon paper around here."

The Xerox was upstairs, but he wasn't going to tell her that.

"As a matter of fact, we are," he said.

He went to his desk, her following.

"Caley, I'd really like to help you . . ."

"But . . ."

"But in order to give you a police document like that, I am going to need something from the director."

He half expected her to pull out a letter.

He turned to Oshefsky. "Jimmy, you ready?"

Oshefsky was replacing a shotgun shell that had fallen off the Christmas tree.

"What do you mean, *something.*"

"Something in writing. Something I can put in the file."

She laughed. "You calling me a liar, Detective?"

"Why do you call me that?"

"Call you what?"

"Detective. You can call me Jack."

"Okay, *Jack.* You calling me a liar? With the director?"

The freckles were red now. She was good and pissed.

"Not at all," he said.

"Then what the hell do you call it, *Jack?"*

He was heading toward the door, leaving her standing near the Christmas tree.

"I call it covering my ass."

They made good time, a straight shot east on Eureka, until they hit a set of railroad tracks and a train two streets before they needed to turn right onto Kraus Street, which was one of the last streets before Eureka ended at Fort. Beyond Fort Street was McClouth Steel and the Detroit River, where the ore boats brought taconite from Marquette and Duluth. Everyone called all these towns Downriver. Prime river frontage choked with old industry. Neighborhoods where you could sit on the porch and watch a steel mill light up the sky at night.

As they waited, Oshefsky talked on the cellular to Trenton PD, which also was sending a car on the warrant. Riker scanned the houses and yards. Bungalows built with postwar GI loans. The large, mature maples on the streets might have looked grand, but all the aluminum siding awnings took away the effect. Ahead, when the flat cars passed, Riker could see the massive McClouth Steel scrap yard a quarter mile away. A crane was moving cubes of compressed scrap onto a conveyor, the metal headed for the blast furnaces.

"Okay," Oshefsky said, hanging up. "They say their car is already there. They're going to circle the block."

"They sent an unmarked car, didn't they?"

They were under strict orders to maintain a news black-out. An assistant county prosecutor had even convinced the district judge to seal the warrant for twenty-four hours. Riker their asses covered, in case the story sprung a leak.

"Yeah, they sent unmarked."

"What did they say about the train?"

"They say we'd have to drive a couple miles to get around it. They say we're better off just waiting for it to pass."

Oshefsky started rapping his fingers nervously on the dash.

"Jimmy," Riker said, eying him. "Don't do that."

Oshefsky leaned back.

"Jack, does anything get you charged up?" he asked.

"Charged up? What do you mean by that?"

"I mean, have you ever seen anything like this before?"

"Sure. On the road patrol. Somebody gets pissed off. Does something crazy. The only difference I see is the scale. This kind of thing, you just try to lay low."

"Lay low?"

"Yeah, do your job. That way if this thing blows up, you'll be occupied. Let the geniuses running this operation take the fall out. Something tells me there's going to be a lot of fall out on this thing."

Five minutes later, the idea of something else exploding dawned on Riker, after he broke the glass window in the side door of the bungalow with the immaculate yard.

Oshefsky and two plainclothes Trenton officers were standing behind him.

"What do you think, Jimmy?" he asked. "Do you think

we ought to call for the bomb squad?" After all, the guy had hot-wired the radar room.

Riker looked over his shoulder at the two Trenton cops, who now stepped back a couple feet.

"You guys don't have a bomb squad, do you?"

"We use the sheriff's."

"Ah, screw it," Riker said. "That would take too much time."

He winced when he reached in, groping for the bolt lock. Inside, his feet crunched on the broken glass.

Up five stairs, to the kitchen. Riker had been in a hundred houses laid out like this.

He could smell cleaning solution. "What is that stuff?"

"Pinesol," Oshefsky said. "My grandmother used it."

"Mine, too. I fucking hate it."

"I banned it in my house," Oshefsky said.

"I just banned my wife," Riker said.

The countertops were vintage sixties Formica, the kitchen cabinets knotty pine. Spotless counters, and floor. Riker noticed the refrigerator. Usually people had all kinds of shit stuck on the fridge with tape and magnets. The old Kenmore looked like it had come from the showroom at Sears.

"Jack, you need to come in here," Oshefsky said.

He was already in the living room.

He was holding a framed photograph when Riker walked in. A wedding shot of a couple. There were other photographs on the TV.

"This must be his lovely bride," Riker said.

"Jesus," one of the Trenton cops said when he saw the woman.

They didn't get a lot of homicides in that part of Downriver, he said.

The first thing Riker noticed about her was her position. She wasn't slumped forward in the chair, or sprawled backward, her arms dangling like an overstuffed rag doll. In his experience with a dozen or so domestic homicides back when he was with the county, family killings usually weren't tidy. Broken dishes and knickknacks. People started throwing before somebody started shooting. He remembered one rural killing where they found bullet holes and blood in every room on the first floor, the guy chasing his old lady all around the house, unable to make a kill shot.

The woman in the chair wasn't messy. The lower half of her body was covered with a fluffy white afghan. Her hands were folded in front of her, like the morticians do it. A modest wedding set, maybe a half karat, glistened on her finger. She faced the TV, as if she were watching it. A basket of neatly folded laundry sat at her feet.

Jack Riker turned to the two Trenton cops. "Do you have your own EMS?"

They nodded.

"I know you're going to want to turn this one over to your evidence people and the medical examiner."

"Yeah, we're gonna do that."

"But if the coroner comes down here from downtown with that goddamn van they drive, every neighbor on the block is going to be outside. And if you call hold off on the evidence crew, that would also be appreciated. We need you to work with us on this."

One of the Trenton cops asked, "You want the EMS to take her out of here like a hospital run?"

"You got it."

"Okay."

"Maybe the M.E. can send someone over to eyeball it before you take her out. But make sure everyone keeps off the goddamn radio. We don't need Detroit media crawling all over this."

One of the Trenton cops went back to the kitchen, looking for a telephone.

Riker looked at the woman again, moving around behind the chair to get a look at the back of her head. The strands

of hair behind her right ear were grouped, as if someone
had wet it and run a comb through it, but not stuck around
to comb it out. He gently pushed her hair aside. He saw a
small-caliber bullet hole like the one he'd seen in the hippie
not two hours ago.

Riker looked at Oshefsky and said, "Kill the old lady.
Put her in front of the tube. Clean up your mess. Make
sure she's nice and warm."

"It's like he still had feelings for her," Oshefsky said,
looking at the wedding picture.

"No way," Riker said.

"What makes you say that?" Oshefsky asked.

Riker pointed to the TV.

"He didn't leave her anything to watch."

They went through the house room by room.

The master bedroom had two single beds, both with
taut slip covers, like a hotel room. Either their sex life
wasn't very robust, Riker thought, or one of them snored
real bad.

On the top shelf of the bedroom closet he found three
shoe boxes that contained spit-shined loafers, oxfords, and
a pair of black wingtips. In the corner, he found a U.S.
Army ammunition box.

Riker sat on the bed and pulled the clasp, still thinking
about that goddamn bomb squad. He cracked the lid and
lifted the ammo box to his nose, checking for the smell of
explosives. The aroma was old and precious, the way he
remembered his father's jewelry box smelling when he'd
sneak into it as a boy and take a peak.

He pulled the items out one by one, laying them out on
the bed. A pair of dog tags. A Distinguished Service Cross.
A pair of aviator's wings. A piece of folded parchment
hugged the side of the box. Riker slid it out and unfolded
the paper. A certificate with an FAA seal.

This is to certify that Laurel Kring has qualified at Full Performance Level in air traffic control for the Federal Aviation Administration.

It was signed by the director, one of those signatures done by a machine.

From the bottom Riker pulled an old photograph, its blues faded to purple, its reds transformed by time into browns. An awkward adolescent standing next to a silver-haired man. They were both holding a black model airplane, some kind of streamlined black jet. The man was smiling, the kid pensive.

Riker looked into the ammo box. A yellow newspaper clipping lay on the bottom. It had been years, but he still recognized the type style and lay out of *Stars and Stripes*. The headline:

MARINES OVERRUN AT BUNGAROW BAY
Entire Company Nearly Wiped Out

Everyone talked about Bungarow Bay when he was in the highlands. Back when he was living day to day, trying to put enough days together to get through a one-year tour. The story from the *Stars and Stripes*. They called the base Liberty Bridge, later "Bungled Bay."

"What's that?" Oshefsky asked, sitting on the bed, setting down a file folder he was carrying.

"Clipping, about Nam," he said, handing it to him.

Oshefsky read it.

"What's this about?"

"A real fuck up."

"You mean a slaughter."

"That's not the whole story."

"You were there?"

"Near there. In the highlands. We all heard about it, though."

"So what happened?"

"What that story doesn't say was there had been race riots at bases at Quant Tri and Tuyhoa. You didn't read about those back here in the states. Nobody did."

"I don't get it."

"Well, they were worried about them at Liberty Bridge, so the command got the bright idea to lock all the firearms down in an A-frame in the center of the barracks. When the NVA hit, only a few GIs got to their weapons."

The *Stars and Stripes* story reported only three Marines had survived the assault. Riker picked up the Distinguished Service Cross, rubbing it between his fingers, flashing on some old faces. Old friends. Old enemies.

"We need to get this guy's military record," he said.

Oshefsky reached for the file folder he'd brought in with him.

"No need," he said. "I found this in a file cabinet in the other room. Discharge papers. Service stuff. He was a Marine."

After EMS took the body away, a neighbor knocked at the side door. She said she'd called the police thinking someone was breaking in, but was told by the Trenton dispatcher that they *were* the police. She said she was Mrs. Kring's only friend and she wanted to know if there was anything she could do to help.

Oshefsky invited her in, telling to watch out for the broken glass. Riker closed the swinging door to the living room and asked her to sit at the kitchen table.

"Has there been . . . a homicide?" she asked.

She was about forty.

"What makes you say that?" Riker asked.

"It's him, isn't it? Laurel. He did something."

"Well, there has been an assault," Riker said. "That's all I can really share with you right now. We're here as part of a larger investigation. Why do you ask?"

"You know they had no friends. Or, *he* didn't. *He* spent all his time out there."

She was pointing out the window to the garage.

"What's out there?" Oshefsky asked.

"I don't know. He never wanted her in the garage. She said he kept it locked. Has there been a homicide?"

"There's been an assault," Riker said again.

The neighbor's eyes moved back and forth quickly, as if she was pulling a dozen different stories from various locations on the inside of her head.

"What are you trying to tell us?" Riker asked.

"She was an abused woman, I think," she said.

Oshefsky began taking notes.

"How so?"

"Well, I don't know how much I should tell you. I don't want none of this getting back. I mean, I have to live here. He scares me. He always has."

Riker motioned to Oshefsky to stop writing.

"You have our word on that," he said.

"Okay, I mean, he never hit her or anything, that I know of. But, you know, like they say on the talk shows, you know abuse can come in a lot of forms. Whenever I was here, I didn't stick around. You know how you get that feeling, the way somebody looks at you."

"Go on," Riker said.

"Well, if looks could kill, that's what I was always feeling from him."

"How about work?" Oshefsky said. "Did she say anything about that?"

"I don't think things were going good for him. That's kind of the way she made it sound. She was scared, really."

"Of what?" Riker asked.

"Well, remember when that guy went nuts at the Royal Oak Post Office? She said he couldn't get enough of that. And, then he ordered cable. Before that, he *never* wanted cable."

"What would cable have to do with it?" Oshefsky asked.

"Well, they got the cable, which like I said, he had always been adamantly against. He *hated* movies, she said. *Hated* comedies, especially. She said she liked comedies. Sometimes, when he was at work, we'd sit around and watch Lucy. She really liked that."

"You were saying about him and the cable," Riker said, nudging her back on track.

"Right. Well, he got the cable but watched only the documentaries. You know, A&E. Discovery Channel stuff. He liked that show about the airplanes and the military they have. But mainly, she said, he was all the time looking for shows about people who kill lots of people."

"Serial killers?" Oshefsky offered.

"No. Again, like that guy in Royal Oak. Well, this was really scaring her."

"Why didn't she leave?" Oshefsky asked.

"Are you kidding me?" the neighbor said. "You guys are men. You don't understand."

"What do you mean?" Riker asked.

"You gotta be a woman to understand. You don't leave a guy like Laurel."

It was odd that the door was unlocked, considering the way the place was fortified, considering what the neighbor had said. If there was a bomb, this was going to be it, Riker decided. He turned the knob, then kicked the door open, bailing out rather awkwardly, falling on the grass as he did.

Oshefsky didn't laugh. Riker appreciated that.

From the doorway they could hear something running.

Oshefsky poked his head inside.

"It's just a computer," he said.

Inside, Riker stood momentarily in the center of the converted garage, looking up at the black model, the same one he'd seen in the photograph. He could see now that it was the X-15. It flew prominently over the two dozen other aircraft suspended around the room.

"Jack, look." Oshefsky was already at a book shelf.

Three shelves were stacked with crime books. Riker ran his fingers across titles like *Mass Murderers, Beyond the Crime Lab,* and *The Encyclopedia of Modern Murder.* There were other titles from obscure publishers, books you get in *Soldier of Fortune: The Anarchist Cookbook, The Modern Technique of the Pistol, Techniques of Harrassment, Screw Unto Others.*

Riker pulled out a paperback called *Fighting Back on the Job (Beat the Boss).* He thumbed through a few pages, noticing a section "How to Keep Your Job."

"He must have not read all of this one," he said.

"Jesus, Jack," Oshefsky said.

The room had three workstations: A reloading table. An old school teacher's desk, which had the computer. A drawing board lined with model-making tools. Each was lit by its own mechanical lamp. The walls were unpainted drywall. No bulletin boards or posters. Only the patterns of the spackled nails and drywall tape.

Riker went to the modeling table. On the back edge of the drawing board were several dozen spray cans and bottles of paint. Both in neat rows. On the right side, a stand of a half dozen Exacto knives. There was a Dremel Moto Tool.

Oshefsky walked over.

"What kind of guy in his forties still builds models?" Oshefsky asked.

"Hey, everybody needs a hobby," Riker said.

"What about you, Jack?"

"I gave mine up."

Oshefsky had a point.

"Pretty good, isn't he?" Oshefsky said. Then he walked over to the reloading table.

Riker stayed, looking at a two-foot-long model of a DC-9 in the middle of the table. A cutaway design that revealed the cabin interior. It was meticulously detailed. A half dozen small plastic passengers had been carefully painted and glued into the airliner's seats. A shoe box behind the plane was full of mold channels and seam burs the model-maker had cut off with the Exacto knives. In the scrap heap, Riker saw a small unpainted figure like those glued in the cutaway cabin. He fished it out. It was a flight attendant carrying a tray.

"He must have just finished this one before he flipped," he said.

"Hey, Jack, what do you know about ballistics?" Oshefsky asked.

Riker tossed the figurine back into the box and walked over to Oshefsky.

"I know my Colt takes a .38."

"Well, I've done some reloading," Oshefsky said.

He started picking up molds and lining them up on the table.

"This is for a .357. And here, this big boy, is a .44 caliber. Magnum. And here, this is a .38 caliber, like your Colt. These are all loads for handguns. Now, over here we have metal jackets. You mold those in the lead and you can put some real stopping power on that lead."

"SWAT will appreciate that."

Oshefsky picked up another mold, holding it between his thumb and forefinger. "And then we have this guy."

"What's that?"

"This looks like a .223. That's a favorite for assault rifles."

Riker thought Oshefsky was showing some real savvy.

"So we're looking potentially at four handguns and an AK-47 or something?"

Oshefsky nodded.

"I'm sure SWAT's also going to be happy to hear about that."

Riker motioned toward the school teacher's desk. "Nothing in there?"

"Just pencils. Paper. Junk, mainly."

Riker walked to the desk. It was clean, except for a white cafeteria-style coffee cup filled with pencils. There also was a small note pad.

"I wonder why he left this running?" Riker asked, patting the computer monitor.

"A lot of people do that."

Riker saw a slip of paper sitting on top of the processor unit. He picked it up. There were numbers: "903,29040." Then the letters: "label*flyin."

"I wonder what this is?" he said, showing Oshefsky.

"Looks to me like a Compuserv address and password."

"What's that?"

"Oh, it's a national on-line service. Your computer hooks up to it through the phone line." Oshefsky chuckled. "Jesus, Jack. What century did they beam you in from?"

Riker slipped the paper into his shirt pocket. "Maybe we can hook this up back at the hangar."

"You *get* stuff from Compuserv. Weather reports. Stocks. News accounts. Stuff like that. He wouldn't be sending anything there that we could really find."

Riker looked at the computer again. "Still, let's take the whole thing with us. Maybe you can check out what's in here later."

"I was going to suggest that," Oshefsky said.

"Is that right?" Riker said sarcastically.

Oshefsky began looking behind the computer, his eyes following the wires to the wall outlet.

Riker asked, "So, computer genius, why *do* people leave it running? You'd think that would burn it up."

Oshefsky was on his hands and knees, crawling under the desk.

"Actually that saves the equipment. Keeps the temperature uniform, they say. Saves the solder joints. Saves the hard drive."

"But the screen here isn't on," Riker said. "The screen is blank."

"No, they call that a screen saver," he said, his voice muffled by the desk. "That saves the monitor. Before I pull the plug here, touch one of the keys. You should see that monitor go on."

Riker reached down and poked the key with a question mark.

The screen flashed.

"Hey, Jimmy," Riker said. "Don't pull that plug yet."

"Why not?" Jack Riker was looking at a letter now.

It began: "To Whom It May Concern:"

Sixteen

Stupek ignored the ringing telephone, letting Conrad finish his tirade about the two, worthless goddamn police psychologists who ought to have their fucking heads examined for leaving town without informing the department.

When it was over, Stupek said, "Okay, then, call the behavioral science section of the state police. Explain our situation. Maybe they can send somebody down here from Lansing."

Stupek picked up the ringing phone.

It was James P. Rains.

Stupek's first inclination was to tell the director of airports to do something goddamn productive. Have airport catering send over food and coffee for the EOC. That's all he'd tell him.

Vince Stupek had learned a hard lesson. Sharing knowledge with people in power outside the crisis operation was a dangerous thing. The next time he attended a training seminar, he was going to suggest they put that in their book.

Rains sounded troubled.

"Lieutenant, you ought to know about a series of telephone conversations I've been having with the FAA in Washington," he said. "The administration is questioning our jurisdiction. Specifically, lieutenant, *your* jurisdiction. They suggest that the jurisdiction on this matter rightfully belongs to the federal government, meaning that this is a matter that should be handled by the FBI."

"We have the buildings," Stupek said.

"Yes, they conceded that. But they also are saying that interstate air traffic is involved."

Stupek told him the feds were puffing.

"Besides, the FBI doesn't have a local SWAT," he added. "They run everything out of Quantico."

"That's what I understand. But they say they've already conferred with the bureau and they're prepared to scramble a team for a joint operation. They say they can be set up here in less three hours. But, I thought I should get your input first."

"It's repetitive. They're going to repeat everything we've done here so far," Stupek said.

And, he thought, for what? Sit around and have meetings. Drink coffee. Foster a spirit of genuine cooperation among local and federal police agencies. Valuable time spent jacking each other off as they stacked up another layer of troops and EOC command.

Stupek wanted to derail the proposal. Give Rains something to really think about.

"Four hours from Quantico," he said. "That's impressive."

"I thought so," Rains said.

"But they may stay longer than you expect. They certainly did in Waco."

"These are the same people who did Waco?"

"Yes, sir, they are."

Rains said nothing. Stupek hoped James P. Rains was thinking about his precious control tower. He hoped he was thinking about it in flames.

"Well," he finally said, "it's my understanding that if the FAA wants to be strident, they can do what they damn well please. I don't think we're at that stage yet. I think they're looking for an official request, from myself or the county executive."

Stupek figured Rains had already called Mackinaw Island. Rains would never walk out on that plank alone.

"So, what does the executive say?" he asked.

"He still has full confidence in the department. He thinks the county should get the credit for resolving this."

"We haven't resolved it yet," Stupek said. "But we will, if we are left alone to do our jobs."

Stupek remembered hearing those exact words on the hostage phone monitor. He remembered hearing them from Kring.

"Nevertheless, the county executive suggests that we— and these were his words exactly—he suggests that we 'throw the FAA some kind of bone.' He believes that will hold them until he gets here."

"He's coming?"

"His plane is probably leaving northern Michigan as we speak. He feels, at this point, he needs to be personally involved."

Stupek held his tongue. He didn't know what was worse. The feds arriving or the direct meddling of a former boss. Half the people working in EOC had served under Marlon Ladd when he was sheriff.

"He should be landing in two hours at Willow Run," Rains said.

"Why not land here?" Stupek said bitterly. "Hell, everybody else is."

Rains didn't answer. He went back to the FBI.

"In the meantime, the executive is wondering if you could pursue getting the FBI involved in some kind of limited support capacity. He believes that would go a long way in assuring the FAA that federal interests are represented."

Stupek thought about it a moment, then asked Rains to hold.

He called Conrad, who'd headed back the CNT.

"You found a psychologist yet?" he asked.

"The troopers are working on it," Conrad said.

"Call me before you have them send anybody," Stupek said.

He punched Rains back up on the line.

"Okay, I'll tell you what we need from the FBI. See if they can send a police psychologist. For our negotiating team. They use a lot of behavioral science people. They should have somebody close."

"Just a psychologist?" Rains said. "Isn't there anything else you need?"

"Yeah, there is," Stupek said. "Sandwiches. Coffee. It's getting near dinner time."

When Captain Thomas Reidy stopped all drinking for two weeks last year one of his buddies, somebody who wasn't in his business, asked him, "How's it going."

"Oh, I don't miss the scotch, really," he said. "I'm just not sure I can live without throwing up."

In the 727's bathroom, Reidy heard the cargo doors being slammed shut in the plane's belly after he hit the flush button, covering the stainless steel toilet with blue water once more. He'd fought his stomach all the way to Memphis and managed to put its churning out of his mind for the Atlanta landing. He'd endured the passengers, nodding and smiling cordially as they filed off. Then he'd gone straight for the airplane lav to do what had to be done.

He should have done it sooner. Put the finger down his throat and made it happen.

Reidy washed the sweat off his face, then added two drops of Visine to his eyes. Puking always put the red back in. He owed a lot to the guys who invented those drops. Visine always took it out.

When he opened the door, the cabin attendant was stowing foil packs of peanuts.

"You okay?" she said. "Sounded pretty serious."

He inhaled and exhaled deeply, like an outdoorsman taking in mountain air.

"I think they poisoned me at the layover," he said, working very hard to sound nonchalant. "Pretty embarrassing, isn't it? But I think that was the last of it, peaches."

He'd flown with the stew before, but never made a move. She wasn't particularly good looking, in the classic sense. Had a narrow face and long nose, kind of like Marilyn Quayle. But she had very sexy small wrists and thin ankles. She had legs that became progressively curvaceous from the ankle, culminating in an ass that was shaped like a Georgia peach.

"Why do you always call me that?" she asked, innocently.

She couldn't have been much older than voting age.

"Because you're so sweet."

She batted her eyes, then glanced down at the floor. "Oh, c'mon. You're just saying that."

"No," he said. Very sincere now. "In fact, things have really changed, you know. A lot of the women . . ."

He made sure to say *women*.

". . . I fly with these days are so, how do you say it?"

"Bitchy?"

"You said it, not me."

"Hey, I have to work with them, too."

When she reached for another handful of peanuts, he glanced at her hemline. He thought about the chick at the guitar player's crib, how he'd failed to get the job done. He thought what it might be like to climb those legs and explore the peaks and valleys shrouded under that official Northwest Airlines maroon.

"Say, so are you staying in Miami, or coming back with us tonight?"

"I'm coming back. But I'm not working. Of course, nobody is."

"That's right."

She touched his arm. "You know, Captain, if you're sick,

why don't you just call in when we get to Miami. Ride back."

"No, I'm fine."

In fact, he was better. Good enough to make some kind of move. They had fifteen minutes before take off. Other attendants were picking up the cabin.

"What are you going to do in Miami?" he asked.

"Oh, I don't know. Probably head to the lounge with a book."

"In four hours you can read two books."

"Yeah. But you know how it is."

"Sure do. Never the time to see what you'd like to see."

"I get lost."

"I used to. But, hey, fifteen years, you get to know some towns."

"Really?"

"Miami's pretty good. Especially at night."

"I wouldn't know where to start," she said.

Passengers were starting to board now. He knew the co-pilot was probably wondering where the hell he was. He decided to take his shot.

"Well, I'll tell you, if my condition continues to improve, I might be able to show you a couple of places."

"Places?"

She was genuinely curious.

"Well, clubs, I mean. Music. You like good music?"

"Depends what kind."

"Blues clubs, mainly. I know a real good blues club only fifteen minutes from the airport."

"Really? I *love* the blues."

He was feeling *much* better now. He was hoping she would say that.

At 4 P.M., Terry Grice turned TRACON over to the second shift supervisor and returned to her office to call both the EOC and the director of airports. Traffic was flowing smoothly, she told James P. Rains. Handoffs from Cleveland Center to TRACON had resumed to normal numbers. Handoffs between the new tower and TRACON were glitch free. In fact, TRACON and the tower had managed to get through the mid-day push with less than a half dozen delays. They often exceeded that on a normal day.

"Even the weather seems to be cooperating," she said.

They had a three thousand foot ceiling and a fifteen-knot wind out of the west.

After she hung up, Grice looked out the window. Light flurries swirled around the parking structures, but nothing was sticking. She found herself wishing for an ice storm or full-blown blizzard whipped up by the warm waters of Lake Michigan. The local saying went: "You don't like the Michigan weather, stay for a couple hours. It'll change." For the first time in her career, she found herself wishing for weather that would shut Detroit Metropolitan Airport down.

In front of her lay Laurel Kring's personnel file. That had taken some time to get. She'd ordered it sent over from the FAA annex in Romulus, then copied it for the police. It was maybe a quarter-inch thick, which was thin for an FAA employee with more than twenty years.

Until today, Grice's knowledge of the controller was limited to what she had observed or heard. She knew he'd been a Traconite for years, but had also worked the tower. Cleage and Roberts had taken Kring off of air traffic control when Cleage decided after two retirements that they could save money by combining the training coordinator and ATC reg update and distribution slot into one job classification. He ordered the old tower canteen remodeled into a training and materials room and put Kring in charge. The position was a nonmanagement desk assignment, but considered by many a low-stress plum. Kring assigned trainees to tower and radar room positions at facilities throughout southern Michigan and tested them on their skills. Grice guessed Cleage awarded Kring the assignment because he was one of the few FPLs around who had been certified to work both the tower and radar, not common anymore in a field that had become more specialized in recent years.

Kring also kept veteran controllers up to date by distributing regulation manual revisions called *CHANGE*. The volume of printed material churned out by Washington was mind numbing. This year alone, the FAA had revised six hundred pages of specific regulations dealing with everything from controller terminology to the exact way staff notified supervisors of a developing traffic problem. Increasingly, the FAA was relying less on individual judgment and more on new technology and standard practices. Controllers were expected to absorb and implement the continually evolving changes, delivered to them three or four times a year in one-inch-thick volumes that read like life insurance policies.

He had always been very quiet. They hadn't exchanged more than a dozen sentences since she came over from the Kalamazoo facility. They'd never worked together in the radar room. And in recent months, she had very little to do with the facility's training arm. Sometimes, he'd drop by her office with an armful of *CHANGE* books. He had an annoying habit of dropping them abruptly on her credenza. The most striking feature about him, now that she thought about it, was that he was one of the few staffers who didn't call her by that stupid nickname "Mom."

Grice took a deep breath, then opened the personnel file. After hearing the Traconites talk about the siege, she realized she'd badly misjudged Laurel Kring. Now she was about to find out how much.

His application for federal employment made up the first six pages. Married. No children. He'd applied straight out of the service. He'd filled out the "previous employment" section with temporary high school jobs, but he'd earned bonus points, been given special consideration, because he

was a veteran. Attached was a letter of recommendation from his commanding officer. One sentence in particular jumped out: "I found particularly that the hotter the action in the field, the more Corporal Kring responded with coolness and resolve."

On the last page of the application Grice found something both curious and disturbing. Under a question about past violations of "laws regulating firearms or explosives" the applicant had checked "No." But asked if he'd ever committed a felony, he'd checked "Yes." The application indicated there had been a background check, but there was no note explaining his approval as a candidate despite his admission of a criminal record.

Grice turned the page to the results of Kring's application tests to the FAA Academy in Oklahoma City. The exam had three subtests. The first evaluated controller aptitudes, measuring the candidate's ability to discern compass headings, altitudes, and distances between aircraft. The second measured his ability to comprehend spatial relationships. The third evaluated his knowledge of air traffic control work. He'd scored in the mid-nineties on his knowledge of air traffic control. But on the controller aptitude and spacial relationship exams he'd hit perfect scores. There was no way for an applicant to study himself into a high score on the spacial relationships subtest. Scoring depended entirely on IQ. Grice was not surprised to see he'd graduated in the top 1 percent of his class.

This man did not belong in a desk job, she thought.

Grice began leafing forward, through administrative paperwork, assignment notices, and step pay increases. Kring had moved around between facilities in southern Michigan early on. He'd been at Metro for fifteen years. He was making top pay for an FPL.

She looked for paperwork for 1981, the year of the PATCO strike. Kring had not walked out with his union. No wonder he kept to himself, she thought. Most scabs moved into management or took retirements in years after the walk out. Many had difficulty relating to the young crowd that the academy churned out to staff America's control towers and radar rooms.

In the pages for 1988, Grice was surprised to find a subpoena. The National Transportation Safety Board had called Kring and four other controllers to testify at a hearing on the crash of flight two twenty-five. A one-page hearing summary was attached. Kring was working local control in the tower the night of the accident. All ATC personnel had followed correct protocol, the safety board determined. The flight crew caused the crash when pilots failed to lower the MD-80's flaps, the board ruled.

At the end of the personnel file, Grice found documentation on Kring's recent reassignment, and another surprise. He'd been hit with an over-the-shoulder, conducted by none other than Roberts, who was sharply critical of Kring's work on approach control. In the supervisor's opinion, Kring had violated a *CHANGE* reg that limited the number of airplanes a controller could have lined up for landings. The last paragraph was the most damaging. Knowing Robert's personality, Grice guessed what happened was a two-way street.

Roberts wrote: "When Kring was advised by writer that he was exceeding new *CHANGE* guidelines as outlined in 7110.65H CHG 1, particularly sections 5-70 through 5-79, he became belligerent, questioning the writer's credentials, then the CHG regulation itself."

Kring bitches about the new regs, so Cleage and Roberts pull him from what he does best and put him in charge of distributing them. It was plain punitive, she thought.

Grice looked back out the window, staring at the new tower in the distance.

"Nice move, Captain Queeg," she said.

Kring had included a one-page letter of protest in his personnel file. It was somewhat rambling. It was typed and signed.

"I also can't help but think that I'm being singled out," the last lines concluded. "This punitive action comes despite complete exoneration by relevant agencies and investigative personnel."

She thought, punished for what? What exoneration? Was he talking about the flight two twenty-five investigation? That was years ago. Now she wondered if Cleage and Roberts had their reasons for getting him off the front line. If they did, why hadn't he been sent for counseling, or stress evaluation?

She turned the page and found more paperwork. Kring had taken advantage in the past year of the FAA's Fam Flight project, an arrangement with the airlines that allowed controllers to ride in the jumper seats of crews to familiarize themselves with the cockpit's point of view. He'd taken four such flights, his last a month ago.

The final few pages covered a performance review made in August. Despite his protest of the transfer, Kring seemed to take to his new duties well. A summary included by the local FAA personnel director praised Kring for utilizing the Fam Flight program, which he'd used partly to attend regional training seminars.

"And," the personnel director wrote, "Mr. Kring's decision to familiarize himself with the program at the Department of Interdisciplinary Technology at Eastern Michigan University showed great initiative and foresight."

Grice turned the page over. There was nothing more.

She flipped the page back.

Department of Interdisciplinary Technology. She was the technology person at the facility, but she'd never heard of that program at that school.

She picked up the telephone and called the personnel director at the annex. Per the request of the police, she'd told people there nothing about the tower crisis.

"Grace," she said to his secretary. "Is Carl in?"

"No, he left early for the holiday."

"Didn't you get the file you wanted?"

"No, I got it. Thanks."

She paused, then continued, "Grace, do you have anything over there about a training program connected with something called interdisciplinary technology?"

"At Monroney?" she asked.

"No, not Oklahoma City. This is at EMU. Eastern Michigan University."

"Oh, yeah. I think I remembering starting a file on that."

"Could you tell me what it is?"

"Hang on."

When she returned she said, "Okay. Here it is. We got a brochure and a synopsis here. Let's see."

Reading now. "The department of interdisciplinary technology coordinates fields of communication, criminal justice, sociology, psychology, and engineering to offer students cross training in graduate studies in highly specialized disciplines as well as offers training seminars in these fields to professionals currently working in these disciplines."

"Grace," Grice said. "What else do you have there?"

"Okay, here's a blank registration form. Something called an EOC exercise."

"A what?"

"Oh, yeah. Okay. I remember this. They called over here looking for clearance so they could use Willow Run for this. But I transferred the man to the hub director."

"Clearance for what, Grace?"

"Yeah. Okay. This is the outfit that puts on those police training exercises. Carl was talking about it this summer. I guess they had police agencies out at Willow Run from all over the country. The people at Eastern put it on. They needed permission to use one of the old towers out there."

What kind of exercise?

"Grace, why did they need a tower?"

"Some kind of make-believe thing. They pretended some

cult or something had taken over the tower and wanted to see how long it took a SWAT team to get them out. If you want to know more, you ought to talk to Laurel Kring."

She was stunned for a few seconds.

"Why Laurel Kring?"

"Yeah, okay, here's a copy of the three hundred dollar voucher I was going to put through the training budget. But as I remember now the university ended up waiving it."

"They waived what, Grace?"

"Well, when they got permission to use the tower, they waived the training fee."

"For what? For who?"

"For Laurel. That's why you should talk to him. As far as I know, he was there."

Seventeen

Riker watched Oshefsky pull away from the J.M. Davey, Kring's computer riding like a prisoner in the back seat of the department Dodge.

The TOC wanted them to swing by the terminal on their way back from the search on Kraus Street. Pick up an FBI police psychologist named Morton Ressler at Gate 26E and bring him to the hangar, Conrad said.

"You just get that stuff back," Riker told Oshefsky. "I'll bring the shrinker over in a cab."

When Riker reached the gate people were already pouring off the 4:10 P.M. flight from Washington in clumps. He stood by the gate door, saying "Ressler" when people came by who he thought looked the part.

"Looking for me?"

Riker turned and saw a man in a thick cardigan sweater. He was wearing corduroys and Hush Puppies. Somewhere between fifty and sixty, Riker guessed. He had a thick dark cigar in his mouth. It was unlit.

"Dr. Ressler?"

He had an eager handshake.

"Please, call me Mort," he said. "Unless, of course, you're like some of my academic friends. They find *Mort* is uncomfortably close to the Latin root for death."

Ressler laughed. Loud.

Jesus, Riker thought.

He introduced himself and they began walking.

"The bureau contacted me on the flight," Kessler continued. "To my good fortune, actually. When the flight crew found out I was with the bureau, they gave me an empty seat they had in first class. Rather nice for someone who is a little claustrophobic. I was the first one off the plane."

"You were on your way already?"

"My daughter lives in Grosse Pointe. The holiday, you know."

"You have bags, then?" Riker asked.

He held up a small carry on. "Just this."

Riker saw a courtesy cart coming up the concourse. He hijacked it with his badge, the two of them taking seats in the back. The driver turned on a warning beeper and began winding his way through the terminal crowd.

"I have many questions," Ressler said. "Just exactly where is your *situation* here at the airport?"

"They didn't tell you?"

"They were rather vague."

"They must have gotten word to you on the crew's radio."

"Only to have me call in on the cellular."

Riker quietly gave him a quick summary. He didn't want to give the guy driving the courtesy cart something to shoot his mouth off about during his next break.

"So he knocked out the radar room and took the tower at the same time?" Ressler asked.

Riker nodded.

Ressler asked, "So what about the air traffic? My flight wasn't delayed."

"Your flight was en route."

"But we landed. You said he had the tower."

Riker just looked at him, letting him put it together.

They were entering the terminal now. A snack bar was on the right.

"Stop," Ressler said.

He jumped off and began walking toward the concession.

Riker followed.

"Ressler," he said. "We're gonna grab a cab outside."

Ressler was already telling a concession worker his order. He wanted a couple of hot dogs and a black coffee. When he was done, he turned around, the wet end of his unlit cigar sticking out of his breast pocket.

There was anger in his eyes.

"Detective Riker, before we go *anywhere* I'm going to eat. I'd like you to join me. In fact, I'm buying."

"They'll have food at the hangar."

"And they'll have many distractions, if it's anything like other operations I've seen. You look like a sane man. I'd rather talk to one sane man right now than a half dozen of questionable mental stability."

"Ressler, we're running a little short on time."

He paid for his order, then turned around again.

"You're doing intelligence on the perpetrator, right?"

Riker nodded.

"There's nothing we can do there that we can't do right here. I need you to sit down and eat with me. More importantly, I need you to tell me exactly what in the hell is going on over there."

Riker spent the first five minutes talking about the airport chain of command. How they'd insisted on keeping the siege under raps. How they had this director of airports who couldn't make a decision. How the county executive was probably calling the shots from a resort island three hundred miles to the north.

He hadn't known Ressler ten minutes, but the way he'd put on the brakes, also told him the shrinker had been burned before by bad command decisions. That alone brought a certain measure of trust.

When Riker was done, Ressler said, "Well, as you know, we had our problems in Waco."

"You were involved in that?"

"Some of us tried. There was an entire group in behavioral science that told them they were courting disaster. Blasting the compound with speakers and all that kind of crap. But there's a certain mentality on the tactical side. They had the ear of the top people in justice. Once that happened, well, you know the rest."

Ressler finished his coffee in one long slug, then wiped his lips carefully with a napkin.

"Tell me about this hostage taker," he said.

Riker told him what he found in the house. The wife. The war medal. The clipping in the ammo box. The models. He backtracked and told them what the other controllers said.

"Pretty typical," Ressler said. "The amazing part is that none of it ever filters up to management."

"Why not?" Riker asked.

"It's the keeping of such secrets that give us our identity in the workplace. In short, management is not in the same club."

He wanted to know Riker's thoughts on the *Stars and Stripes* clipping.

"A lot of GIs blamed the people in charge for Liberty Bridge," he said. "They blamed the West Pointers. Some also blamed the spades, the riots."

"So, you were there?"

Riker nodded. "Near there. In the highlands. Army infantry."

"Do we know what the hostage taker did?"

"We have some military records. I just sent them over to the EOC. Tactical ground control."

"That's infantry?"

"Well, he was a Marine. But we had a similar job in our army units."

"And that entailed?"

"A chopper would drop one of these guys into a hot zone with a radio. They did ground-based air control."

"To what purpose?"

"You'd have a bunch of GIs pinned, or injured. Or bodies. We lost a lot of guys just picking up bodies. That was the policy. You left nobody, dead or alive. These guys orchestrated air strikes against the enemy while at the same time bringing in the choppers to get your ass out. We had a guy in our company. I remember his handle. Gun Smoke. He was pretty creative. You had to be. The NVA, particularly, became hip to American tactics near the end."

Ressler pulled the cigar out of his sweater and rolled it between his lips.

"Go ahead," he said. "Tell me more."

"Well, the NVA wasn't stupid. They'd pound the shit out of the area where the OV-10s were flying. Because when you had people down and injured, an OV-10 would always scout the area first. It was your basic observation chopper. It would drop a smoke marker, then the medivacs would head for the smoke. But so would the Gooks, sometimes with everything they had. A good tactical guy could get you out. A bad one just got you killed."

"Tell me about the good ones."

"Our guy got real creative. Instead of one smoke marker, he'd have them drop a bunch. Different locations and different colors. Red smoke. White smoke. Then he'd radio our location according to the color. Nothing really too complicated, now that I think about it. But not bad, considering we were all a bunch of goddamn kids. It worked, most of the time."

Ressler pulled the cigar out of his mouth and looked Riker in the eyes.

"Tell me about the time it didn't," he said.

He was pretty perceptive.

"Six of us were pinned down in a tree line," Riker said. "Five guys ran to the chopper. Got on all right. But then it got hit and blew. Our tactics guy didn't make it back, either."

"How did you get out?"

"I worked my way back alone. Five miles to our base."

"Why didn't you go in the first place?" Ressler said, leaning forward.

Riker glanced down at the table, then back to Ressler's penetrating stare.

"I didn't like the color of the smoke."

Ressler slid the cigar back into his teeth, and started talking through the side of his mouth. "Well, twenty some years is a little long for posttraumatic stress disorder for your hostage taker, especially after twenty some years of productive work. But all this certainly tells us that he's got some real experience at being under fire."

Riker remembered the letter on the computer. Oshefsky had made a print out. He pulled it out of his jacket pocket and handed it over the table.

"We also found this at the guy's house," he said.

Morton Ressler pushed aside a paper plate smeared with mustard and chili sauce, laying the letter out in front of him.

To Whom It May Concern:

I want to make clear at the very beginning that what I do has nothing to do with my wife. She has always been there for me, but she has indirectly suffered the indignities that I have, simply because she has had to live with the results. It was never my intention to bring her harm. A virtuous woman deserves no less. Therefore, I have chosen to spare her this ordeal and its aftermath. Please see that she has a proper burial. I have left the necessary funds in our savings account at the Dearborn Federal Credit Union. These are to be dispersed to her sister, Julie Ann Spulik. Her address and phone number are listed in the Seattle book. What I do, I do with no malice to the general public. They place their trust in those of us with the skills to look after their welfare, and we are bound by duty to provide nothing less than our personal best. But our's has become a world that is not motivated by the pursuit of excellence, but by incompetence and individual appetites. Those of us who struggle, do so not against our own limitations, but against the distracted pursuits of those who have been placed in charge, but fail to do their jobs. In the name of these abominations I have been mistreated by those who have been deemed managers. But I am not alone. Many innocent people have been harmed. It is in their name, that I do what must be done. The truth must be known. My only fear is that even then, it will only resound as a clattering cymbal in a chorus of incompetency. But a man does what he must, in spite of obstacles and dangers and personal consequences—and that is the basis of all human morality.

"There are no paragraphs," Ressler said.

"Yeah, I noticed that," Riker agreed. "But pretty good, don't you think? He's not using words like that, from what I understand, on the hostage phone."

"This letter is *coherent,* though obscure in content."

"So?"

"He is very self-centered, very inward. He thinks very clearly, but he feels no empathy to provide those of us on the outside with any guideposts to help follow his logic. He's a man all wrapped up in himself. And that makes for a very small package. Rather adolescent, really. The models you spoke of. That's adolescent. He's *also* a plagiarist."

"How do you mean."

"This last line, it's JFK. From *Profiles in Courage.* For all his espoused superiority, he's really lacking. He takes another man's words, but feels a need to parade them as his own. This is somewhat typical pathology."

Ressler was starting to lose him. Riker checked his watch and stood up.

"Ressler, we've got to get over to the hangar."

"The hangar?"

"Yeah, that's where we've set up our EOC."

As they circled the access road in the cab, Riker pointed out the new control tower. It seemed more remote than Riker had ever remembered it. It seemed taller, sitting out there in the junction of runways six and three center.

Ressler's cigar remained unlit.

"Maybe the hack here's got some matches," Riker suggested.

"Oh, no. I never light them. I gave up the habit."

"That's a hell of cigar you're not smoking."

Ressler held it up so he could see the ring. "Te-Amo. Mexican. It means *I love you* in Spanish. Simply an oral fixation, or I'm fooling myself. Maybe I'm getting something from a trickle of nicotine down my throat."

The cigar ring reminded Riker of Kring's wife. The way she was tucked in on that easy chair.

"Ressler, how does a guy put a bullet threw his wife's head and then write her a love letter?"

"Do you remember Charles Whitman?"

"The name sounds familiar," Riker said.

"Austin, 1966. He was the sniper in the clock tower of the University of Texas. A sensational case for its day."

"Oh, yeah. I remember."

"Well, on the night before his rampage began he wrote what some would call a suicide note, saying he could not understand his violent behavior and that he intended to murder his wife. He was interrupted by friends who dropped by. He spent a couple of hours talking quite normally to them. After they left, he went to his mother's house. Stabbed her to death and left a note saying he loved her with all his heart. Went home. Killed his wife. Finished his note. The next morning he killed nine people from the tower's observation deck. Wounded another eight. He was a vet. A superb marksman, but a poor problem solver."

Ressler pointed his cigar at the distant tower. "Kind of like our fellow out there."

"But they say the guy is a top controller," Riker pointed out.

"Perhaps. But no, he's not a very good problem solver. The cab pulled into the Nomad's parking lot.

"What makes you say that?" Riker asked.

"If he was, he wouldn't need to take hostages, would he?" Ressler said.

Eighteen

They tacked the blueprints and a field survey on a sheet of plywood, then propped it up against the west wall of the Nomad's hangar.

Reed Johnson, the SWAT field commander, was waiting there as a dozen team leaders, information handlers and SWAT cops gathered in front of him. He was a tall, thin black man, late thirties with penetrating eyes. Off the job, he sang bass in a doo-wop group that performed at local street rod gatherings. He didn't do this for money, but for the love of the art form, and the women he met along the way.

Johnson switched on a laser pointer, its red dot landing on the field survey.

"Nice toy, Reed," somebody said. "You get that at Toys 'R Us?"

Johnson turned the pointer, putting the red dot in the center of the smartass's forehead.

"I got one like it on another piece of equipment," he said, referring to his MP-5. "Wanna see that one, too?"

When the chatter subsided, Johnson said, "Okay, here's what we're looking at. We've got about four hours into this now, so this is based on our tactical capabilities and what the TOC has been able to find out so far."

Johnson waited until everybody was looking, particularly Stupek, Thompson, and Conrad.

"Tactically speaking, our HT has three zones of defense

around his position," he began. "All three will be difficult to negotiate, but not necessarily impossible. All three zones have their own set of problems. And all three, the first in particular, will require extended tactical maneuvers over a considerable length of time."

He spoke from the diaphragm, his voice booming. He wanted to make himself heard over the departing flights outside on three center. Johnson pointed the laser pointer at the tower, then motioned outward as if he were drawing spokes of a wheel.

"The first zone, the outer perimeter, starts at the tower base and extends to a radius of from four to eight hundred yards to the secured and enclosed airport buildings on the north, *and* on the east to the elevated ridge along Eureka Road at the south. This area is flat and exposed, so the HT has complete visual surveillance of this zone from his position in the tower, as demonstrated by his threats on tape sent over by dispatch. *However,* we also believe, according to interviews conducted by the TOC of FAA tower personnel, that the HT also has the considerable advantage of electronic surveillance with ground-oriented radar located in the tower itself. This possibility would prohibit any kind of concentrated SWAT movement, even under the cover of night, and *especially* the SWAT assault vehicle."

"Assuming it would start," somebody cracked.

When the laughter subsided, Vince Stupek asked, "How effective is the ground radar?"

"It's known as ASDE, or Airport Surface Detection Equipment. They use it primarily for ground control when the airport is socked in with fog. It can pick up a man walking down that access road from Eureka, if that's what you're asking, Vince. This particular device also has a number of features, we're told, including a nifty little option that allows the user to set it up so that it shows only moving targets. Furthermore, it has zoom capability. Its range can be set as far out as the entire airport property, or collapse down to a range of two hundred yards."

"I can see more than you think," Conrad said.

"What's that?" Johnson said.

"That's what he said on the phone."

"Right, very difficult," Johnson said. "But *not* impregnable. Fortunately, airport engineers blessed us with a shallow drainage ditch along this access road here." He traced a line from the Eureka check point, where Riker found the dead security guards, to the tower parking lot.

"Under the cover of night, we can avoid the radar by crawling in this depression. But it *will* take time. We're gonna be on our bellies. We're lookin' at a distance of twenty-four hundred yards, about a mile and a half. We believe there may be water in this ditch, which means that they will also have to carry with them dry provisions for when they arrive at this staging point here."

The red dot landed on the new fire house under construction.

"Furthermore, the weather service tells us that temperatures are expected to dip below freezing tonight, so that is something to consider in terms of the timing of this assault. The firehouse here is incomplete, unheated, and real goddamn drafty. *However,* strategically, the firehouse is a godsend. There is ample cover for sniper positions, with a clear view of the tower cab through the north and east vistas, though we do have some unknowns in ballistics and accuracy, considering the thickness of that tower glass."

Stupek asked, "So how long are we talking about here, from the time SWAT leaves the check point at Eureka Road to the staging area?"

"An hour minimum. Then, any major assault should follow within a window of no more than two hours of their arrival. After that, the cold is going to become a factor."

Somebody asked, "Why not a Trojan horse?"

Thompson, the TOC leader, spoke up. "That's out. They

used a gutted bottled water truck making a delivery in the EMU training exercise at Willow Run. He's going to expect a scam like that."

"Does anybody know what Kring did in the drill?" a familiar voice said from the back of the group.

Several people turned around. Jack Riker and Morton Ressler had walked in behind them, unnoticed.

"Not yet," Thompson said. "We got that from one of our SWAT people who helped in the drill, but we weren't involved much more than that."

Riker introduced the FBI psychologist.

When he was done, Johnson continued, "So, if the negotiator is able to talk the HT out of the tower, or if he requests transportation out with his hostages, we should be in good shape from our first zone penetration as he and the hostages exit the building."

Stupek pointed to the board. "Let's say he doesn't come down. Let's presume there is no sniper shot into the tower cab, what next?"

Johnson went back to the field survey with his pointer.

"Well, that takes us into what I'm referring to as the HT's second defense zone. This zone extends from the doors at the tower base to a radius of one hundred yards. And this is where it gets real tricky. Now, we think we *can* defeat his ground radar capabilities with a fast low run across this parking lot here, *if* the HT has the ASDE on one of its extended ranges. Apparently sensitivity is reduced the closer you get to the radar's center. *But* that doesn't help us if he happens to be sight seeing out the window. Also, the tower has security camera locations on these doors here and here—*as well as* a tower cam with a ninety-degree view of the parking lot from the north side. The monitors are in the tower cab and *are* operational, we're told. And all the doors at the base have electronic locks."

"Can we pull the plug?" Stupek asked.

"No, unfortunately. Because of the FAA's past problems with the airport power supply, this facility's electrical is entirely self-contained with a number of built-in redundancies. *Furthermore,* if we cut the power, we still have to get up those tower stairs. He could waste everybody before we ever made two flights."

Johnson surveyed the men in front of him. Waiting for suggestions. Waiting for something he or his men might have overlooked.

None came.

He continued, *"But,* we are not completely shit out of luck. Fortunately, we know from Detective Riker here that this south door is easily accessible due to some bad workmanship."

Some turned to Riker.

He shrugged.

"Feds put the lock in backward. I opened it with my Visa card."

Johnson continued, "We believe we can negotiate the parking lot and slip a half dozen SWAT people through the south door in less than ten seconds. But *obviously,* we're going to need a diversion."

Johnson looked everybody over again.

"I *am* open for suggestions. But remember, he knows the drill. He's familiar with the training. He's going to be expecting something."

"What kind of diversion did they use in the Willow Run drill?" Conrad asked.

Thompson answered. "They moved a half dozen snipers in clear view on one side of the tower. It drew him to one window. SWAT came out of the bottled water truck on the other side."

Conrad laughed. "What the fuck was the water truck doing delivering water in that situation?"

"I don't know," Thompson said impatiently. "I don't

work there. I didn't design the goddamn thing. It's a goddamn university drill. What do you expect?"

Stupek turned to Conrad. "Can you work somebody on the phone. Can you get something from the inside?"

"You mean a hostage?"

"Yeah, those people up there are used to working under pressure. Do you think you can get one of the hostages on the line and maybe set up some kind of internal diversion?"

"This guy places everything close to his chest," Conrad said.

Morton Ressler interrupted. "I take it this assault would not be able to take place until, when?"

"Later this evening," Johnson said. "Before twenty-four hundred."

Ressler moved forward. "You're going to run into the Stockholm problem," he said.

"That soon?" Stupek asked.

"In this situation. Under *these* conditions. With this hostage personnel, who are already under considerable stress controlling traffic. In my opinion, *absolutely*."

Everyone heard about the Stockholm syndrome in training. It was first identified in a barricaded gunmen situation in a Swedish bank in 1973. Two criminals held four bank employees hostages for one hundred and thirty-one hours before finally surrendering. As time wore on, the need to survive caused hostages to sympathize with their captors. They developed negative attitudes toward authorities. Anyone unfamiliar with that case, had only to remember Patty Hearst.

"Any suggestions, Dr. Ressler?" Stupek asked.

"I'd like to see your hostage profiles first. I'd also like to see everything you've gathered on this man."

"All right," Stupek said. "Let's put the diversion aside, just for the time being."

He looked at Johnson. "What about once SWAT is in the tower?"

"Right, and this is our third zone," Johnson said.

He moved over to the blue prints, using the laser pointer again.

"This stairwell is easily accessible, and it dumps out into *this* level here where the ASDE radar units are located. We know these floor schematics are good because everything here has been confirmed by Detective Riker. The tower also features a trap door at the top, but it is largely useless for our purposes because we have no way to reach it without being detected through the glass in the cab. *However,* the distance from the stairwell, up the spiral staircase to the cab is less than thirty feet. This is short, all things considered. Certainly short enough for us to storm the door and the stairs. We can hit the cab with smoke and shock grenades and, if with some luck, walk out of this thing with no casualties, except for the HT, of course."

"So the last zone will be the easiest," Stupek said.

"Well, on paper at least," Johnson said. "And *that* is an assumption. According to TOC intelligence, we *are* dealing with a trained veteran here familiar with combat situations. My guess is that he's not going to let us in that cab that easy. We have a pretty good handle on his firepower. But I'd sure like to know where the surprises are."

Stupek turned to Conrad. "Tuck, what does Tommy think the odds are of him cutting loose somebody?"

"He doesn't think he can get any kind of handle on this guy until we try to negotiate the airport back."

"What about the kids?"

"Well, he doesn't think he was expecting the kids."

Ressler spoke up. "I would say the children are not part of his fantasy."

"What's that?" Stupek said.

The psychologist walked farther forward. "On the way over, your detective did brief me enough to make me believe that this man has put a great deal of thought into this. His sabotage of the radar room, timed with his assault.

He's likely been planning it for many weeks, more like many months. But he did not plan for the children. They were not part of the fantasy. As a matter of fact, it's very likely you find yourself in this difficult situation *entirely* because of those children."

Ressler stopped, looking around. He seemed reluctant to distract from Johnson's presentation.

"Go ahead," Stupek said.

"You see, as a result of the numerous problems at the Postal Service and other situations in the private sector, we've made an effort in the Behavioral Science Section in recent years to learn more about the workplace killer. I, myself, have interviewed a number of these men—and they tend to me mostly male, though not exclusively—who have survived their own assaults."

Stupek crossed his arms. He didn't doubt Ressler's expertise. He hoped he would put it into terms everyone could understand.

"Feel free to explain," he said.

"For an *extended* period of time, the preparation for the assault provides the thrust of the catharsis for the workplace killer. He may even dabble in some relatively harmless antisocial behavior before he lashes out."

"How about making bogus radio broadcasts to aircraft?" Riker asked. "We've had some trouble here with that."

"Yes, exactly," Ressler said.

"What's a catharsis?" somebody asked.

"His emotional *release*. In fact, in the beginning, the perpetrator does not really believe that he will indeed make an actual assault. But over and over he finds himself fantasizing, working detail after detail. In the beginning, his gratification may come from picking out weapons. Or drawing diagrams. He studies literature. Watches documentaries of others who have committed mass murder. In our case here, he goes one more step. He attends a training exercise. As unusual as that appears, *that* does not surprise me, really. The training exercise just happened to be available, like a book he might find in the crime section of his local bookstore."

"You don't think he took the training to anticipate our moves?" Johnson asked.

"Not necessarily. It may not have been a defensive effort, just another step in the amplification of his fantasy. But in time, something happens to these people. Wishful thinking in a damaged psyche eventually transforms into an irresistible force of its own. In time, he may see himself as having no choice but to carry the fantasy out. To the man, the workplace killers I've interviewed all told me of committing the act with an otherworldly-type mind-set. Of watching themselves shooting. As if they were outside observers."

Stupek wanted to nudge Ressler back on track. "You were saying about the children."

"The children have never had a place in the scenario he repeatedly rehearsed in his mind. Unlike the move to the new tower, the holiday, the staffing, the crisis response by authorities, he would have had *no way* of knowing the children would be there. My first impression is that your man planned to commit great carnage in that control tower, *until* he came upon the children. *That* is what stopped him. The children shocked him out of this abject state, and he *stopped*."

Ressler had a Te-Amo in his hand now, waving it like an instructor would a pencil.

"Stopped what?" Stupek asked.

"Shooting. Killing. Venting. Ultimately, most of these end in suicide. But he never got that far. *That* is why your victim count remains relatively low."

Ressler turned to Conrad. "He has not told your primary negotiator what he wants, has he?"

Conrad nodded, somewhat impressed by the accurate

perception of someone who had just walked through the door.

"No, he hasn't," Ressler continued. "You see, he can't tell you what he wants because he doesn't know what he wants."

"He keeps saying he wants to be left alone," Conrad said.

"Of course he does. He needs time to build a new fantasy. Perhaps some kind of new final stand. Suicide by police. Going out in a blaze of glory. Who knows? But it will take him time. And the presence of those children will only complicate the situation for him."

Ressler pointed his cigar at Stupek. "You have a real opportunity here, Lieutenant. I believe you can negotiate the release of those children. He doesn't want them. They're in his way—psychologically, at least."

"What do you think he's going to want?" Conrad asked.

"More importantly," Ressler said. "What does he *need?*"

"Obviously, he wants the tower," Stupek said. "The tower and the traffic. Getting the traffic was his first move."

Ressler was brainstorming. "Exactly. He's improvising, driven by his basic need. He *needs* to prove to everyone his professional skills. *Needs* to prove he can run that tower better than the management he despises. I don't believe the people in those airplanes are in *any* danger whatsoever. In fact, they're probably safer now than under the authorities whom he despises for their incompetency. It's all in his letter."

Stupek studied the psychologist. He was thinking that despite himself, James P. Rains, may have managed to contribute.

Ressler stuck the Te-Amo in between his front molars, talking out of the corner of his mouth.

"*That* is your answer, gentlemen. To *both* of your problems. Let him keep the airport, but get those kids and anybody else you can in return."

"And the diversion?" Johnson said.

"Just think about it," Ressler said. "If your job was to control airplanes. No, if it were to *manage* people who controlled airplanes, what might absolutely captivate your attention for an extended period of time?"

Nineteen

Caley Harmon listened to the erratic chorus of holiday traffic outside. A screeching panic stop. Somebody flooring it off the light. A lone junker chugging along, bringing up the rear. The office for Local 2757 of the International Brotherhood of Teamsters was neither large nor luxurious, nor were its walls very thick.

She'd been waiting at her desk for an hour now for the director of airports to return her call. She'd skipped her regular Wednesday meeting to wait.

Harmon walked to the window and pushed aside a vertical blind. She watched the drivers, picking out the ones she thought looked crazed. She'd always found the winter holidays somewhat depressing. It was the way everyone raced around, trying to get to a state of mind on time.

And here she was. *Pushing.*

Back at her desk, she spotted the wallet card she'd shoved under the glass desktop. It was the Serenity Prayer: *". . . grant me the serenity to accept the things I cannot change, the courage to change the things I can and the wisdom to know the difference."*

Nikki Delesandro.

Go home, she told herself. Or catch the end of the meeting. Enjoy the holiday at her parents'. Wait until Monday to get the letter from Rains. Do something really brave on Friday, she told herself, like let go, and take the day off.

But that was not her nature. Her nature was to push.

A couple years ago, she'd stopped saying she was a "Teamsters official" when somebody asked her what she did. She'd become weary of the image it conjured, like she was on some kind of free ride. In Detroit, people thought of Local 299, Hoffa's old outfit. They thought of the pension fund and the big conventions in Vegas. She had to admit, though, she'd learned a few moves from those old steel haulers. "The name's got clout with the starched shirt crowd," a Hoffa contemporary told her once. "Honey, don't be afraid to fucking use it." He told her that at a convention in Vegas, in fact.

Local 2757 represented all attendants working Northwest Airline's Detroit-Memphis commuter base, the airline's largest. Nearly twenty-six hundred passed through Metro every couple of days. Their names and biographies were in a six-inch-thick computer printout on her credenza. An attendant could make nearly forty thousand a year with full seniority. Decent money *for a woman,* as some were still apt to say, though a third were now men. From many, she'd heard every kind of complaint or problem, from grievances over high time to golden girls claiming the cabin air was putting the wrinkles in their skin.

They had elected her president four years ago, quite a vote of confidence considering she'd only been flying ten years at the time. They said they voted for her because she took shit from nobody. Others said it was because of the turnaround she'd made in her own life. She hadn't let them down on both fronts. She pushed for better employee assistance programs. She fought for age discrimination language in the current contract. She won scheduling reforms to prevent attendants from being stranded in distant cities, simply because they couldn't find a nonworking return to base because of overbooked flights.

Caley Harmon had been preparing for years, without really knowing. Blue-collar kid from Corktown, Detroit's old Irish neighborhood. Her father moved them to Dearborn when he made union steward at Detroit Diesel. He paid for college, but she partied her way out by the first Christmas break. The lure of excitement drew her into aviation. She'd wanted to see Miami and San Francisco and New York.

After she sobered up, she realized the only thing she knew about those towns were the locations of the best bars. A series of bad cross-country relationships. Flying on amphetamines. Weekends with Tanquary and tonic. Never lost many work days, or even spilled one drink on a passenger. She should have realized she was in trouble when they invented the plastic half-gallon liquor containers. She discovered you could light them with a match and they'd burn into a small balls of plastic. She thought that was the world's greatest invention. She no longer had to worry about what her neighbors thought when she dumped those clanking glass bottles in the condo's trash.

That's how screwed up her thinking was. Five years ago, a jetbag with ten years sobriety took her to her first meeting. She still hit AA twice a week.

"Why do you still go after five years," somebody asked her recently. "You still want to drink?"

"The urge is history," she said. "But reality keeps coming. It's reality that will drive every drunk back."

When she hit a couple meetings a week she didn't push so much.

That's what she liked about the local. It gave her access to the people in trouble. If the flying public knew about what some of those airline uniforms were hiding, it would scare them half to death. Two in ten. That's what the statistics said. Two in ten Americans had some kind of problem, or were on their way to one. All the drunk driving laws and health fads weren't going to change the genetics. Profession had nothing to do with it. The tables had taught Caley Harmon that. She'd heard doctors talk about drinking to relieve stress. She'd heard line workers say they drank to relieve boredom. She once heard a bricklayer say he drank because of the dust in the mortar. He maintained beer was the only thing that quenched his thirst.

Nikki Delesandro had her own reasons. Another bright Detroit girl doing with her body what she should have been doing with her brains. She'd stopped by Harmon's office the week before she disappeared, wondering if she considered it unusual to take four blue Valium to find sleep on the other side of two time zones.

"Sounds perfectly reasonable to me," she told her. "But the only other people who agree with me all sit at the tables now."

Harmon told her she could get her into treatment, with no company ramifications. But she wanted time to think it out. She thought herself right out of it. The next day, she left on a five-day trip to the West Coast.

Ever since, Caley Harmon had been second-guessing herself. Maybe she should have pushed harder, taken the girl herself to the treatment center.

But now, she was telling herself to let go.

The wisdom to know the difference.

Caley Harmon also knew she wasn't the first alkie who had trouble finding the balance. But the bottom line was that Nikki Delesandro never got her shot.

When the phone rang just after 5 P.M., it brought only more trouble. Another attendant in her directory. She could put a face to the voice on the line, a young stewardess not two years out of the charm farm.

"Caley, my purse," the attendant began.

Someone had snatched her purse while she was walking in her civvies in Concourse E after her last leg of an Orlando trip. The guy bumped into her in a crowd. It took her a minute before she even realized it was gone.

"Now slow down," Harmon said.

She was sniffling.

"Call me stupid, Caley," she said. "But I had five hundred in cash in that purse, not to mention all my plastic. This was going to be my weekend to get it all *done.*"

"Get what done?"

"Christmas crap, you know. I've bidded myself to Bejesus and back next month. I'm flying night and day."

Harmon left her purse at a bar once. She remembered she left it the next morning, but she couldn't recall the name of the bar.

"It feels like you've lost half your life," she said. "Getting the ID cards. That's the worst."

"No, that's not the worst part," the attendant said. "The *worst* part has been trying to deal with the airport police."

"How so?"

"Well, first I couldn't find a cop in the terminal. You'd think with the holiday, they'd put some extra people on duty. But I did not see *one cop!* Only outside. Directing traffic. And you know they're not going to give me the time of day."

There always were airport police standing around in the terminals, Harmon thought. She must have missed them in the crowd.

"Well, at this point, you probably should go over there," she suggested. "The department is just up the road here, on Middlebelt."

The attendant was mad now.

"Oh no. That's why I'm calling. I've got a travel rider on my policy, but the insurance company said it has to have a police report."

"Okay."

"So, when I couldn't find a cop, I took the shuttle to the lot and picked up my car. I drive over to the department. There on Middlebelt. Jesus, the place is a real crap hole over there. They could use some paint."

"I know. I've been there."

"I go into the reception area. You know, where they have the old bowling trophies in that glass case."

"Okay."

"And, get this, there's no one there."

"There's nobody working the window?"

"Not just that. I figure what the hey, I'll just find somebody. I go down the hall. Room by room. And I mean this place was *deserted*. At three in the afternoon. It was like the Terminator had been there."

"Did you try the detective bureau?"

"Yeah. The only thing there was the ugliest Christmas tree I've ever seen in my life."

"There's got to be *somebody*."

"Well, on my way out. I go down there, and now there is somebody at the front window. A woman cop. She says she stepped away for a second. I asked to make out a report."

"And?"

"And she said that was not possible."

"Not possible? What do you mean, it's a formality."

"That's what I told her. But she said there was nobody to help me and she was busy. I'd have to come back on *Monday*."

"Did you ask her where everybody was?"

"Yeah, but I couldn't get a straight answer."

"Did you ask her *why* no one was around to take the report."

"Yeah, and she got real dikey. She says, 'Hey, take a break, sister, it's Thanksgiving. Cops deserve a holiday, too.' "

Jesus, Harmon thought, what kind of operation were they running?

The young attendant pleaded. "Caley, you gotta help me. Do you know anybody over there?"

Harmon cradled the phone under her shoulder, stretching the chord as she walked over to her coat tree.

"Yeah," she said. "I know somebody. Give me your home number."

Detective Riker, she thought. Busy, my ass.

* * *

Lefty Thompson dropped the folder of documents on one of the tables where Riker was sitting in the TOC.

"Most of this you already know. But you might want to familiarize yourself with this entire file. They're looking for somebody to work full time with the negotiation team when they start to move in on this guy. You seem to know more about this guy than anybody at this point, I think it ought to be you."

"Do I have a choice?" Riker asked.

"Yeah, you got a choice."

Riker liked his mobility. He liked being able to get out of that goddamn hangar if he had to. In the CNT, he'd probably spend most of his time waiting for the red light on that hostage phone.

"Let me know what you want to do," Thompson said, sitting down at a nearby table.

The TOC was quiet, considering.

Thompson had sent Oshefsky to Eastern Michigan for the paperwork from the Willow Run drill. Others were informing hostage families, gathering more pictures and background. Every few minutes a SWAT intelligence officer came in and out, checking information on the poster boards. A few photos were up, as well as Kring's wedding picture he'd brought from Kraus Street. Somebody had circled it with a marker with four inward lines, suggesting cross hairs, then wrote: "Our man."

SWAT, Riker thought. Only SWAT did shit like that.

Kring's computer was plugged in and running. Empty coffee cups and yellow legal pads nearby. Earlier, Oshefsky had checked the machine but said he'd found little more than something he called "program files."

"What are those?" Riker asked.

"Software. They run the computer, Jack."

Behind the glass window marked OSC, Riker could see,

but not hear, Vince Stupek. He was giving somebody hell
on the telephone, his forehead creased. Dealing with James
P. Rains and the rest of county, Riker guessed. Stupek was
a good cop. But watching him only reaffirmed Riker's long-
time policy of not seeking or spending too much time with
the people who supervised them. He would just as soon
leap into a vat of shit.

He opened the folder filled with documents and information gathered by other investigators. An FAA personnel
file. A driving record. A LEIN (Law Enforcement Information Network) printout. A record check with the Michigan crime network. A printout of the number of weapons
registered to one Laurel Kring.

Riker pulled out the printouts from Michigan and LEIN.
"Shit," he said to Thompson. "He's got a sheet."

Thompson was reading interview summaries and other
paperwork.

"Yeah, we got some hits. A fed, can you imagine?"

"How?"

"I need you to check. Everybody else is out and about."

There was one entry on the LEIN:

**Arr: 10/16/69 Felonious Assault. Berkley, CA PD.
Conv: 10/18/69 Aggravated assault. Berkley District
Court. Sen. Susp.**

Translation: Arrested by Berkley police in the fall of
1969, but convicted of a lesser charge and did no time.
Pled out, Riker guessed.

He went to the FAA personnel file, still thinking, you
don't get a goddamn high-security job with a police record.

He found the "yes" box checked under the background
check.

Riker picked up the phone and got the number for Berkley PD. What the hell, he thought, he'd connected on longer
shots.

Another phone call, a 510 area code.

"Records section," he asked.

"Just a moment."

"This is records."

After he asked, the woman in records said, yes, they indexed old felonies. "But our file won't tell you much more than the charge, the location, and the arresting officer," she added.

He gave her what he had from the LEIN. He waited on hold for five minutes.

When she picked up again she said, "Yes, Laurel Kring. I have it here. He was arrested in Sproul Plaza, that's the edge there of the U of C campus. The arresting officer on this case is now one of our captains. He's working out front, but I can't guarantee you the condition of his memory."

"I'll take my chances," he said. "And thanks."

She transferred him.

Riker made some small talk, then emphasized that this man Kring was into some serious stuff now, and they needed all the help he could provide.

"What did you say that date was?"

"October 16, 1969."

There was a pause.

"You know you make, what, several thousand arrests in a career?"

"At least," Riker said.

"But some you *do* remember. You *do* remember the crazy ones. I remember my daughter also was born that week. I wasn't there, though. I spent the night at the goddamn station because a bunch of hippies had a war protest that day. One of many. We were the center of the universe for that crap. They used to call us Bezerkley back then."

"You remember this arrest?"

"I remember collaring a GI. A Marine, I think it was. The hippies had filled the street. Chanting. All that stuff.

We had everybody back then. Krishnas. SDS. Jesus freaks. We were running a regular fucking zoo here back then. That day, we had a group of soldiers there on the sidewalk. If I remember correctly, I think they'd just shipped in at Oakland and come up to check out the exhibits."

"Kring was a Marine."

"Well, that's probably the guy I arrested. Names, you're asking too much."

"Arrested for what?"

"The protesters had lined the demonstration with women. They used to do that, figuring we'd keep the sticks off the hippie broads. Anyway, the guy I collared was standing alone on the sidewalk. Full uniform. When one of the gals spit on him. Calling him a Nazi. I don't know if you remember, but these people didn't respect shit."

Riker remembered.

"And you arrested the Marine?"

"I had to. After she spit on him, he just goddamn decked her. Knocked her clean on her ass. The place went nuts, so I cuffed him and got him to the wagon. It was for his protection, really. Then the hippie pressed charges. But I can't say I blame the guy, really. I think he got a break from the judge."

"Yeah," Riker said. "It looks like he did."

After Riker hung up, Thompson looked over.

"Anything?"

"He decked a broad in a war protest," Riker said. "I guess the FAA figured he was honest and cut him some slack."

Thompson shrugged.

"What about Romulus? There's a disorderly in Romulus. Just last year."

"I know," Riker said. "I was saving the worst for last."

After five minutes on the phone with Romulus PD, Riker was thinking all kinds of things he wanted to tell the prick lieutenant on the other end of the line. Like how was it

that he could call all the way out to Berkeley fucking California and have a very pleasant and informative conversation about a suspect, but when he called Romulus PD only
a couple miles down the goddamn road they had to jerk
him around.

"So, you're telling me you can't give me any details
unless I personally come over there and clear it with your
chief?" Riker finally said.

"I'm telling you that I have the report in front of me,
but can only tell you that the arrest was for disorderly persons last November tenth. The subject paid his fine and
has no outstanding warrants."

Riker looked out the window at the Nomads parking lot.
Saw all the cars parked there, their rear bumpers facing
him. He remembered the plate he'd made early in the day.

He remembered Spencer Davis.

"I'll tell you what, Lieutenant, you're a man, right?"

"What do you think?"

"And I'm a man."

"If you say so."

"Man to man, I'm going to make you a deal."

"A deal?"

"Yeah, a *deal.*"

"You can try."

"It's my understanding, you're looking for a certain 1994
Taurus stolen from one of your finest establishments there
in the city of Romulus, the old village section."

"We are?"

"You are. Trust me. It came over the wire earlier today.
What would you say if I told you that I know where that
Taurus is and can have it waiting in our impound for you
by this time tomorrow. Would that make you forget about
the book over there for a couple of seconds and tell me
what you can about this arrest?"

He heard the lieutenant yell to an underling for paperwork on a certain stolen Taurus.

Not ten seconds later he said, "Okay, that car was stolen from the Landing Strip. Yeah we're still looking for that. Where is it?"

"Good shape. Still has its wheel covers. But I want the disorderly."

"It was at the Landing Strip."

"I know the car was stolen from the tittie bar. What about the suspect?"

"It was at the Landing Strip."

"The disorderly?"

"Yeah. I guess this guy slugged a dancer and went at it with the bouncers. We wrote him for illegal parking, too."

When Riker hung up, he put on his coat.

Thompson now was rereading Laurel Kring's farewell note. "Riker, we ought to talk to this sister," he said. "I talked to Trenton. They said Seattle PD delivered the bad news."

Riker handed him the Kring file.

"When I get back. That disorderly was at the same club where he took the Taurus."

"The tittie bar?"

"Yeah, I'm going up there and poke around."

Riker pulled Laurel Kring's airport ID picture off the TOC board.

"Maybe I'll have Oshefsky call this sister," Thompson said.

"Whatever," said Riker.

Thompson looked at him skeptically.

"Jack, watch what you poke up there, okay?"

Caley Harmon pulled out on middlebelt right behind two airport police patrol cars heading south. She thought they would turn into the department, but they slowed before then and turned into the Nomad's lot. As they did, a Dodge darted out in front of her, scattering gravel, pebbles bouncing off her grill.

"I'll be damned," she muttered under her breath.

She saw Jack Riker behind the wheel.

She expected him to turn into the next driveway, the airport police. When he kept going, she punched the accelerator.

Pull up to him at the next light at Eureka, she thought. Or outright pull him over. A Teamster pulling over a cop. She started laughing out loud at the prospect.

She followed him for nearly three miles, thinking, this is crazy. Caley, you've gone goddamn nuts. You really need a meeting.

They went south, then west, around the airport, ending up in Romulus, the old village section.

She was going to stop and turn around, but then she saw his blinker go on. Ahead on the left she saw a convenience store. He passed that driveway. All that was left was the brick night club with the big bright awning.

He turned in.

She did a U across four lanes.

Before she sped off, fuming, she read the canopy, just to make sure it hadn't changed ownership.

THE LANDING STRIP—FEMALE ENTERTAINMENT, it read.

Twenty

Inside the Landing Strip, the music was loud and the big bouncer at the door seemed to have a hard time hearing what he was trying to tell him. The guy had a big neck and a look on his face that said *I think you might be full of shit,* so Riker showed him some department metal.

"Where's the manager?" Riker shouted over Rod Stewart.

He pointed to a door at the back of the club.

The club was jammed with suits. They sat at tables around the stage and in the shadows of booths along the walls. Some eyes were on the dancer with the garrison cap working the brass pole. Other customers were under girls doing lap dances, most of them smiling, trying to look casual about being dry humped in public.

It was a different perspective, being there on official business, Riker decided. It looked more decadent from the outside looking in. A real sin pit. The view gave him a crazy idea: Flash the metal and make all the guys with light color slacks stand up for a pants check. Tell the ones with wet spots he was hauling them in on a health ordinance.

Still smiling to himself, he knocked at the manager's door.

The guy was wearing a black double-breasted suit jacket. Had his hair moused back with the wet look. Couldn't have been more than thirty.

Riker gave him the date. Showed him the picture.

"Yes, I remember that sonovabitch, alright," he said. "I pressed the case. *I* was quite upset. You don't come in here and hit one of my girls."

"Does the stripper still work here?"

"My girls aren't strippers. They're *dancers*."

"Okay, does the dancer still work here?"

He pointed to the stage. "That's her, working the north pole up there."

"North pole?"

"Yes, that's the north pole. The south pole is on the other side of the stage."

Riker nodded his head, giving the man the courtesy of acknowledging what must be an important differentiation in his business.

"Well, do you think I could talk to Santa's little helper there at the north pole when she gets done?"

"I have no problem with that. Grab a table there. I'll buy you a drink while you wait."

Riker asked for a coffee and took a seat near the neon outline of the jet liner, catching the last couple minutes of the dancer's show. She was petite, but had a big face that at some angles seemed at odds with her small frame. She used her eyes a lot when she danced. A lot of contact and a surly look that bordered on a sneer. When their eyes met, he would have thought she was staring right into him, had he not known it was all part of her act.

Afterward, the manager sent her over. She sat down topless, pulling on the rest of her costume, a jacket, over her very erect nipples as he introduced himself.

"I just need to talk to you for just a couple of minutes about an assault I understand took place here about a year ago," he said after the formalities.

"The creep that tossed me around?"

He nodded.

She poked her hand through the sleeve and extended it.

"I'm Tea."

"Tea?" Dancers picked some odd working names.

"Yeah, as in Coffee, Tea, or me. With me you get both."

She giggled, moving her shoulders back and forth, showing off her chest and the jacket.

He looked over the costume, now that she was wearing all of it. She was wearing an old Delta Airlines stewardess outfit. The garrison cap was something stews wore in the fifties.

"Flying theme," she said, matter of factly. "Like it?"

"It's very creative."

"A gimmick always helps, especially if mother nature shorted you a little, if you know what I mean." She popped her chest. "I think it's healthier than implants. Besides I don't think they look natural, do you?"

"I wouldn't know."

"Yes you would. Just watch the girls with them. You can tell they got silicon bags because they never move."

Fascinating, Riker thought. "Anyway, you were saying?"

"I've got all the uniforms. Delta. Northwest. American. United. I go to the same uniform store the real ones do. But I found this one, this is my first, at a garage sale. *Hey,* it's my favorite, because it's what gave me the idea."

Let her talk, he told himself. "That's showing real enterprise," he said.

She lit a cigarette.

"Of course, I've altered them a little bit. But not too much. There was a pilot in here, or at least he said he was a pilot, he told me I could get into deep trouble. Do you think? You're a cop, tell me? I guess they got copyrights or patents on them or something."

Riker smiled. "I don't think you have to worry about anybody from my department coming in here and locking you up for that."

The coffee came.

"Hey, he drank coffee," she said.

"This guy," Riker said, pulling Laurel Kring's ID shot from his lapel pocket.

She held it up, catching the incidental light from one of the stage spots.

"Yeah, that's him. He scared me pretty bad."

"Does he still look like that?"

"As much as I look like my driver's license."

"How did he assault you?"

"It was more than that. I had one of the guys walk me to the car and follow me home that night. *Hey,* what did he do? Kill somebody? That guy's a killer. I'm telling you, he had a lot of hate in him."

"We're not sure. But you even remember what he was drinking. That's good."

"Yeah, you remember somebody like that. He was really intense. When I first sat down with the guy, actually, I kinda felt sorry for the guy. Sitting there real quiet. Alone. *Hey,* you want a real drink? I'm buying."

Riker shook his head.

She leaned closer. "Actually," she said, "you guys who drink coffee get skunk breath. It makes for a tough lap dance, you know what I mean?"

Riker leaned back. "I'll be sure and remember that."

"So, you saw him in here a lot?" he asked.

"Oh no. Just that once. After that, they banned him. But I don't think he ever tried to come back."

Riker wanted the entire story.

She told him how she dropped by Kring's table. Tried to give him a free dance. How he hurled her a good ten or fifteen feet through the air.

"Did you say anything to him, right before that?"

She took a deep hit on her cigarette. *"Hey,* I was just doing my thing. I just told him to loosen up. I was just looking at him. Right before. You know, it's kind of my trademark. Like the uniforms. This thing I do with my eyes. Most guys like it."

"I'm sure."

"Most guys like what they see."

Riker was intrigued. He didn't think that was because where he was or who he was with. The girl obviously had a close encounter, he told himself. Maybe she could tell him something.

He pushed on.

"I'm sure you meet a lot of assholes in this business," he said.

"It comes with the territory."

"But you say this guy really scared you," he said. "Why?"

She took another hit of the cigarette and exhaled slowly.

"It was what he called me. After he pushed me. I'll tell you, *that,* more than what he did, got his ass thrown in jail."

"What did he call you?"

"After he pushed me he stood up, stood over me. Screaming. I swear foam was coming out of his mouth."

"Foam?"

"Well, at least it seemed that way."

"What did he call you?"

She seemed embarrassed to reveal it.

Finally she said, *"Drunken slut.* He kept repeating it. Over and over. *Drunken slut. Drunken slut.* I mean, if he's going to call me that, hey, I'm a *dancer."*

"I understand," Riker said. "You're working."

"He was crazy."

"Sounds like he had a temper."

"No crazy. When they took him outside he was still screaming and pointing, calling me that. I'm not a slut. I'm not a drunk."

She took another hit on the cigarette and smiled. "I'm going to college."

Yeah, they all had stage names and were all going to

college. They were all going to become doctors and lawyers and CPAs.

Back at the TOC, Jimmy Oshefsky was typing in commands on Kring's computer when Riker walked in.

"Jack, you're not going to believe it," he said, keeping his eyes on the monitor. "I just got back from Eastern. We found out what Kring was doing at the Willow Run drill."

"What's that," Riker said, taking off his coat.

Oshefsky stopped typing and looked up.

"They had him coordinating intelligence on their negotiation team. Lefty said he offered you that job."

"I don't think I want it."

"Shit. Why not?"

Riker motioned with his head toward the lounge and the hangar. "I don't want to be stuck in there."

"Shit, I'll take it then. That ought to be pretty good when SWAT makes its move."

Riker sat down. "Where is he?"

"Who?"

"Thompson."

"CNT briefing. I think they're going to try and make a deal for the kids."

"Jimmy, you got any gum?"

He handed Riker a stick.

Riker sat down to type out a summary of the interview with the dancer. He'd add it to Kring's file.

"What are you doing?" he asked, nodding in the direction of the computer. "I thought you said there was nothing there."

"I thought I better check his Compuserv software. I found some files there. Looks like the guy spent a lot of time in the aviation forum. Also a forum on model making."

"Sounds Roman."

"No, it's a place where people exchange information. In his case, airplane stories and stuff like that."

"They have a place just for people who make models?"

"They have a lot of forums. Any subject. Just about anything you want."

Oshefsky turned off the computer.

"Man, you really don't know shit about computers, do you?"

"And don't want to."

"Why?"

Riker started typing.

"Already have too much computing going on in my own head."

Riker stopped, looking around for a central file on Kring.

"Where's Kring's file."

Oshefsky motioned toward the lounge. "Lefty took to the shrinker."

He knew two patrolman had been sent over to interview Kring's fellow workers over at the FAA.

"Did those guys write up anything?"

Oshefsky pointed. "They put it all on the board."

Riker looked up. Saw the words *quiet* and *mellow* under a heading labeled "Personality."

"Mellow? That's all the fuck they came back with?"

Oshefsky nodded.

"Where are they now?"

"Who knows."

"Were you here when they unloaded?"

"Yeah."

"Did anybody say anything about Kring's personal habits?"

"What do you mean?"

Riker nearly lost his temper. "I mean was he fucking anybody, Jimmy. Was the guy cheating on his wife? Was his wife fucking someone? Specifically, another airport worker. A ticket agent. Flight attendant. Somebody like that."

"Jesus Christ, Jack, I don't know. Who put a bug up your ass?"

Riker went back to the typing. These group efforts, he thought. They never functioned smoothly. Maybe he needed to take the job Thompson offered. Maybe he could consolidate everything and people could talk to *him,* instead of reading some report. Maybe he just shouldn't have gone to a bar. Spending time around booze, particularly people drinking it, sometimes put him on edge.

Oshefsky started putting on his jacket.

Riker looked up. "You want that CNT job you ought to talk to Vince," he said. "I'll put in a word for you, if you want."

Stupek was still in his office, pacing with his Styrofoam cup in one hand, the telephone in the other.

"When I get back," Oshefsky said.

"Where you going?"

"Put out a fire. The parents of those kids are over at the department."

"What kids?"

"The hostages. We talked to the parents earlier, but I guess they drove over. Any suggestions what I tell them?"

"I don't know," he said. "Last time I tried that at this airport, I wasn't very good at that."

Riker turned away from the banquet table.

"Jimmy," he said. "Forget it, okay?"

"Forget what?"

"What I said."

"We all know you're an asshole. Don't worry about it."

Riker was thinking. Three women. Three assaults.

"There's something more to this guy we're not getting here. That's what I was trying to ask."

"What you mean, something more?"

"That's the bug," Riker said. "I don't goddamn know."

Twenty-one

They had been talking now for fifteen minutes. Monsorta had repeated the same message every few minutes as if it were on a tape loop: Three hours without an incident weren't enough. The evening push was coming, four hours of heavy traffic. Airport officials weren't satisfied. They needed further evidence of good faith.

"Bat, I'm running out of arguments here on this end with these people," Monsorta said. "I think they're losing patience."

It was a precarious balancing act. Make the hostage taker believe they wanted control of the airport back, when in fact they wanted him to keep it. They wanted Kring in charge of the tower to enable a diversion. But they wanted him to pay for the privilege by releasing hostages. That would both save lives and give them inside intelligence for the SWAT attack.

Morton Ressler believed the strategy was so convoluted, Kring would never discern it, despite his involvement in the drill at the Willow Run. The problem was Kring had put nothing on the table. He seemed perfectly content right where he was.

Ressler passed a note down the bar, reminding Monsorta what they had discussed before he picked up the hostage phone.

There was one word: *"Need."*

Monsorta was sharpening the ash on his smoke into a

point as he talked to Kring. There had been none of the histrionics earlier in the day.

"You know, Bat, there's one more thing. You and I have been talking since, when?"

"We've been talking entirely too much."

He ignored that. "The early afternoon? And I still don't know where you're going with all this."

"Where I'm going? I'm not going anywhere."

"You've got people up there who are going to get hungry."

"We have plenty of food."

"But they're going to get tired, too. If that happens, and, God forbid, somebody makes a mistake, and there's an accident, that's not going to be on my conscience. And I don't think that's what you want."

"You don't know what I want."

"You got that right, Bat. You got that right."

Monsorta changed his tone, as if he were angry at a well-meaning friend who was letting him down.

"You know I'm workin' here, Bat. Trying to help you out. But we're going to blow it here. You see, I'm the only thing right now that stands between you and these people taking that tower right away from you."

"We've already discussed that."

"Yes, we have. But do you think this thing can go on forever? I need to know. I need to know *now.*"

"Know what?"

"What you *want.*"

"I want people to *fucking understand.*"

"Understand what?"

"That it's not *our* fault."

Monsorta looked down at Ressler. He was nodding.

"What is not your fault?"

"That the system is breaking down."

"What system?"

"It's too technical."

"Try me."

"The system is corrupted. By outsiders."

"What system?"

"The ATC. The administration. Regional. National. The United States Congress. The President. God. The cosmos. The whole *fucking* thing is rotten to the core. How's that for starters?"

"I can buy that. How about being a little more specific."

He launched into a technical dissertation on traffic control devices, speaking quietly but rapidly, as if he was discussing a spec sheet with a group of electrical engineers.

Monsorta let him go. He had no idea what he was talking about.

After a pause, he said, "Major Tom, do you know what TEACUS is?"

"I can't say I do."

"That's one from the U.S. *fucking* Congress. They pushed it."

"They don't know . . ."

"Do you know what phraseology is?"

"I think . . ."

"No, you don't. *Phraseology* can cost you your goddamn job, today. *Fucking* regs written by *fucking* bureaucrats. Assholes in Washington who can't even park their *fucking* cars between the lines, let alone line up a push, Major Tom."

Morton Ressler was rolling his cigar in his mouth. Good, he thought, let the guy vent. Find a handle.

"What about your union?" Monsorta asked.

"What about it?"

"Can't they . . ."

"They can't do shit. The union only adds to the problem."

"How?"

"Putting out the big lie to the public."

"What lie?"

"That we're stressed-out. That we're gonna *crack* any minute."

The irony of the words were not lost on anybody listening.

"Isn't that what the PATCO thing was about?"

"When's the last time you ever read *traffic control error?*"

"In what?"

"Crashes. Sure goddamn, near misses maybe. But the operative word there, Major Tom, is *miss."*

"I don't understand the connection. Help me with it."

"Can't you *fucking* see? The union puts out the word to the media. Stressed-out controllers. People read the media. Congress reads the people. Then they put more regs over our heads. You want stress, *that* is your stress."

"They're in the worry business, all right."

"They should be worrying about the people working in those goddamn planes. That's where *your* problem is."

"So what do you think we should do about it?"

"I'm going to *fucking* show them."

"How?"

"I'm showing them right now."

Monsorta looked down at Ressler again. He decided to plant a seed.

"You're showing the people who run this airport, but that's *all* your showing."

"That's not enough?"

"It's like that story they told us in school. If a tree falls in a field and nobody was there to hear it, did it really fall? What I'm saying is that right now, all we got here is that falling tree."

"The message will get out. Give it time."

"No, Bat, that's the one critical miscalculation you seem to be making."

"Is that right?"

"Yeah, I think it is. Hey, I can talk to you all day and

night, if need be. But these people here. Jesus, they want their airport back."

"In time, they'll get their *fucking* airport."

Time for a little more leash.

"No, that's simply not going to work. That's just not going to be good enough."

"Is that right?"

"I'm afraid it is."

Monsorta lowered his voice, as if they were sharing a secret.

"You know, between you and me, some of these people down here just don't give a damn. They don't care about the airport or hostages or how anything looks. They care *only* about their jobs. And what they do, they do very well. I'm sure you can appreciate that."

Silence.

"Bat, I'm going to take a time-out here. But you think about what I've been saying, then you call me with some ideas on how you think we can resolve this thing, other-wise . . ."

He wanted Kring to fill in the blank.

"Otherwise what?"

"Otherwise, I just don't see how we can go on."

Monsorta butted his cigarette as he hung up.

He spun the bar stool toward the men at the other end of the bar. "Christ, I don't know if he's cagy, or he's just plain fucking nuts."

"He *speaks*," Ressler said. "That was very good."

"But will he bite?"

Ressler pulled the Te-Amo out of his mouth.

"I predict he'll be back on the line within ten."

The woman wearing an apron with "Cook Armed and Dangerous" emblazoned across the chest poked her finger into the breast of the turkey on her refrigerator's bottom shelf. The skin was rubbery and soft, but felt hard and very cold underneath.

"I hope this thaws in time," she yelled.

Her husband, a line inspector with Boeing, was in the living room.

He did not answer her. He never did.

She washed her hands at the sink, thinking about how her mother did this, how she had the same worries, the same holiday check lists. Somehow it always got done.

The spell was broken when she looked up at the window. Mount Rainier. You didn't often see Mount Rainier in November in Seattle. But there it was, its snow cap was poking out of the clouds churning at its base.

She yelled again. "Hey, honey, you can see Rainier."

He walked into the kitchen, carrying a portable phone. He handed it to her, it's red light was on.

"I never hear that ringer," she said, wiping her hands on her apron. "Who is it?"

He shrugged his shoulders and peaked out the window, then left the kitchen, still not saying a word.

"Julie Ann Spulik? Is it Mrs. Spulik?"

A telephone solicitor, she thought.

"Yes it is, but I don't buy anything over the phone. And I do all my giving through the United Way."

"I'm not a salesman, ma'am. My name is Jack Riker, I'm a detective sergeant here at Detroit Metropolitan Airport."

There was a pause.

"Didn't the Seattle police tell you to expect a call from us?"

"The Seattle police? I haven't talked to the police. Who *is* this?"

A longer pause.

"I'm sorry to bother you ma'am like this on the phone. Like I said, I'm with the detective bureau here with the police at the Detroit airport, where your brother-in-law

Laurel Kring works. You should have had a visit by now from Seattle PD by now."

"No one has been here. What is this about?"

She heard him sigh.

"I guess they ran into a problem. We generally don't do this over the phone."

"Do what? What's happened. Has something happened to Laurel?"

Another pause.

"It's your sister, Mrs. Spulik."

Another pause.

"We found her today in her home in Trenton."

"Found her?"

"She'd been assaulted."

"How?' "'

"She'd been shot."

"Shot? My, God."

"Yes, we tried to do everything we could for her, but . . . I'm sorry."

"My God, who? I mean, how?"

"We believe her husband is responsible."

Julie Ann Spulik yelled her husband's name.

"Would you like me to call back later?" he asked.

She sat down at the kitchen table. Her husband didn't come.

"No, please," she said. "Tell me what happened."

He told her what was happening at the airport. He told her about the letter he left.

"What can you tell me about your sister, about Laurel?" he asked.

"I haven't seen her in ten years," she said. "You see, he'd never let her come out. And, she always discouraged us coming to visit."

"Why's that?"

"He was . . . quirky. I didn't really know him. I'm not sure anybody did."

"Did she express any concerns, about her safety?" he asked.

She could think of only questions, now.

"You say he's taken over the tower?"

"Yes."

"What does he want?"

"That's what we're trying to find out. That's why I'm calling."

She said she had received letters.

"In one, my sister did mention something. She said she was worried. She was worried he was going to do *something*. But she never feared for herself. Like I said, he had a lot of quirks. Twenty years, you learn to live with them, I guess."

"Was your sister ever a flight attendant?"

"God no. She wasn't the type."

"What did she do?"

"Served him. Catered to his every need, as far as I could tell."

"Can you tell me more about their relationship?"

She tried to remember the early years, before she moved west.

"I think in some ways, she was the mother he never had. His mother wasn't there for him, I remember her saying that."

"Was his mother a stewardess?"

"God no. She was a bar fly, I heard. I guess she also slept around quite a bit, too. That was after his father . . . Well, the guy just one day got up and left. They never saw him again. He had an uncle who kind of took him under his wing."

"Is he alive?"

"No."

"Did she indicate to you in any of her letters that he might be having an affair?"

"God no. Was he?"

"It's just a routine question."

She thought, who was this man on the phone?

"Detective . . ."

"Riker."

"Detective Riker, I don't know why you are asking me these questions," she said. She knew she sounded angry.

"Ma'am, I know this is hard, and crass, and there's no way to prepare for a phone call like this out of the blue. That's why Seattle police were supposed to visit you. But right now, we have a real crisis on our hands here. And I have records here of at least two assaults on women over the years. Now your sister. I'm just wondering if he was having some kind of problem with women."

"The last time I saw Laurel, he had problems with *everybody.*"

"You saw him? When?"

"Well, he was out here only about a month or so ago. Stopped in for the afternoon. He came out here on some kind of flight with the FAA. But he had to go back that night."

"And."

"He was very bitter. About his job. About the government. About the flight he took. He talked a lot about that plane crash you had out there a few years ago."

"Flight two twenty-five?"

"I don't know the number. He said he *knew* things. That there was a lot more to it than met the eye. He was telling my husband. They were talking about some equipment. He works for Boeing. But he wouldn't go into it much more than that. I don't know. We just had coffee and talked, but he was so—oppressive. I was kind of glad when he left."

He asked for dates. He asked for names of friends or other next of kin. She didn't think she was very helpful.

Her husband finally came into the kitchen, saying the Seattle police were at the front door asking for her.

My *sister,* she thought. The sonovabitch killed my sister.

It was sinking in now.

"Are you going to kill him?" she asked the detective named Riker.

"We have trained personnel for this kind of thing," he said. "We try to minimize losses."

"Well, don't minimize it too much," she said.

Five minutes later, Riker walked into the Nomad's lounge for the first time, thinking for a second that the CNT was headed straight for conduct unbecoming. They all were sitting together on bar stools, hunch shouldered. They looked like a bunch of cops out on a major drunk.

Closer, he saw the monitor.

He listened to Kring making demands.

He wanted continued control of the air traffic—both in-bounds and outbounds.

He wanted a reporter. No, make that two reporters. One print and one TV. He wanted a specific writer from the Detroit *News,* a cranky local columnist named Pete Meyers. For years, readers had been following Meyers's different looks as well as his ranting and ravings. Mustache, beard, clean shaven. With hat. Without hat. The point was, his picture was in the paper every day.

"And I want a TV person I can recognize," Kring said. "And I don't want some goddamn ditsy bitch."

"So when do you think we can do this?" Monsorta said. "It's going to take some time on our end to contact these people."

"After midnight."

He wasn't done.

"Have them go over to the FAA offices in L.C. Smith first," he demanded. "Over there, they'll find four shelf feet of *CHANGE* regulations issued in the past three years."

He wanted the reporters to bring those.

"I want people to see them," he said.

"How about food?" Monsorta offered. "You know we can get you some pizza. The food up there can't be that great."

Everyone was thinking, they could put somebody from tactics in a Dominoes uniform.

"Didn't you hear the story about pizza in Naples, Major Tom?" Kring said.

"I can't say that I did."

"Yeah, I guess some terrorists who took an airplane sent out for pizza, but the SWAT team there ate some. They killed one passenger for every slice."

It was an old story that made the rounds in tactics circles. Kring must have picked up the story in the Willow Run drill.

"Are you willing to pay those prices?" he said.

Monsorta said nothing.

"Okay," the negotiator finally said. "So here's the deal. You get the airport until the reporters come. We get you these documents. Now, I think we need to talk about how to do this real safe, so nobody gets hurt when you walk out of there."

"No, Major Tom, that just gets you to midnight. That's when a bat really needs his radar."

Playing games again.

"I'm not following you."

"I've got to see how the interview goes."

"No, I can't do it," Monsorta said. "I've got to have more than that."

They negotiated the point for five minutes. Monsorta started with the release of all the hostages, acquiescing to the freeing of all nonessential tower personnel, meaning the children and Gerry Russell. The TOC wanted the observations of an adult hostage, if at all possible.

Kring held firm.

"The rep stays," he said. "He's got to look after his *people,* doesn't he, Major Tom?"

In time, they came up with a tentative deal. He'd release the two children within the hour. If he was satisfied with the interviews, they would work out a way to release everyone and he'd come out, unarmed.

"Bat, I need to run this by my people," Monsorta said.

After the red light went off on the hostage phone, Riker asked, "Has he ever mentioned anything about flight two twenty-five?"

"About what?"

"The crash a few years back. You know, the MD-80 that went down out here under the freeway."

"No, he hasn't said anything about that."

Ressler spun his stool around. He was curious.

"I read about it in his personnel file. You found something more?"

"Only that he bitched about it to his sister-in-law a month ago. We're talking *years* later. This guy has a long memory."

"And there was the safety board inquiry in the file," Ressler said. "He seems to have taken it quite personally, hasn't he?"

"Right," Riker said. "What do you think?"

"I think he has a fixation. It's common in this sort of thing."

Conrad spoke up. "How common?"

"Often this kind of perpetrator becomes fixated on a coworker, or an event. It has symbolic value, really. Represents the essence of their rage. Our hostage taker seems fixated on incompetence. What better example than a crew that forgot to set its flaps?"

"You have a point," Riker said. "But he hinted to his sister-in-law he knew things that hadn't been made public."

"Of course he did."

Riker asked him to explain.

"What we have here is a person who is paranoid," Ressler said. "He is also clinically depressed. Now, we know people get depressed all the time, but that doesn't necessarily lead to violent acts. With clinical depression, most don't know why they're depressed. But add paranoia, and now this person finds a reason for his mental state. This makes them very dangerous because paranoia creates a target. In this case, the supervisors, in the tower."

Nobody wanted to argue with that.

"What about the women?" Riker asked. "You saw the file. Two assaults. The stripper a year ago. Then his wife. You know, we do have a flight attendant missing here at the airport."

"Can you connect them?"

On a hunch, Riker had already tried, using the personnel file records and a date Julie Ann Spulik had provided. The only thing they had in common was they were both on the West Coast in the same week. But Kring had flown back from Seattle on the Fam Flight, Delesandro from LA. They had left on different days.

"Not really," Riker said.

"Look," Ressler said, confidently. "This kind of personality is going to have difficulty in any kind of intimate relationship with the opposite sex. In fact, it very well contributes to his low self-esteem. As for any sort of past homicides, now you're talking serial assault. This kind of perpetrator doesn't do that. They lash out. It doesn't fit the profile."

Monsorta threw in his two cents. "You know, I don't think he watches much TV, either," he said.

"What does that have to do with anything?" Conrad asked.

"He doesn't want that film crew until after midnight."

"So."

He reached for another cigarette.

"Most want to go live."

The phone rang, but it wasn't the hostage line. It was inside.

Conrad picked it up.

"Jack, they want you in the OSC's office," he said.

Twenty-two

Riker could think of a half-dozen different reasons why Vince Stupek might want him in his office, but none of them had anything to do with the other men waiting there.

Stupek was sitting at his desk with his hands folded. Riker saw no sign of his Copenhagen or his Styrofoam cup.

"Jack, you know the director of airports?" he said.

Riker nodded.

"And, I don't have to introduce you to the county executive."

The executive put forth his hand, shaking Riker's vigorously. But Riker felt nothing. The man simply had pressed a lot of flesh.

"I'm trying to recall the last time we talked," Ladd said, sitting back down. "It was at the old department, was it not?"

Stupek was pointing to the wall facing Ladd and Rains. "Jack, have a seat."

Riker didn't like the fact Stupek was offering him a chair. That meant he was staying awhile.

Ladd was still waiting for an answer to his question.

Riker nodded. "Yeah, it was the department."

Ladd knew where and *when*. The former deputies who guarded him during the campaign used to talk about Ladd's memory, how he could work an entire banquet room, recalling a couple hundred names and occupations a night.

"But I'm trying to recall the circumstances."

Ladd was leaning forward, his elbows on his knees, his hands and index fingers forming a pyramid that peaked just under his upper lip.

"Your office."

"What was the case?"

"It was the day you shipped me out here."

"Yes, that's right," he said, sitting back.

Riker had always thought Marlon Ladd was a disingenuous sonovabitch. He was a bottom feeder with a couple of university degrees and good taste in suits. He was surprised to see him wearing a sweater.

Stupek spoke up.

"Jack, we've developed somewhat of a problem here."

"Problem?"

"I guess you've had some contact with the local Teamsters. An official named Harmon, is it?"

Riker glanced at all three men in the room, but their eyes told him nothing.

"Yeah, Caley Harmon. I'm all too familiar with her."

Rains said, "She was over at your department several times today, seeking a file on that missing stewardess."

"Yeah, that's right."

"And did you know that I gave her my blessings, in terms of you releasing that to her?"

"Yeah, she mentioned it."

"So, why didn't you give it to her, Detective Riker?"

Riker looked at Stupek, but he remained silent.

He looked Rains in the eyes.

"Well at the time I was a little occupied. Still am, like everyone else. What's this all about?"

Ladd leaned forward, resting his elbows on his knees again.

"Jack, when I came in from Willow Run," Ladd said, "I found Ms. Harmon over at the director's office when I arrived. She was quite upset."

Jack. Riker didn't like the way Ladd said *Jack.*

Rains said, "Apparently, in the process of seeking this file that you were to copy and deliver—"

"I don't do deliveries."

Rains began again. "In her attempt to locate you, she saw you pull into one of the local clubs here. One of the topless places in Romulus. Figured you were drinking on duty. This, of course, upset her greatly."

Ladd interrupted. "It was my understanding that you'd gotten a handle on that problem, Jack."

Riker could feel the blood pounding his jugular vein. He didn't know who he wanted first. The two stiffs across from him or that crazy union broad.

"It *is* handled," he said, trying to keep his voice steady. "I was working this investigation."

Stupek interjected, "I told them you were working, Jack."

"Your man holding hostages up that tower ripped off a car from that place," Riker continued. "He also assaulted a woman there a year ago. Maybe you'd have preferred I just have a little chat with them on the phone?"

Rains interjected, asking innocently, "Why would he take a car?"

Ladd held on his hand. Rains fell immediately silent.

"Look, Jack, that's not the point," the executive said calmly. "I was not implying a problem."

No, Riker thought, you just thought you'd bring an old one up.

Riker glared. "Then what's your point?"

"Well, that's what we've been exploring here. Because she was so upset, she could have gone over to the depart-ment. There was a hostage family in the lobby over there, from what I understand. You realize, that's all it would take? Then we'd have no end of trouble."

Riker laughed. He had to laugh, or he was going to say or do something he might later regret.

"Look, how long do you people think you can keep the

lid on this goddamn thing, anyway? If not her, it's going to be somebody else."

Stupek said, "No one's blaming you, Jack. I'm not, at least."

"Then what the fuck is the problem?" Riker asked. "I've got things to do."

Ladd stood up and walked to the window, looking at a couple of investigators adding more information on the hostage boards.

"The International Brotherhood of Teamsters is always a problem," Ladd said. "They've been a problem for people trying to get anything done in this town for years."

Rains elaborated. "As you can imagine, Detective Riker, the Teamsters have quite a bit of clout here at this airport. They not only have the attendants, they have the drivers of the fuel trucks."

Ladd turned around. "What the director is trying to say is that she can shut *everything* down."

"But she doesn't know anything," Riker said.

"And we're not going to give her the opportunity," Ladd said. "It would only complicate your situation."

It's not my situation, Riker thought. It's yours.

He wanted out of that office.

"Look, maybe I should have given her the goddamn file," Riker said. "It was a judgment thing."

"It always is, Jack," Ladd said. "It always is."

Riker looked at Stupek. "I think I'm going to take that job on the CNT. I've got some ideas on this guy."

"Jack . . ."

"Down the home stretch, I think I should be involved in that."

". . . your off it."

"I'm not on it, yet."

"You're outta here," Stupek said. "That's what they're saying."

He turned to Rains, then Ladd.

"For what? Failing to run a goddamn Zerox?"

"Jack, this isn't punitive," the executive said. "We need you for a special assignment."

Jesus, here it comes, Riker thought.

"We need you to keep the lid on the Teamsters."

"A lid?"

"We need you to look after this—lady."

"Look after her? You mean baby sit?"

"I wouldn't call it that."

"What *do* you call it?"

"We want you to give her what she wants. Keep her occupied. Until we all can get through this."

"Occupy her where?" Riker asked. "At the DB?"

"For Chrisakes no," Ladd said, raising his voice. "Somewhere *away* from this airport."

"What?" Riker said, sarcastically. "Dinner. Drinks. A show. Maybe take in the *Nutcracker* down at the Fox."

"Whatever you need to do," Ladd said.

"I call that baby sitting."

"No, spoon feeding. It's somewhat more skilled. Though, now that I think of it, you probably shouldn't take her for drinks."

Fuck you, Riker thought. Get out. Get out before you take the guy down and your pension with it.

"Where is she?"

"She's at her local," Rains said. "She's expecting you to call her there."

Riker stood up.

"Why me?" he said.

"Because she asked for you, *Jack,"* Ladd said.

Rains added, "And she's expecting that file."

Five minutes later, Stupek stepped outside into the TOC to talk to Riker while he filed the last of his reports on Laurel Kring at one of the folding banquet tables.

"I almost thought for a second you were going to make some kind of move," Stupek said.

"He never showed us anything as sheriff," Riker said. "He hasn't changed."

"For what it's worth, I tried. I tried before they ever called you in."

Riker shuffling a few papers, then handed Stupek the Kring file.

"Vince, this guy. There's something we're not getting here. Look, I know Tommy is real good at what he does. And this guy Ressler makes a lot of sense. But I think Kring's holding out on us. I think he has been from the get go."

"What makes you say that?"

"Well, I mean, even Rains picked it up. In there, he had a point. Why does Kring steal a goddamn car?"

"Ressler says he's evening the score with old enemies. He had problems at that bar."

"Yeah, I know he did. But the car also bought him time. Christ, we didn't even know who we were dealing with until we were half way into this thing."

"You're right. But is that really unusual? In Munich, the Olympic Games, it took them a day before they even knew what they were up against."

"This isn't Munich. This is Detroit."

Stupek sat on the table.

"There's one more thing," Riker continued. "Two twenty-five. He hasn't mentioned it with Tommy."

"Why should he?"

"Well, it's come up. It's in his personnel file. I just talked to his sister-in-law. Out of the blue, he's telling her about it a month ago. But here. His big moment, he doesn't say a goddamn thing."

"So what are you saying?

"Maybe there's something more here than just a work thing."

"Like what?"

"I need time to find out. You'd have to cut me loose."

Stupek glanced back into his office where Ladd and Rains were talking, then back at Riker.

"You know I can't do that."

"Yeah."

"But look, before you go handle this Teamsters broad, I want you to talk to Oshefsky. Try to give him an overview. Have you told the shrinker?"

"Yeah. Why Oshefsky?"

"I'm going to put him on the CNT. But all this may not even matter in a couple of hours."

"What you mean?" Riker asked.

"I get the feeling he's going to pull the plug on us."

"Ladd?"

Stupek nodded. "He's been talking about the hostage rescue team in from Quantico."

"After all this work? What are they going to do differently?"

"I'd like to believe it was because he used to be with the bureau."

"But we've known him too long, haven't we?" Riker said.

Back inside the OSC's office, Marlon Ladd had one more question about Jack Riker.

"Lieutenant, he's not going to try anything creative is he? Jack Riker was never a team player. Not when he worked for me, at least."

"He's a cop," Stupek said. "He follows orders. You folks seem to be the ones with all the ideas around here."

Ladd let the insult go without comment.

"Actually, I would have preferred someone else," he continued. "But he is in charge of that investigation apparently, and I thought it best he should go. My only concern is his state of mind."

Stupek fished his Copenhagen out of his shirt pocket. The hell with protocol, he thought.

"I can vouch for him," Stupek said.

"Well, he *looks* better now. I'll give you that much."

Rains spoke up. "I'm not sure I'm following everybody here."

Ladd turned to the director. "Our Detective Riker was a very talented investigator, but he developed a serious drinking problem. I personally transferred him to the airport because I felt he would be out of harm's way."

"Didn't you have a treatment program?" Rains asked.

"We did things a little differently back then," Ladd said. "We've all come a long way in that area, haven't we?"

Rains nodded enthusiastically.

"Like I said," Stupek said. "You don't have to worry about Jack Riker. The airport's lucky to have him."

Rains leaned forward, looking him in the eyes.

"Lieutenant, there's not a whole lot I don't find out about. Especially when my people start doing things across county lines."

Stupek did not know the story had traveled that far up the county pipeline.

"That was five years ago," he said.

"But troubling, nonetheless."

Rains said, "I'm sorry. Again, I don't understand."

Ladd leaned back and turned to Rains.

"As I was saying, there was a problem. But apparently, things got much worse before they got better."

"Jesus, do we really need to go into this?" Stupek said. He saw no reason for Ladd to trash Riker in front of the director. "I think the man is entitled to a certain amount of privacy."

"What he did was very public," Ladd said. "Or, *could* have been."

"That story doesn't get told," Stupek said. "Around *this* department, at least."

"Well, more people know about it than you think."

"Know what?" Rains demanded.

Ladd leaned forward again.

"You ever drive out M-14, Jim? Between the western suburbs and Ann Arbor?"

Stupek reached down into the trash basket for his cup.

"Sure," Rains said. "All the time."

"Have you noticed that large cemetery, near the freeway, about half way out?"

Rains nodded.

"It's my understanding that four years ago our Detective Riker was located out there. I believe it was Washtenaw County that got the run, was it not, Lieutenant?"

Stupek spit, not answering.

"Anyway, Detective Riker was extremely drunk and let's just say not showing due respect for the dead."

"He was blacked out," Stupek said. "He didn't remember. I know, because I told him the next morning."

"You were involved in that fiasco?" Ladd asked.

"I picked him up from Washtenaw."

"I still don't understand," Rains said.

"When a Washtenaw cruiser picked Detective Riker up he was drinking out there with the gravestones," Ladd said. "He was tampering with the graves of some people who'd died here at Metro, before you came on board, Jim."

"He was at the *memorial,*" Stupek said. Goddamnit, he thought, at least get it right.

"What kind of memorial?" Rains asked.

Stupek explained. "A group of us here, and in EMS. People who worked in this hangar, doing the ID work. We put up money for a memorial. For what was left at this hangar. The unidentifiable body parts from flight two twenty-five."

Ladd crossed his arms. "Well, needless to say, he was

detained. Fortunately, he knew the deputies. No charges were filed. Professional courtesy still counts for something in Washtenaw County, apparently."

"The important thing is he did something about his problem," Rains offered. "Alcoholism *is* a disease, Marlon."

"Yes, but what he was doing may hint at something deeper," Ladd said.

Rains looked at both men. "What was he doing?" he asked.

Ladd turned to Stupek. "Lieutenant, you want to tell him? I want to get this right."

Stupek glared. Riker didn't deserve this. Nobody did.

Ladd went ahead.

"They found our Detective Riker out there talking nonsense," he said. "And they found him digging."

"Digging?"

"Yes, with a shovel, no less."

Twenty-three

His nephew was asleep, his head on the table. Candy wrappers and juice cans and empty Dorito bags lay around his head and shoulders. His niece rested her chin on her hands, at the window sill, watching aircraft land in the rows of blue lights.

Earlier, at dinner time, the boy had been up and down the tower cab stairs ten times, shuttling cash and vending machine meals back and forth. Kring called down the orders on the tower intercom. Russell and the girl miked the cold hamburgers and burritos. He tried to make a game of it, like they were staffing a drive-through. It kept their questions at bay. It would have worked even better, if it hadn't been for that screaming Robo alarm.

Russell rubbed his niece's shoulders.

"How's it going kiddo?"

She looked up, still keeping her chin on her knuckles.

"It's going," she said.

He could see a DC-10 releasing its brakes and beginning its roll on three left.

"Uncle Gerry?"

"Yeah, kiddo."

"You think we're going to have to sleep here tonight?"

"I don't know."

"I hope not."

"I hope not, too."

Russell had thought about making some kind of run. He

even timed the Robo. It always sounded for exactly sixty seconds. Have the boy turn the alarm *off* when he returned from a food run at sixty seconds. They make a break for the stairs. Then Russell realized the way the food orders were coming in one-minute intervals. It was as if Kring *expected* to hear the alarm every minute as another order went up. Russell had no idea which order would be the last one. And if they did run, there was still another Robo alarm waiting for them at the stairway door at the other end of the hall. Russell would have written the entire setup off to luck, had it been anybody else.

But Laurel Kring was a controller. For some, it was more than a simple job description.

Until he stopped coming six months ago, Kring had been in his office maybe two dozen times in the past two years, Russell guessed. He came asking for something the Professional Flight Controllers Association could not give him. He incessantly questioned changes in procedures made at the Washington level, wanting to embark on mind-numbing philosophical discussions on controller terminology and technical advances. Recently, he complained about management, as others had. But Kring's objections were nebulous, nothing that Russell could work up into a formal grievance.

He finally told him, "Laurel. If they short you on overtime, or you are having scheduling conflicts, I can help you. If you feel you, specifically, have been wronged, then we can work with that. But we don't make ATC policy here, we only make sure it's applied without prejudice."

When he heard Kring had been transferred from TRACON, Russell was surprised when he did not show up at the local, demanding formal action. He'd guessed maybe the eccentric controller had finally found his nitch in the philosophical duties of training and policy implementation.

Now, he knew Kring had simply isolated.

Jesus, I'm not a goddamn psychologist, Russell kept tell-

ing himself. But he couldn't shake the feeling that he'd
made a terrible mistake in judgment.

Russell flinched as the Robo alarm went off outside. He
looked at his watch. It was 7:40 P.M. He peaked out the
window of the break room door, half expecting to see a
SWAT team.

He saw Laurel Kring, walking toward him down the hall.

He was strutting. Russell swore he'd even caught him
smirking. Gone was the parka, and the wild eyes he saw
when he first stormed up the tower cab stairs. He was wearing a khaki photographer's vest, one of those with pockets
and webbed compartments you could buy at Eddie Bauer.
The pockets bulged with guns and ammunition. He carried
a rifle on his shoulder. He was wearing the revolver with
the big barrel in a leather holster on his hip.

Like some kind of cowboy, Russell thought.

He stepped back from the door as Kring switched off
the alarm.

Russell thought, where were the others? He would have
heard shots. Or would he?

When Kring opened the door, Russell's nephew looked
up from his nap.

"I want all of you upstairs," Kring said.

The negotiation was textbook. Kring saying that the children must exit the door at the tower base and walk nearly
a mile to the Eureka Road gate. Monsorta insisting they
be picked up by two policeman in the parking lot.

"Jesus, Bat," he said. "It's cold out there. You can't expect those kids to make that walk out there in the dark."

It took five minutes to find the compromise. The children would be released at the tower door. They could be
picked up by one airport official fifty feet from the entrance of the parking lot, just beyond the firehouse under

construction. The vehicle must be a compact, Kring insisted, and a two-door at that.

They'd scheduled the rendezvous for 8:30 P.M.

"Sounds good," Stupek said.

Stupek went to the hangar and talked to Reed Johnson. The FBI team from Quantico was coming, he told him. At 9:30 P.M., a group of two dozen SWAT personnel, negotiators, and tactical commanders were expected to arrive by government jet at the executive terminal. Shortly thereafter, they would assume airport police roles and positions in the EOC. Ladd had made the official request to the bureau.

"I want to emphasize, this will be a cooperative effort," Ladd had said.

Time spent *cooperating,* Stupek had unsuccessfully argued, only sapped effort and planning aimed directly at getting the primary goal: getting that tower back with minimal bloodshed. Stupek talked with the FBI commander on the phone intercom, Ladd and Rains at his side. Ladd agreed when the FBI commander requested all local assault strategy be put on hold. That meant scrapping the plan to send a half dozen SWAT cops crawling toward the tower in the wet drainage ditch.

"This isn't about cooperation or tactics or any of that happy crap," Stupek complained bitterly. "This is about Ladd covering his ass. This thing blows up, he wants the FBI there to blame."

"Unless we get there first," Johnson said.

He had an idea.

Five minutes later, when Stupek reached his office, James P. Rains was gone. He'd gone back to the terminal to put out routine fires, Ladd said. Ladd looked somewhat anxious. That's how Stupek wanted it, a little on edge, a little eager.

Vince Stupek was ready to do a little negotiating of his own.

"Good news," Stupek said. "He's going to turn lose the kids."

And bringing in the FBI was fine, Stupek said. His SWAT team would cooperate fully. "But the devil is now in the details," he added. "You need to make some choices."

Ladd wanted to know how so.

"We still have to be prepared to honor our negotiator's deal," he said. "The hostage taker is expecting a TV reporter sometime after midnight. He expects Pete Meyers from the newspaper as well. I think we need to proceed on that."

"How do you mean?"

"We need to contact a local station. Find someone willing on their staff."

"The FBI may not want to do that."

"The FBI may not have much of a choice, or somebody in that tower may pay a price."

"You're going to allow this madman to go on TV?" Ladd asked.

"At that hour, they'll have to shoot tape. He's said nothing about it being live."

"What about Meyers?"

"Already checked. He's out of town."

"So, the other?"

"We're going to need a reporter awfully hungry for an exclusive. When it's over, he gets the story first. We at least need somebody on standby, depending on what the team from Quantico wants to do."

"I know the general manager of one of the stations here," Ladd said. "Let me call them and see what we can work out."

Ladd paused. "But what if something goes wrong? They'll devour us with sound bites if a reporter gets hurt."

"Well, that's my point. We'd planned to have SWAT in place by then. In fact, we were considering running the big diversion right before the interview. Of course, waiting for the bureau, the timing now is not—doable."

Stupek wanted Ladd to see what kind of house of cards he'd pulled down with the request to the FBI. He had an opening now, so he took it.

"I should also point out that with the release of these kids, we have an opportunity to end this very simply, before the FBI arrives."

"What kind of opportunity?" Ladd asked.

"One we may not get again."

Ladd parked his two index fingers under his lip, ready to listen.

Stupek continued, "SWAT is confident that they can transport our best sniper close to the scene just before they pick up the kids. He can then take a position in the firehouse, where there's the very real possibility he may get a good view for a shot."

Specifically, Reed Johnson had already told him earlier, they would remove the front passenger door off a Ford Escort. As the vehicle came to a stop just before the firehouse, the sniper, crouched onto the floor, would roll out into the cover of darkness, making his way fifty feet to a pile of I beams, then to the west facade of the building where he could conceal himself. The car would then back out of the area with the children.

"From his elevation, the HT will see only a door *opening* on the passenger side," Johnson said. "That's why we need the air conditioning. We'll send our driver out to meet the children, which ought to provide a sufficient distraction for the sniper to make his move. As for the ground radar, according to information from the TOC it is ineffective this close to the tower base. So our boy upstairs has no way of knowing our man was ever there."

Ladd was intrigued.

"One bullet," Stupek said. "And you've got your airport back."

* * *

Gary Paquin got his first rifle in St. Ignace, the day after three schools of white fish tried to run through his father's gil nets north of Waugoshance Point. The old man brought home two brand new Ruger 1022 semiautomatics, one for him and one for his twin brother. The catch was that good, more than fifty boxes.

He was ten years old.

"We both used those guns for years," Paquin explained to the rookie who was asking him all the questions in the hangar. "Squirrel. Rabbit. Poached my share of deer."

He could hit a running rabbit.

"The magazine on that rifle held ten rounds. The old man never gave us more than that. Shit, man, we were poor fucking Indians. My brother always went home early. I always tried to come home with a bag of game and at least one round."

"In the clip?" the rookie asked.

Four other SWAT members turned to look, critically. They were all sitting in the hangar, cleaning guns and telling lies, observing the SWAT motto: Hurry up and wait.

"You mean the *magazine*," Paquin said. "You put *clips* on ties and paper. You put a *magazine* in a gun."

"Sorry," the rookie said. "The *magazine*."

"The point is," Paquin continued, "It's not necessarily the weapon, or your eye sight, or even, to a certain extent, practice."

"What is it?"

"Patience. To pick your shot. You either got it or you don't."

The rookie nodded, satisfied with the story.

Paquin was oiling a Remington model 700 sniper rifle. He wanted the .308, a military caliber with a lot of powder and velocity. He was reasonably sure all three would accurately penetrate that control tower glass.

"So just how good are you with that thing?" he asked.

"No match," Paquin said.

"C'mon, that's pushing it, don't you think."

"No," he said, now that he had him sucked in. "A kitchen match, man. A human being standing a thousand yards away is about the same view you'd have of a kitchen match at a hundred feet."

"You gotta be able to hit it?"

"No, not hit it. Light it. That's how good."

Paquin was putting the bolt back into the Remington when Reed Johnson hung up the phone on the other side of the hangar and walked over.

"Paquin, how you Indians do in the cold?" he asked.

Twenty-four

Stupek met Reed Johnson and the sniper in front of the poster board for Kring in the TOC. Gary Paquin was carrying a down-filled camo jacket and an armful of other clothes.

"We're a little short here on markers," Johnson said, eying the board.

The board listed Kring's physical description. Under *clothing,* the space was blank. They had an ancient wedding picture of Kring. They had a copy of his airport ID photo. It confirmed TOC interviews with fellow workers. There was a small scar near the corner of Kring's mouth.

"Will the scar show?" Stupek asked.

Paquin was unbuttoning his regular SWAT issue uniform.

"On a nice clear bright day, sure," he said. "Up there. Out there. Who knows?"

"You've got copies of the photos," Johnson said.

"Yeah, but I have some real misgivings about the airport ID."

"What do you mean?" Stupek asked.

"Put it this way," he said. "How do you feel about the photograph on your operator's license?"

"We should be able to get something more when we debrief the kids," Johnson said.

"How about the car?" Stupek asked.

"They've already got the door off," Johnson said. "It's ready to go."

Paquin was stripped down to his boxers now.

"Toss me those thermals," he said to Stupek.

Stupek asked Johnson, "Reed, you're reasonably sure we can come up with something current on our man up there from those kids?"

"Reasonably. We can ask them in the car on the clothes, then radio it in to Gary here. Or maybe we'll get lucky, and our man will show his face outside."

"What if we don't get either?"

Johnson looked at Paquin. He was pulling up a pair of long johns.

"What?" he said, stopping.

Johnson laughed, then said, "Then sometime tomorrow morning we're going to have to find a way to thaw out this Indian's ass."

As the controllers went about their work, Gerry Russell stood in front of Laurel Kring's command station, pleading.

"For Chrisakes, if you refuse to use the elevator, send somebody with them," he said. "You can't send those kids down those dark stairs alone. Then, you want them to walk three hundred yards across that parking lot. These kids are *scared,* Laurel."

The tower cab was dark, standard procedure for evening control. Illumination came from the different colors of LEDs on the equipment and small directional lights at the work stations. Kring was sitting at his command post, his hands folded in front of him, the security monitors and the ASDE casting an otherworldly glow on his face.

Kring looked at the girl. The boy was standing next to her, just watching.

"Tell your uncle you're not scared," he said.

She began to sniffle.

"You're going home," Kring said. "I hope you enjoyed your tour."

"I want to stay with my Uncle Gerry," she said.

She was looking right at him.

His cocky demeanor seemed to change instantly. He lowered his head, bouncing his forehead a couple of times on his folded hands in frustration.

Then he looked at Russell.

"Just what do you suggest, Uncle Rep?" he said.

"Let me walk them out of here to the car. Then I'll come back. That simple."

"How do I know that?"

"You don't. But you're still in control here. That wouldn't change."

Kring bounced his forehead on his hands again twice.

He composed himself with a deep breath.

"Okay," he said. "To the car. But any closer than fifty feet, you're going to have to deal with this."

He held up the rifle.

At eight twenty-five Kring identified a light green radar blip on the ASDE screen. It was slowly making its way on the access road from the Eureka gate toward the tower.

He walked to the window, using field glasses to confirm the target, that it was alone.

He turned to Russell, "Okay. Go."

Russell sent the children first, following them down the narrow tower cab staircase, then down the hall to the main stairwell, setting off both Robo alarms. They could hear the Robos wailing above as they hurried down the steps, the sound of their feet on the stairs echoing, the noises blending into a hellish mix.

Near the bottom, Russell could feel his heart beating, but he didn't think that had anything to do with the stairs.

A blast of cold wind greeted them when they pushed open the tower door.

"Walk slowly now," he told the children.

He could see the headlights of the compact as it pulled to a stop a hundred yards away.

The debate raged in his head for most the distance. He could easily leave, make a dash for the car, be out of harm's way. Nothing but his word to a madman was keeping him, he told himself, then the other side would make its pitch. His people were in that tower. Maybe *he* was responsible. Maybe he should have seen the warning signs.

Fifty feet. Russell stopped. A man in a plain down jacket was getting out of the car.

"Go ahead, kids," he said.

They hesitated.

"Go," he said, sternly.

A 737 was releasing on three center. When its engines faded, a voice came back through the darkness.

"Who are you?"

"Gerry Russell."

"Are you coming?"

In the final analysis, the thought of Kring up there with that rifle, ended the debate.

"I can't."

"Can he hear us?"

"I don't think so."

The kids walking to the car now.

"What is Mr. Kring wearing?"

Russell thought it odd he would call him *mister.*

"A tan vest, with a lot of pockets."

The man was in front of the car now, his body silhouetted by the compact's lights.

"Why?" Russell yelled.

He didn't answer.

Five seconds later, the man in the down jacket hustled the children into the compact, through the driver's door.

As Russell turned around, it backed out from where it came.

Five minutes later, when he reached the top of the stair-

well, Gerry Russell was hot and winded. He took off his
coat and carried it with him up the spiral staircase to the
cab.

Kring was waiting, his feet on his desk, polishing the
large revolver.

"Man of your word, Uncle Rep. I'm impressed."

He was still out of breath.

"You're perspiring."

"I know."

Kring had mischief in his eyes.

"But you need to stay warm," he said. "That's what my
mother always used to say."

"I'm fine. This coat's too heavy."

Kring stood up, and began unloading his vest. One handgun, then another. Several boxes of ammunition.

A couple of the controllers moving traffic glanced in
their direction, but continued about their work.

Kring took off the vest and tossed it.

It landed on Russell's shoes.

"Put it on," he said.

"No, that's okay."

"Put it on," Kring barked.

Russell reached down and slowly slid on the garment.

"And, I want you to stand over there at that east window."

He motioned with the revolver.

On his way over, Russell put it all together with what
the guy had said below.

Gary Paquin had the white adult male in the parking lot
in the cross hairs of the Starlight scope, until he heard the
guy say his name with his left ear. The right ear had a
headset.

Then, he hustled to the northwest corner of the fire
house. There he found a small doorway that opened to the

north, facing the airport. The first level had been skinned
and insulated, above him, the ceiling sheeted. Maybe later
he'd explore the second level, get a spot he could watch
without freezing. But for now, he knew he could step
through the doorway, sneak and peak just around the building's corner.

From his breast pocket, Paquin pulled out the Xerox of
the photographs in the TOC, scanning them with his pen-
light. He decided the wedding picture was absolutely
worthless, unless the HT showed up at that window in the
same tux. He'd made a mental check list from the poster
board in the TOC. Laurel Kring. Five feet ten inches. Likely
armed with a large-caliber pistol. Brown hair, cut just above
the ear. Small scar at the junction of his right lower lip.
He'd brought the AN-PVS-4 Starlight for the dim conditions in the tower cab. What he gained in brightness with
the infrared, he lost in detail.

In his business, you couldn't have it both ways.

The Indian wanted at least two markers. A resemblance
and a weapon. Preferably the scar and a weapons. That
would be best.

The headset crackled.

"Target is wearing a tan vest."

Something more to work with.

He went through the north door, moving along the edge
of the building to the corner. Very slowly he slid the 30-06
around the building corner.

He began breathing heavily when he saw the tan vest,
as big as all hell at the east window. He could hear his
heart pounding in his head. He remembered the way the
big swamp bucks in the UP used to make his heart pound.

Relax, he told himself. Let it pass.

Paquin studied the angle. He could only see the target
from breast up. He had his view filled with a nice head
shot, like one of those old portraits with the oval frame.

Scar? No, not from this angle.

The figure turned. *Could* be the guy in the photo.
Maybe.
Maybe he saw a scar. Maybe not.
But he had the vest.
His finger lightly caressed the trigger.
Patience, he told himself.
Pick your shot.

Twenty-five

He'd asked her to meet him at a bar in Dearborn named Miller's around 8 P.M., a place known for its quarter pounders. He arrived a couple minutes early and reserved the stool next to him with a copy of the Delesandro file. He hadn't bothered to get a table. He wouldn't have to look at her that way.

The bartender came.

Caley Harmon sat down.

She ordered a basket of fries and a Vernor's.

Riker ordered nothing.

"Can I bring you a beer?" the bartender asked.

He'd already spotted the Windsor Canadian, standing at attention with the other bottles in front of the mirror. He'd always liked the picture of that Mounty on the back label. He'd always liked the slogan underneath.

"Just a Coke," he said.

She was surprised he wasn't drinking.

"I thought you said you were hungry," he said.

She'd said she was famished when he called her.

"I am," she said. "I just don't feel like eating."

That made a lot of goddamn sense, he thought. Maybe he should have taken her to the Landing Strip. The thought had crossed his mind, just to piss her off. But even he wasn't that crass.

She turned toward him on the bar stool, putting her elbow on the bar like she'd done it a lot of times that way before.

The sensors from the Holter monitor had started itching, like old skin under a plaster cast. The last entry he'd made was after his meeting with Marlon Ladd. It read: *Extremely pissed.*

"So, did you enjoy yourself?" she asked.

"What do you mean?"

"Earlier. The Landing Strip. I saw you driving in."

"I was working."

"So were the girls."

"I was working this tower case."

Bullshit, she thought.

"What kind of connection?"

"I can't talk about that."

"Why not?"

"You make a habit of stalking cops?" he asked back. "Or do you call it surveillance where you come from?"

"I was leaving my office. I was just trying to catch you. Avoid a phone call."

Bullshit, he thought. Who chases cops?

The soft drinks came.

"You know, you don't have to clean up your act on my account," she said.

"What are you talking about?"

"C'mon, a Coke?"

"What about it? I don't drink on duty."

"I don't drink on duty," she said mockingly.

He thought, what is this broad's problem?

"You know, I wasn't born yesterday," she continued. "I've known a few cops. Major leaguers. You get pulled over. You flash a badge. On duty or off."

He looked over at her.

"I thought you were anxious to read this file," he said.

It was sitting next to the condiment caddie.

"I am," Caley Harmon said. "But I don't feel like reading it now."

Riker shook his head.

"You're hungry, but you don't feel like eating. You're screaming for the file, but you don't want to read it. You know, you're really fucked up. Did anyone ever tell you that?"

She laughed. Loud.

"Is that right?" she said.

He should have kept his mouth shut. But he was rolling now.

"You come into my office today, demanding a goddamn ongoing police investigation. Privileged material. Material that could be damaging to certain people in the wrong hands . . ."

"I wonder if it's in the right hands."

". . . think you deserve to have it. Why? Because the goddamn missing girl paid some union dues?"

"That's bullshit."

"Or is it because you can cost some people some money by telling a couple thousand airplane waitresses to take a walk?"

"We have *men* working, too."

"I'm sorry, flying waitresses and waiters. You're throwing your goddamn weight around, which is fine. Until it starts fucking with things I need to do!"

"Is that right?"

They were both shouting now.

"Folks."

The bartender was standing there with their sodas.

"You sure you guys don't want a drink?" he asked.

They both looked at him. They both waved him off at once.

"I wasn't trying to *fuck* with your case," she said, quietly now. "I was trying to *help*."

"Save it," he said, turning back toward the mirror.

Nobody said anything for a few seconds. She opened the Delesandro file, then closed it.

"Detective Riker," she said. "Do you like working at the airport?" She was looking straight ahead herself.

"Not particularly."

"Always, or something you've grown to dislike."

"Let's just say I've never been particularly thrilled about the place."

"Why's that?"

Jesus Christ, he thought. What fucking difference did it make?

"It's a pipe," he said.

"A pipe? I don't understand."

"It's like working at a bus station. It's bigger and the people dress a little better, but the same old shit flows through it day after day. Week after week."

"So, if you don't really like your job, wouldn't you say that might effect how you do it?"

"That doesn't apply here. It doesn't apply in any case."

"Why not?"

"Because things *do* come along. The Delesandro case, whether you choose to believe it or not, is one of those more interesting cases. That may very well be one reason I'm not particularly enamored with you all over it."

"So why are you here?"

"You asked for me."

"I did?"

When he turned she was looking at him with genuine bemusement.

Fucking Ladd, Riker thought.

She started to get up.

"Hey, where you going?" he said.

Standing now, reaching in her purse and the file.

"Back to the airport."

"What about your—fries?"

She tossed five bucks on the table.

"Be my guest."

Let him stay and get shit faced, she thought. That's what he really wanted.

When she started to walk, he grabbed her arm.

"No, stay," he said. "Look, you have no idea. It's been a real long day."

She pulled her arm away.

"I'll bet it has. I know just how long they can get."

"What is that supposed to mean?"

She pointed to the fries. "You know, you really ought to eat those. They'll coat your stomach."

He spun around on the stool.

"You know, *Mizz* Harmon, I don't know what your problem is, but I'm getting just a little irritated at these references to my personal habits, so I'm gonna set the record straight, okay. I *don't* drink. I retired champion, you follow what I'm saying? So in the future, in the interest of us working together on this thing, if there is to be a future, I'd appreciate it if you would cut the lush crap. It's not doing a whole lot for what little is left of my police career."

She started to backtrack toward the bar stool.

"You don't drink at all?"

He held up the Coke.

"What about those bottles under your tree?"

He shook his head. "Like I told the other guy, at one time they wouldn't last me a week. Like I'm telling you, I retired champion. I was lucky to be on my feet."

"How long?"

"It's been five years."

"Why didn't you tell me?"

"Why should I?"

She smiled.

"It's been five years for me, too."

She kept saying two words.

"Yes . . ."

". . . Good."

"Yes . . ."

". . . Good."

Yes, she was good. He'd had few women with so little inhibition.

He was almost there.

"Pull out," she said.

But he didn't understand.

"Pull out."

"God, what?"

There now.

"Pull out."

"What, baby?"

"Pull out"

"Jesus."

"Come on me. On my back."

"What?"

"Pull out!"

He collapsed forward, his chin landing on the pillow just above her right shoulder.

She started giggling, while he was out of breath.

"Captain," she said. "When I say pull out, you gotta pull back on your stick."

Christ, he thought. *Really* uninhibited.

"Peaches, you should have told me you were into aerials," Thomas Reidy said.

He rolled over. Laughing. Picked up the bottle of Korbel Brut he'd stuffed into the plastic ice bucket at the Motel Six and took a swig. Offered her some.

"I lied," she said, taking a sip.

"What?"

"I don't think I like the blues. In fact, I'm not sure I'd even know it if I heard it."

He'd already guessed as much. They had made it to the blues bar by cab, but at 7 P.M. no one was there but a couple of regulars at the bar. It had taken Reidy no less than forty-two minutes—he had timed it—to make his move, suggesting straight out they find a motel near the Miami airport.

"You ought to," he said, sitting up now to light a cigarette.

"What's it sound like?"

"You ever heard B.B. King?"

She turned on her side, propping her head up with her elbow. Showing him the length of her body, like an exquisite nude. Uninhibited. If she kept that pose, he'd be ready to go again in ten.

"No."

"How 'bout Robert Cray?"

"No."

He'd started with the old cats, worked his way up to a contemporary. He tried the white rockers.

"Okay, have you ever heard Eric Clapton?"

He was looking at her face now. Shit, he thought, a little plastic surgery and she could bump two points. Damn near hit a nine or ten.

"No."

"You haven't heard of Eric Clapton?"

She was looking at him coyly, her right finger running circles around her nipple.

"Yeah, him I've heard of. 'Layla,' right."

"No, that's not blues," he said, exhaling smoke.

"You know, if we hustle after we land back in Detroit, I know a place in Taylor. Called Cisco's. We could probably catch the last set."

"I've always listened to country, really."

Country, he thought. He *hated* country. Even with the nose job, he'd have to knock off a full point for that.

He offered her more Korbel.

"What are your plans?" he asked. "When we get back."

"I don't know, it ought to be some party."

She handed him back the bottle.

"The flight?"

"Yeah. You know, the company ought to provide us with cabin attendants."

"No, they should give you passengers. Let them serve you guys, for a change."

"Well, they better leave the drink cart. I've never been on one of these before."

"I've never flown one. But knowing the company, they'll probably strip the stock. Still, I wish I didn't have to work it."

She took the Korbel from him.

"Captain, you still gotta get us back safe and sound."

He took a swig.

"A half bottle of champagne, there's more alcohol in a week-old bottle of orange juice."

She began touching him.

"I wouldn't be with you, Captain, if I didn't think you could handle it."

"So what *are* your plans when we get back."

"Bed," she said, coy again.

He kissed her breast.

"Me, too, peaches. Me, too."

He jumped to his feet.

"I gotta pee, first," he said.

"Details. Details."

After he pissed, he checked his eyes. Pretty clear. Maybe a little yellow. Before he left, he'd hit them again with the Visine. The hangover of the morning wasn't even a memory now. He was just a little tired. But one more roll with the leggy blond, he might be outright bushed.

Thomas Reidy opened his shoulder satchel, pulling out his black leather shaving kit. At the bottom of the compartment for dry accessories, he saw the folded rectangle of slick magazine paper.

Yes, he thought. Last night. He knew they hadn't dipped into that.

"Captain," she said from the bed. "We're running out of time."

"Coming."

He fished out the little package with his fingers, laying it on the sink, first making very sure there was no water there. On the outside was a paragraph from the *Playboy* interview. He unfolded it, exposing the inside. Inside, was a nude of the Playmate of the Year, a full gram, it looked like, laying across her breasts. His dealer always packaged his goods on the charms of Hefner's best.

"Well, hello, honey," he said quietly.

He dipped his well-manicured thumb nail into the coke and took a quick hit.

No tired flight home now.

"Captain. What are you doing in there?"

Hell, he'd be razor sharp.

Twenty-six

Oshefsky met the escort at the department, taking the two children to be reunited with their parents briefly, then up to the DB to be debriefed. Lefty Thompson had suggested the DB, considering the hangar was in chaos from the invasion of the Federal Bureau of Investigation hostage rescue team.

When he was done, Thompson said, he'd have to turn over the results of the interview to the FBI.

"Like our tree?" Oshefsky asked.

"It's pretty ugly," the girl said.

The boy said nothing.

Oshefsky smiled. "I agree."

"I guess you got some tour, huh?" Oshefsky began. "Were you scared?"

"Sometimes," the girl said.

After five minutes of chit chat, Oshefsky went for the specifics. The number of people in the tower. The number of weapons they saw. He was working from an extensive hostage debriefing check list he'd brought over from the TOC.

Their answers gave him a pretty complete picture of conditions of the tower, considering the children's ages.

He asked about any anti-intrusion devices.

"Alarms," Oshefsky explained. "Things like that."

"Two things he hung on the doors, that had sirens," the girl said.

The boy interrupted, speaking as if his older sister was misinformed.

"No, they're called Robo alarms," he said.

"Robo alarms?"

"Yeah, you can get them in the U.S. Calvary catalogue."

"You get that?" Oshefsky asked.

"My dad does, but I read it all the time."

They talked about Kring's clothing. The girl said she'd seen him only in a tan parka and a tan vest.

"Any other distinguishing marks or anything you saw on this man?" Oshefsky asked.

"He had a cut or something here," she said, pointing to her mouth.

"That's all?"

She nodded.

"He had funny hair," the boy said.

"No he didn't," she said.

"Yes, he did. You just didn't see it. You were too busy *talking.*"

Hair. Oshefsky hadn't heard anything from the employee interviews about hair.

"What do you mean?" he asked.

He circled his own head as if he was drawing a halo.

"On top?"

"Yeah, he has a spot up here. With no hair. In the back."

"A bald spot?"

The boy nodded. "Yeah."

Oshefsky picked up the phone. He thought the sniper should know about that.

Russell was having some difficulty understanding the blithe atmosphere in the control tower. Kring had his feet up, leaning back deeply into the swivel chair, gloating like some kind of third world dictator. They had a lull in traffic.

Mike Garcia was on break. Kring had put him on center stage.

"Okay, funny man," Kring said. "Now, I want to hear somethin' with spooks."

Garcia looked around to see who was listening.

"That's okay," Kring said. "There aren't any up here."

Garcia lowered his voice a little. As if it really mattered.

"Okay. Here it is: Hang gliding, right? Big new flying sport a few years back."

"Right," Kring said.

Russell looked slowly in the direction of the parking lot.

"Turn around," Kring barked.

He looked back at Garcia. "Go ahead, funny man."

Garcia started again.

"Hang gliding, right? So there's this black dude. A black yuppie, okay. He's trying to move up in the Atlanta office of IBM, but not really having much luck. He figures shit, man. My problem is I need to take up some kind of white man sport. Show these white motherfuckers I'm with the program. So, he decides he's gonna learn to hang glide, man. He gets the equipment. Takes the classes. Learns to glide. Then invites the local vice president out to the boon-docks with him to show off."

"Okay," Kring said.

"So, the black dude shoves off from this hilltop. But what he doesn't know is that down near the bottom there's these two rednecks who are goose huntin'. They're sittin' down there in the trees waitin' for somethin' to fly over, when all of a sudden they see this big shape in the sky comin' there way. Look up. Man, they unload their weapons. Bam! Bam! Bam!"

Russell flinched.

Garcia gave the story a dramatic pause, his hands out.

"Well, the shadow of this thing passes over the red necks and keeps right on going. The one redneck says to the other, 'Hey man, what the hell was that?' The other red neck is reloading his gun and he says, 'I don't know man, but we sure made it drop that nigger it was hangin' onto.' "

The two men laughed, Kring almost hysterically. There was laughter in other parts of the room.

"Garcia," somebody said. "You know that was real bad."

Kring was wiping his eyes.

Just one big happy family, Russell thought. Almost.

"Hey, I guess you're going to have to write Garcia up for that one, Captain Queeg," Kring said, still smiling, but with a certain amount of venom.

Cleage looked down at his shoes.

Russell had watched Garcia climb into Kring's good graces by dumping on Cleage for the last fifteen minutes, before he started with the jokes. He'd guessed the others in the tower had aligned themselves with Kring while he was below in the break room.

The strain was showing on Cleage. He'd been traffic co-ordinator all day.

"How 'bout it, Captain," Garcia said, feeling his oats a little now. "You gonna write me up?"

Cleage looked up, making eye contact with everybody.

"What's said here, stays here," he said.

"You're goddamn right it will," Kring said, grinning.

Russell figured this was his opening.

"Laurel," he said. "When are we going to get outta here?"

"We got to finish second shift here, Uncle Rep," he said. The shift ended at 1 A.M.

"Then what? You know, this can't go on forever."

Russell could feel others eyeing him critically. He knew he was upsetting the equilibrium, but he pushed on.

"Laurel, why don't you let me work something out here with the authorities. I think I can guarantee your safety."

He was still grinning.

"You think you can do that, huh?"

"Yeah, I really think I can."

The smile fell from his face.

"You fucking never did a goddamn thing for me before. You haven't done shit for half of these men."

Kring picked up the Ruger, waving it in his direction.

"You're not too far afield from the captain over here, Uncle Rep," he said, louder now. "Why don't you go over now and sit by him. Maybe you two belong together."

Russell walked over toward a seat.

When he sat he felt a hand hit his shoulder. He looked up and saw Garcia, glaring down at him.

"Russell," Garcia said. "Why don't you just shut the fuck up."

The FBI commander was a humorless lifer of fifty or so. Accompanied by the county executive, he'd shown up in Stupek's OSC office in light brown trousers and matching shirt, the shade color coordinated with the camo pattern of his assault team's uniforms. He wore a cotton baseball cap. The real thing, no cheap plastic connector on the back. On the front, embroidered in official United States government blue was "FBI," and below that HRT, for hostage rescue team. Across the bill in gold were two lines of scrambled eggs.

They met up with his team leaders and went room to room in the hangar. As Stupek walked them quickly through every phase of the EOC, then Scrambled Eggs grabbed for everything he could.

"We want to work with the bureau," Ladd kept saying.

What Ladd was saying was *take it all,* as far as Stupek could determine. As Stupek predicted, Ladd was eager to sell the entire operation out.

Vince Stupek could hardly blame the FBI guy. If it were him, walking in cold, he'd want his own people brought up to snuff, then he'd want them on the job.

When all the meetings and briefings were over, only Tommy Monsorta and Jimmy Oshefsky were left working in the Nomads, and the airport police SWAT team.

It was Morton Ressler's opinion that Tommy Monsorta had made a connection with Laurel Kring. "At this stage, after nearly twelve hours in that high-stress environment, his emotional condition will be such that he may act rashly," Ressler had argued. "I don't think you can afford to upset that cart."

"So we don't have the time to establish new rapport with one of our men," Scrambled Eggs said.

Ressler nodded. "In my opinion, yes."

The FBI debriefed Oshefsky about the children, then sent two agents over to reinterview the kids. Oshefsky would have been free to leave like the rest of the investigators, until Stupek suggested it just might be a good idea to have someone around who actually knew the airport.

"Good idea," one of the FBI agents said. "We can always use him to run stuff around."

Everywhere else there was new personnel, a new bowl of alphabet soup. Lefty Thompson had been put in charge of something called perimeter control. That meant he'd command a couple of cruisers at the gate on Eureka Road to keep out the curious once a raid went down.

After more meetings, Stupek met with Scrambled Eggs and Marlon Ladd in his office. The FBI wanted the airport police SWAT team to stick around.

"I think your plan is basically a sound one," Scrambled Eggs said. "With *some* alterations."

"You want to move sooner or later?" Stupek asked.

"Let's just say the director wants this airport clear by day break."

"You mean Rains?"

Ladd answered, "Vince, the director of the Federal Aviation Administration."

Stupek wondered to himself when the U.S. Congress was going to check in as well.

"The request for media coverage affords us a real opportunity. And we think, especially considering we have two tactics units, yours and ours, available now, that we can send two units. We'll move one group of men in the drainage ditch. Conceal a small *elite* group in the TV truck."

Stupek had considered that idea earlier himself. He already guessed which group would be crawling in that wet ditch. But he'd also decided he wasn't going to spend the night sitting under the fluorescent lights in that Nomad's office.

"I'd like to move out with our SWAT," he said. "You won't be needing me here."

"Good," Scrambled Eggs said. "We're going to have a tactics briefing here in a couple of minutes, and we'll want your input, of course."

Stupek turned to Ladd. "You were able to get the TV reporter?"

Ladd nodded. "Yes and no. Channel seven is providing us one of their trucks, but they don't want their reporter in harm's way."

"Well work with that," Scrambled Eggs said. "And we want to keep your sniper in position. Your people indicated he's had no sign of the target, but he could help us on the intelligence side."

"Fine."

Stupek wanted to know what they were planning. He didn't want to wait for the briefing.

He said, "You've got a TV truck, but you're not going to send in the reporter . . ."

"Or a film crew, for that matter," Scrambled Eggs said. "We plan to use *our* people in those roles."

"You know he's got a TV up there," Stupek said.

Scrambled eggs nodded.

"You know he wants to see a familiar face," Stupek.

"We'll let him see the reporter's face in his security camera, but he won't go up. That's if we can't lure him outside first for the interview."

"I wouldn't count on it."

"And we're not."

"What happens when he realizes he's not getting the real thing."

The FBI man pulled off his hat and pushed his hair back, as if he we was becoming bored with all the questions.

"Lieutenant," he said, "under our plan, he'll never get that chance."

Twenty-seven

The condominium was not far from the old Ford Motor proving grounds. It was a modified New England town house in used red brick, with colonial white sash work, inspired by Greenfield Village and the Ford Museum just up Rotunda Drive.

Heading into the kitchen, she wondered if he wanted espresso.

"Isn't that what you get in Greektown, with the mud in the bottom?" Riker asked.

"No. *That's* turkish."

He said he usually drank regular, although the coffee in the DB sometimes got so burnt it looked like the stuff in Greektown. She more or less said he was getting espresso anyway, whether he liked it or not.

He took a seat on her overstuffed couch. The place was smart, but very comfortable. Hardwood floors and area rugs. Some primitive furniture and more recent antiques.

Jack Riker had lied his way into her apartment. If you're going to lie, tell only one, and build it on a foundation of truth. He'd learned that from criminals. He learned that stealing time from the county when he needed to slip off for a couple hours of drinks.

He'd told her that indeed he was investigating a suspect on the Delesandro case. He said he was a federal employee. That was the lie. This would keep her off track about what was really going on at the airport, but allow him one more shot. He did this after they began talking about flight two twenty-five back at Miller's and she mentioned she'd saved all the news coverage. He couldn't shake the feeling that crash held secrets about the man in the tower.

"I made you a double," she said, handing him a tiny cup.

"This is a double?" he said, examining it. "This left over from your tea set as a kid."

"It's called demitasse, Jack."

"I know," he said. "I'm just pulling your chain."

"I'm going to get into some jeans," she said.

When she returned from her bedroom she was wearing faded denim and a black turtleneck. She went to a roll-top desk where there was a computer and rummaged through the lower cabinet. Then she plopped down cross-legged on the floor, across from him at the coffee table. She dropped a thick manila envelope there.

Looking at her, he decided maybe he had the best assignment of the night.

"Well?" she said, looking up.

She caught him staring. "What?"

"The espresso. You like it?"

As a matter of fact he did. "It's good. Thanks."

She pulled out several handfuls of clippings from the envelope and began putting them in two piles. They were already starting to discolor from age.

"You don't like change, do you?" she asked.

"What do you mean?"

"The coffee. Your routines back at the department. People intruding on your territory. That's okay. Most us alkies don't deal with it well."

Shit, he thought. He hoped she wasn't going to go into the AA stuff again. He thought they'd covered that back at the bar.

"I don't particularly like most people. It's a cop deal, I guess."

"Is it?"

"What about you?"

"People are okay. I just don't like being pushed around. That's me. But it has nothing to do with the job, when you get right down to it."

"Maybe you're right."

She looked up from the two stacks of stories.

"Can I ask a personal question?" she said.

"You can try."

"What made you quit?"

He pointed to the clippings.

"The crash," he said. "It took me a little lower than I really wanted to go."

"What was it like? Before you quit?"

He wasn't sure he wanted to go into this. The only reason she'd got this much out of him was because the way she looked, he guessed. *That* was stupid. Beautiful woman shows up, a man lets down all his defenses. Tells her things he'd never tell anyone else. Why? To get laid?

Something also told him there was something more there. She could be obnoxious, all right. But he also liked the way she came straight at him. He liked the way she wasn't afraid to say what she thought.

"I guess it's none of my business, is it?" she said.

"No, it's okay."

"So . . ."

"The last few years, being pissed off was kind of a perpetual state."

"At what?"

"The department. The bosses. The scumbags. My ex. The world. Waking up. You name it."

"You drank to relieve it."

"It helped."

"So what do you do now?"

"I don't hang out it in bars. I don't hang with the same people."

"But the last time I checked, the world hasn't improved a whole lot."

"Yeah, in some ways it's worse."

"Did you go into treatment?"

He shook his head.

"And you don't go to meetings?"

"I do okay on my own."

She grabbed their cups and got up. "You want another one?"

"Sure," he said. "Another double."

She had a small pot already made in her kitchen. He watched her go there. He liked the way she walked.

When she returned she said, "Well I'm just trying not to be a horse thief."

"A what?"

"They always say around the tables you sober up a horse thief, you know what you got?"

He shook his head.

"A sober horse thief."

"I'm not sure I understand."

"That's why I go to meetings. I'm told you can dry out, but if you don't change, you're limited by what you have left when you quit."

She pulled a stack of clippings toward her.

"But what do I know," she said. "I'm just a union hack."

"Maybe quite a bit," he said.

She divided the clippings between them, giving him three special sections devoted to the crash. He vaguely remembered one or two of them from newsstands, or maybe he'd spotted them on desks in the department in the days after the crash.

"Jesus," he said. "I had no idea there was this much."

"Yeah, there's a lot. Didn't you follow this?"

"You don't follow it if you're trying to forget it."

The first section showed a color photo of the crash site, nearly as wide as the paper and as deep as the fold. The photo was a vista of gray and black debris covering Middlebelt Road, highlighted by patches of yellow.

The cutline read: "Yellow plastic marks where parts of bodies were found."

Inside, several stories speculated causes:

JETLINERS ENGINE TYPE HAD FOUR RECENT FAILURES

and,

FAA SUSPECTED ENGINE

The section opened to eight pages of victims bios and photographs. A high school football picture. An executive's corporate portrait. Dozens of head shots, most cropped from family photographs. There was an insert featuring the crew. A pilot. A copilot. Four flight attendants. The dead also included an off-duty pilot and a flight attendant who had hitched a ride home on the doomed flight.

Riker didn't recognize any of them, but he remembered some of the family names.

"What are we looking for?" Harmon asked.

"All the theories on the cause of the crash," he said.

"Why?"

"I think it might have something to do with the guy's MO."

"Who is this guy?"

"I can't tell you that."

She grabbed his hand. "Shit, Jack, trust me a little, will ya? I trusted you, didn't I?"

His eyes asked how.

"I brought you over here, didn't I?" she said.

"Laurel Kring," he said. "He's a controller. He was working the night of the crash."

Riker knew he was getting dangerously close. Answer questions as they came. Tell only one lie, he told himself.

As they read through the clippings, they began comparing notes. By the first week, a debate already was raging over the cause of the crash. The investigators focused increasingly on the flap settings when the recovery of the black box data record showed the flaps were set at zero, a low-lift setting intended for high-altitude flight. Yet, no flap warning alarm was heard on the black box's cockpit tape.

One story reported there had been a series of distractions during the crew's preflight checklist.

"It says here: 'The black box showed the crew had four interruptions,'" Harmon said, reading now. "'Two from the control tower about weather. A third when the captain missed his taxiway and had to turn around.'"

"Those first two might have been Kring," Riker said. "He was on local control, if I remember right. What's the fourth?"

She read onto the jump page.

"It doesn't say."

She pulled out another story.

"Here's the copilot quoted from the jet behind two twenty-five that night on the runway," she said. "He says as far as he could recall that the jet's flaps appeared to be set correctly."

"Where did he say that?"

"The safety board hearing. Months later. There was a real pissing match between the NTSB and the Airline Pilots Association. I remember all this. They took it right into the hearing. The safety board claimed in the end the pilots had disabled the flap alarm because it was annoying. You can't blame the APA for fighting that theory tooth and nail."

She spread out a half dozen stories.

"Here, these are all the hearing stories. But I think I

might be missing a couple. These dates look a little spread out."

Riker had another story.

"Here's the transcript of the cockpit tape," he said.

He read. "This might be Kring here. Just talking about wind speed. Looks like they changed runways."

He handed it to her.

"This is your business," he said. "You should be reading this."

She became excited when she read the clip.

"I get it," she said. "Now I see where you're going, Jack. Yes, he went after a flight attendant, because he thinks one caused the crash?"

"What are you talking about?"

"You see this note here with the story. There's a forty-two-second gap. I think that was the fourth distraction. I remember this, too, now that I think about it. They never released it."

"Why?" Riker asked.

"They said it was irrelevant."

"What was it?"

"The pilot was having a chat with one of the attendants."

"About what?"

"I only heard rumors. But they were all over the airport. You know, give a bunch of bored people a gap, they'll fill it in."

"So fill it."

"Well," she said. "There was some talk that they were having an affair, and she'd told him it was over. That's why he forgot to check off on the flaps."

She reached across the table and slapped him on the shoulder.

"I told you I could help you," she said, smiling broadly.

"Is it true?"

"I don't know. Supposedly, the head of the local APA had a bootleg copy of the tape."

"Can we get it?"

"On the night before Thanksgiving?"

"I've got his home phone number, but it's back at my office."

It made sense to Riker, but not for the case he was thinking about. Not for the siege in the tower.

"I wonder why he took it all so personal," he said, trying to get back to what he really wanted.

She pointed to the clippings from the NTSB hearings.

"You ever been to a safety board hearing?" she asked.

Riker shook his head.

"It's very public. It's a big show."

Riker motioned for the clippings.

"Let me see those."

She shook her head. "He's not in these. But I'm missing a couple."

She stood up. "C'mon."

He followed her over to the roll-top desk.

"Grab that chair over there and pull up a seat," she said.

She turned the computer on.

"I can get into the Detroit *Free Press* library," she said. "We can get those missing stories through Compuserv."

He sat down next to her.

"Christ, you've got that, too?"

"You mean Compuserv?"

"Yeah. One of the other detectives was telling me about it."

"Most people with personal computers do."

In a minute, she had the *Free Press* library up on the screen.

She typed in a date range and the search words: "225." "NTSB." Hearing. The service produced a list of stories.

She highlighted one: "TOWER PERSONNEL SAY 225 LOOKED FINE."

"Let's look at this."

In seconds, the text scrolled onto her screen.

"Here," she said, pointing.

The story didn't say much more than the hearing. Kring's name was mentioned as a witness.

"You don't strike me as the high-tech type," he said.

"I wasn't, but I got hooked. I got this thing so I could bid flights. I still work a trip now and then, just to keep in touch."

Riker knew about bidding from the Delesandro investigation. Every month pilots and flight attendants requested certain trips they wanted to work.

"*This* helps you bid?"

She went over to the printer to get a copy of the story.

"Yeah, that's why I got Compuserv. Northwest worked out a special deal. You can hook up into SLICK, the Northwest computer in Minneapolis. You used to have to do it at the terminal, but now any attendant with a computer hooked into a phone line can do it now from home."

"So this does the schedules?" he asked.

She sat back down, the printout in her hand.

"Yep. If two people want the same flight, it goes with the seniority. Follows the contract. I think the name fits, don't you?"

She handed him the paper. He folded it and put it in his lapel pocket, sliding it in next to the Holter monitor log. At the bottom of the pocket, he felt something else.

He pulled out the paper. It was the slip with the numbers from Kring's workshop. He decided to let her have a crack at it. Maybe Oshefsky had missed something.

"Can you get into there with this?" he said, showing it to her.

She glanced at first, but did a double take.

"Where the hell did you get that?" she said.

Stick with one lie, he told himself. But sooner or later, he'd have some real explaining to do.

"From the controller," he said.

"I thought you said you haven't arrested him yet."

"We haven't. But we did a search warrant on his house today. Like I told you at the bar, we're looking for evidence."

She seemed a little miffed. "Well, that's a Compuserv address and probably a password. But where did you get those other numbers?"

"They were on there. Why?"

She hesitated. "Well, I could be wrong, but I'd swear that first set is a passport number. And that second one, that looks like one of our seniority numbers."

"For who?"

"For SLICK."

She started typing in commands. "When you bid flights you log onto Compuserv," she said, matter of factly. "Then you go to a special section, where you bid. But you have to have security clearance to get there."

"What kind of clearance."

"You have to use your passport number. Then you use your seniority number as your password."

He still wasn't sure he was following her. The computer stuff had him confused.

"Why would Kring need that?"

She grabbed the paper out of his hand.

"He wouldn't. He shouldn't even have it in fact."

She returned to the computer again, her fingers flying over the keys.

"What are you doing?" he asked.

"I'm going to log on to Compuserv again using this address and password," she said.

Her eyes scanned the screen. A box appeared on the display.

"Welcome to Compuserv," it read.

"Okay, we're in," she said. "His number and password are good."

She began typing again, looking over at the paper from Kring's work shop.

"Now, I'm going to enter this and see if I can get into SLICK."

She sat back, waiting, tapping her hands on the edge of the roll-top with anticipation. They watched the screen change colors a couple of times, then went to an unadorned black background with bright white text.

"I think these numbers are going to do it," she said.

They waited

Another two seconds.

"Jack, dammit, look!" she said.

"I see it."

The Northwest computer greeting was in the center of the screen.

"Welcome to SLICK, Nikki Delesandro," it read.

Twenty-eight

Terry Grice thought about the question from the FBI man with the scrambled eggs on his cap. She was sitting in the same office she was in earlier in the Nomad's hangar, but looking at new faces.

"Well," she began. "We *could* close runways twelve left and twelve right and pile everything onto three center. That will concentrate both inbounds and outbounds, despite the light traffic at that hour. We call that shooting the gap."

"Shooting the gap?" another FBI man asked.

"Right. As you land one aircraft, you send another from the same runway. The trick is to never have them cross paths. If you want them really busy up there, that would do it. It requires a lot of coordination in the tower, but it's perfectly safe. Our people do it all the time."

"Why would you close the other runways?" Scrambled Eggs asked.

"Routine runway maintenance. Wind sheers. Strong cross wind. Once we lost our landing lights."

"What about shutting the lights down?" somebody asked.

"Too obvious," Scrambled Eggs said.

"What about the wind sheers?" somebody else said. "Is there any way to rig the equipment."

"The indicator is in the tower," Grice said. "The measuring stations are located at airport perimeters. Plus, there's one at mid-field. That would take some doing."

She looked at the FBI commander.

"Why don't we start with you telling us what you're trying to do. That might help."

He said they were going to make an assault on the tower. They had a time. They were going to do it sometime after midnight.

She felt her heart sink.

"That's not much time," she said.

"I know. We're already moving one SWAT team in position. We have another waiting. We don't have much time. Like I asked you earlier, we want that tower entirely *occupied*. We're open to ideas."

"Has this been cleared with Washington?" she asked.

Scrambled Eggs nodded.

"With *our* people? The FAA?"

He nodded again.

Grice wanted to help, but she didn't want anyone hurt. "I don't want to endanger my people," she said.

Scrambled Eggs said, "You want to help them, Ms. Grice, then you need to help us."

She remembered walking from the Nomad's hangar, the brisk west wind in her face.

"Well, sometimes, the National Weather Service issues high wind advisories," she began.

"Go on."

"They get that in the tower on a video hook up. It comes straight from the weather service office here. All night we've had this front moving in, so it wouldn't be unexpected. Yes, if you could have the weather service issue a high wind advisory. Pin a time to it. That alone should make the tower supervisor move everything to three center. It's our east-west runway. If I was in charge of that tower, I'd want to be ahead of the game. I'd want my planes landing and taking off into the prevailing wind."

Scrambled Eggs looked at one of the other men in the room.

"Contact the weather service," he said. "See if we can make that happen."

He left the room.

"That may be good, Ms. Grice," he said. "But isn't there some kind of equipment failure beyond their control up there?"

She looked around the room. A half dozen strangers in crisp uniforms. All with the same government-issue clipboards. She knew she was putting her people's lives in the hands of a half-dozen men she didn't know.

"Well, we have been having a lot of problems with ASR-9, our local radar. In fact, that's what started this mess."

"Go on."

"I suppose we could shut down the radar. But then, they'd lose it in the tower. They have an ASR-9 scope up there for low-visibility conditions. We'd switch over to a backup system, like we did earlier today. Something called CENRAP. It tracks the flight by beacons in the aircraft. They'd still be landing airplanes, but they'd have to coordinate closely with our radar room."

"Ms. Grice, short of crashing an airplane, I need one hell of a diversion. Something that will have every person in that tower hopping, especially the man who thinks he's in charge."

"They'd be pretty busy without the ASR-9," she said.

"The wind thing's better," somebody else added.

The FBI man thought for a couple of seconds.

"Maybe you've got something there," he said. "What did you call that, Ms. Grice?"

"Shooting the gap."

He nodded. "Maybe we could do both," he said.

So far, the drainage ditch had been true to the specs on the county blueprint. Two feet deep, three feet wide, and at least four hundred more soggy yards to go ahead in the darkness. They had not come across any standing water. Stupek counted that as the only good news in the last hour.

He crawled to the bank, keeping his head low.

"Okay, let's break," he said.

Johnson and the four other SWAT cops behind him slowed and stopped, looking for dryer ground. The flurries off and on during the day hadn't accumulated into anything, but had managed to give the grass a good soaking. The temperature, when they left the Eureka Road check point at twenty-three hundred, had just reached freezing.

Stupek rolled over on his back, resting on the backpack that carried a dry set of clothes, an H&K MP-5 submachine gun and an incendiary device for use in a tower raid. He doubted he'd get a chance to use it.

Stupek fished his Copenhagen out of his flak vest.

"I guess I fucked up," Johnson said, catching his breath.

"How's that?" Stupek said, packing his lip.

"My mother wanted me to go to college, but I wanted to be a cop."

Stupek slipped the Copenhagen into his lip and turned. "You'd rather be behind a desk?"

"Not necessarily. But if I went to college I could have applied to the *Federal Bureau of Investigation*. Maybe then I'd be riding to this gig in a nice warm van, instead of crawling in this motherfucking ditch."

Stupek smoldered in silence. That's why he'd gone with SWAT. Maybe crawling in the ditch, he wouldn't think about it too much.

"I better check in with the Indian," Johnson said. "Tell him we'll be there in about thirty."

Johnson keyed his radio. He had a head set.

When he was done talking to the sniper, Stupek asked how he was doing.

"He says he left us the first floor of the firehouse," Johnson said. "He's gone to the second level."

"Why upstairs?"

"He's still looking for a shot."

"He won't get it."

"I think you're right."

"No, this asshole is way too smart."

Stupek looked up at the sky, seeing only darkness.

Johnson turned over on his side, facing him.

"We're not gonna get any of this, are we, Vince?"

"You were at the briefing, if they get that phony film crew through the tower door, they're not going to fuck around. They'll hit those stairs, then they'll go in hard."

"I don't like it."

"It's not our call," Stupek said.

He spit out all the dip. Then tossed the can into the darkness. It tasted bitter, unsatisfying.

"It must be the lights," Stupek said.

"The what?"

"The *lights*. Guys like Ladd and Rains, they spend too much time under those lights. My old man always said fluorescent lighting ruined your eyes. But I'm beginning to think it makes your brain rot."

"At least we got those kids out of there," Johnson said.

"We might have got 'em all," Stupek said. "But they just couldn't help themselves. They had to micro-manage our ass. They couldn't just leave us the fuck alone."

"You better be careful, Lieutenant," Johnson said. "That kind of talk is dangerous in these parts."

"Fuck 'em, who's listening."

"I'll never tell."

Stupek turned over, ready to resume the crawl.

"Then what are you talking about, Johnson?"

"I'm talking about the guy in the tower."

"What about him?"

"For a second there you sounded just like the man."

* * *

Tommy Monsorta felt it was his duty to argue the hostage taker's case. If he didn't do that, he wouldn't be able to believe in what he did. And *believing* really had nothing to do with conscience, in the conventional sense. Simply, it was the mark of a good negotiator. He had to be able to believe in his own line of crap. Tommy Monsorta considered *that* his talent—something he was fortunate enough to find a place for in police work, instead of used car sales or ponzi schemes.

"Okay," he told the FBI commander. "You're saying if I can get him to come down to the first floor, do the interviews there and walk out, we're gonna let him walk out of there."

"That's right," Scrambled Eggs said. "After a little persuasion, the reporter has agreed to the first floor only. But he says he *will not* go up into the tower."

The TV reporter was with the airport police. The FBI didn't want him seeing the EOC.

"What about the columnist?"

"We don't have one. We've got a look-alike and a Detroit *News* advertising car standing by over at your department."

"Why advertising?"

"It's got the paper logo on the door."

"So I gotta get him to do the TV interview," Monsorta concluded. "Or, you're sending the phonies to the top?"

Scrambled Eggs nodded.

When Monsorta picked up the phone he didn't feel particularly comfortable, not with the FBI guy behind his back.

He swiveled in the bar stool. "Hey," he said. "You gotta cut me some room here. I get claustrophobia when people stand to close."

He pointed to the end of the bar where Ressler, three dozen FBI HRT members, Marlon Ladd, and Jimmy Oshefsky were sitting. The FBI commander walked slowly over, then turned around.

"Remember, we need that time nailed down on the interview," Scrambled Eggs said. "Everything revolves around that."

Monsorta picked up the hostage telephone.

"Okay, Bat," he said when he answered. "We're about ready to go on this end."

"Did you get Pete Meyers?"

"He's on his way."

"Did you get a TV crew?"

"They're coming out from Southfield. Should be here soon."

"Did you get the *CHANGE* regs?"

"We have them, too. You were right. There's a lot. The TV people are going to pick them up. Bring them."

"Very good, Major Tom."

Kring sounded relaxed, confident.

"Now about these interviews, Bat, these news people are pretty nervous. You can understand that, can't you?"

"I suppose."

"I was thinking . . ."

"No, I'm not coming out. You should know me better than that."

"I was thinking maybe of some kind of neutral location."

"Such as?"

"How about the first floor of the tower. I understand you have administrative offices down there."

"Forget it."

"How about . . ."

"Look, Major Tom, you don't seem to *fucking* understand. We've got work up here to do."

"I'll have to have some assurances . . ."

"You'll have the elevator, and that's all you'll get."

Monsorta looked down at the FBI man. His face was expressionless, but his hand motioned an OK sign.

"All right," Monsorta said. "We can have them there at midnight. And the agreement was you'd send down the union representative, Mr. Russell."

"After the interview."

"Yes, after . . ."

"He can leave with the TV crew, but that's going to be later, rather than earlier. I want the reporters at twelve fifty-five."

"I thought you said midnight."

"I said sometime after midnight. That's fifty-five minutes after midnight, to be exact."

"Why not earlier?"

"My people need to finish their shift."

"And after that, I've got to have some assurances. That was the deal."

"You're getting the rep."

"I thought we were going to end this thing."

"We are. But you haven't delivered the reporters yet. Who did you get from the TV station? I need a name."

"A name?"

"Hold on for a second, Bat. Let me check."

Monsorta covered the phone and looked down the bar. One of the FBI men passed him a name.

He read it to Kring.

"Shit, I'm not talking to him," Kring said. "He's a fucking nigger."

"You said no women, Bat. You didn't say anything about that."

The profile information gathered by Riker and the TOC had fallen through the cracks during the change of guard.

The FBI commander was motioning with his hands, mouthing *we'll get somebody else.*

"We'll get somebody else," Monsorta said.

"You blew it."

"It's not a problem . . ."

"You *fucking* blew it."

"Bat, how were we supposed to know?"

Kring let out a long sigh.

"Major Tom, your people are letting you down."

Monsorta tried to recover.

"Okay, who do you want? We still got time."

"Nobody."

"Maybe this is providence. I'm not so sure I even want a TV crew, now."

"Bat, you . . ."

"No, in fact, I think, in general, when you're talking about TV *journalists,* you're talking about a pretty lousy lot."

Monsorta didn't want to push the issue. He knew if he looked too eager, that would tip off they had SWAT coming.

"We have the news truck. We can get the reporter. It's your call, Bat."

"I don't know," he said.

"Shit," the FBI man said under his breath. He paced away from the monitor, then paced back.

"Okay, Bat," Monsorta said. "What's it gonna take to get this done?"

There was a long pause.

"Okay, if you can get a new *newsman.* And Pete Meyers. I want to see them at twelve fifty-five. *Sharp.*"

The light went off on the AT&T hostage phone.

After Monsorta hung up, somebody said, "How the hell are we going to get a new newsman?"

"We're not," Scrambled Eggs said.

Twenty-nine

Jack Riker sped toward Metro on I-94, snow flurries coming at him in his headlights like the tips of white hot darts.

It hadn't taken long to tie Kring and Delesandro together. Riker called Julie Spulik on the coast from Harmon's condo. Kring's connection was in LA. They'd been on the same flight back to Detroit.

"Maybe they got to talking," Harmon speculated. "That's a long flight."

He remembered the dancer at the Landing Strip. Maybe she tried to pick him up. Maybe that set him off.

Riker checked his mirror. He could see Caley Harmon's headlights behind him. He'd thought up a couple of relatively inconsequential errands for her, so he could avoid more questions. He wanted that bootleg cockpit tape from the Airline Pilots Association. He was pretty sure what was on it. Kring probably had heard it. The pilot was probably screwing the stew.

"Can you also get some official printouts, some kind of records?" he'd also asked Harmon. "I need them for Kring's Seattle and LA flights."

She said she could get them from the Northwest computer.

"Fine," he'd said. "Before you go, though, leave the tape at my department. Leave it at the front desk. Call me when you have everything."

He gave her his pager number.

Riker did toy with telling her everything, end the goddamn charade. But he also knew if he crossed up Ladd,
he'd find a way to screw him, probably go after his pension
for insubordination. His police union might eventually pre-
vail, but he knew the executive and his attorneys could tie
him up for years in court.

He also considered contacting the OEC by phone, Morton
Ressler, specifically. But what was he going to tell him?
Kring's connection with Delesandro only further complicated the picture. Kring probably lifted the computer numbers from the missing attendant's purse. But what good were
they? Why should Kring care about the work schedules of
a couple thousand flight attendants? What good did it do
him in that tower? He remembered the book Kring had on
his shelf about locating people. Maybe Kring was stalking
attendants. Or, maybe he was just a techno freak playing
with another high-tech toy. Ressler's words kept coming
back. *We're not dealing with a serial killer here.* He knew
this for certain: He had Kring tied to four assaults on women
now, assuming he'd done Delesandro and dumped her somewhere. He thought, so what were they dealing with, Ressler?
He wanted an answer to that.

Riker saw the Middlebelt exit, the overpass of the crash.
He took it, for the first time in years. On the slope, he saw
a couple of wreaths and a white cross. Years later, families
were still remembering what happened there on that hill.

He turned on Lucas Drive. Harmon continued on toward
her office.

Riker was headed to the terminals. He was headed to
L.C. Smith, the old tower. He was looking for answers. He
wanted a solid theory before he took what he had to Vince
Stupek and put it all on the line.

Ten minutes later, he discovered the FAA offices in
Smith locked down, so he started buzzing the intercom at
the door.

When a voice answered he said, "Jack Riker, airport police. Here to see Terry Grice."

After a pause, a voice came back, "Hang on. She'll be
right down."

He waited five minutes, spending the time looking at
the titles of books in the Christian Science Reading Room
across the hall in the terminal mezzanine.

He heard a voice behind him. "Detective Riker, do we
have a problem?"

Her head was poking out the door.

He walked back over across the polished floor.

She lowered her voice. "Please, I'm very busy trying to
plan the radar failure you requested. Is there a change in
plans? Is there a problem? You could have just called."

"Radar failure?"

"You folks wanted one for a diversion. For your SWAT
people at twelve fifty-five."

The assault must be going down, he thought. He had
less than an hour.

"No, there's no problem. Can I come in? I just need a
second or two. I'm working a different aspect of the case."

She motioned him into the reception area, then sat down
on the empty receptionist's desk. The only people working
were upstairs in TRACON.

"Ms. Grice, I've come across some evidence that leads
me to believe Laurel Kring is responsible for the disappearance of a flight attendant from this airport a month
ago."

She looked too stressed-out to be surprised.

"Jesus, what next?" she said.

"And, I think somehow all this is connected to the crash
of flight two twenty-five six years ago."

"Laurel was working the tower when . . ."

"I know what he was doing. I saw it in his personnel
file. Did you ever hear him talk about it?"

"We had few words. Besides, I wasn't assigned to this facility at that time. I was in Kalamazoo."

"Do you know if he ever blamed anyone in particular for the accident? Made any kind of threats?"

"Not that I know of. But apparently, there's a few of us around here who apparently didn't know quite a bit about Laurel."

"What about the controllers I spoke with earlier?"

"They've gone home."

She thought about it for a second. She remembered a name from Kring's personnel file.

"You know, I do have somebody upstairs who was working the tower the night of that accident. He's just come in for night duty."

"Where is he?"

She got up and started toward the inner offices.

"C'mon, he's in the break room," she said, as he followed. "I'll show you, but I've got to get back to TRACON. And don't take too long. He's scheduled to go on soon."

Caley Harmon met the APA president at his house in Belleville. He came to the door in a jogging suit with the bootleg cassette tape. She was collecting on an old favor. She'd rounded up some attendants for him once as character witnesses when one of his pilots was stuck on a bogus sexual harassment case.

"Caley, I don't know why you want this, but . . ."

"I'll fill you in after the holiday," she said.

She dropped off the tape with the front desk at the airport police, then headed toward the terminals. She'd been thinking about Nikki Delesandro's password, wondering what other assaults Riker's suspect had planned for her membership. At the Northwest In Flight office, where attendants checked in for their trips, she could get the records the detective wanted. She could also gain more detailed access to SLICK and poke around a little bit.

She found a spot in the short-term lot. It was a ten minute walk down the long connector that linked the two terminals. The holiday rush, for all practical purposes, was over. There were very few passengers and a crew of janitors with push brooms.

In Flight was on the first level in Concourse E. She entered through an unmarked door and took a small service elevator down.

In Flight had dressing rooms, a TV lounge, and two walls of mailboxes where attendants received their company memos and mail.

One Northwest supervisor was working behind the desk where attendants checked in for their trips. They went way back. The super was a former attendant who'd moved up the company ranks rather than spend her forties balancing trays.

The super looked up from a paperback.

"Jeeze oh pete," she said. "Has your sex life gone to hell, Caley? What brings you in here at this hour?"

"We all have to make certain sacrifices," she said.

She went directly to one of the bid computer terminals. There were four of them on waist-high counters with no chairs, a setup that encouraged attendants to bid and move on. Harmon didn't want to get into a lot of chitchat. She knew the super was bored and primed to talk up a storm.

She kept her eyes on the computer, pulling out Delesandro's passport and seniority numbers to sign on.

"How goes the battle?"

"It goes."

Welcome to SLICK, Nikki Delesandro.

Harmon punched in a request for a list of the attendant's flights the previous month.

"Say, that was some trouble earlier this day, huh?" the super said.

"What trouble? I'm out of the loop over there in Romulus."

"Radar went down. They had a two-hour hold. I guess it was a real mess."

Delesandro's schedule came up, the last entry being the flight from LA.

"Yeah," the super continued. "You'd think they'd have solved that with the new tower."

"You'd think."

Harmon glanced up briefly. The super had gone back to her book.

Now, at the bottom of the terminal screen was a message:

View November Bids? Y(N)

She'd checked Delesandro's November bids earlier in the month, after police put forth the theory that the attendant would sooner or later show back up at work. She'd found nothing then, and promptly informed him of the same.

She pressed "Y" anyway.

A new page appeared. A date, and a confirmation:

Flight 260, Miami to Detroit—departing MIA at 9:50 p.m., arriving at DTW at 12:50.

The date struck her more than anything. That flight was arriving tonight.

She looked up at the super.

"Say, you don't know if the company would have reassigned Nikki Delesandro's passport and seniority number, do you?"

The super looked up. "You mean the missing girl?"

Harmon nodded.

"I don't see how they could. The feds give out the passport number."

"Yeah, I guess you're right."

"So, you've got a late flight coming in from Miami. I didn't think Northwest ran a Florida route that late."

"We don't."

She pointed to the screen. "Then, what's this two sixty here?"

"That's a mandated return. They had to run it because of the holiday."

"Mandated return?"

"That's what we call it. You know, you Teamsters put it in the contract, remember. The return to base provision. We had so many people at southern connections and regular flights were so full, the company had to provide an aircraft to get everybody home for the holiday."

"No passengers?"

"No, just a hundred or so attendants and a few pilots. Passenger bookings were so thick this year, it's been available for three weeks."

"Arriving tonight, at twelve fifty?"

"Yep, gate E-5. That ought to be some trip, huh?"

The guy was sitting with a stainless steel Stanley thermos and a large brown bag. In front of him he had a Tupperware filled with fruit cocktail. In his late forties. A mustache and a thinning widow's peak. He was wearing a flannel shirt. He reminded Riker of the old school, the controllers he guarded during the riot.

After Riker introduced himself, he offered him a cup.

"No thanks," he said.

The guy went back to the fruit. Relaxed, as if it was just another day.

"They got their goddamn hands full up there, don't they?" he said.

Riker nodded.

"I wouldn't want to be on the shit end of the stick with Laurel," he said. "Nope, not with Kring."

"You know him, then?"

"Worked with him for years. I'm the only FPL here with more seniority."

"You thought he was dangerous."

"Shit," he said. He chuckled. "I've been predicting something like this for years."

"Why didn't anybody tell somebody?"

The guy took his time answering, stabbing the last cherry in the Tupperware and sliding it into his mouth.

"Nobody'd listen," he said. "Not this new crowd. That's why I like this shift. Been on it four years. After midnight, you don't have to put up with all their bullshit."

Riker could tell the guy knew a lot. But he was going to make him come and get it, one question at a time.

"So, if you've been here for some time, you know about two twenty-five."

"Shit, man, I was there."

"Working."

He nodded.

"Where?"

"In the tower. Laurel was there, too."

Jesus, Riker thought. He had a dozen questions now.

"Tell me."

"I was working ground control. I brought the MD-80 over from the north terminal, then handed it off to Laurel. But I'll tell you, those guys really had their heads up their asses. Missed a runway. They thought it was pretty funny."

"Who?"

"The crew. But hey, it happens. Some people work a job a long time, they get sloppy. But you can't get *too* sloppy. Not in this business, at least."

He unscrewed the top off the thermos.

"You sure you don't want some?"

"No thanks. Gives me the shakes this late."

The guy shook his head. "No, man. This is bouillon. Learned that from my old man. He bombed Germany in a B-25. Lot of hours to Dresden and back. They never drank coffee. Too much coffee, you go to pieces. Then on the way back, you fall asleep."

Nice history lesson, Riker thought. But he was running out of time.

"What about the crash?"

"What about it?"

"How did Kring react."

"He pulled the handle."

"What handle?"

"It's just a figure of speech. He picked up the phone to crash-fire-rescue, but he did it *before* the fireball. I remember that. He knew goddamn well that MD-80 was in trouble. Laurel knows his airplanes."

"Did he blame anyone?"

"Not at first. I think he would have been okay with it, if it hadn't been for that safety board hearing."

"The hearing cleared you guys."

"Yeah, but you would have never known it. Me, I didn't care. I knew what we did. But Laurel wasn't real comfortable on the stand there. Not with the pilot's widow and all those people in the audience."

Riker asked him for more detail.

"Well, they just worked him over real good."

"About what?"

"They questioned his terminology in the transmissions. Tried to get him to say he was pushing the flight. You know, questioning his separation on the departures. But he was legal. At one point they did get out the regs. Made him read them. Made him compare the regs to what he said on the tape."

"Have you heard the cockpit tape? From the black box?"

The controller shook his head. "Heard *about* it."

"The deleted conversation between the pilot and the attendant?"

"Yeah, everybody figured he was jumping her bones. Hey, it happens. These people are adults."

"What about Kring? Did he know about that."

The controller popped the lid back on his fruit container. "Yeah, he knew about it."

"What did he say?" Riker asked.

"Just one thing. It was after the safety board, in fact."

"What?"

"Said he'd like to pull the handle on all those bitches one day."

Thirty

Five minutes before his flight plan called for him to re-move the MD-80 from autopilot and begin his descent into DTW, Thomas Reidy made one last trip to the lav. On his way out, he wiped his nostrils with his thumb and index finger. This was an unconscious habit, started a couple a years ago when he worried he might have left a trace of the white powder on his nose.

The gal he called Peaches was sitting with the rowdy group of attendants who had commandeered the drink cart at the back of the jet. She reached out and squeezed his ass as he passed.

"Blues, or whatever," he said to her, winking.

"Whatever," she said, winking back.

"Hey, Captain," somebody yelled. "Aren't you supposed to be flying this rocket."

"Nature called," he said.

He endured a dozen wisecracks on his way back to the flight deck. He passed more than a hundred attendants. Some were still in uniform, others in their civvies. Some were sleeping. Others had their noses in paperbacks.

"Excuse me, Captain," a gay attendant said, imperson-ating a concerned passenger. "When are we due to arrive?"

Reidy ignored him. Metro was reporting fifteen-knot winds and flurries. He saw no reason for delay.

By the time Thomas Reidy reached the first-class sec-tion, he could feel the coke draining down his throat. Cocaine made Thomas Reidy feel confident, in control. When he felt like this, he could fly that big bird under the Ambassador Bridge.

He was already anticipating last call at Cisco's.

"Everything under control?" somebody in first class sniped.

At the flight deck door, he turned around and mockingly saluted his fellow employees, placing his hand palm up on the left side of his head.

The safety board hearing. Delesandro. The LA flight. Her disappearance. Kring's threat.

When he was done telling them everything, Marlon Ladd said, "Some admirable leg work, Jack, considering the circumstances."

He was a patronizing sonovabitch.

"You're not worried he may pose a threat up there?" Riker asked.

"At this juncture, it's not a concern," Scrambled Eggs said. "Traffic is very light, largely cargo. The man says he wants to be interviewed. And we're going to give him what he wants."

Riker wanted to see Ressler. He just wanted five minutes with the psychologist and his smokeless cigars.

"I'm sorry, we have an assault to run here, Detective. At this point, you're information is largely irrelevant."

Ladd wanted to know why he wasn't with the Teamster official, but he was already headed for the door when he asked.

Largely irrelevant.

Jack Riker had been feeling that way since the day he first showed up at the big pipe.

Five minutes later, he parked the department Dodge right in front of the goddamn canopy.

"This is valet parking only, sir."

"Police business," he said.

Police business, until he opened the door. Then, Jack Riker considered himself done for the night.

Inside, his pager went off. He pulled it out of his coat pocket and glanced at the number, recognized it as the Teamster's office. He never even looked at the pay phone near the coat check to see if it was free.

At the inner door he paused, listening for a few seconds to the sounds of the bass bleeding through.

"Fuck it."

The music hit him with a blast of air filled with perfume and the smell of beer and liquor. Ahead, two naked women worked both brass poles. Others worked the booths.

He went straight for a small empty table away from the stage. Jack Riker hadn't come to the Landing Strip for the show.

A waitress showed up. She had on the black tights and the leotard buried up the middle of her ass.

"Windsor Canadian."

"On the rocks?"

"And the bottle."

He wanted to see that Mounty. He wanted to say hello to his old friend.

When she brought it, she leaned over.

"You know, honey, that's going to be more than a hundred dollars in here."

"What, do I look like the kind of guy that can't afford it?" he said.

She walked off, pissed.

Riker knew that if he started, that bottle was going to cost a hell of a lot more than that.

The beeper went off again.

"Goddamnit."

He didn't bother to even look at the number this time.

Riker poured the Canadian, studying the way the whiskey filled the cracks and crevices between the ice, savoring the moment, or maybe snuffing the last voices of an internal debate.

"Don't ever let the debate start. If that happens, you've already lost it." That's what a reformed alkie told him once.

The debate started back at the Nomad's hangar. Maybe it started before that.

Riker spun the bottle around, looking for the logo. The Mounty was sitting on his horse, his shoulder's back, tall in his saddle.

Underneath was the slogan: "One Canadian stands alone."

He'd always liked those words. But he was thinking about what Harmon had said about the meetings. The slogan seemed like an empty promise now.

The worst day in aviation, he thought. He'd managed to get most of it there on the Holter monitor log. Phantom controller. The Teamster. Stolen car. The EOC. Missing women. Dead women. And Kring. Idle threats, and real threats. All for what, to get a lousy TV interview?

He knew they'd take Kring out of that tower in a bag.

Riker eyed the whiskey, thinking of other body bags.

He heard the club DJ say: "And now gentlemen, let's put your hands together for our very own Tea."

He turned to the stage. She must have come back in to work a double. Another show. A different uniform. They were flooding the stage with dry ice vapors.

The spots kept changing colors.

Red. White.

He put both hands around the glass of Canadian. But for reasons that eluded him, couldn't take his eyes off her show.

That phony stew dancing in the clouds. Or was it smoke?

Red smoke. White smoke.

He was thinking about Kring and smoke markers in the highlands when his pager started beeping at him again.

* * *

He watched the green blips accumulate directly south of the tower on the ASDE. Small green cells heading for one glowing spot on the screen, as if sperm clustering around an egg.

Insignificant, he thought.

And worthless.

They were all goddamn worthless. Their SWAT teams, their tactics. He'd seen them play the game.

He picked up the phone.

"Major Tom," he said. "You insult me."

"Insult you?"

They were insulting him at the Eureka Road checkpoint. The ground radar revealed vehicles, full of police personnel probably, were gathering there.

"Move them, Major Tom, or there is no deal."

"We need to secure the perimeter."

They talked.

"You need your news people, and that's all you need," he demanded.

So much talk. It bored him now.

When he hung up, the green blips moved again, dispersing. Only two radar targets remained, and the occasional traffic streaming by on Eureka Road.

He closed his eyes, sensing things around him. He could feel the movement in the tower, and he could feel the tower moving in the November wind.

He tossed his head back, then opened his eyes, looking at the black sky behind him. He began thinking, this must have been what it was like for Crossfield, when he crossed from the blue into the outer darkness. Flying those clipped wings.

Doing it alone.

They shouldn't have done this to him. There are certain things a boy shouldn't have to witness. There are certain things a boy shouldn't have to see. He blamed his father as much as his mother. A spineless man.

He had the backbone, but it was their cruelty now.

He was helpless to stop it, only shape it.

He knew this feeling.

Sky above, earth below. In the jungle now.

Send the choppers in for Charlie. Burn the skin of the back of those fucking Gooks. Watch the Huey make the grass dance.

Keep them guessing with the colors. Keep them guessing with the smoke.

"Captain Queeg," he barked. "You tired?"

The worthless goddamn hub director had been doing traffic coordination for more than ten straight hours. Actually, he'd impressed him slightly. He'd done a workmanlike job.

"Yes," Cleage said. "I'm tired. I think we're all tired."

They had a lull.

Cleage walked over.

"You know Laurel, I realize now," he said.

"Realize what, Captain."

"Maybe I could have done things better for you folks up here."

He liked that. He liked seeing him trying to kiss ass, trying to save his worthless fucking life.

"You done good, Captain. Soon I'm gonna step in for you. I'm gonna give you a break."

He'd been planning his break for a week.

Garcia turned around. He was watching the north sky.

"You want me to watch him, Laurel?"

He reached into his satchel and tossed the wire wraps to Garcia.

Kring nodded. "I want you to tie him up."

He looked at the digital clock.

He pointed the Ruger at the rep, sitting in the chair. "Tie him up, too."

He directed Garcia to put them back to back, looping their wrists together. The spic was really showing him something. The spic was okay.

"Why?" the rep said.

"Shut the fuck up!"

He took a deep breath. He could feel himself transforming. Soon the whole world would know.

"They're sending someone up here in a few minutes," he said. "I'm going to talk to a reporter. If nobody fucks up, you're all going home after second shift."

He heard a cheer. He didn't think it was in his mind.

The woman at feeder control walked over.

"Laurel, you need to come look at the weather screen. They're predicting some real stiff easterlies."

"What about sheers?" he asked.

"Nothing yet," she said.

He got up, carrying the Ruger with him. He checked the sheer equipment, then went to the west vista. Saw the flurries bouncing off the glass.

He was reaching out now. His mind expanding across the control area. He saw a hundred vectors, a hundred different possibilities. He had plans and contingencies. He had *redundancy*. Chaos only brought more possibilities. They had trained him well for that.

He had two runways open. Twelve left. Twelve right.

"Fed Ex 1020, cross twelve left, turn left, then hold short of twelve left," the ground controller said.

There were cargo flights leaving every few minutes. That was all he needed.

"Do you have anything left from Northwest," he asked the feeder.

She held up a strip. "Just this one. Two sixty out of Miami. Our last commercial before the red eyes. Ought to touch down at twelve forty-five."

He nodded.

"Laurel," she said. "Should we move everything to runways six and twenty-seven?"

Thinking.

He'd been expecting something from them all night. Now he had it.

Let them have their ruse. Let them do his work for him.

"Yes. Take pending inbounds, then notify TRACON. Let's shoot the gap."

"Christ, Laurel," Cleage said. "You're going to need somebody to coordinate if you're going to do that."

"Don't worry, Captain," he said. "I'm going to coordinate."

He could do it blind. Play all the instruments at once, just like Rhaasand Roland Kirk.

Thirty-one

Thirty minutes past midnight, upon Grice's order, the tech threw the circuit breaker on the ASR-9, blanking all the radar screens in TRACON and the new tower. They could be on CENRAP in less than a minute. With all the equipment failures in the past, everyone knew the drill well.

The FBI had asked her to make the call to the tower. The crisis team felt it would reenforce the authenticity of the diversion. She'd rehearsed what to say, but she could feel her hand trembling.

"Just be yourself," an FBI special agent told her.

"If I did that, I'd have only questions," she said.

It had been thirteen hours since the last radar failure. It had been thirteen hours since it all began.

She picked up the shout line.

"Tower."

She recognized his voice. He sounded very calm. He didn't sound at all like the madman she had heard on the tape earlier.

"ASR-9 out," she said. "We're moving to CENRAP."

"Another failure?" he said.

"We came up short on suppressors after we lost it earlier today. We've still got everything lined up for runway twenty-seven. Do you want a fifteen-minute hold?"

There was a long pause.

"We can handle it," he said. "Are you ready?"

"We have two freight carriers and just took a handoff from Cleveland Center, an inbound Northwest flight."

"I saw the strips. That's not what I meant."

She didn't know what to say.

The agent standing next to her in the dark radar leaned into her free ear. "Respond," he whispered.

"Ready for what, Laurel?"

"For the shift change. When we get out of here."

After she hung up, she started looking for volunteers.

Tommy Monsorta was enjoying a cigarette.

Oshefsky hung up the outside line in the CNT and said, "That was the radar room. He bought it. He's talking about a shift change, of all things. The FAA is rounding up replacements."

"Maybe this is going to work," Marlon Ladd said.

"And maybe he doesn't think they'll give him holiday pay," Monsorta said, exhaling.

The red light on the AT&T hostage phone began blinking.

He picked up.

"I told you *fucking* twelve fifty-five and not a goddamn minute sooner!"

He was shouting.

FBI CNT personnel, standing in small groups around the lounge, jogged over to the monitor.

"I don't understand, Bat," Monsorta said. He cradled the phone on his shoulder and raised his hands, signaling to everyone he truly didn't.

"I see a goddamn car, coming from Eureka. You're gonna blow it, *Major Tom.*"

The "Miller Time" clock read almost twelve forty. The FBI agents were shaking their heads.

"We didn't send the reporters, Bat," Monsorta said. "I don't understand. What car?"

"Coming from Eureka. I can see his headlights now."

"Hold on, Bat. We're checking on that."

Monsorta motioned with his right hand: *Give me god-damn something to work with.*

Before he got an answer, Kring yelled again, "I want answers, Major Tom. I want answers now!"

Improvise. Tell him anything before he blows.

"We think it's one of your people, Bat," Monsorta said calmly.

"My people?"

"You didn't want any security at that gate, remember, Bat. When you don't have security, things like this happen. Maybe somebody didn't get the message at the FAA. We think it's one of your people showing up for work."

There was a pause. Monsorta could hear him saying something to another controller. Kring sounded like he already had his hands full directing air traffic.

An agent ran into the room. He was telling the FBI commander something, gesturing with both hands.

"Bat, you with me? Bat?"

"Yeah."

"Now work with us on this. We're gonna try to get that car back, okay?"

He began shouting again. "No more cars! I see another car and I'm ending this!"

"Okay, Bat. No more cars."

Monsorta angrily snuffed his smoke, covered the phone and turned to the people around the monitor. "What the hell is going on? Who the hell is it?"

The FBI commander stepped forward.

"We don't know. Some stupid sonovabitch just sped through the gate over there."

Vince Stupek was sitting with his back to a pile of I beams on the south corner of the new firehouse, watching

a 727 with Federal Express colors rocket past and lift off
on a runway not three hundred yards away. A minute later,
landing lights appeared over the trees to the east of the
airport. From his angle, the landing jet seemed to hover
like a UFO.

Johnson tapped him on the shoulder. "Hey Vince, come
up here and look, I think it's going down."

Stupek motioned to the rest of the SWAT team to stay
down, then peaked over the beams. He saw headlights approaching on the access road. The vehicle was moving at
a pretty good clip.

He looked at his watch. "Shit, aren't they going to tell
us a goddamn thing? They're early. Get the EOC on the
radio."

Johnson lowered himself to the ground, using his hand
to shield his headset microphone from the wind.

"That's a car," Stupek said. "I wonder what happened
to the TV crew."

The sedan glided into the lot and parked in the handi-
capped spot in front of the tower door.

When Stupek didn't see a newspaper logo on the door,
he pulled Johnson up by his flak jacket.

"Reed, look," Stupek said. "Where have you seen that
car before?"

Thomas Reidy was finishing his wide bank turn, the
wings of the MD-80 bumping and flexing on the thermals
rising from the Detroit River. Below to his left, he could
see the lights of the Ford Rouge Plant twinkling through
the broken clouds. When he leveled, the nose of the MD-80
was lined up with the east end of runway twenty-seven,
twenty miles ahead.

"Northwest two sixty, descend and maintain three thousand," said the approach controller in his left ear. The sen-

tence sounded like one word. A lot of them mumbled fast like that.

Behind him, Reidy could hear attendants in first class, partying, singing some sixties tune.

"What is the name of that song?" he asked the copilot.

He kept his eyes on the instrument panel. " 'Hooked on a Feeling,' B.J. Thomas."

"I wonder what B.J. stands for."

"Yeah, I'll bet he didn't go by that in school."

Reidy sniffed, then said, "Well hello, Detroit."

Through the broken clouds ahead, he could see Metro's landing lights.

A minute later, DTW air traffic control checked in again.

"Northwest two sixty, RVR is forty-five hundred. Cleared for approach. Contact tower on 124.05."

"Did you get that?" the copilot said.

"Every word."

Thomas Reidy was feeling good.

He switched the radio frequency. "Northwest two sixty to tower."

The controller came right back.

"Northwest, report the outer marker. Wind 090 at fifteen knots. Runway twenty-seven, RVR forty-five hundred." A slow talker.

Reidy reduced his air speed, then lowered his flaps several degrees.

A new voice broke in on the tower frequency.

"Northwest two sixty, this is Detroit terminal radar control. We have a situation here. Abort. Repeat, abort landing."

His tone was urgent and deliberate. It didn't sound like the speed demon he had a minute earlier.

The copilot turned, "Christ, what the hell was that?"

The tower voice cut in, "Northwest two sixty, ignore unauthorized transmission."

The other one was right behind him. "Negative two sixty,

abort! Switch to 118.4 and pull out and go around. I repeat, pull out and await further instruction on 118.4."

"Northwest two sixty, this is Metro tower. I repeat, ignore unauthorized transmission. Everything's oakie dokie. Cleared to land on twenty-seven."

Reidy looked over at the copilot. "Did you see that letter to airmen?"

"About the phantom controller?"

Reidy nodded. "Well, I think we've just heard from him."

"Maybe we better go around, recontact TRACON on a different frequency."

"That's another ten or fifteen minutes, partner, by the time we get done fucking around." Reidy was thinking about a cold one at Cisco's.

"Yeah, but maybe we ought to do it."

Reidy saw the airfield again.

"Fuck 'em," he said, nudging the MD-80 down.

He was wearing his own head set now. He was ready to switch from the local control frequency over to the one for ground control.

"Everybody," Laurel Kring barked, motioning with the Ruger. "Over there by the stairs."

"Laurel," the local controller said. "We've got traffic coming in."

"The Bat's got the traffic!" he shouted.

When nobody moved, he fired one round through the ceiling. Everyone ditched their head sets, scrambling, then accumulating in a group at the top of the stairs.

"Fed Ex one twenty, proceed to runway six," he said. "Then wait for further instructions."

"Laurel," somebody said. "You've got an inbound coming in at twenty-seven."

He knew that. You're goddamn right he did.

Some of them were working their way down the stairs now.

Fuck 'em. He didn't care. He didn't need them now.

"Go," he said, waving the Ruger. "Get the fuck out of here."

He walked over to Cleage and Russell. He pulled out a pocket knife and cut apart their wrists.

"Go, Uncle Rep," he said.

They both got up.

He aimed the Ruger at Cleage.

"Captain Queeg, you're fucking staying here."

Cleage sat back down.

He eyed the CENRAP screen, then the ASDE. He could see blips of vehicles accumulating at the Eureka Road checkpoint, but that didn't matter now.

The Bat's radar was tuned to the incoming flight.

The Fed Ex jet waiting at the foot of the runway.

"Fed Ex one twenty, hold for my signal."

He knew one twenty would need three quarters of the runway to get airborne. He knew two sixty needed half the runway to slow and brake.

It was simple geometry. A matter of time, velocity and distance. Two lines meeting. Closing the gap.

At more than two hundred knots.

Ten miles out, below the cloud ceiling, Metro's lights were hitting Reidy's eyes like blowing sand. The strobes at the foot of the runway were flashing, the directional string everyone called the rabbit because they ran in sequence like a running hare.

"Goddamn, those are bright," he said to the copilot.

Reidy didn't know if that was from the cold November air, or all that Visine.

"Tower, Northwest two sixty, turn down the lights, please."

"Do you want the approach lights down, sir?" the controller came back.

"No, the rabbit."

They were at two thousand feet now. He lowered the flaps to their landing setting. The MD-80 became very buoyant, bobbing up and down in the head wind.

"Tower, Northwest two sixty, will you kill those goddamn lights?"

Shit, he couldn't see beyond the foot of the runway.

"Maybe we better go around, Tom," the copilot said.

He felt like the big jet was sewn to his pants. It made him think of a joke. "Hey, partner, you know why broads like to ride horses so much?"

"No," the copilot said, irritated Reidy was ignoring his advice.

"It's the only time a woman can put something that big between her legs and still keep it under control."

"Northwest two sixty, pull out and go around! I repeat, pull out and go around!"

The phantom again.

"I'm not going to listen to that noise," Reidy said, turning the radio volume down to nothing.

Lights or no lights, he'd goddamn do the rest himself.

"Are you nuts four sixty, or are you just drunk," Stupek had said. "You're gonna get yourself and everyone else killed up there."

Riker had talked to him on his handheld, when he was running up the stairs.

"The interview is smoke," he'd said. "This whole thing is about a flight."

He'd given them the number he got from Caley Harmon. He'd given them much of the story as he could on his way up those 350 steps, before he ran out of wind.

Now, he was just outside the door, at the top of the

stairwell. He needed just a few seconds. His lungs ached and his calves and upper thighs were cramping.

An alarm started screaming. The door flew open and he was almost knocked down by a half-dozen controllers scrambling for the stairs.

Riker grabbed the guy with the Red Wings jersey.

"What's he got up there?"

"Guns," he said. "And Cleage. He's gonna put a flight into the farm."

He slipped Riker's grasp like a bad tackle and stumbled down the stairwell. Riker went through the door and found the tower cab stairs.

He looked up, but saw only darkness at the top.

He felt his breast pocket, then took off his jacket. He took off his gun and placed it on the stairs. It would serve him better there.

Up. Slowly.

The Robo alarm was still sounding.

One step at a time.

At the top, he peaked into the tower cab. Kring was looking out the north window, the .44 magnum in his left hand, pointed in the general direction of Dale Cleage. Cleage looked spaced-out, depressed even. He was sitting hunch shouldered in a chair.

Riker walked into the cab, his hands high above his head.

Calmly now.

"Laurel Kring."

The controller turned rapidly, aiming the revolver at him. He was wearing a headset.

"Jack Riker, Kring. Airport police. I'm unarmed."

Riker stretched his arms higher.

"What do you want?"

Kring's eyes were darting between the window, Riker, and the radar screens.

Talk now.

"I want to talk."

Kring eyed the screens again.

"The time for talking is over."

He pressed something on the console.

"Fed Ex 160, cleared for takeoff. Start your roll now."

Kring ripped off the headset with one hand, throwing it down at the south window. He took four steps forward. Four aggressive steps, then he stopped suddenly, even with Cleage.

Riker stepped backward, maintaining eye contact.

Keep talking.

"Look, Laurel, I understand."

"Understand what?"

Spencer Davis.

"You're a man, right?"

He took another step back, Kring one forward. In his peripheral vision, he could see Cleage was eyeing the headset.

"You're fucking right I am."

"And I'm a man."

Kring's brow furrowed.

"Then I think we should talk this over man to man."

Riker maintained eye contact, even as Cleage bolted for the headset.

"Fed Ex one sixty. Inbound! Abort! Abort!"

Kring spun around, firing three times at the hub director as he ran to the east side of the tower cab, trying to escape his draw. Before Cleage went down into a heap, one of the tower windows shattered from a stray, falling like a sheet of ice.

Kring spun around, aiming the Ruger at him now.

Both of them. Waiting.

Riker saw a jet descend from the east, through the open window, as ringing filled his ears. He waited for an explosion, or a fireball. He only had to see Laurel Kring's face to know Cleage's message had gotten through.

Riker put his hands up higher. He could feel the cold wind hitting his wet armpits.

He sidestepped to his right toward Cleage.

Kring quickly closed the distance between them, putting the gun not a foot from Riker's forehead.

His eyes were wild now.

Talk, Riker told himself.

"Laurel, listen to me. You didn't want that."

"You don't know," he said.

The ringing gave way to sirens, coming from the terminal area. The outbound jet must have skidded off the runway.

Riker could see the hammer was back.

Do what you came up here to do.

"Laurel, listen. I know about flight two twenty-five."

Kring blinked twice.

"I worked all the bodies."

"Bodies?"

"I worked the hangar. I was there."

Kring cocked his head, like a goddamn dog.

Keep talking.

"I don't know what that accident did to you. But I know what it did to me."

Kring was listening. At least Riker thought he was. His eyes had gone from wild to vacant.

"It's not our fault."

"Wrong, Detective *Jack.*"

"No, somebody just screwed up. It *happens.* I've got the proof."

The bore on the .44 looked like an endless black hole. But the black hole was starting to shake.

"Proof?"

"Yeah, in my shirt pocket. I've got the tape. It's all on there, man."

Riker slowly lowered his hand to his shirt. He pulled out the tape then held it to his right, at arm's length, only a couple feet from the open window.

"There's a gap."

"No, this is the complete tape, Laurel. Listen to me, it's all on here."

He'd played it on the car deck on the way over. It was there, all right.

"Play it."

"What?"

He screamed. "Play it!"

Kring's eyes were darting at his Holter monitor.

Shit, Riker thought, he doubted that goddamn thing would play an audio tape.

Give the guy something to go home with. Give him back his dignity, as warped as it was at that.

"You put down the gun, and I'll play it."

Kring blinked rapidly, three or four times.

"Give it to me," he said, motioning with his fingers.

"No, man, this has got to be a fair trade. You grab for it, you shoot, it's out this window."

He challenged him.

"C'mon Laurel, be a man. I came up here like one. I came up here unarmed. Put down the gun. And you can play the tape yourself."

His grip seemed to relax on the revolver.

Keep talking.

"Laurel, you want to walk out of here, not really knowing what all this was for? Put down the gun. Play the tape. And we'll walk out of here together, okay? We'll play this thing for everybody. Just you and me."

Kring lowered the gun halfway.

Riker unbuckled the Holter unit, pulling the cassette out. He loaded the tape. He motioned with his head to his left, to the feeder controller's table.

"It's cued right up, man. You set the gun there. And I'm going to set this down."

Riker placed the player on the table with his left hand as Kring set down the gun next to it with his right.

Kring picked up the player.

Riker was thinking about his next move. He was thinking about the other weapons he could see bulging in the guy's vest.

They were face to face, only two feet apart.

Kring hesitated.

Riker wondered if he really wanted to know the truth.

"Go ahead, play it, Laurel."

Kring looked down at the unit, then pressed the play button.

There was only slow motion garble.

Three seconds into it, Kring reached for his neck.

As Riker spun away, looking for that pistol, he saw the controller falling backward, against the open window.

He was holding Riker's clip-on, looking at it with an expression of bemusement, when Riker heard the sniper's shot and saw his forehead explode.

Thirty-two

He parked under a sign "police vehicles only" outside Detroit police headquarters. He figured his dash placard was good in that league, if not at the airport. He only had to walk a block to the New Hellas Cafe.

Only a couple of pedestrians were on Monroe at two thirty in the morning, but the street wasn't quiet. Greek music blasted out of a small speaker over the doorways of a restaurant called the Golden Fleece. That's one of the things he always liked about Greektown, people didn't even have to be around, but you still felt like somewhere there was something going on.

He poked his head inside the Athens Bar, his old haunt. It was dead, nothing like he remembered it. All the hoods must have gone on to a new haunt. Or maybe they were all in graves. Maybe they were all in jail. Only two men were at the bar rail, sitting hunch shouldered. One head turned, eyeing him briefly. The other never took his eyes off his drink. A couple of contenders, he thought, working on last call.

He turned around and moved on. He'd worn only his sport jacket. There was no wind on Monroe Street. Or now it was at Jack Riker's back.

Caley Harmon and Mort Ressler were waiting for him in a booth near the wall at the New Hellas Cafe. He'd suggested the Hellas. He knew that the restaurant was one of the few places in Wayne County where you could get a fine Greek meal well into the early morning hours. He'd learned that many years ago when he worked at the sheriff's department headquarters down the street.

A couple dozen other people were in the restaurant. Mostly couples. Low lit. More Greek music. Pictures of the Acropolis and other classic structures everywhere. As he reached the booth, a waiter lit a flaming cheese dish called Saginaki at a nearby table and yelled "Oopa!" as it combusted like a flash pot. Riker felt the wave of heat hit his face.

Harmon and Ressler both looked up, smiling.

"Maybe Kring should have come here," Riker said. "He could have got his fire ball for under five bucks."

He sat across from Harmon, Ressler sliding over.

"My daughter has told me for years about this place," the FBI psychologist said. "Thank you for inviting me."

"Yes, I'm famished," Harmon said.

Riker leaned toward her. "But will you eat, *Mizz* Harmon?"

He felt her kick his leg under the table.

The waiter took their orders. A couple plates of mousaka. Ressler wanted the squid in wine sauce. Greek salads. A Coke. A Vernor's. Ressler wanted a glass of Retsina, the wine that Riker said tasted like cedar shingles.

"You've had cedar shingles?" Ressler asked.

"I've chewed on a few," Riker said.

After the server brought a basket of bread, Harmon asked, "So, did you get a chance to talk to the executive?"

Riker shook his head. "I saw him at the Nomads hangar, but he was kind of tied up with news people. Christ, they got out there quick."

"Really?" she said.

Ressler chimed in. "Detective Riker's gracious invitation for dinner was a godsend really. I was looking for an excuse to leave. A few of those media people seemed to already know quite a bit about the day's events."

"Ladd was doing a lot of explaining," Riker said.

"Such as?" Harmon asked.

"Mainly, they had to do with why he'd decided to put thousands of holiday travelers at risk."

"I wonder how they found out about that," Ressler said. "I thought you had a news blackout all day."

"We did," Riker said, looking at Caley.

She didn't look up. She was buttering her bread.

Ressler patted Riker's forearm. "It's me that should be apologizing, Detective."

"To the news media?" Riker said. "Shit, they're just looking for a story."

"No, to you, Detective. I was wrong about Kring. I underestimated the sexual nature of his disorder. Unfortunately, psychology isn't a precise science. In fact, some aspects of it aren't science at all."

Riker wouldn't have any of it. "You just didn't have all the information. You would have made the same call."

Ressler chewed on some of the crusty bread. "This is very good," he said, holding up a piece.

Harmon asked, "What about Nikki Delesandro, doctor?"

"What about her?"

"What do you think happened?"

He chewed with one side, talked with the other. "No doubt, she made some advances toward him on the flight. They probably went out for a drink. He was dabbling, just as he did at your local topless bar. He may have resented his mother's promiscuity, but afterall . . ." He leaned closer toward Harmon, almost whispering, "Every man has needs."

"So he *killed* her?" she asked.

Ressler leaned back, wiping butter from his lips with a napkin. "Her advances only excited an elaborate mosaic of disfunction and maternal resentment. Yes, he no doubt killed her. I'd check local motels. Or, perhaps, Detective Riker, you should look for trace evidence in his car. She was the beginning, so to speak. She was going to make his fantasy a reality."

Ressler took a healthy drink of the Retsina.

"To what?" Harmon asked.

"When he discovered the information concerning the flight computer, when he found out about the courtesy return from Miami, he found an object for his rage. It was too much for him to resist."

Harmon wasn't satisfied. "What about her body? Or her car, for that matter?"

Riker touched Harmon's hand. "On Monday, I'm going to put a couple patrolmen on that. We're gonna check all the plates in the parking structures."

"And you're going to let me know, *Detective Riker,*" she said.

She kicked him under the table again.

"Of course," he said.

The meals came. They talked subjects unrelated to what had happened that day. They laughed a lot, as Ressler launched into a pretty elaborate dissertation about the predatory practices of sea squid.

Nobody wanted to spoil a good meal.

When the check came, Riker, reaching for his wallet, remembered the cassette.

"Here," he said, handing it to Harmon.

"Did it help?" she asked.

"It almost cost me my life, but then again, it might have saved it. I don't know. I still haven't decided which."

"Did you listen to it?" she asked.

Riker nodded.

Ressler was searching for a Te-Amo. "Yes, how graphic is it, detective?"

"Graphic? Not at all."

He stuck the cigar in his mouth.

"Back at the hangar, you told me Kring thought there was conversation of a sexual nature on the tape."

"Right. He thought there was."

"Well, Jack, is there?" Harmon asked.

She kicked him again.

Damn, he wished she'd stop doing that.

"No. There's nothing. The pilot and the stew . . ." He began again. "The pilot and the *flight attendant* were comparing notes."

"About what?" Ressler demanded.

"About their kids. That was it."

Ressler said, "Of course, he heard a rumor and believed it."

"Right," Riker said. "It was all in Kring's mind."

"It always is," Ressler said. "It always is."

The psychologist stood, reaching for his coat. "Well, I'd better get going. My daughter is expecting me."

"She's waiting up for you?" Harmon asked.

"I told her to leave the key under the mat, but knowing her, she'll still be waiting."

They watched as Morton Ressler produced a pack of matches and lit the Te-Amo.

"Besides," he continued, once he had it stoked, "I'm afraid this fine Mexican cigar might very well clear the place out."

"I thought you didn't smoke those," Riker said.

"I don't," he said. "Except on national holidays."

Then they watched him disappear into the night.

They talked awhile. About people they knew, about the people they no longer saw from their drinking days. She talked about new places she'd gone, new people she'd met.

"I call them adventures in sobriety," she said.

She was still wearing the black turtleneck. He liked the contrast between the sweater, her fair skin, and her long raven hair.

When he looked into her eyes, she said, "By the way, what took you so long to answer when I paged you? I tried three damn times."

"I'm glad you did."

"But I was going crazy. I thought he was going to do something to my girls at the gate."

"Girls, or *women?*"

Another kick, more playful this time.

"You didn't answer my question."

Riker thought of the Mounty on the bottle. "I was doing further research."

"On what?"

"I guess I was teetering."

"Between what?"

"Well, the way things turned out, I guess between exultation and despair."

She didn't ask for the details. She didn't need to. He could tell she'd been there.

Caley grasped his hand, but she didn't let go.

"You know there's a hell of a good meeting down here."

"In Greektown?"

She nodded. "Every Saturday at that church right up the street. Why don't you come with me?"

Riker thought about it. "I might do that."

She leaned back. "Coffee?"

He shook his head. "There's mud in the bottom of the stuff they serve here."

"I was thinking about mine. My place. It doesn't have mud."

"I know," he said. "But look at me."

"You look fine."

He undid one button, displaying the wires and patches of the Holter rig.

"All day I've been carrying around all this on my chest."

She laughed.

He said, "I guess they're not going to get what they want, are they? I lost the goddamn log. The recorder is in pieces."

She stood up, reaching for her coat.

"C'mon," she said.

He looked up.

"Some things you can't do all by yourself," she said. "There's too much pain involved."

"Like what?"

"Ripping those off. I'm painlessly fast."

"Well, as long as you're going to put it that way . . ." he said.

WILLIAM W. JOHNSTONE
THE ASHES SERIES

WINGMAN
BY MACK MALONEY

WINGMAN   (0-8217-2015-5, $3.95)

#2 THE CIRCLE WAR   (0-8217-2120-8, $3.95)

#5 THE TWISTED CROSS   (0-8217-2553-X, $3.95)

#6 THE FINAL STORM   (0-8217-2655-2, $3.95)

#7 FREEDOM EXPRESS   (0-8217-4022-9, $3.99)

ALSO BY MACK MALONEY:

WAR HEAVEN   (0-8217-3414-8, $4.95)

HORROR FROM HAUTALA

SHADES OF NIGHT   (0-8217-5097-6, $4.99)
Stalked by a madman, Lara DeSalvo is unaware that she is
most in danger in the one place she thinks she is safe—
home.

TWILIGHT TIME   (0-8217-4713-4, $4.99)
Jeff Wagner comes home for his sister's funeral and uncov-
ers long-buried memories of childhood sexual abuse and
murder.

DARK SILENCE   (0-8217-3923-9, $5.99)
Dianne Fraser fights for her family—and her sanity—
against the evil forces that haunt an abandoned mill.

COLD WHISPER   (0-8217-3464-4, $5.95)
Tully can make Sarah's wishes come true, but Sarah lives
in terror because Tully doesn't understand that some wishes
aren't meant to come true.

LITTLE BROTHERS   (0-8217-4020-2, $4.50)
Kip saw the "little brothers" kill his mother five years ago.
Now they have returned, and this time there will be no es-
cape.

MOONBOG   (0-8217-3356-7, $4.95)
Someone—or some*thing*—is killing the children in the little
town of Holland, Maine.

---

*Available wherever paperbacks are sold, or order direct from the
Publisher. Send cover price plus 50¢ per copy for mailing and
handling to Penguin USA, P.O. Box 999, c/o Dept. 17109,
Bergenfield, NJ 07621. Residents of New York and Tennessee
must include sales tax. DO NOT SEND CASH.*